The womb-emptying society.

society.

Irene Garzón.

ISBN: 978-1-8380645-1-8

To my Lecherito, for giving me wings.
To my Lecheritas, for believing we've got them.

To those women and babies who have had a joyous birth, but
especially to all those who did not.

Foreword. We in western culture, love drama. Set the drama in a hospital with the attendant emergencies, people in uniform, and love triangles and we can't get enough. Exploring the human condition through emotional drama AND physical medical conditions is compelling. It's because at our foundation, we are all storytellers and story-listeners. The human brain has tremendous powers of reasoning, deducing patterns out of a hundred seemingly unrelated facts, and finding meaning in the chaos of lived experience.

In this extraordinary book, Irene Garzón has gifted us exactly this opportunity. With the first paragraph, witnessing a shift change on a busy hospital ward between sleep-deprived midwives and their caffeinated replacements, we step behind a curtain rarely explored in modern society. We're whisked into the dramatic and engrossing world of heartache and loss, the shock of unplanned pregnancy, the pain and triumph of labor. We see the struggle of relationships in the doctors', midwives', nurses', administrators' AND new parents' perspectives. These disparate perspectives weave together realistic birth stories, universal love stories and ultimately color the process of being human during one of life's peak experiences.

I was moved to tears several times reading the families' struggles, even as a veteran midwife of two decades, because these challenges are mostly manufactured by the systemic injustices present in the modern-day maternity world. But as a maternal child health investigator with a public health degree in MCH systems, I celebrate this seminal work as the bright spotlight it intends to be - shedding light into the dark underbelly of institutionalized, corporatized, healthcare for-profit. Even when profit is not corrupting the system, western obstetrics firmly rooted in misogynistic patriarchy has distorted the most basic human right of passage into the unnatural medico-surgical event we now think is normal.

Following the engrossing and enlightening stories in this book, Irene has given even the most reluctant reader a toehold. Climbing through a labyrinth of emotional complexity, her characters feel so realistic, it is relatively impossible to put down. The birth scenes take us deeper into not just understanding the process, but also to understanding the complex challenges present for all.

Irene has tackled this topic like none before her. Even without the modern neurological research proving storytelling is the best way to capture people's attention, bake information into their memories, and forge close, personal bonds, we intuitively know humans inherently crave and seek out great stories almost as much as food and water. As the writer and storyteller, Francesca Lia Block said, "Think about the word destroy. Do you know what it is? De-story. Destroy. Destory. You see. And restore. That's re-story. Do you know that only two things have been proven to help survivors? Massage is one. Telling their story is another. Being touched and touching. Telling your story is touching. It sets you free." Irene has set so many stories free in this novel and in doing so, she is touching our hearts and our collective passion to see the change - to re-story; restore the sovereignty of the birth person to own their birth process.

Irene's midwife heart has birthed a gem. This glittering beacon of transformation in the depths of systemic struggle will resonate with so many readers. Mothers hesitant about the unknown, midwives struggling to maintain their humanity and ultimately policy makers and change makers hungry for another way through will all resonate with this humble and courageous offering.

Brené Brown agrees, "Courage is a heart word. The root of the word courage is cor - the Latin word for heart. In one of its earliest forms, the word courage meant "To speak one's mind by telling all one's heart." Thank you, Irene, for speaking your whole heart with us. Seen through her lens, the messy and ugly and beautiful bits of birth have blended with her quiet and courageous intention to paint a new worldview of what's possible in pregnancy, birth and parenting. The world is lucky to have such a visionary leader willing to tell us stories from her beautiful heart.

With love,
Augustine Colebrook, MA-MCHS
MidwiferyWisdom.com

Note from the author to the English edition.

I first published this book in 2015 and I cannot even tell you how many times I've reread it since then. Especially the English edition, as I have reviewed it many times. Please bear in mind English is not my first language, so my revision might not have been very accurate. Isabel Ferrán, a good friend of mine, has translated it and she is also Spanish so you might find a bit of a Spanish accent as you read along. Overall, we really hope you enjoy it.

It took me about 8 years to write it, which means I started around 2007.

My dad was an obstetrician and my mum was a literature teacher. When I was 15 and I had to choose to study either science or languages, I did not want to choose. I loved both and choosing one meant leaving the other behind. I chose science and the other part always weighed on me.

I've always written. I've always enjoyed telling stories.

If any of the stories you read sound unrealistic to you, please realise you are very privileged to be in a country where women are not treated this way.

So many women have come to me to tell me their story was very similar to Estela, Sol, Sarah, Elena's... Some of them have shared their experiences with me and, with a lot of sorrow, I must admit that reality overtakes fiction by far.

Irene Garzón.

Week 5

Maternity Hospital 7.55 am.

Ana grabs her handbag from the car and hurries to get changed into her scrubs. She is in the nick of time once more. No matter what time her children get up, she always ends up running.

"Humph! This is crowded," she muses as she walks to the dressing room. Minutes later, she enters the staff room pulling her hair into a ponytail.

"I am here, Marta. Don't you look tired! Bad night, was it?" says Ana to the midwife who has been on the night shift.

"Six deliveries, two of them C-sections. Everything's done, the delivery room is being cleaned, the last section has just gone to the ward. I think you're getting the diabetic for the induction.[1] Have a good shift, I'm going home to die."

"Have a good rest, sweetie."

Ana starts making coffee, for this morning she did not have the time for it. Besides, now that Luis has lost his job, instead of helping at home it feels as if she has one more child to look after. But well, it has been less than ten days, and then he did not see it coming at all. It was all of a sudden, after ten solid years of working for them, but… There are no new orders, either we make some cuts or we will be bankrupt, of course, we will be firing top people too … Sure, top people too, but it had to be Luis, it couldn't be useless Vince, or Michael, who's a cocky bastard and besides is wasting the firm's money; but, of course, he is the boss' nephew… those never get fired, do they?

"Girls, I made coffee, who wants some?"

"I want one, I'm freezing and I left my cardigan at home," says Cande, another midwife.

"But it's not cold in here, c'mon."

---

[1] Labour induction: procedure aiming to provoke contractions by artificial methods to stimulate childbirth.

"Yeah, well, I like my cardigan on. I miss it if I'm not wearing it."

"Ana, you'll be getting the induction," interrupts Leyre, the admissions nurse. "An induction for gestational diabetes. This one's going to be a section, I'm telling you. Fat as a cow, she is."

"Ok, I'll take her. I'll get everything ready, put her on the monitor and then let them decide," she says as she takes a last sip of coffee.

Delivery Room 2. 08:30 am.

"Good morning, Madam," says Ana.

"Hello, good morning. I'm Miriam. Are you the midwife?"

"Yes, love, that's me."

"I'm a bit nervous. It's my first baby, you know. A boy. Esteban, like his dad," says Miriam hurriedly.

"Lovely, darling… look, now I have to monitor the baby, it may annoy you a little…"

"All right, I will help you as much as I can… as long as my baby is born all right…"

"Right, put your legs up here and try to relax."

"Ouch! What is that?"

"Easy, lady, I barely touched you."

"Ouch! Ok, sorry, I'm just very nervous, this is my first… My husband has children already, but I don't, and, well, I am very nervous, you know…"

"No, no, not like that, relax, we cannot do anything if you don't," nags the midwife. "Relax; put your bottom on the bed. I can't do this if you don't cooperate."

Miriam flinches again.

"Madam, please! What was your name again?"

"Miriam," she replies in a small voice.

"Miriam, this is hopeless. Either you relax or I'll have to call the doctor; and he is much less delicate than me, alright? I am being veeeery delicate."

"Yes, sorry… just nerves."

"Yes, I do know you are nervous; I do this several times a day, you know, Miriam? And with people far more cooperative than you are, let me tell you. Shall I call the doctor?"

"No, no, I can relax, give me a minute, I can do it," she says as she closes her eyes and inhales deeply.

"Bottom down, Miriam, put your bottom down; relax, please! For heaven's sake, no way, I'm calling the doctor because I can't monitor you."

"Wait, could you call my husband, please?"

"No. Your husband can't come in until we're finished monitoring you."

"Yeah, but I'd be far more at ease with him here," argues Miriam once alone in the room.

Miriam is left alone for a few minutes in the delivery room. As she tries to unwind, she gets more and more tense... *Damn, that was hurting... what will the doctor be like? I'm so jittery, and, getting someone's fingers inside your fanny, suddenly like that, hurts. She might do it several times a day, but I don't...,* she thinks.

Maternity Hospital.

Delivery Room 2.

"Good morning, Madam!" Miriam hears behind her. "I'm Doctor Casona."

A woman, thank God! Miriam thinks. "Good morning, Doctor."

"The midwife tells me you're a bit fretful and she cannot put the internal monitor on."

"Yes, a bit, Doctor. I do want to cooperate but it's my first and I'm very nervous... it's a boy. I'm calling him Esteban after his father."

"Ahh, fine, fine... You know what we are going to do now?" asks Dr. Casona once she is at Miriam's bedside.

"Well, getting my baby out, isn't it?"

"Well, it's you who will be getting that baby out; but do you know the steps we will follow to do that?"

"No, doctor."

"Well, we are going to induce your labour: we risk the baby getting too large if we allow you to reach full term," explains the obstetrician.

"Due to the '*diabetis*'."

"That's right, due to the gestational diabetes. So, at this stage we're trying to break the bag of waters around the baby; after that, we'll give you some medicine to make your womb start contracting. This will take quite a lot of time, you might not have your baby until tomorrow; or it might not even work."

"And what if it doesn't?"

"If it doesn't, we'll have to perform a Cesarean section on you. But so far, we will be going step by step and try for you to give birth to Esteban. Now, put your bottom down as much as you can. That's it, very good. Now you will notice a bit of pressure, it's my fingers; you relax, I'll do it softly. That's right, that's fine… you told me it was your first child, didn't you?" the doctor says, as she softly introduces her fingers inside Miriam's vagina.

"Yes, my first; well, Julio has two from a former marriage, but this is our first."

"Didn't you tell me he'll be called after his dad?"

"Yes; his name is Julio Esteban, but we call him Julio, so the child will be Esteban. Besides, my sister married a bloke called Esteban and the poor thing was widowed some months after marrying him… so sad, they were so happy, you know? So, I feel thrilled to call the baby Esteban."

"Well, that's done," says Nuria Casona, taking her gloves off.

"Already? Really? I didn't even notice! Thank you, Doctor."

"So, stiff as a board with me and soft as butter with the doctor, were we?" states Ana, the midwife. "Nothing better than threatening women with the doctor to make them relax. You've been lucky, Dr. Casona treats her patients wonderfully."

"Well, Miriam, all the best, and I expect to see you with baby Esteban in your arms very soon."

"Thank you, Doctor, thank you very much," a frankly relieved Miriam replies.

Maternity Hospital.
Doctors' Office. 08:55 am.

"Hi, how are things?" asks Laura, an Obstetrics consultant, who is just starting her on-call.

"Fine. It's been a quiet night, but you're in for a busy, busy morning," replies Elena, the consultant on call the previous night.

"How so?" asks Laura as she hangs her handbag in the coat rack.

"I'll tell you in a minute. The junior doctors are starting today, so, the moment they are here I'll handover to you. We will let them join the party from their first day, shall we?"

"They'll have to get moving then, we're starting right now."

"C'mon, Laura, remember your first day? Give them a chance, they're bound to feel a bit lost." Elena replies.

"Anyone know anything about them?" Ángela, the registrar says.

"Male and female methinks." Elena tells her.

"I don't know where men get the idea to become obstetricians," says Laura as she tidies her scrubs up. "Hundreds of specialties to choose from, and they have to choose this one… frankly, I think some of them should get themselves checked. Do you know any female urologist? 'Cause I don't…"

"You're right," Elena says. "I don't think men would readily accept showing their privates to a woman. She might get to do some surgery, but nobody would go to her clinic."

"I knew I was making the wrong choice…" says Ángela. "I'd be twiddling my thumbs in Urology."

"Yes, but: would you really exchange this for sick, infected, smelly, revolting penises?"

"Well, not really," she replies with a disgusted face.

"Hi, I'm Abel, I start my internship today," says a young man as he comes into the room.

"Hello Abel; I am Laura, the consultant on call this morning: did you find us easily?" "I did but parking took ages; I never thought I'd have to queue to park."

"Meh, many people work here and this is peak time. Please excuse me, we were discussing something interesting here, let's say it's some kind of survey: why did you choose obs and gyne?"

Ángela pokes Elena's arm: they both make efforts not to laugh.

"Well, because 'Cardio' was all taken and after the body's engine, reproduction is what I find more interesting."

"And why not Urology?" Laura asks.

"C'mon, are you trying to compare a man's role to a woman's one in reproduction? I'm thrilled by the fetus formation, embryology, development and delivery. I find it the most beautiful area in medicine. And, as I myself cannot give birth, at least here I can participate."

"You could have become a midwife, couldn't you?"

"Hey, you leave him be: why didn't you become one anyway? Poor chap, you are giving him the third degree and he still has his backpack on. I am Elena, the consultant who was here last night," she says as she warmly kisses him on both cheeks. "Don't worry, Laura just got out of the wrong side of bed."

"Well, I wasn't that harsh, was I?" apologizes Laura.

"Do you find it normal to pester the boy like that the minute he comes through the door?" scolds Elena.

"Well, excuse me, Abel, it wasn't my intention…"

"Don't worry, it's all right," he replies with a smile.

"Hello! Hi, Abel! Hi everyone, I am Julia, Abel's mate."

"I'm Laura, the consultant on call this morning: welcome."

"Wow, aren't we a big bunch today! Lots of new faces!" says Carlos as he enters the office. "I am a consultant. Let's start, people on the night shift must be dying to go home."

"Who's missing?" Laura asks.

"Nuria, who was monitoring number 2, a diabetic of the worst kind. This afternoon's C-section is my guess," says Elena.

"And is she already in labour ward for an afternoon C-section?" Julia, the new trainee doc asks.

"No, no. She's here for an induction, but a diabetic that fat is very likely to end up with a C-section, they are useless at dieting. Well, you'll see what happens."

"Hi, Nuria!" Ángela greets the newcomer. "These are our new colleagues; guys, this is Nuria Casona: stick to her if you want to learn this profession well. She's a great obstetrician. One of the best."

"Thank you; Ángela, darling. Please don't stick too much just now, I'm about to go home," she says as she takes a seat.

"Ok, let's start," says Elena.

"Room 1 is empty, woman just delivered, it's getting cleaned."

"Room 2 is the induction for diabetes I was telling you about: Nuria, how is she?"

"Quite well, frankly, she had a rather favourable cervix, I think she has possibilities."

"Nuria is always very optimistic in cases like this." Elena states.

"Cases like this?" Laura smiles. "In every single one. When I was doing my training, Nuria was already a consultant and I remember she expected every woman to deliver."

"Well, all women have that capacity... and if we wouldn't trust that capacity, we would be performing many more C-sections; and 20% is about enough, is it not?"

"Yes, Nuria, but if you get a dwarf, diabetic with a breech presentation[2], you do induce her."

"Well, I'd have to study the case…"

"See?" Laura laughs. "Seriously now, guys: this is the woman you'll be learning most from."

"Ok, let's go on, I want to go home" says Elena, and she goes on with the shift change.

"Room 3 all right, an induction already in labour, 6cm. at 7:00am."

"4 has just started labour. One of those who wants a natural birth. 3-4cm., and she is with our *'flower power'*, so, well, we will see how that ends."

"Who is the *'flower power'*?" asks Abel.

"Pff, one of those natural birth crusaders who studied in the UK and is absolutely pro natural birth. A total pain in the neck. Every time we get into the delivery room she questions and casts doubts on every single decision we make. You'll soon be meeting her, you will see…" Laura says and carries on. "And in room 5 an induction, a Chinese girl who doesn't speak a word of Spanish and is complaining lots, but we cannot give her an epidural."

"Why not?"

"Anaesthetists refuse to give one to people who don't speak Spanish because they don't know what they're saying."

"And if she needs a C-section doesn't she need to sign a consent?"

---

[2] When the baby presents bottom first.

"Yes, but as that is supposed to be vital we can always say it was necessary and the woman was told what she was signing."

"And how was she told if she only speaks Chinese?"

"Well, no idea, but a section is excusable as it was necessary to save her life. And as an epidural is not a vital need, she doesn't get one."

"Couldn't it be translated into several languages?" asks Julia.

"Yeah, fine, that and every possible test you may need in a hospital," Laura retorts. "These are public services, we are not that affluent. You will see, just wait…"

"Well, guys, I'm leaving, I'm sooo knackered, I'm going straight home" Nuria says.

"I'll go with you," says Ángela.

"Good shift to you all."

"Thank you. Have a good rest."

Maternity Hospital.

Delivery Room 4. 9:00 am.

"Hello Dolores, I am Celia, your midwife; how are you?"

"Fine; a bit frightened, but fine."

"What do they call you at home?"

"Loli," she says smiling faintly.

"Very well, Loli. I'm told you want us to do everything we can so you have a delivery as natural as possible."

"Yes, I'd love to; I've been gathering information and I think it's the best for the baby. I've made my own birth-plan[3] and I'd like to stick to it as much as possible."

"Very well, I'll have a look at it and we'll see how we can achieve it. Will you tell me what's been happening so far, or are you tired of explaining the same again and again? If you want, reading your medical records will be enough so far."

Loli starts having a contraction that very moment. "Can I stand up?" she asks.

"Of course, you can, you're the boss here" says the midwife as she helps her to do it. "I am here to help you, but you are the leader of what is happening in this room."

---

[3] birth plans are lists elaborated by the mother stating her birth preferences and wishes related to her care during labour.

Loli stands up smiling at Celia, closes her eyes and her smile grows larger as she thinks, *how lucky! I really like this midwife.* As the contraction fades away, Loli opens her eyes and asks, "how much longer will you be staying here?"

"Until much after you've had your baby." Celia smiles.

"Am I having my baby with you?"

"Yes, we'll do all we can so that you do. Are you on your own?"

"My husband went to the canteen to have some breakfast."

"Will there be someone else at your delivery?"

"No, but they only allow one birth partner, don't they?

"As I told you, you choose. If there's somebody else you'd like to be present and everything's going fine, I don't have any problem for them to be here. If we don't stand out too much, they'll leave us alone."

"Thank you so much, Celia, I'm thrilled you are my midwife: I have heard so many horror stories about this hospital I was afraid to be stuck with one of the 'obnoxious ones'. I'm ecstatic that you are with me."

"I'm also glad to be able to help you. It's also a pleasure for us being able to help someone who wants to deliver naturally and knows about it." Celia says with a wink. Soon after, Celia tells her, "look, Loli, as your baby is perfectly fine I'm taking this monitor off and we'll just be listening to your baby from time to time, so that you can move freely. Got any music?"

"Yes, we brought some. It's in the baby's bag, don't bother, Raúl will look for it when he comes."

"Well then, I'll put out the light: a relaxing atmosphere will help you loosen up and dilate."

"When will you check my dilation?"

"Whenever you ask me."

"But the person in triage told me they would do it every two hours here in the delivery room."

"It's not necessary, but if you want it like that I will do it. We'll see, ok? We can know how labour is progressing without a vaginal examination. If I see anything awry I'll let you know, right?"

"I think I've won the lottery with you: how lucky I am! Thank you."

"You're welcome, Loli. And the other star of the story, what do we know about him/her?"

"That "shim" is a much-desired baby, and his father and I are anxious to meet "shim" already."

"Don't you know if it's a boy or a girl?"

"No, we didn't want to. We wanted to keep the surprise till the end."

Raúl comes into the room just then and he shakes Celia's hand to greet her.

"Hello, Raúl. I am Celia, the midwife who will help you deliver your son or daughter," she says as she shakes Raúl's hand.

"Hello, pleased to meet you."

"Raúl, darling, she's charming, we've been very lucky: she's one of us," Loli tells her husband.

"Well, we are a team." Celia replies.

"Yes, but listening to my friends and sisters-in-law's deliveries is so distressing that… we came ready for the worst and we've been so lucky…"

"Well, delivering with someone like you is very gratifying for me too, as I told you. Have you thought how you want to know the baby's sex? Do you want to discover it yourselves, or shall I tell you?"

"We haven't thought about it, I don't think we mind much…"

"Well, we'll see when the moment comes, then."

"Raúl, please, look for the music and give it to Celia."

Maternity Hospital.

Delivery Room 2. 11:00am.

Ana comes into the delivery room where Miriam is with her husband. "May I stand up?" Miriam asks.

"Yes, let me help you" replies Ana going towards her. "These cables can be annoying, I know."

Miriam gets up as the midwife rearranges the monitors. "Couldn't you take them off for a while?" she asks.

"No, I certainly can't, because you are on the oxytocin[4] drip and we need to know how your baby is coping all the time."

"And what if I need to pee? Do I go to the toilet with the machines on?"

[4] Drug used to provoke uterine contractions in order to start labour artificially.

"'Course not, just ring the bell and the assistant will come with the bedpan."

"But I'm very particular about being able to pee in private. I won't be able to do it in front of anyone! Can't you unplug me for just a sec?"

"No, can't you see you are completely wired? You have the belly monitors and the drip to your arm; there is no way. If you want to pee you do it here to make things easy. How are those pains going? You noticing them already?"

"Yes, I do, yes… and they hurt quite a bit really." she says, rubbing her belly.

"Huh, that's nothing, just you wait until you get them really long and hard… I'll increase the oxytocin a little bit, we have to get it into full swing for you to deliver. I'll be back in a short while, shall I tell Feli to come with the bedpan?"

"No, I'm not feeling like it yet, thank you." Miriam replies.

Ana goes out the door and Miriam tells her husband, "Sheesh, if this is nothing I don't want to think what's coming… the minute she's back I'm asking her if I can get that *'pidural'* thing, I cannot take these pains much longer!"

"Sure, you will, whatever you want, love! It didn't work well for Marga with Dani and with Carla, well, she didn't even have the time," her husband replies.

"From what the midwife says I'll be having plenty of time, we'll be staying here a long time; and I can't take much more of this."

"Marga had to cope with it. Something didn't work well with the anaesthesia and it hurt the same…"

"Julio, dear, do you think I feel like hearing about your ex's labours right now?"

"Sorry, you're right… it's only that, as I've been here before…"

"No, you haven't been here with me, it's not the same, so don't compare."

"Right. I'll shut up."

"Oww, gimme your hand, a pain's coming."

Miriam grabs her husband's hand as the contraction comes. When it gets milder, Julio jokes, "they'd better give you that epidural soon or you'll crack my fingers."

"Yeah, well, you have no idea how this hurts," his wife smiles.

"You just crack my fingers as much and as hard as you need, love."

When Ana comes back into Miriam's delivery room she approaches the monitor and remarks, "Well, it looks as if things are finally livening up, aren't they? How are you doing?"

"Gah, not very well I think: when can I get my *'pidural'*?"

"Whenever you want. Shall I get everything ready and call the anaesthetist?" asks the midwife.

"Yes, please, this is hurting lots."

Ana puts Miriam's drip on free flow and exits through the door.

Maternity Hospital.
Delivery Room 2. 11:40am.

"Good morning, Ma'am, I'm the anaesthetist coming to give you your epidural."

"Oh, good!" Miriam sighs with relief.

"You get out, please," the midwife tells Julio. "We'll call you when she's ready. If you want to eat something, do it now. This'll take about twenty minutes."

"All right Ma'am, you have to sit as I tell you and don't move at all," the anaesthetist tells Miriam.

"And what if I get a contraction?"

"You don't move, but you tell us it's coming. How much weight did you gain in your pregnancy?"

"12 kilos, more or less."

"So, you were already roly poly before you got pregnant."

"Yes, I've always been a bit overweight," smiles Miriam.

"That's no good, Ma'am; not for you, nor for the baby or the epidural, excess fat makes it a more difficult and dangerous technique."

Miriam looks at the midwife, who whispers, "just don't listen to him," as she grimaces at the anaesthetist disapprovingly.

"Well, Miriam, now you cannot move at all; tell me when a contraction comes, but just don't move, will you?"

"Ok," says Miriam, and just then she bounces with a start.

"Ma'am, what are you doing!? Don't move, I told you!"

"Sorry, I just noticed something weird, like an electric shock." Miriam apologizes.

"Where?" the anaesthetist asks angrily.

"In… in my left buttock."

"Well, that's normal, don't move again."
The anaesthetist finishes the epidural and says, "It's been easier than I expected; with your obesity, I thought it would be harder. Now you'll start to feel relief, little by little. The normal, the ideal, is for you to feel the contractions, but without the pain. Don't expect to feel numb from the waist down, ok?"
"Ok. Thank you, Doctor."

Maternity Hospital.
 Delivery room 4. 11:50 am.
"You're doing fine, Loli, you're doing wonderfully; look, it's been two hours, shall I monitor you?"
"Is it really necessary?"
"No, it isn't, baby's perfect and you are doing very well."
"Let's wait a bit, then."
"The doctors are about to do their round, let me do the talking, right?"
"Sure."
"Do you feel like pushing?"
"No, but with the pain I feel like pooing."
"Good! That's your baby's head pushing down. Should the doctors ask, you don't feel like pooing, right?"
"Right," she replies with a grin.
"But… is the baby coming?" Raúl asks, astonished.
"Soon, we're nearly there," the midwife replies smiling.
Just then a group of four people comes into the delivery room.
"Hello, we are the team on call today: how are you doing?" Laura, the consultant, asks Celia.
"Good, everything's fine," the midwife replies.
"That's off, is it?" Laura asks pointing at the monitor.
"Yes, we're intermittently monitoring; it's all written here," Celia replies, pointing at Loli's records.
"Aren't you going to examine her?"
"I just did, just when you came in, I had no time to write it down."
"And, how is she?"
"6 cm. dilation, fully effaced cervix, head at -1. Looks very well."
"Ok, just monitor her for a while to see how she's doing."
"But she's doing fine, I told you…" Celia replies.

"Yes, but we need a long CTG[5] trace every two hours," Laura interrupts. "You know the intermittent monitoring protocol goes like that."

"Ok, I'll do it right now."

"All the best, I wish you a quick labour," Laura tells Loli as the three junior doctors follow her out the door.

"She hardly looked at me, did she?" Loli tells Celia.

Celia smiles at her.

"Have I really dilated 6 cm. already?" Loli asks once the on-call team has left.

"I think you have, and more, possibly. We'll listen for a long time after your contraction has passed to see how your baby's doing. I'm going to monitor you for a while for their peace of mind."

"Aw, after being without them, these belts feel really uncomfortable now," Loli complains.

"Just for a little while, ok? The minute we check baby's all right, I'll take them off."

During the next few contractions, all that can be heard is Loli's breathing, mingled with her chanting as she contracts. She is sitting on a stool, while Raúl acts as her lean-to sitting on the ball.

Celia watches from a corner. The noises Loli is starting to make tell her the baby's head is coming down and Loli is now near full dilation.[6] *We'll be seeing this baby very soon,* she thinks as she starts hearing the first involuntary pushes Loli makes with her contractions.

"I am pushing, I just can't help it. And I think I'm going to poo."

"Don't worry, you're doing splendidly. Do as your body tells you, but without forcing. Just listen to what it asks from you, your body is telling you what you have to do."

"And what if I poo?" she asks, frightened.

"It's not poo, it's the baby's head. The feeling is exactly the same, but your bowel is probably empty. And if you do poo, there's no problem either. Relax."

[5] Cardiotocograph: Technical means of recording the fetal heartbeat and the uterine contractions during pregnancy.

[6] Full dilatation: when the cervix is completely opened for the baby to pass through into the vagina.

"Right. I've had some diarrhoea since yesterday…"

"You are doing beautifully, go on like this. I'm going to take the monitor off so you can be more at ease."

"Wait, here comes another… this one's very tight, I cannot push. I'm going to poo, I just can't…"

"Relax, Loli," Celia says as she touches Loli's arm. "Let it carry you away, let go. Let shim out, help shim, don't avoid it out of shame. Don't fight. Relax your jaw."

Just then, Loli gives a long push and Celia can see the baby's scalp.

"Lovely, go on, you're doing just fine."

Loli closes her eyes between contractions; she is tired and keeping all her might for the pushing.

"If you want, you may attempt to touch your baby's head in the next contraction."

"Is shim already there?"

"Yes, can't you notice?"

"Yes, I can feel shim going up and down, is that his head?"

"Yes."

"Have you seen it?"

"Yes."

"Has he got a lot of hair?"

"Not much, really." Celia smiles.

She looks up to Raúl and they both smile. "A baldie," Raúl says, kissing his wife.

Loli closes her eyes again and she stands up briskly.

"I don't know how to stand, I feel so uncomfortable…"

"There is no comfortable position right now," Celia says, "how do you want to be?"

"I'm not sure."

"Sitting on the bed, lying on your side, on your knees, standing up holding Raúl…?"

"I'm not sure, it may sound silly, but I'd like to be hanging, pulling from something, putting my arms up…"

"That's normal, but here, in this delivery room we have nothing for you to hang from; why don't you try hanging from Raúl's neck and squatting when the contraction comes?"

"Ok. Get going, here comes another one," she tells her husband hurrying him up with a hand gesture. "Ooouuch," she pushes with the contraction. Celia bends down and sees how the baby moves forward: *baby will be here in a matter of minutes.*

"He's coming, she's coming!" Loli repeats. "Come, baby, mama's here and wants to meet you. Do come out, mama loves you a lot, please come."

"Raúl, want us to shift places for you to catch the baby?" Celia suggests.

"No!" Loli says clutching him. "You stay here with me. Don't leave me, darling, don't go."

"Easy, Loli, I won't move."

Another push and the baby's head comes out, while Loli pants. With the next contraction she pushes again and the baby is born.

Celia, who is kneeling on the floor with a cloth in her hands to catch the baby, passes him to his parents; Loli takes him and presses him against her breast.

"My sweet, my beautiful baby," she says between tears and sweat, simultaneously moved by emotion and with a huge grin. "Look, Raúl, look, my love, our baby, look how open his eyes are…" Loli looks at her husband: she has never seen him so moved. They kiss.

"Look, look how beautiful he is… It's a boy! Raúl, it's a boy."

"I love you so much, my dear…"

"Me too. I love you a lot."

They kiss again.

"Does he look like an Álvaro?"

"He does. Does he? If you want, yes."

"Let's see… Álvaro, Álvaro… I think he likes it."

"So, Álvaro it is."

"Hi Álvaro, we are Mum and Dad."

"Look, he's got your thumb!"

"How beautiful he is, isn't he?"

"I love you, I love you a lot."

Meanwhile, Celia is still in her corner, her heart full of joy because she's done it again: another couple has been able to receive their baby the way everyone deserves, and again she has witnessed this moment. The biggest moment of love a family may experience, and she is so lucky helping make it happen. Not interfering in the process but joining in, not being one too many in the room. Moments like this are what make this constant struggle with colleagues and doctors worth it. When she succeeds, she feels on cloud nine for being able to witness a moment, that sadly, many workmates will never experience.

How shocking it must be, she thinks. *Helping to give birth and never seeing a physiological one in your life, and, besides, not even be aware of it. They are convinced a natural birth is merely a child coming out of a vagina…*

"Thank you so much, Celia." Loli says a few minutes later.

"No, thank you for allowing me to be here and join the moment of Álvaro's birth. Happy birthday, Álvaro!" she says approaching them. "What a fine way to be born, isn't it, without even crying a bit, not a sound. Not many babies are born without crying nowadays."

"It's true!" says Raúl. "He hasn't shed a single tear. But don't they get smacked and put upside down?"

"No, not anymore; well, it's been proved they don't need it, even if they still do it in some places. But: can you imagine what a welcome that is? All you know is your mother's inside, and being born must be quite a shock already to get shaken and smacked on top of everything else. What a baby needs more, the only thing to make his birth as best as possible, is staying bonded to his mother all the time. Everything we do here (weighing and measuring him), should get done in the postnatal ward, or at least a few hours after the baby has been born."

Loli gives Celia a kiss, "Thank you, Celia, thank you very much. Thank you for making it possible, I know without you this would not have been so wonderful. You don't know how grateful I am."

"It's been wonderful for me, too. I'm thrilled that it's been as you dreamt it would."

Suddenly the door opens and two doctors come in, switching the light on.

"What?" Laura exclaims. "I was just coming to ask you if Abel could watch a birth on his first day and the baby is already born! Didn't you tell us she was 6 cm dilated a short while ago?"

"Yes, but…" Celia replies. "Turn the light off, please."

"Come on, it's too dark in here. Oh, the placenta is not out yet," remarks the obstetrician when she gets in front of Loli.

"Well, she gave birth two minutes ago; go see if Abel can watch another birth somewhere else," Celia adds.

"Well, congratulations," says Laura as both go away, somewhat upset.

"Just as well they didn't come before, isn't it? They would have spoiled the moment, but it's all right. We've been so lucky, darling!"

"Well, yes. It's unusual giving birth before the junior doctors get wind of it and want to come and take your baby off," smiles Celia.

"Thank you again, Celia. Thanks, and a zillion more thanks. I will never be able to thank you enough for what you've given us. You are a great person: I knew since I saw you come into the room."

Loli and Celia hug each other and Loli gives Celia a big kiss with tear-swollen eyes.

Maternity Hospital.
Delivery Room 2. 12:15 pm.
Julio comes into the Delivery Room.

"About time, they've been looking for you for a while and you were missing." Miriam scolds.

"I was outside, smoking."

"So, I told the girl, that if you weren't there you'd be having a puff somewhere."

"How is it going? Not hurting anymore?" Julio asks his wife as he sits by her side.

"No, I'm feeling great. But the anaesthetist was stupid."

"How come?

"He called me a roly poly, and he scolded me for budging. As if I had done it on purpose…!"

"Well, take it easy, you know doctors can be brash… though I'd like to see them as patients, we'd sure be getting a good laugh!" Julio looks at the monitor and then at his wife, "don't you notice anything?" he asks.

"Like what?"

"You are having a very strong contraction. Look, 125, 127…"

Miriam looks at the monitor, touches her belly and says calmly, "no, I can't feel anything. What a wonder this 'pidural' thing is, really…"

Maternity Hospital.

Staff Room. 12:15 pm.

Ana is in the staff room having a coffee and leafing through a magazine when Celia comes in. "How are you, Anita?" she asks.

"All right, I have an easy day."

"What do you have?"

"Just an induction for the whole day. She was very green and she just got an epidural."

"Who is she? The diabetic woman?" Celia asks.

"Yes, but I don't think she'll go into labour, or at least not with me. I'll be examining her now, after lunch. And you? Do you have anyone?"

"My delivery room is being cleaned. I've just had the most beautiful birth… I still have goosebumps."

"The one with the birth plan?"

"Yes, that one."

"Without epidural?"

"Yes, the way she wanted. She's on cloud nine now, oxytocin-high."

"Well I'm glad, because these ones are the best candidates to end up with the whole lot; those who shout 'me, I'm having a natural birth', and ten minutes after they are screaming for the epidural and ending in theatre… I always start to tremble whenever I get one of them."

"Why?"

"Because I think they're jinxed and they have the worst labours in the end; at least, the ones I get…"

"Have you ever thought it's maybe us who unconsciously add that load to them?" Celia asks her.

"Me? I follow the same procedure with every woman."

"I mean it's maybe us, due to the way we see things, getting on the defensive, thinking they are not going to give birth, and we give up too soon and try to make them give up too."

"Don't know, I don't think I treat them any differently than I treat the rest. I give them what I have to give them and what they ask me for, within some limits, that is. What I won't do is intermittent monitoring, letting them into the shower, massaging them... I don't get paid to do that. If they want, they can get one of them doulas..."[7]

"Wow, it's the first time I hear a midwife speak in favour of doulas," says Noemí, a student midwife who's just come into the staff room.

"No, I'm not saying I approve of them," replies Ana, "but I think some things are not our responsibility. If a woman wants a massage, or her feet fondled, she may well hire someone for the job, because that's not a part of mine as a midwife. What I don't find right is doulas tutoring antenatal classes, for instance: that is unqualified practice and I think it's indictable. Or them speaking about breastfeeding just because they took a ten-minute course."

"Well, of course that's unqualified practice," says Celia, "but it's true that anyone dares expressing their views on breastfeeding, even the plumber if you ask me."

"Personally, I think you're wrong, Ana." Noemí says, "I do think that supporting and taking care of women in labour is a part of our job, a fundamental part, and that if we gave more massages, spent more time inside the delivery rooms with the women, listened to their requests and did as much as possible to give it to them, we would have much less intervention, many more normal births and much more satisfaction, both from the women and from ourselves."

"No way, you say that because you have the eagerness of the beginner and are ready to take anything. But when you have spent some years into this you'll lose all that, just wait and see," Ana replies.

---

[7] A woman, typically without formal obstetric training, who is employed to provide guidance and support to a pregnant woman during labour & after birth.

"Or maybe not," Celia interrupts. "That depends on each person's temperament. I come here every day eager to do as much as possible for women to give birth as they want, for them to decide and to have a joyful birth. And whenever I get a well-informed woman who knows what she wants, I get a high and enjoy it so much more."

"And if that woman ends up getting the whole enchilada, what then?" replies Ana.

"Then I suffer a lot and I feel immensely sorry for her; but I have the consolation, to call it something, of having done all I could to give her what she wanted."

"And which you finally could not give her." Ana interrupts.

"But I tried to."

"So, you do it for you."

"No, Ana, it's not that. I do it for her, to help her get what she wanted, it's really much more satisfactory to work like that." Celia insists.

"Well, I don't see it. If a woman has a normal labour, I'll be as pleased as Punch. And if it ends badly, well, those things happen; but if I haven't been breaking my neck there, that's just trouble I have spared myself."

"But can't you see that if you break your neck, as you put it, that woman has less probability of ending with a C-section?"

"Oh, yeah? Says who? Do you really think you have that much capacity to influence women's labours? Then, what happens with those we mentioned before, who come with their birth-plan and their natural birth intentions and end up with synto, epidural, forceps, episio and a third-degree tear?[8] According to you, they should give birth because you've done your best: is it your fault then that woman ends up like that?"

"No, I don't think it's my fault. It's nobody's fault, or maybe it's everyone's: it's not having given her the right ambience, having had many interruptions, not having given her what she needed… many factors can have an influence."

---

[8] Synto: synthetic oxytocin; forceps: metal tool to extract the baby's head; episiotomy: cut done in the vagina to ease the baby's birth; third degree tearing: tear affecting the anal sphincter.

"Look, Celia, you do what you want. Sing with them, give them massages and invoke every delivery Goddess: if it makes you happier, I'm fine with it. Myself, I completely forget about work as I go out that door home with my family at the end of the day. And I prefer a thousand times to get an induction with a closed cervix when I get here, because that means I will probably have a much easier shift, than having a mother wanting a natural birth and rosehip oil massages, even if she finally has a textbook delivery."

"Well, that sounds more like not wanting to work than anything." Celia replies.

"Yes, the law of minimum effort. And at the end of the month we will be getting the same pay, won't we?" says Ana standing up. "Believe me, Celia, the sooner you admit defeat, the better: it will save you a lot of pain."

"I find it a bleak life philosophy, to tell you the truth: don't make more effort than strictly necessary because it's worthless. It's not, it's worth it, Ana! And the feeling that remains when someone gets what they want because of your effort and your collaboration is one of the reasons that make me get up to come here…"

"Up to you. Whenever we work together, you can keep the hippies and I'll be getting all the inductions, what do you think?" says Ana patting Celia's shoulder as she gets out of the room. "And everyone will be happy."

Celia looks at Noemí with a resigned expression, and Noemí says, "We'll never change anything that way. No student likes to be her mentee, because they learn nothing. She won't let us do anything except for legs up, directed pushes, perineal manipulation…"

"Well, there are more and more young midwives willing to change things, and these old ones are getting retired little by little…"

"But Ana is young!" Noemí complains.

"Yes, but she's a one off, most of the last generation midwives arrive eager to do things well. One thing at a time, Noemí, one thing at a time…" Celia tries to comfort her.

Maternity Hospital.
Staff Room. 12:20pm.

Ana is sitting at the computer when Julio, Miriam's husband, comes in looking alarmed, "Baby's heart's gone down to eighty!" he says frightened.

Ana stands up and follows Julio to the Delivery Room. As she gets in she sees Ángela, a registrar, with one of the junior doctors. Miriam is already lying on her side, and the baby's beat is at 90 per minute.

Miriam looks scaredly at Ana and her husband and asks, "what's going on? Is the baby all right?"

"Take a deep breath, Miriam," Ana says, "don't speak."

They keep silent and all that can be heard is the baby's heartbeat. "Do I stop the Oxytocin?" Ana asks, her finger already on the button that stops the infusion.

"Yes, yes, stop it." Ángela replies.

"But, what's up? Please say something," Miriam insists.

"Baby didn't like the epidural. He's reacting in a way we don't like," replies the doctor.

"But is he all right?"

"Yes, that's not uncommon; he's already recovering. It happens to most babies some minutes after their moms get the epidural. Look, he's better now," replies the midwife as the heartbeat starts to get quicker.

"Wait for ten minutes and start the Oxytocin again. Half the dose she had before, and go on increasing it. Let's see if we can get this baby delivered one of these days," the obstetrician tells Ana.

"Is he going to take days?" Julio asks startled.

"Just a manner of speaking, don't fret. Tomorrow at the latest. If you don't dilate sufficiently in some hours," she says looking at Miriam, "you'll be getting a C-section. When are you going to examine her?" Ángela asks Ana.

"At two o'clock," she replies.

"Ok, full swing then," she says as they leave the Delivery Room.

Maternity Hospital.

Delivery Room 2. 14:00pm.

"Well, against all odds, you are in labour," Ana tells Miriam while performing a vaginal examination. "You have dilated 5 centimetres., soft cervix… Very well, all is very well."

"5 cm.? And I have to reach how many?"

"Ten."

"And then the baby will be born?"

"No, then another phase of labour starts where the baby comes down. And when he's down enough then we'll start pushing. We still have some hours to reach that stage, but I didn't think you'd get into labour this soon."

I'm running to the toilet, I just noticed something. I'm sure this is it, you'll see how I've got it. I lock the door and I repeat the routine that has become ritual since I started worrying: I close my eyes, I sit on the toilet and as I pee I open them very slowly, little by little and… *"This can't be true: clean, not even a little discharge. Can't be true, I did notice something coming out a minute ago, I even felt a bit of a tummy ache…*

"God, please help me. I know I have misbehaved and I should have gone to the hospital when that condom split, but don't punish me this way. I've learnt, I promise it won't happen again, but it's enough, I've learnt the lesson, don't make me suffer anymore. Why doesn't my period come? Send it to me, please, I need to have it, I need some peace. Five days; it can't be. It must be something else, it's late for some other reason, something else, and if I don't take it easy I will never get it. This just can't happen to me, it was just the once, everybody has some condom trouble sometime. I just can't be pregnant, I simply can't. It couldn't happen to me. Relax, Elena".

"It-just-can't-be," she says out loud separating every word as she hits her lower abdomen with each one. "Come, fucking period, do come!"

After getting out of the shower, Elena looks at herself in the mirror. She takes her breasts in her hands and squeezes them: they don't hurt, they feel taut as they do when her period is due, only they don't hurt. And her nipples look bigger. Suddenly, she starts sobbing and she knows she must do something, she's got to buy a pregnancy test and clear any doubts, because she can't go on like this.

"I'm pregnant. Fuck, fuck, FUCK, shit! Fuck it, Javi, how could you not realize your condom had slipped out? Dammit! you should know! Wasn't it such a shitty thing to use? 'It doesn't feel the same, you lose a lot of sensitivity…' Then, you're supposed to realize it! Bastard, if you have done this on purpose, I'm killing you, I swear I will." Elena thinks.

Elena texts Paula, her best friend, and walks to her house to meet her.

"I'm worried I might be pregnant," she tells her friend.

"Surely not, Elena, easy, don't worry."

"But I'm never late… well, I usually am, but not THIS late."

"Have you done a test?"

"No, I'm so frightened it may come out positive..."

"C'mon, don't be silly. Just do it and put an end to this agony; then you'll be able to rest."

"And what if it's positive?" she asks, terrified.

"Well, then if you were pregnant, which you surely aren't, the sooner you know, the better, isn't it? What's more, we are going to buy one of those widgets straightaway and that's that."

"But you buy it, will you? I'm so frightened someone recognises me and tells my mother…"

"Don't worry, I'll go get it. Just let's go to some chemist's that's not downtown to avoid meeting anyone."

"Thanks so much, Paula, thank God you're here…"

"Don't worry, you'll see it's just a scare. Have you told Javi?"

"No, I don't want to worry him unless I'm sure."

"Damn, girl, if you're going through this he should be, too," her friend rebukes.

"Yeah, and besides it was his fault... I just don't want to, ok? I wouldn't have told you either if it wasn't because I need your help."

"But you know you can tell me anything, I'm your best friend, Ele."

"Yes, yes, it's not that. It's just that the fact of telling anyone makes it more real. It might be silly, but it feels as if by not telling it it's not real, it's just in my head; but if I say it out loud, the possibility of it being real is there. It's totally absurd, I know," she says looking down to the floor.

"Ok, relax, let's go for it. Got any money?" Paula asks her friend.

"Yes, well, how much does it cost?"

"No idea, how much do you have?"

"Twenty quid."

"I have twelve, I guess it will do."

Soon after, Paula comes back with the pregnancy test hiding in her handbag. "Done. Let's go to a bar and be over with it," she says, grabbing her friend's arm.

"What? No way! I need to do it when I'm ready, and I'm not, not yet. It took me a lot to get to the point of buying it, I cannot do it yet."

"And what if someone at your house finds it?"

"I'll be careful, I'll keep it well hidden."

"Fine. Just tell me. If you need anything, whatever, just call me and I'll come by your place, ok?"

"Right, Pau," Elena says as she hugs her. "Thanks so much, dear, I'm glad I've told you, you're a darling. Thank you for being my best friend."

"I love you lots, and I want you to know I'll always be by your side, right?"

"Thank you so much," she says, and she breaks into tears.

"C'mon, Ele, cool it. You'll see how this comes to nothing. And if it doesn't, we'll find a solution," Paula tries to comfort her.

"But my parents will kill me, I swear they'll kill me. If I am, I'd rather die before telling them."

"C'mon, calm down. Never say die! We'll find a way to solve it." Paula says while hugging her friend warmly.

"Thank you, Pau, thank you very much," says Elena as she gets calmer in her friend's arms.

After leaving Paula at her home, **Elena** goes back to hers, thinking: *This is such rotten luck, because if I'm not, I'm going through hell just for being late for some reason I don't even know. And if I am… No, it can't be, this can't be happening to me, I just can't be. Look at that Gómez girl, or Paloma, they've been having sex with half the college and nothing ever happened to them. No, this can't happen to me. Look, God, there are simply many more people in the world who deserve this much more than me. And what about all those couples desperate to have a baby? Send mine to them so everyone will be happy. I don't want to go through an abortion, God, I promise you I will be much more careful from now on. I've learnt, I've got the lesson from all this with this scare and this shock, but I think it's enough, isn't it? Send my period to me, God, I cannot take it anymore…*

Maternity Hospital.
Delivery Room 2. 16:30pm.
"Something's coming out from between my legs," Miriam tells Ana when she comes into the room to watch the monitor.
"Must be a little water, lady."
"Dunno, I'm all numb…" says Miriam.
Ana lifts the sheets and blankets; she cannot believe what she sees: it's undoubtedly Miriam's baby's head. She runs out to the corridor and screams, "Send me an assistant to Room 2, fast!"
She puts on some gloves as fast as she can and tells Miriam, "Don't push with the pains, how come you did without telling me?"
"But I didn't!" she replies, "I just told you when I noticed something down there. What's up?"
"Your baby's being born, that's what's up," the midwife retorts. The maternity assistant comes in just then, and Ana blurts out, "she's delivering, where were you? Quick, put her on lithotomy.[9] Don't push, don't push. Blow, Miriam, your baby's coming out and we have nothing ready."
"I'm not pushing, I'm really not…"

---

[9] Lithotomy: position where the woman lies on her back with her legs up in stirrups.

Just then Miriam's baby is born, on the bed, with no time to do anything.

Ana cleans his face with a gauze and taking a cloth, covers him and gives him to his mother. Miriam takes him, astounded, and smothers her baby in kisses. "Esteban, Esteban, my beautiful boy. Look, Julio, look how beautiful he is. And how swift! Just like that, without any notice…"

"Well, I think it's a yes, but if it's a no that's no problem, right?" says Soledad with a smile on her face. She's both happy and nervous.

"You'll see it's a yes, darling. Piss there on the stick and let's see what it says," says Sonia, her wife.

"It's great! I never thought this could happen in my life. Me having a baby with the person I love the most in the world! and here we are, just about to do the test that's going to tell us we are going to be mothers."

"I love you lots, Sol."

"I love you too, Son."

"Two stripes, Sol. Two stripes!"

Soledad looks up to meet Sonia's bright eyes.

"We are going to have a baby, my love. We are going to be mothers!"

"Yes, my dear, I am pregnant with our baby," replies Soledad full of joy.

"Sol, you're going to be the best mother in the world."

"So are you. This is one lucky baby, it's got a fantastic pair of mothers."

"I love you, my darling, you make me very happy."

"You do, too. I love you," Soledad replies as she hugs her wife.

"Shall we go this weekend to see my brother and María and tell them?" Sonia asks.

"Yes! But María's going to kill me, wait and see," Soledad retorts.

"How come?"

"Because since school she was forever talking about having babies, she's always wanted one so much... And now here comes me, her best friend, the lesbian, the one who didn't want babies, getting pregnant before she does…"

"Well, I don't think she will mind that much. Life doesn't happen as you plan it, things simply happen… besides, I don't think they will take long. My brother has always been very fond of children, and they've been desperate for one for some time. It would be great if both babies are just some months apart! My mother will be thrilled with so many grandchildren around."

Elena goes into her home and meets her mother.
"Hello, dear, what's wrong?" says her mother as she comes in.
"Nothing's wrong, Mom, I was just minding my own business."
"But did anything happen? You don't look well," says her mother, worried.
"Of course not, Mom! I'm all right," says Elena kissing her.
"Start setting the table then, lunch's ready."
"And Dad?" Elena asks.
"He's coming, just went down to the cellar for a second."
Elena keeps the pregnancy test inside a handbag she doesn't use anymore and sets the table as her father comes from the cellar with a bottle of wine.
"Hello dear, how are you?"
"Fine, Dad, and you?"
"Very well, dear," he says as he positions his face to get her kiss.
The three of them sit around the table as the news headlines start on the TV. This new abortion law has them rather upset.
"It's incredible!" says Elena's father. "Can you believe that a sixteen-year-old child, because they are children, may get an abortion without telling her parents? That's outrageous! Then, what are we parents for? To pay for everything while you can do whatever you please? Even killing our grandkids without our knowledge…"
"And what's the difference between sixteen and eighteen?" Elena says.
"An awful lot," her father replies. "At eighteen you are already of legal age and you are free and responsible for your actions. Until then, I am the one responsible for them; so, I should be the one to decide, because you are still a child."

"That's a ridiculous law. You can't go to jail if you are under eighteen, but you can kill at sixteen," says her mother.

"But Mom, abortion is not considered killing; if it was, girls over eighteen would go to jail and they don't, you are mixing things up."

"So, I'm mixing things up, am I? You do not believe that abortion is a crime, then?"

"Well, I'm not so sure about it, Mom."

"What do you mean you are not so sure?" her mother asks unbelieving. "Is it killing a baby or is it not?"

"Well, Mom, not a baby. You kill a being who, should that pregnancy progress, would become a baby."

"Hence, that's killing, my dear."

"Well, maybe that's killing for you, Mom. But for a woman in a terrible situation that might be the only answer…"

"She can put him up for adoption. There are thousands of families desperate for having a child."

"But Mom, think of the anguish of that woman who doesn't want to have a child, but is going to gestate it for nine months and give birth to give it up for other people to be their parents. For that person, that's probably much more agonizing than an abortion."

"But dear, are you telling me you are pro-abortion?"

"Not pro-abortion the way you put it; but I'm trying to make you see that there are more perspectives and that often the things you propose don't adjust to other people's realities."

"What's absolutely shameful," says Elena's father, "is the fact that minors may have an abortion without their parent's knowledge. What is the world coming to? Come on, if I'd ever find out one of my children is having an abortion without telling me I could kill her."

"And if we told you you'd let us do it?"

"Of course not, that is sheer madness, and besides, with the education we have given you, none of you will ever find yourselves in that situation," he retorts angrily.

"Dear, you won't happen to be sleeping with that boy, will you?" intervenes her mother.

"Mom, he's not 'that boy', he's my boyfriend and his name is Javi." Elena replies irritated. "And, what's the matter? I cannot just have an opinion opposed to yours without it being a personal matter? I'm just trying for you to open your minds a bit more, to put yourselves in someone else's shoes: it's easy to criticize people from the side-lines when you've never had a problem in your life."

"And we've worked hard for it, neither your father nor I got anything for free."

"Well, I'm sorry then, but I can't understand you, because right now you are the shining example of why an abortion without their parent's consent is the only way out for many girls: from what you both just said, if I got pregnant you'd kill me. Then, what options do I have if I do?"

"Don't talk nonsense: you are not getting pregnant, because you are not doing anything. Which is what you've been taught at home."

"But we are not talking about me, Mom. We are talking about the zillions of girls who cannot count on their parents, who cannot tell them about these matters, because they would really kill them if they knew, or would throw them out of the house or whatever."

"They would have well deserved it. Those are not the things to be thinking at that age, which is for studying and not for boyfriends and such nonsense," her father replies.

"You blow me away sometimes, you really do. Sometimes I find it hard to believe I come from such intolerant genes."

"But dear, what do you mean? Your mother and I are not intolerant. But we are talking murder here, and of a totally defenceless creature at that, which no one will defend if we don't, because even their own mothers want to get rid of them…"

"Wow, fantastic; just imagine then I get raped and get pregnant: do I get an abortion, or do I have the child of a damned rapist, considering my child, your grandkid, will have half the DNA of that punk?"

"Well, dear, that's totally different," says Elena's father.

"How come is different? There's an innocent life, a fetus inside me; so, what should we do with it? According to you, if I have an abortion it will be a murder. Just the same as if I have one because I got pregnant from Javi."

"But that's different, because if you've been raped… Of course, we wouldn't be having a child at home to remind you what you went through. In that case I do think it's justified."

"And why is it justified to kill that fetus and not another one? It's just as innocent and defenceless as the rest; however, that doesn't seem so bad now and is even justifiable…"

"Look, Elena, you are taking things out of all proportion here. That is simply not going to happen," says her father visibly angry.

"And if it does?"

"Well, if it happened it would be very unfortunate for you to get pregnant, and I'm sure you'd be given that pill at the Hospital just in case."

"Ok, then imagine I don't tell you until a month has passed because I'm ashamed and it's too late for the pill."

"Enough, Elena. This conversation is over for today," her father blurts out.

"Always the same story, whenever I corner you, you just bellow a couple of times, you make me shut up and that's that, discussion ended."

"Enough, I said; how do you dare to be so rude to your parents?"

"That's just it, Dad, you…"

"Shut up! Go to your room and let us not mention this matter ever again," says her father enraged.

"But…"

"Elena, this conversation is over and that's that."

Elena gets up from the table and banging the door goes to her room to cry.

Let's get down to it. It's the best thing to do. I get it done and then I can relax, because I can't take more uncertainty; and if it's a yes, it's a yes, and if it's a no I'll finally relax. These last days have been frantic... Elena thinks as she reads the instructions carefully and follows the steps on the leaflet. She closes the test and her eyes and tries to relax. A couple of minutes go by until she opens her eyes and her hand. *I'm not pregnant.* She looks at the instructions in disbelief, and checks the test again: -negative-, she breathes with relief. *No, I knew it, how could I be pregnant! It would have been the worst of luck if it happened to me. Phew, just as well. Thank you, God, thank you, even if you are a bit of a bastard, aren't you, I've been through hell. How can some people think you don't exist...? You do know how to put everyone in their place. It was useful to me, I reckon, I will never play the fool anymore, ever. Thank you, God, thank you. Next time I have a scare, if there ever is, because from now on I'm going to be awfully careful, I will go to A&E to get the morning after pill and that's that.*

May it be too early? I can't lose anything for trying. I buy it and I do it and that way I'll get some peace." María thinks. *"But this is just our first try and I'm just a few days late. If that counts as being late at all, but... so what? I don't care, I need to know.*

After coming from the chemist, María goes to the bathroom, reads the whole leaflet, does the test and waits. "I'd better be," she tells herself, "for with the price of this thing I'm not going to buy one each time I'm late."
"Well, that's it, then. How long has it been? Let's see: two stripes, two stripes mean... pregnant! It can't be, I don't think the three minutes are over yet. It will surely change afterwards. I'll leave it a bit more. Wow! It can't be. Don't get your hopes high, María, just don't, for then comes the disappointment and it'll be worse. Sure, you get the two stripes first and then it changes and it's a no. Go to the kitchen, make yourself a cup of tea. Wait a little and then go check again."

María heats the water. Two minutes in the microwave, and meanwhile she chooses her tea. 'Ping', the microwave sounds, and as if pushed by a spring, she runs to the bathroom. "Just as when I last saw it. Two stripes. I'm pregnant. The waiting time has passed now, for sure. I can't believe it. I'm going to have a baby."

She sits on the edge of the tub and sees herself in the mirror. She looks at herself, "I can't believe it. I'm going to have a baby. I must call Guille. No, I'd better tell him when he comes home. What time is it?" she says, looking at her watch, "still two or three hours before he does. I'll hold on and wait for him."

"I'm calling Mom to tell her. But, what am I doing? Guille will kill me if I tell her first. Gee, I'm having a baby! I can't remember ever being so happy. I don't even think I have!" she presses her hands to her belly and caresses it. "I know you're there. Hello baby, It's Mom here. Everything will be alright, you'll see. I'm dying to get to know you. Just you wait till Daddy knows. He'll be ecstatic.

"Argh, I want to tell him, I sooo want to tell him. But I must wait, I want to see his face when I do. I have to be able to wait".

María gets up and goes to the sitting room; there, she lies on the sofa and while holding her tummy she talks to her baby. She can't believe it.

The phone rings. It's Guille. "I can't tell him as much as I want to. Please keep your mouth shut. María, hold your horses, you don't want to regret it later."

"Hello," she answers as she takes the phone to her ear.

"Hello tootsie, how are you?"

"Fine, just fine, and you?"

"Fine. Listen, I had thought we could invite Sonia and Soledad for supper at home. Son just called me to tell me they're here, they arrived a while ago, and as it's been quite a long time since we met…"

"Can't it be some other day?"

"Why? Any problem with you?"

"No, noo, but I'm a little tired and I had already put my pyjamas on… Couldn't we make it tomorrow? How long are they staying?"

"I guess for the weekend. I'll check if they want to come tomorrow."

"Ok, fine."

"Are you truly all right?"

"Yes, don't be boring, I told you I was just tired and eager for you to come home…"

"All right, all right. I'll call them and we can meet tomorrow. I hope they don't mind."

"They don't mind what? Guille, have you already invited them?"

"Yes, but never mind, I'll tell them you are tired and that's that. Don't worry."

"No, I do worry: now I'll look like a fool, it will seem as if I didn't want to see them."

"But don't be silly, María, anyone can understand you're feeling tired. Besides, if we're going to meet, today or tomorrow is the same. C'mon, don't worry. I'll call them and fix everything. Want me to take anything home?"

"No, we don't need anything. I've got all we need for supper."

"Shall I bring some beers?"

"Well, if you feel like it…"

"But what's wrong with you?"

"Nothing's wrong, I'm just feeling a bit listless."

"Well, do I bring the beers or not?"

"Yes, bring them. We can always drink them later."

"Ok. See you in a while. I'll be off around half-past seven. If you recall something, gimme a ring, ok?"

"Ok. I love you."

"Me too. See you later."

"Gosh, I almost told him. I'm hopeless at keeping secrets, I've always been. And besides, we almost had an argument. Well, that's it, then: I should and I could and I did it, more or less."

19:50h.

"María! I'm home, where are you?"

"Upstairs, in the bathroom."

Guille notices something weird as he goes up the corridor. *That light? Candles, are they?* he wonders, intrigued.

"Hello darling, what's all this?" he asks, getting inside the bathroom.

"Nothing, I just felt like a relaxing bath with you."

"Mmmmh… did you? The last time we had a bath together was… I can't even remember."

"Never mind that, take your clothes off and get in."

"I'll go down for a couple of beers and we'll drink them here, ok?"

"Just bring the one, I don't want any."

"What a pleasure!" Guille says as he gets a foot into the water. *I'm enjoying this moment so much,* María thinks, *I'm telling you in a minute, I can't hold it on anymore, and at the same time I'm enjoying this moment so… I feel powerful with what I'm going to tell you. As you accommodate yourself in the tub, you talk about what a good idea it was to delay meeting Sonia and Soledad, that they'll be coming tomorrow for lunch, that they thought it was all right…*

"Why are you looking at me like that?" Guille asks his wife.

"Because I love you and I'm very happy and I very much wanted to tell you."

"I love you too, my darling. I'm thrilled to be with you. You make me very happy."

"Well, I can make you even happier."

"I don't think so. It's not possible to be happier than this. You're all I need."

"In nine months or so we'll be one more."

"What? Are you sure?" he asks, incredulous.

"Yes."

Just then Guille swoops on María and hugs her and kisses her and half the water in the tub goes out of it.

"Hahaha, watch out, you fool, you'll drown me," María laughs.

"But, how is it possible? Just like that, so soon, how do you know? Have you been to the doctor's?"

"No, not yet, I just did the test some hours ago."

"But are those tests reliable?"

"Sure! Well, at least that's what it says on the leaflet…"

"We are going to be parents, María. We are going to have a baby. Oh my God, I can't believe it. Are you all right?"

"Sure, of course, I'm perfect."

"So that's why you were tired this afternoon."

"No, I'm not tired. I told you that because I didn't want to tell you over the phone, but I didn't want to wait till tomorrow either. It was an excuse not to have the girls for supper. I wanted us to be alone."

Just then, Guille puts his head under the water and starts kissing María's belly as he yells to the baby underwater.

"Hahaha stop it, you silly thing, you'll drown yet," says María among guffaws.

"But why did you do the test, are you feeling poorly?" he asks after getting his head out of the water.

"Nooo, I'm fine. I was a few days late and I went to have the test done, I thought it was impossible, but look what I found!"

"I love you lots, my darling."

"Me too."

They remain hugging, holding their hands over María's belly, in silence for a while, enjoying the moment.

"Right, Guille says we'd better meet tomorrow for lunch, María's feeling a bit off colour today," Sonia tells her wife after putting down the phone.

"Off colour like what? Is she sick?" Soledad asks.

"No idea, he didn't say, but it didn't seem important."

"Well, we should find out, we don't want her passing it on to me now we have to be extra-careful with all the viruses out there."

"...Says the pregnant lady with the chorizo slice in her hand," rebukes Sonia sarcastically.

"Well, one thing is to have some chorizo from time to time and another is spending the afternoon with someone we know is sick."

"Ok, ok, I'll find out what's wrong with María, but you should keep an eye on what you eat now. They say you shouldn't eat raw things, they might cause fetal malformations and such."

"Quite, but chorizo is not raw, it's cured, isn't it?"

"Right, but it's uncooked, and in case it has some bug or whatever it's easier for you to catch it than from something that has undergone some temperature."

"But c'mon, Sonia, how many times have you got sick from eating chorizo?"

"No, Soledad, things are not like that and you know it. We have gone through this a lot. We decided you would be the pregnant one because you are the youngest and healthiest of the two, but now that we are going to have a baby you should take maximum care of yourself."

"All right, all right, I'll be taking care, but I don't get what's wrong in having some chorizo from time to time…"

"Well, I just told you, so don't be pig-headed. Anyway, you'll see I'm right and the doctor will tell you when you're pregnant you cannot eat chorizo or ham or seafood or pâté… well, several things. Oh, and I will be taking care of Frida from now on."

"But, what are you telling me? Suddenly all the thrill from being pregnant is going down the drain, instead of a baby I seem to have a time-bomb attached. You just tell me I must stop swimming now and I'll die. But I may still stroke Frida, may I?"

"I'm not sure. The best we can do is ask for an appointment with the doctor and he will tell us what we can and we can't do."

"I'm devastated, you know, don't you?"

"Well, maybe all I've told you is already outdated and now you can eat anything and sleep with the cat. Don't worry, you'll see how it's not that bad. And I promise I will make it up for every single thing you cannot eat."

"So, what do we do? Shall we go to a private doctor?" Soledad asks.

"No way. Why should we? We don't have insurance and they cost the earth."

"Right, but if we pay we'll get a better treatment."

"What next? And why should we have to adapt to a hypothetically homophobic obstetrician?"

"Fine, fine. I just thought it would be easier. But wait and see if we get an old ignorant one, because I'm very sensitive of late…"

"Well, let's not anticipate. We can ask for an appointment and we'll see, and if we get a nasty one we'll ask to be referred."

María wakes up to Guille's kisses. There's a smell of coffee. María smiles and stretches in the bed as she starts opening her eyes.

"Mmmm… I love you lots. This is what I call waking up… you have some months ahead for doing it every day, don't you?"

"And here you have the second part: your breakfast in bed with your adoring husband," he says as he takes a tray from the floor and places it on the bed.

"Oh, wow, Guille, this is great! Thanks a lot."

They both start to eat and Guille says, "will it be a boy or a girl?"

"Well, so far it must be a tiny and still undefined lentil."

"It's us who don't know, but the baby is already what it is, the one we will be having in our arms in some months' time. It is already a boy or a girl, isn't it?"

"I don't know, I guess so. I had never thought about it. You're right," María agrees, "we already have our baby, it just needs to grow, but it's already in here whoever it is," says María, touching her tummy. "How good, what joy!"

"What shall we do about your sister and Sol?" María asks.

"Well, nothing, what are we supposed to do? We aren't telling them not to come today either, are we?" Guille says.

"No, but shouldn't we tell our parents first?"

"Well, Miss Protocol, it's not like we are going to make a list to see who we tell in the first and second place, is it? We'll go telling people, just like that."

"Yes, but you know my mother, these things are important for her."

"So, call her if you want."

"Yeah, but she could make us cancel lunch with the girls to go somewhere with her and Dad."

"So, don't call her…"

"Well, all right. We'll tell her whenever."

"Darling."

"What?" María asks.

"We are going to be parents."

"Yes, my dear."

"I can't really believe it." Guille says. "Look, what do you think about going to a baby's shop and having a look around for some clothes?"

"Great! But we won't buy anything, right?"

"Or maybe yes, babe, we'll see," says Guille hopefully.

"Hello," greets Elena hugging Javi from behind as she comes into the cafeteria. "I love you," she tells him with a huge grin.

"How happy you are!" her boyfriend says, surprised, "what happened?"

Elena asks for a cappuccino, sits in front of Javi and tells him, "I've had some very good news today. I had been worried for the last couple of days because my period wasn't coming, but everything's all right now."

"You're always worrying over nothing, why shouldn't you get your period?"

"Well, due to that time when the condom slipped out, loverboy."

"Fuck, but that was just the once, that happens to everyone all the time and no problem. And that was our only time. You are totally paranoid, aren't you?"

"Look here, boy," Elena says angrily, "I've been through hell these days, absolutely overwhelmed, thinking of committing suicide if I was pregnant, and besides I've gone through this alone not to worry you, and when I do tell you, you call me paranoid."

"Hey, hey, hey... plain to see you've got your period, darling, it hit you hard this time, didn't it? I'm telling you not to stress, it's over. Elena, you shouldn't have suffered so much because the possibilities of this happening to us were minimal. And, on the other hand, if you were going through such hell, you should have told me the minute you started worrying, shouldn't you? I'm your boyfriend. I'm here for good and for bad things, am I not? You always take things so seriously, it's difficult to believe you've gone through this alone."

"I told Paula," she replies somewhat angrily.

"Fuck, woman, you tell Paula something like this before you tell me? I can't believe it," Javi says, offended.

"That's it, you always get the story to revolve around you. I don't know how you do it, but at the end you are always the subject in every story and I have to end up feeling terrible and apologizing," Elena replies.

"What?" bellows Javi, "you mean you're worried you might be preg…"

"Ssssht, lower your voice," whispers Elena.

"You tell your best friend before you tell your boyfriend and I have to find it well and normal?"

"I didn't want to worry you unnecessarily and I found it easier to tell Paula because as she is not involved she wouldn't mind so much. You'll find it silly, but the fact of telling you made it more real, as if by telling you something that was just a worry it would become a reality."

"But, as I had much to do with your worry, I think I had a right to know, didn't I?"

"Look, I don't know, Javi, I don't know if you had a right or not. And, you know what? You're just proving I shouldn't have told you, because I was happy and now you've got me in a bad mood. You're so selfish. Here I come happy as Larry to tell you that I've had a false alarm and there's nothing for you to worry about, and you get mad at me for not having told you before and tell me I'm paranoid and such. Well, thanks for so much consideration on your side, for thinking of you, for not wanting to worry you for a suspicion that, in the end, came to nothing."

"Really, you get impossible when you are in your moontime. There's no way to talk with you," Javi replies.

"Stop saying that, stupid! You say it just to annoy me. Besides, I'm not having my period, you genius."

"But, didn't you say you did, and everything was a false alarm?"

"I did not. It was a false alarm all right, but not because I got my period, but because I did a pregnancy test and it was negative."

"You got to the point of doing a pregnancy test without telling me? I can't believe it, mate. That's trust for you. This way, we are going to be wonderful as a couple. Besides, those tests fail a lot. My sister had to do several until she got a positive, so they are not that reliable either."

"Go to hell, you moron! piss off and don't you ever dare call me," says Elena rising from the table, "thank God I'm not pregnant, because if I were I'd be having the child of a first-class idiot. Fuck you, stupid."

"Hello, girls, come in, come in! How are you?" says María as she hugs and kisses Sonia and Sol.

"Very well, and you?"

"Splendid!" replies María.

"Are you feeling better?" Sol asks her.

"Better?" María asks, surprised.

"Guille told us yesterday you were a bit off, that's why we are coming today."

"Oh, that was nothing, I just had quite a day… Guille, they're here! Come in, I'll tell you in a minute."

"Hello, beauties," greets Guille, "sis, how are you?" he says, kissing Sonia.

"Very well, gorgeous, and you?"

"Very well, very happy. Some wine?" Guille asks.

"Thank you," his sister replies.

Guille comes back with a tray with the wine bottle, three empty glasses

and a glass of grape juice.

"And that juice?" says Sol, "not for me, is it?"

"How could it, we all know you're a total alkie!" says María with a smile, "It's for me."

"And since when are you not drinking wine?" Sol asks her best friend.

"Well…" hesitates María looking at Guille, "since yesterday."

"How come?" Sonia asks.

"Because yesterday we knew that we are going to have a baby!" says María.

"Gee!" Sol screams. "Congrats! I'm so happy for you!"

They all kiss and hug and Guille says, moved, "You are going to be aunties!"

"Yeah!" yells Sonia, "and so are you, too!"

"What?" says María, incredulous.

"We're pregnant too!"

"No!" says María looking at Sol in astonishment.

"Yes, I'm pregnant too!" says Sol excitedly.

Both friends hug and María tells her, "I'm so thrilled for us both! Lifelong friends, then we end up being family and now we'll live our pregnancy together! We'll be mothers and aunts of the same children at the same time!"

"Great, let's call Oprah and start the babies' layettes," laughs Guille as he hugs his sister. "These two can't believe it, but us? Who would have imagined we'd become parents at the same time!"

"I'm terribly happy for you, little sister," says Guille, still hugging Sonia.

"So am I, Guille, so am I. Does Mom know?"

"No, we still haven't told her. And you?"

"Not yet. Who tells her first?" she asks her brother.

"So, we'll tell her at the same time," Guille replies, "well, we'll talk about that later.

Let's make a toast for us and our babies!"

"Guille, bring another grape juice, please," María tells her husband as she gives Sol her glass.

"You see how it was for me in the end?" smiles Sol taking the juice.

"As for you, I know you did it on purpose… always trying to steal the show from me no matter how. You even had my sister in law knock you up just to up me: you're jealous, that's what you are!" jokes María.

"C'mon, c'mon, don't say nonsense, you know you are always the first at everything; so, for once, we're even!"

"I'm soo happy, really, really! Yesterday I thought I was the happiest woman in the world, but I'm even happier today. It's wonderful. I love you lots, Sol."

"Me too," replies Sol as both hug again.

"Well," Sonia says, "how shall we tell Mom and Dad?"

"Let's call them now and tell them, shall we?" her brother replies.

"I'm not sure, we'd better wait a bit or they'll be here in a matter of minutes. Let's enjoy supper first and then we'll tell them. Shall we tell them together or separately?"

"No idea, whatever you think best. Maybe we'd better do it separately to avoid overlapping both good news, this way they'd enjoy them more."

"Right. And who tells them first?" asks Sonia.

"I think you should. That way she'll be happier with both news."

Sonia raises her eyebrow, "what do you mean?" she asks, surprised.

"Because you know Mom, and as your baby is not genetically our family it could well be that mine outshines yours in her eyes."

"Fuck it, you just shocked me to the core! Don't you think that theory is a bit twisted? I'm going to have a baby, just like you, and I guess Mom and Dad will be just as happy about yours as about mine, won't they?"

"They sure will, Son, please excuse me. It's just that, well, Mom usually reacts in the most unsuspected way… but I don't think she'll be that frivolous about something like this."

"What's wrong?" Sol asks her wife. "You look upset, what's happened, Son?"

"Nothing, that I'm a complete moron. I have said something that was just a guess and I've put my foot in. I'm sorry, Son, I'm absolutely stupid," says a visibly downcast Guille.

"What's up?" worries María.

"Nothing, nothing," says Sonia, "just some silly nonsense."

"Well, tell us, because we are worried. Guille, what happened?" María insists.

"Well, talking about who would be telling our parents first I've told her she'd better be first, because as the child is not biologically hers our parents would be equally happy for both."

"But that's completely stupid," his wife retorts.

"Totally and utterly," says Guille, "I don't even know how I came to think something like that. I'm awfully sorry, I'm a big mouth and I can't think how I came out with such nonsense. I'm sorry, Sonia, I really am."

"Well, that's that," Sonia appeases him, "it's not such a big deal. The truth is I was surprised you could even think something like that. I hadn't even thought of that, and the fact that you have, and at such an early stage, just when you've got wind that Sol's pregnant... that you may think Mom would love my child less than yours because I didn't put a sperm cell… just baffled me."

"No, no and no. I don't want you to think that," Guille retorts, "I wasn't saying that. Don't misinterpret me because that's not what I said. There was no bad intention whatsoever in my words. I just thought it would be better if you told her first for her to feel happy about your baby first and then I would tell her so that she'd feel happy for mine too, because being the way she is maybe she would...

"Oh God, I don't even know why I said it. My intentions were good, and in the end, I don't know how, I've fucked it up. Forgive me, Son, really, not my intention at all."

"Good, that's right, don't worry. We don't want this celebration to turn into an annoyance for a silly matter. Let's have supper and forget it, everything's right," says Sonia hugging and kissing her brother.

"I love you and I'm sorry," he replies.

"Come on, forget it once for all."

"I've had a row with Javi," Elena tells Paula as she picks up the phone...

"How come?"

"Same old story, he seems to think the world revolves around him and everything else is secondary. I told him that I was worried, that it had been a false alarm and he got angry because I told you but not him. When I did it for him in the first place!"

"Well, he may be somewhat right, don't you think?"

"No, I don't. I think it's for me to decide who I tell things to or don't."

"Well, but if you're worried you might be pregnant and don't tell the other party involved, I can understand him not liking it."

"Hey, you're supposed to be on my side, you know?"

"Always, but I can understand him not appreciating it."

"I don't know. If I had had an abortion without telling him, or if I simply had been pregnant and hadn't told him, that, I understand; but if I wasn't sure and I didn't want to worry him until I knew for certain..."

"Sure, you're the mistress of your own decisions and everyone does what they want. I'm just saying his not liking it is not that difficult to understand. I don't think it's such a big deal this time, and as you know I'm not his biggest fan."

"Well, today he's just a moron, right?"

"Right; are you going to call him?"

"No, I'm still pissed off and I don't want to be the one to call. I don't even know if I'm answering the phone if he does."

"As you want. Shall we go out tomorrow?"

"Yes, we'll talk tomorrow. Kiss."

"Another one for you."

Without letting go of the phone, Elena rings Javi.

"Hi. How are you?" asks Javi.

"Slightly less livid. And you?"

"I'm fine. Longing to see you."

"You are, are you? You could have called me."

"After everything you told me yesterday? No, it wasn't for me to call."

"I'm sorry."

"Me too."

"I love you."

"I love you too. When are we meeting?"

"This afternoon?"

"Shall I pick you up at…?"

"Seven."

"See you later, gorgeous."

"See you then, my love."

Week 6

"You're pregnant, Lorena!"

"Impossible," she says, absolutely certain.

"You can see it here quite clearly. Against all odds, and with this minimum ovarian tissue you have, you are pregnant. Congratulations to the future mum and, believe me, I never thought I'd be saying this so early and so easily, without any kind of stimulation; when did you stop taking the pill?"

"I never did."

"I can't believe it. Yours is a case fit for publishing. Are you telling me you got pregnant on the pill and with minimal ovarian tissue?"

"Well, as you said I had few possibilities I didn't quite control it, I forgot to take it some days…"

"Great, just half a dozen eggs and you are putting them at risk like that. Sorry. I'm very happy for you. You're happy, aren't you?"

"Sure, of course. Just a bit shocked, I wasn't expecting it. But yes," Lorena lies.

"Lorena, this is probably your only chance to become a mother. You've been very lucky. You must take good care of yourself now, will you? Do you have anyone to care for you?"

"Well, yes, I guess, I'm not sure…"

"Do you have a partner, Lorena?"

"No, I can't really say I do."

"But do you know who the father is?"

"Yes, I do," she replies visibly offended by the question.

"Well, you will know how and when to tell him, if you do," retorts the doctor embarrassed, realizing how inappropriate his question was. "Get these tests done and I'll see you in a month, ok?"

"Fine, thank you," she says taking the papers from the doctor and getting up.

After leaving the doctor's, Lorena goes quickly to her place. She needs to think, to sort out her ideas. She puts her hands around her belly. "Pregnant," she whispers. She had got so used to the idea that this would never happen she doesn't even know whether she is happy with the news or not. "I'm pregnant," she repeats.

"I can't tell him. If I do, I know what will happen. Well. I have time to decide. I'll let some days go by and then I'll see everything more clearly. This is insane! I never thought it would be so difficult. I don't even know if I want to be a mother, fuck it, these doctors are the limit. They tell you something is practically impossible and then when it happens they say: 'How great, congratulations!' Holy crap! if I had known I could get pregnant, maybe I'd have looked forward to it, but now… now I don't know."

Lorena picks up the phone and puts it back on the table. "No, if I can't think alone, talking with Luci won't help either. Or maybe yes, or no, what do I know?" she says as she presses the 'call' key.

"Hello, princess," comes the reply from the other side.

"Hi Luci. Listen, could you drop by?"

"I'm at the supermarket. Could be there in an hour, is that right?"

"Perfect, get something and we'll have supper here."

"What would you like?"

"I don't care, anything not too spicy; it's impossible to sleep after one of your dinners."

"You ungrateful bitch. It's a Marmite sandwich for you."

"Mmmm, I love Marmite."

"See you."

"Bye."

"Good grief, that lift's not working again; it's more often on the blink than not, dear. And you pay maintenance fees for that?" complains Luci as she walks through the door loaded with shopping bags.

"Well, at least I've got a lift, you don't have any," Lorena says kissing her.

"Yeah, but I live on the first floor and besides I don't pay half as much as you do."

"Fine, we'll go to your place next time, you whiner."

"So, look, I've brought some eggs and potatoes and I'm making a Spanish omelette for you, just like my mom's," she says, leaving the bags on the kitchen counter. "Do you have any onions? A good omelette must have onion, it's not the same without, is it?"

"I do, here you are. But I really like it more without it, you know?" Lorena says.

"Come on, don't say nonsense. Do you have any complaints about my omelette?"

"Not a single one, your omelette's splendid; that's why I think it must be simply glorious without onion."

"Can you believe it? Spanish omelette with onion has lots more taste and it's much juicier. And it has that special touch only onion and no other ingredient can give."

"All right, with onion it will be… it will be divine, being yours," Lorena says condescendingly.

"No, you spoiled the fun, I'm not putting it."

"Well, we're not going to start defending what we don't want just to do what the other says. You are the omelette chef, so we'll do as you say and that's final."

"Thanks, Lorena, I'm really very pro-onion."

"You can say that again… you dice an onion and fry it while you think about what to cook, don't you?"

"Hahahaha, don't exaggerate, hahaha," Luci guffaws.

"I'm pregnant."

"What?" says Luci as her smile fades away from her face.

"I'm pregnant."

"Yes, I heard you, it was an automatic response. But, are you sure? Didn't you say it was impossible for you to get pregnant?"

"Yes, that's what the doctor said, but…"

"Just what we needed, a miracle. And do you know whose child it is?"

"His, of course."

"The Mister's?"

"Yes."

"But are you certain?"

"Yes, Luci, of course I am. It's his, he's the only one I use nothing with. That's what we agreed from the start."

"And what are you going to do? Does he know?"

"Luci, please! I'm in a state of shock, don't ask so many questions, let me speak and I'll tell you."

"Sorry, you got me by surprise. I couldn't even begin to imagine something like this."

"Imagine me when I got the news… I called you the minute I knew. I still don't know what to think. I've always been used to the idea that I'd never have children of my own, so I feel completely out of depth. If I were a normal woman I would have gone to get an abortion straight from the doctor's, I wouldn't have even called you, I think. But suddenly I'm pregnant, and this is my only chance to be a mother, and it makes me consider many things, Luci. There's a baby inside me I don't know if I love, but he'll be the only one, you get it?"

"Yes, my dear, of course I get it. How difficult! And what will you live on later, when you have it?"

"I have a nest egg."

"Yes, but a flat doesn't pay itself, and a child means lots of expenses. And no one must see you pregnant, you'll have to disappear the minute you start showing. I don't know, Lorena, I don't want to stress you, but there are a good many things you have to think about."

"I know. So far there's time, I have to think about it and see what I can do."

"Are you telling him?"

"No. I don't think so, I can't."

"You might ask him for help."

"I don't know, I don't think so. I'm not going to show up telling him I'm expecting his child and asking for money to support him."

"Well, you could; he'd be doing whatever you ask him for, as his situation is very delicate, as is yours. More so now you have proof, and a huge one, of his infidelity. More than that Lewinski girl!"

"I don't like it one bit when you talk about him like that. He's always been very good to me, and to you too, when he's asked for you to come with us."

"Yeah, well, I'm just saying you could have that child and dedicate yourself just to him if you tell him. He would support you even if it was just to keep your mouth shut."

"I don't know, Luci. I'll think about it, I still don't know if I want to leave this life and this job. I like what I do, you earn heaps of money, you live the life of Riley and I like the luxury it gives me. The trips, the presents, the suppers, the hotels... I'd have to leave it all behind. I couldn't do this with a child. And then what? He will grow and he will wonder why his mother doesn't work, where does she get the money, and what do I tell him? That his rich daddy is paying for everything in exchange of no one knowing he's his son? I don't know, I'm in a mess. I have to think everything very well. I don't want a child, I don't want a baby, it ruins my whole life and it took me a lot to get it right. I was so certain I'd never have any! And nevertheless, since the doctor told me I keep getting images in my head of this baby, when he'll be here with me, as if I already knew I'm having it. As if there was something inside me that had already decided and now all I had to do was get used to the idea. I'm very glad you've come, you're my best friend and I feel very happy to have you."

"I'm also very happy that you called me, and to be here. You know I'll help you in everything I can. For a start I'm going to make you this omelette without onion; it's the minimum I can do for you," she says as she hugs her.

"Thank you, Luci," Lorena says as tears start to run down her face.

Elena and her boyfriend are hugging in the car. They've just had sex and none of them is speaking. A bit later, Javi asks, "what are you thinking?"

"That I still haven't got my period."

"How late are you?"

"Eleven days."

"How long are you going to wait?"

"I don't know, I don't know... I've been more relaxed since I did the test, but I'm beginning to get nervous. I don't understand why I don't menstruate if the test was negative; I should get it for once so that I could calm down."

"Why don't we go to a chemist's and do another one?"

"I don't want to, Javi. I don't want to go through all that anxiety again, I want to wait a bit more. Since I knew it was negative I feel safe, and if I do the test again…"

"If you did the test again we'd find out for sure and we'd all get our peace of mind."

"All?"

"Just a way of speaking, Ele."

"Ahh, I thought you might have told someone," says Elena looking at her boyfriend. "You haven't told anyone, have you?"

"No, I haven't told anyone. Elena, I truly think you must do the test again. Doing it won't change anything, we'll simply know whether it's a yes or a no and I think the sooner we know, the better."

Elena remains silent for a while, deep in thought, and she finally replies, "all right, then. Let's buy it and we'll see when I do it, right?"

"Right. You'll see how you sleep better tonight."

Javi gets out of the chemist's and gets into the car "Where are we going? To 'Pancho's'?"

"Good, the gang might be there, I'll call Pau."

"No, Ele, where are we going to do the test."

"Now?"

"Yes, now."

"Not to 'Pancho's' then, somewhere no one knows us."

"Anywhere around here, then."

"But I don't want to go to a cafeteria and wait there for the result."

"Then go in, get it done and come back and we'll wait in the car for it."

"I'm ashamed to go in and not have anything…"

"Where do you want to go?"

"To a vacant lot, or to a kerb or the way to hell… I'd do it on the street, really, I just don't want to see anybody."

As Javi drives on, Elena opens the box and starts reading the instructions.

"Well, it's just like the other: two stripes, pregnant."

Javi stops the car and Elena sighs before opening the car door and getting out. She comes back straight away with the test in her hands. They both await in silence for a couple of minutes.

"You'll see how it will be a no," says Javi breaking the silence.

"And if it's a yes?" Elena asks, terrified.

"If it's a yes we'll find a solution; don't worry. We'll see the way to do it."

Elena opens her hands and there they are, "two stripes," she whispers. "No, no, no. Shit, Javi! I'm pregnant."

Javi holds her tightly as Elena starts crying.

"Hey, hey, babe, easy, don't cry. It's going to be alright, we'll find a way out of it," Javi breaks his hold and takes her face in his hands. "Look at me, Ele. It will be alright, you'll see how we find a solution."

"My parents will kill me, Javi, they're going to kill me…"

"No, they won't because they will never know. I'll find everything out and take care of it all, right?"

"But how are we going to do it? In a hospital I'd find people who know me, they'll know for sure, it's not that easy."

"And can't we do it somewhere else, paying?"

"No idea."

"Sure, we can. Now take it easy, you'll see how we'll find a solution, and fast. Don't worry, darling, we are together in this and you'll see how we get out of it without a problem."

"I'm frightened."

"What of?" Javi feigns surprise. "Everything's going to be alright, really. You'll see how we'll sort this out in no time," he says as he holds her again. The truth is he is also frightened, he has no idea where to start and not a clue what to do. *What a shit!* he thinks as he kisses his girlfriend and dries her tears.

After leaving Elena at her home, Javi sits in his room in front of the computer and starts looking for information on abortion. *Well, we can, we can…* he thinks, looking at the screen. *At the hospital, and if we pay, in these two clinics too. Right. I'll tell her tomorrow. Shit, what a fuck-up. Once, just once, a condom slips out… Look at Pablo, he's never had a single problem, and he's playing with fire all the time. Fucking hell!*

Javi sends Elena a message: "Can u talk? I ⬜ u."
The phone rings straight away.
"Hello," says Elena.
"Hello darling, how are you?"
"Fine; worried, but fine."
"Well, don't worry because I've found a solution. I think the best we can do is to go to a private clinic, because you get everything done in one day there. You have to spend a night out, but you can manage to do it over the weekend; tell your parents you're going somewhere with your friends, and that's it."
"And what is it like?"
"There are several ways to do it. One is with pills: you go home, have the abortion and go back to the clinic the following day. With the other, they put you to sleep and it's like a vacuum cleaner. But any of them takes just a few hours."
"I prefer the pills."
"Right, we'll see if you can choose and if you can't then whichever will do."
"Thank you, J."
"Right ho, Ele. Don't worry about anything, you'll see how quickly we'll arrange this. Tomorrow morning I'll call these two places and we'll see which is best, we'll ask for an appointment and we'll be there when they tell us."
"And what about the dough, do we know anything?"
"Not much, in the clinics' webs they don't mention it, but some forums mention it's between 300-400€."
"Fine, I thought it'd be much more. I have some savings, so there's no problem."
"So do I. Of course, we'll go Dutch, this concerns us both."
"I love you."
"I love you too, princess. Sleep tight, we're much closer to the solution now. Everything will be over in a few days."
"Gosh, thank you so much. I don't know what I would have done without you, my love."
"Well, you wouldn't be in this situation for a start," jokes Javi.
"C'mon, no kidding, you know what I mean, others would have run away the minute they had known. But you, after everything I called you, have forgiven me and are helping me a lot."

"That's because I love you and because this is happening to me, too. I can't understand how some chaps are such cowards they can leave their girlfriends in the lurch when things fall flat. Only a sook would do that."

"Well darling, I love you and thank you so much again. I'll try to get some sleep, you do the same. You'll tell me tomorrow. We can call together if you want."

"No, I will, that way we won't have to wait till the afternoon, and the sooner we know what to do, the better."

"Right. Did I tell you I love you?"

"Not for a while."

"I love you."

"So do I, babe," Elena says, smiling.

"Me too, darling. See you tomorrow."

"Bye."

Elena goes to bed feeling very upset. How can she be pregnant? With all the pains they always took, what bad luck. *I've got a baby inside me. How awful!* she thinks. All her life pointing at the girls who got pregnant at secondary school, and now it's herself. Even if she's in university now, *what's the difference between 19 and 17? It's the same shit*. At least she's lucky enough not to have to tell her parents. *If this happened to me before I was 18 I'd have killed myself*, she thinks as tears run down her face. *I'm sorry, I'm very sorry, baby. I simply can't. I can't have a child now. I can't assume the change in my life, the shame, the responsibility. I don't want to, I don't want you. You shouldn't be in my belly. You are just some cells, you can't feel anything yet. I'm not going to hurt you. It's early yet, you won't feel anything. I'll have a child when I'm ready. Now, it just can't be. I'm very sorry, baby. If I could turn back time I swear I would, but I can't. I can't have you, I can't be a mother. I can't even tell my parents… even if I feel tempted to, they were so silly about the matter the other day I feel like telling them, just to say: "So, this would never happen to me, would it? And what shall we do now? Shall we have an abortion? Or else we let everyone know I'm pregnant?" You mind so much about your social position, about what people will tell, you'd be very ready to make me have an abortion. And even so you'd probably go on thinking your daughter may have one, but it shouldn't be legalized. Well, what's the point? It's my life, and this is forever, and even if you really deserve it I'm not telling you. Some people can count on their family and some people just can't: their parents just want to show off their successful kids studying at Oxford, taking a Master in the U.S.A. and having a PhD's tennis-playing boyfriend. But a pregnant daughter gets no help nor backing. It's all making her miserable, humiliating her, crushing her and deciding for her, to keep on living their fucking lives where appearances are everything. It's decided. I can't count on you, so please don't count on me either.*

Lorena gets out of the shower; she can't stop feeling her belly and thinking of the future. She still can't believe it, she feels like she's in an Almodóvar film: the barren call-girl who gets pregnant by a high office married politician. "Gee, I think I could call him and send him the idea: hear, Pedro, call Penélope because I have an idea you'll love for a film."
The phone rings and as she goes towards it her face darkens in seeing the name on the screen. *It's him,* she thinks inhaling deeply and answering the call.
"UNICEF, hello? Good morning, my name is Lorena."
"Good morning, princess."
"Hello Doctor, how are you?"
"Very well, and you?"
"Fine, happy to hear your voice. As usual. What can I do for you?"
"I want to see you. I miss you and I'd love to spend some days with you. We are leaving in ten days for a country hotel in a small village near Ávila, what do you think?"
"I think it's great. I also want to see you very much. We haven't met for months, I miss you. I'm thrilled you called. Could you send me the details when you have them?"
"I already do, I'm sending you the train ticket and I'll pick you up in Ávila. We'll go by car from there."
"Where are we going exactly?"
"To Gredos and that's all I'm telling, I want it to be a surprise."
"Friday can't come soon enough. So long, see you soon then, Doctor."
"You'll see how much fun we'll have. See you soon."

"Hello, Luci."
"Hello Lorena, is everything all right?"
"Yes, yes, I'm just calling you to tell you I'm leaving for a weekend with him in the 'Sierra de Gredos', he just called me."
"And have you decided what you'll do?"
"No, I have no idea yet; I haven't decided, but I can't reject this. A whole weekend means a lot of money, and I might be needing it in the future."
"Well, money's money and it's always better to have it than not. Are you telling him?"

"I don't really know. As I said yesterday, I don't think I can tell him anything yet. If I do, I think it will be later. So far, I have to grab the chance and be with him as much as he wants, until I show or I tell him."

"Congratulations, Lorena, you're going to be a mom."

"No, no, don't say it yet, I'm still not a hundred percent sure. I want to spend these days with him and see what happens."

"What do you mean what happens? Is he going to leave his family and go live with you and you'll all be one happy family?" Luci retorts ironically.

"Don't say nonsense! I simply need to know; see what vibrations I get. My life just turned upside down yesterday and I need to consider things from another angle. Everything has changed, and I want to spend a weekend with the father of my… let's say 'chickpea'. Let's call it like that for now, until I can sort out my ideas."

"Well, then I hope you make good use of it and clarify all you need to clarify. On the other hand, I just got a call from Galindo. He's having a party on Saturday and he wants me to come with a friend. Are you coming?"

"That swine?"

"Yes, that swine; you know he's harmless and he pays very well and we can keep the clothes…"

"What clothes?"

"Well, all those clothes he likes us to put on and which come in so handy for other meetings... I'm asking you because you'll want to make some money in your situation. But if you don't want to, I'll call Sam or Jessie."

"Fine. I think I'll go, but I don't want to do anything in public."

"You'll have to do as he tells you, he's the one who's paying."

"He may well take someone from the street then. They'll do anything, and for almost nothing."

"I don't like it when you talk like that, Lorena. Do you think if they could be where we are they'd be doing 10€ blow jobs?"

"Of course not, but there have always been classes, even at this. And remember that we live mainly off the customers looking for exclusivity, and that we can go with them wherever because nobody would ever guess we're paid company. We all have lost a lot going to these kinds of parties and meeting some customer who was thrilled thinking we did that exclusively for him. And things being as they are, we can't afford to lose one thing nor the other."

"Right, but you know how Galindo works. Two for going, and later he'll pay for the extras. Try to get into the private shows, and if he asks you to get into a public one just tell him one of the customers is an old teacher of yours and that's that. He's a swine, but he does respect us: if you say no, it's no. Even if you go home with ten times less money and he doesn't call you again. But until that day comes, it's a lot of money for quite a good job."

"Fine, Luci, I'll be going. I just need to be careful around that kind of situation, and so should you. Saturday afternoon, is it?"

"No, it's for the whole day. They'll pick us up at eleven. You know, swimming pool, jacuzzi, buffet… until three, even if we might be over before that, they usually are totally out of it by ten or eleven. Shall I give you a ring when we get out of my place and pick you up?"

"Right. See you on Saturday."

Week 7

Elena and Paula get out of class. Javi is waiting for them. He kisses his girlfriend and smiles. Shall we go to *'Pancho's'*?
"Sure."
"See you later, Paula," Javi tells Elena's friend.
"No, Pau's coming with us. I want her to be there," his girlfriend says.
"As you want, darling. Sure," Javi says resignedly.

"Well, I've been talking with a clinic one hour from here, in the countryside." Javi starts telling. "They've been ever so nice, they explained everything in detail and all will be done in 48 hours."
"And when?" asks Elena.
"The sooner the better. I think next weekend would be great, because it's a bank holiday, and three days are better than two, just in case. Better to have an extra day, isn't it?"
"What's the holiday?" asks his girlfriend.
"All Saints Day," says Paula.
"No way, I can't make it," says Elena. "We go to my Dad's village every year, to the cemetery. My father would kill me if I say I'm not going. That date is just impossible for me. It'd be almost like saying I won't be home for Christmas. What's the day anyway?"
"Monday," says Javi. "Well, if worse comes to worst we can go there for the weekend. Then, you can go to visit the family graves on Monday."
"It won't be easy. We'd better go the following weekend. There are no feasts whatsoever and it will be much easier for them to let me go."
"Well, as you want. But the sooner the better, you know that."
"And what can I tell them? It's so difficult to find a good excuse to tell my parents… besides, since you're my boyfriend they have me on an even shorter leash," she says looking at Javi.

"Yeah, well, your folks really overstepped the mark, don't they? Frankly, you are at university, you are of age…" her friend remarks.

"Sure they do, Pau, but I'm living at their place and that's what you get. Do you remember how difficult it was for them to let me stay overnight on your birthday? They're awful. And, besides, they think they're doing it for my own good. Oh, well…"

"We can say you're coming to my village for St. Martin's festival, we have the annual slaughtering of the pig."

"That's a good one, Pau! We couldn't find a better excuse!"

"The only thing is that we do it on All Saint's weekend, so that everyone can come and help, it's easier that way…"

"Yes, well, but Elena won't be going, whatever the weekend," replies Javi somewhat sarcastically."

"It's true, how silly of me!" Paula replies blushing, "I was just saying because that's the weekend I'm going to the village, but I'll be here the next one."

"No way, you're coming with me," panics Elena.

"If you want me to go, I'll go," says Paula grabbing her friend's hand.

Javi looks astonished but says nothing. At the end of the day, she's the one who's having the abortion. If she wants her friend there, let her come along.

"So, what are things like? What else do you know?" Elena asks her boyfriend.

"Well, they say that, in principle, we can do the pill thing, but a doctor has to see you beforehand, and they decide which is the best way. He'll give you the pills the first day, then you go home and have the abortion there and the following day you go back to the clinic to check everything's fine and that's all."

"At home? How do you mean at home? I can't go home!"

"I know, love. That's already planned too. There's a small country hotel nearby, we'll take a room there. The people from the clinic themselves told me about it. Apparently, many people do that."

"Aw, all right," says Elena, uncertain.

"What's up?" Javi asks her.

"I'm not convinced about having the abortion in a hotel room: what if I bleed to death there?"

"Ele," Paula chips in, "speaking from my utter ignorance, but I mean, if they do it that way in the clinic, they must know, don't they?"

"Well, I don't really know. What about the vacuum aspirator thing? They do that in the clinic and that's it, isn't it?"

"Yes, they do, but they anaesthetize you, so it's more expensive. And from what I've been reading on the net, the pill method is safer and more comfortable."

"Can't I take the pills and have the abortion at the clinic?"

"Apparently they don't have bedrooms at the clinic. If you have the vacuum method you spend some hours there and then leave."

"Well, I have to think about it, have a look at the pill and vacuum methods myself, and decide."

Saturday 9:30 am.

Lorena's having coffee, fruit juice and a tuna sandwich for breakfast. *I must eat well, we won't be eating anything for the rest of the day… and besides there will be fantastic food all around us… this affair of being pregnant is amazing, I've just known for ten minutes and I'm already eating for two. And eagerly at that…! I don't feel like going at all, but it's just for a few hours. And the truth is the bloke pays well.*

10:30 am.

The phone rings a couple of times and then stops. It's Luci's missed call, they are already downstairs.

Lorena takes her handbag and goes down. She looks at herself in the lift mirror. She feels beautiful. She looks at her stomach and turns sideways, trying to imagine herself with a huge belly. She finds it impossible that it's going to happen in just a few months; nevertheless, she is astonished at the swiftness of her acceptance. She is pregnant and she is going to have a baby. *I'm pregnant, I'm having a baby this summer.*

She gets into the car, kisses Luci and greets the driver.

"How are you, baby?" asks Luci.

"Fine, how are you?"

"Splendid. Happy to spend the day with you."

"I don't really feel like it," says Lorena.

"It's just a while, you'll see. You just keep a low profile. Let Galindo see you from time to time and disappear meanwhile," Luci whispers, gesturing with her eyes towards the driver.

Saturday 11:30 pm.
Lorena and Luci get inside one of the cars waiting at the entrance.
"Let's go home, I'm starving," says Lorena.
"Babe, you don't sound like yourself: you, hungry?"
"Yups, I'm always starving these days," says Lorena winking at her friend.
"What would you like for supper?"
"Pizza, a hamburger, a hot dog, one of Obelix's wild boars... I don't recognise myself, my body's asking for meat, calories..."
"Where do you want to go then?"
"To a burger place to get one of those dishes with chips, onion rings, the works..."
"You won't happen to have a tapeworm or something?" Luci smiles.
"I really want this and I'm letting myself have it. When was the last time you ate anything like that?"
"Can't remember. When I was 18 or 20 I guess."
"Shall we go to the one by your place?"
"Perfect."

Lorena bites into her hamburger and rolls her eyes.
"Yummy! This is scrumptious. So many years going without good things... I'm making up for them in one go! Why do they call it junk food? God, it's simply glorious!"
"You aren't starting to eat worse than ever now after ten solid years of eating healthy, are you? Now is when you should be eating even more healthily."
"Well, if the baby's asking me for this it must be good for him, mustn't it?"
"Yes, but one thing is asking for meat and another is asking for a double hamburger with cheese and bacon and so much ketchup you'll have to pay extra... you'll catch your death and all...!"
"Go ahead and try yours, you'll see how this can't be bad for you."

"You're happy, are you? I'm glad to see you like that," Luci smiles, "It's decided then?"

"Yes, I guess it always has been. It never crossed my mind to take any decision about it. I can't, Luci; something impossible, unthinkable and absolutely life-altering is happening and I cannot change it; well, I could, but I don't want to. I don't know how to explain it, but I know what I mean."

"Somewhat like the Virgin Mary," Luci replies.

"Quite, that's exactly what I mean. Differences aside, a miracle has taken place in my body and I won't decide about it. Something so huge has happened I feel I have no right to change it. I'm going to have a baby, and since I made up my mind I haven't felt bad or unhappy, upset, or fucked up…"

"Well, you were shocked when you told me…"

"Yes, sure it was a real shock and I wasn't myself for a couple of days. I was confused, but that's the logical reaction to what's happening to me. I've never for a minute thought of an abortion since last week; it's been more like a process of accepting what's happened to me."

"I think I understand. I've never considered anything like this, and I'm not sure whether I'd like to be a mother or not. It's not anything I've ever thought about too much, but I think if I got pregnant right now I wouldn't have it. It's not the right moment."

"But that's because you can choose your moment."

"Sure, sure, that's exactly what I was going to say, that if someday I want to have children I'll do it, but that's something you can't do."

"That's why I can't question anything right now, just accept it. But I accept it happily, not resignedly, you see?"

"You're going to be a wonderful mother."

"Well, that's a different story, we'll see about that," she smiles biting her hamburger.

"You will, you'll see."

"I'm going to Paula's village next weekend, she has invited me for the pig slaughtering festival." Elena tells her parents during supper, "I'd love to go, it's a huge event. She talks about it every year, it's almost like Christmas. All the family gathers there, aunts, cousins, grandparents… And even if it's a once in a lifetime, I'd love to go to a pig slaughter fest."

"It's ok by me," Elena's father says, much to her and her mother's surprise. "I won't be here that weekend either. I have that convention. In Ávila. It's silly to have it so near, most of the people going come from Madrid; we could have stayed comfortably at home, but no: you have to pay for everyone's trip, lodging and food just 60 miles from here. It's preposterous."

"But next weekend is All Saints weekend," says his wife disgruntled.

"Yes, I know," her husband adds. "On top of everything, on a long weekend. I've already told Jaime that if they carry on like that this is the last year I'm going."

Elena remains silent. She's got the wrong weekend, but if it can be done that soon, much better.

"Well, I'm not going to the village on my own," Clarisa protests.

"Of course, you aren't, Clarisa. Go to see your parents. They'll be happy to have you there with them for that weekend, won't they? I'm sure they'll be thrilled that you spend All Saints day with them, as we always go to my village since my parents died."

"Well," Clarisa babbles, "I'm sure they'll be delighted, that's for sure. But, what about your parents' graves? Someone must go and tidy them up a bit and put some flowers. We'll be the shame of the village if we don't."

"Of course, dear, don't worry, I'll call Ramona and she will take care of everything."

"Oh, but I will buy the flowers myself; Ramona would fill the graves with carnations and gladioli. You know she hasn't got any taste, the poor woman."

"Of course. You take care of it, much better. Call her and tell her clearly, you'll be sending the flowers and she just has to tidy the graves up. With your taste, they will be the most beautiful in the whole village, as every year," he says as he blows his wife a kiss on top of her head and leaves.

After dinner, Elena calls Javi.

"Hi sweetie."

"Hi Paula: yes, my parents agree that I can go to the pig slaughter fest with you."

"You're with your folks?" asks Javi.

"Yes, great! I'm telling you so that you tell everyone you must that I'll be there. Are we leaving on the 29th or the 30th?"

"Ahh, so it's this weekend already. Perfect. I'll call them and fix everything. You must tell me how you did it! Shall we meet tonight?"

"Yes, see you later, beautiful. Kiss."

Javi is already waiting at *'Pancho's'* when Elena comes in with a huge smile. It's been some time since he saw her smiling. Just as well that everything is more or less under control and will be over in a few days. As Elena approaches his table, Javi sees Paula coming through the door. *Are we fucking ever going to be alone, just the two of us?* he thinks irritated.

"Hi Pau," says Elena on seeing her. "Shall I get you a beer?"

"Yes, please," she replies. "Hi, Javi," she says, sitting down.

"She got to be free this weekend, the long one," Javi tells Paula with a huge grin.

"How?" she asks, astonished.

"She'll be telling us," says Javi as his girlfriend is coming towards them. He grabs her arm and sits her on his lap. "How did you do it? Do tell us, we are so intrigued!"

"It was much easier than I had thought in the end: I told them about the pig slaughter fest and such, but I got the wrong weekend; I said something like 'Paula has invited me over the weekend for the festival, blah, blah, blah…' And suddenly my father says it's all right by him, he's not going to be here either, he's got some convention somewhere; and my mom, dumbfounded, saying that it was All Saints Day, that she didn't want to go to the village on her own… and then my father says that she should go to see her parents. She was delighted with the thought. So of course, I never said I had got the dates wrong."

"Well, I'm happy that everything has gone so beautifully with your parents, but I still have the slaughtering this weekend," Paula replies a bit upset.

"No, Pau, please. You can't do this to me. You have to come with me."

"But now it's going to be me who's not allowed to go. This is one of the most important weekends of the year for my family. We all gather there."

"You have to come no matter how," her friend insists.

"Well, easy, Ele, if Paula can't make it there's no problem either. I'll be there," Javi chips in.

"Yeah, but I just can't believe you'd leave me in the lurch for something like that; to go to a pig slaughter, for Chrissakes!" Elena reproaches her friend.

"Hey, don't you push it, girl. I do want to come with you, I just have no idea whatsoever of what to say at home for them to let me."

"Well, invent an exam or whatever, but you have to come with me. I need you by my side. Don't let me down now."

Paula silently ponders on the exam idea, looking for the best way to tell her mother, who's not going to be happy with the news… she'll do anything for her friend, but this abortion is going to be more costly for her than for Elena in the end."

What a fuckup! she thinks resignedly.

Maternity Hospital.

Delivery Room 1. 14:00.

Celia gets into her delivery room to wait for the woman she'll be looking after. Noemí, the student midwife working with her for the day, comes in right behind her.

Seconds later, the woman arrives on a wheelchair, pushed by the porter. Noemí helps her stand up. "Come, let me help you," she says as she offers her arm for her to lean on. "I am Noemí and this is Celia; we are the midwives' team who'll be here with you."

"Pleased to meet you, I am Dori," she says getting up from the wheelchair. "Wait," says Dori standing still, "contraction."

"Very well," says Noemí softly putting her hand on Dori's belly to feel the intensity of the contraction. "You're doing very well. This was a strong one, wasn't it?"

"Was it?" replies Dori, scared.

"Sure! Don't tell me you don't find them strong!" smiles the student midwife.

"I do, a lot," Dori smiles, relieved, "but I was afraid you'd be telling me that it was too early or they weren't strong enough…"

"They're already strong and I think you're in labour. Did they check your dilation outside?"

"Yes."

"And did they tell you how many centimeters you had dilated?"

"Four, I think."

"Well, then you are in labour already, that's great! I'm going to monitor you for a bit to see how your baby's doing. Is it a boy or a girl?"

"It's a girl."

"Who's here with you?" Celia intervenes.

"My husband."

"Fine, I'll go look for him while Noemí monitors you."

Before long, Dori's husband comes in looking frightened, followed by Celia.

"Hi, I'm Miguel," he says reaching out for Noemí's hand.

"Hi, I'm Noemí, the student midwife. Pleased to meet you."

Miguel approaches his wife and kisses her. "How are you?"

"Fine, I'm already in labour, four centimeters."

"Did they give you the epidural?" Miguel asks his wife.

"No, not yet."

"Will you be wanting it?" Noemí asks.

Just then, another contraction starts and Dori closes her eyes, looks for her husband's hand and starts breathing in a deep, deliberate way. Noemí looks at Celia with an annoyed expression. *I shouldn't have asked her, she's doing so well,* she thinks.

Celia knows what Noemí's thinking and smiles at her.

"Yes, I do, I want it," answers Dori when the contraction has passed.

"Do you have the anaesthesia tests?" asks Noemí looking for them in the medical records. "Yes, here they are. To give you an epidural we need to put an IV line in and give you a couple of bags of fluid and call the anaesthetist once they've gone through, okay?"

"Dori," Celia chips in, "you are doing wonderfully; you are taking it very well, and based on my experience, I think the epidural often means trouble. You don't have to get it right now, and if you still want it in a while, you can have it then. But why don't you try to carry on a bit more just as you're doing so far and we'll see? We'll truly give it to you later if you need it; but, right now, it would be a pity."

"Fine, whatever you tell me, you're the ones who know. So far, I can take it all right."

"Why is epidural troublesome?" asks Miguel.

"Because we start interfering, putting drugs into the body, making it more difficult…"

"Why more difficult?"

"Because bodies are wise and they know perfectly what they have to do to give birth," the midwife explains. "Look how Dori is now: she's standing up, and what does she do with every contraction? She breathes calmly and moves her hips, she rocks her body… just what she has to do to help your daughter being born. And we haven't told her anything. Since she came in, she has done what she felt like doing. She's doing what her body's asking her to do. Pain is leading her and telling her what she should do."

"I can't do it lying down, it's impossible," Dori butts in. "Before, when they were checking how many centimeters I had dilated, I had a contraction while lying down and I thought I was going to die," she tells her husband.

"That's it," Celia continues, "your body's telling you: don't do that, I cannot do it well in that position. However, the epidural takes the pain away, which leads the body towards what it should do while giving birth. With the epidural you tend to lie down and rest. Your body then tries to tell you that position is not right, and how does it do it? As it did earlier when you were lying down: with more pain, for you change that position. But as you cannot feel it, you continue to lie down. Your body can't take it, contractions become less effective: it starts getting tired because what it's doing is not working as it should. Then, as a result, there are no more contractions: the body surrenders. So, we give you oxytocin, one more drug for the system. Now you have contractions again, but you're still lying down, and it's not easy for the baby to know where and how to go, because both gravity and your position are not helping. Often, the baby will get in the pelvis facing the wrong way and you end up with a ventouse[10] or a forceps delivery, or with a C-section, just from getting the epidural."

"Holy shit," says Miguel, "and why don't they tell you all this before?"

"Well, it doesn't always work that way. There are times when, even with the epidural, the baby finds its way all right and is born without any problems. But it's been proven that epidural increases the rate of instrumental births and C-sections."

"All right, I won't take it then," says Dori.

"I didn't mean to frighten you, Dori. It's true epidural doesn't always have these consequences, but it sometimes does. And as you are taking it so well, I think we should try to keep on like that, without an epidural, until you see you really need it because you can't go on."

Dori closes her eyes again and hugs Miguel. Her breathing becomes stronger, they can even hear her give a little push as she pulls Miguel towards her. Noemí looks at Celia and they both smile: "second stage[11] is near; this little girl will be here soon."

---

[10] Ventouse: Suction instrument applied to the baby's head during birth to facilitate its expulsion.

[11] Second stage: Birth phase coming after the complete dilation (10 centimetres) of the cervix in which the baby goes down the birth channel and gets out.

"This one's been much stronger. I don't know if I'll be able to hold on like this much more."

"Not much longer to go now. Have you noticed the baby pushing in that contraction?"

"I noticed I wanted to poo."

"Yes, it feels like pooing, but it's actually the baby's head pressing down. There's not a lot of room down there, so the feeling of something inside wanting to get out is the same, be it poo or baby!"

"Again," Dori's able to articulate as she hugs Miguel again and pushes with the contraction. Just then, a jet of whitish liquid comes out of her vagina. A perplexed Miguel looks at Celia. He doesn't want to move because Dori's leading, and if Dori wants to stay like that so be it.

"Your water just broke," Noemí says as she changes the Inco pads on the floor, "they are clear; baby's happy."

"Now, after this contraction passes, can you lie on the bed and I'll check how dilated you are?"

"Right," Dori says once the contraction has faded, "but if another one comes I don't know if I'll hold on."

"It's all right, you don't have to. If you see you have to stand up, you stand up, as if I wasn't there at all."

Miguel helps Dori to lie on the bed and Noemí puts a pair of sterile gloves on.

"Are you ready?" she asks her.

"Yes."

"Relax your legs, good, and just tell me if a contraction comes or it's uncomfortable or anything… Very well. You are almost completely dilated now; there's just a little bit of cervix left.

"Shall you examine her?" the student asks Celia as she takes the gloves off.

Just then, Dori says, "another one, another one," as she stretches her arms trying to get up.

Once the contraction has passed, Noemí offers Celia a pair of gloves, but she shakes her head in refusal.

"She was almost fully dilated when you examined her, wasn't she? It's very clear, and it would be a pity to disturb her again just to confirm what we already know."

Celia crouches as the next contraction comes. Noemí, nervous, puts the gloves on and asks Celia, "where do I stand? I've never been in a birth with the mother standing up."

"Just get wherever she lets you; in this position the easiest will be from the back. As long as you can put your hands to stop the baby from falling, you're ok."

"And what if she slips off my hands?"

"Don't worry. Take a cloth, it'll make it easier for you," replies Celia passing one to her.

"May I stay like this? May I give birth like this?" asks Dori after the contraction has passed.

"Of course, you can. Would you like to sit on a stool? Or on your knees with a pillow under them?"

"I don't know."

Celia takes the stool, puts it behind Dori and tells Miguel to sit down, as she makes Dori lean back. "That's it, hold her from under her arms. It's not very comfortable but it won't be long. How are you feeling like this, Dori?"

"Yes, it's good."

Noemí takes the brake off the bed and moves it to get in front of Dori who looks at Celia relieved, whispering, "that's better," and smiles.

Celia turns the light off leaving just a spotlight facing the ceiling, "baby likes it better this way."

"So does her mom," Dori whispers, leaning on her husband with her eyes closed.

Another contraction comes and Dori pushes again. "Excellent, Dori, in a moment I'll be telling you whether she has lots of hair or not," Noemí says. "And what's the baby's name?"

"We still don't know, we have two names. When we see her face, we will decide which one suits her best."

At that moment the door opens and the team on call appears. They approach and Laura, the consultant, asks:

"How are you doing?"

"Very well, on second stage," says Noemí.

"Great. How are you taking it?" she asks Dori.

"Fine. I think so, it hurts a lot."

"Why didn't she get an epidural?

"She didn't need it," Celia replies, "she's doing very well."

Laura goes to the monitor where Dori's clinical records are. "9 cm. Is that right?"

"Yes," replies the midwife, "Noemí didn't have time to write the last examination because she just did it a moment ago."

"And, how was she?" Laura asks Noemí.

"Fully dilated," Celia replies.

"Yes, fully," Noemí says.

"Station?"

"-1 but she already has urges to push."

"Very well, let's push, then; are you staying?" Laura asks Julia and Abel, the new doctors.

"Fine," both of them reply.

"Right, ask Dori if she minds, then," Celia retorts.

The two of them look at each other, confused, and Laura tells Dori, "these guys are doctors and now they have to see normal births, they'll be staying here with you to see yours."

"If you don't mind," Celia adds.

"Fine, I don't mind," says Dori, starting to get up as another contraction starts.

"C'mon, very well, very well, go on, go on, go on," Laura says. "Strong, long pushes. Take a deep breath, hold it and push as long as you possibly can." She crouches beside Dori and asks for some gloves to Celia, who replies, "we've just examined her and everything's right. There's no need to disturb her. This is a midwife's birth, we'll call you if we need you."

"I just wanted to know how she is," retorts Laura, upset.

"As we just told you, she is fully dilated and the head is -1, at the spines with pushes," Celia insists firmly.

"All right, you have fifty minutes," says Laura as she goes to the door and leaves.

"Fifty minutes?" asks Miguel, "what for?"

"For her to visit us again," the midwife replies, "but don't worry, this girl will be born by then."

"She's going to take fifty minutes? Oh my God, no! She can't take that long, I won't hold on, she has to be born straight away!" says a desperate Dori.

"Don't worry, it won't take that long; you're doing so well!" says Noemí as she caresses Dori's leg, "you are at the last stretch."

Julia and Abel position themselves behind Noemí.

Along the next contraction, Dori pushes again and the baby's little head starts to show. "Very well, Dori, that's it, we can see your little girl's head, you're doing very well. Wanna see?"

"Is she born already?"

"No, I mean her head; if you want, I can put a mirror in front and when you push, you'll see it."

"I'm not sure."

Celia passes the mirror to Noemí, who puts it on her lap waiting for the next contraction.

Dori pushes again and Noemí positions the mirror. Dori looks at it and then closes her eyes. Miguel crouches to see. "Wow! yes, yes, yes!" he exclaims. "Is that her head?" Noemí nods. Dori opens her eyes as the contraction passes, looks at the mirror and says, "where? I can't see anything."

"You can't see it now," her husband tells her, "but when you were pushing it was sticking out a bit."

In the following contraction, Dori again closes her eyes while pushing. When she opens them she says, "Is she there? I can't see her head. She's going back, she doesn't want to come out."

"Yes, she does," Noemí tells her, "but this is the way babies are born, they advance little by little."

"But why does she go back? I really want her out!"

"She's stretching your perineum little by little, so that you don't tear," the student midwife explains.

"Another one," she says before she starts pushing once again. "Very well; go on, go on, carry on like that, a bit more…" Noemí tells her.

"Don't lead her pushes," Celia whispers to her.

"Oh, yes… old habits die hard," Noemí apologizes.

After some more contractions, Celia asks Noemí to explain 'the fire ring' to Dori.

"Yes; in a moment you'll be having a stinging, burning feeling all around your vulva. It's completely normal, and it's there so that you don't push too strongly and tear."

"Yes, it's already stinging quite a lot."

"Just do as your body says, I may tell you not to push, or to pant if I see you are pushing too strong," Noemí says.

With the next contraction, the baby's head is born. Miguel, moved, looks at the mirror, leaning over Dori's shoulder.

Dori looks down.

"Why doesn't she get out?" she says, frightened.

"It's okay, her body will be here with the next contraction, most babies are born in two contractions."

"But we've been through many more than two," notes Miguel.

"Yes, you're right," smiles Noemí. "I meant that once the head is out, the body will come with the following contraction. It is like this with your first baby; next ones usually come in one go."

The baby's head starts moving and Celia, looking at the doctors, says, "can you see how it rotates on its own?"

"Yes," reply rather shocked Julia & Abel.

Dori pushes again and her baby's arms are born; and, little by little, the rest of her body comes out, and Noemí picks her up with a cloth. Dori looks at her baby, asking worriedly,

"what's wrong? Why doesn't she cry?"

"Nothing's wrong, she's perfect; everything's all right. She doesn't cry because she doesn't need to. Take her."

"Shall I? I don't know if I can, help me."

Noemí helps Dori to hold her baby close to her and she starts telling her welcoming words; Miguel is crying and, moved, crouches and kisses his wife telling her between sobs, "she's beautiful, I love you."

"Look, darling, she's already here, look how beautiful she is, how tiny, is she all right? Has she got everything?" she asks looking at Noemí and Celia.

"I'm sure she does, but we haven't examined her yet," Noemí smiles.

The little girl sneezes.

"Hey, what's up? She's cold, she'll get a cold; cover her," Dori says trying to cover her better.

"Relax, it's just her way to clean her airways; babies sneeze often after they're born."

"How awake she is, her eyes are wide open," Dori tells Miguel.

Julia and Abel stand up and talk about the first birth they've ever seen. Celia makes a sign for them to keep silent.

"Ouch, what's that?" Dori asks startled. "Something's coming out."

"Don't worry, that's the placenta separating; bleeding is normal. Let's help you into bed, you'll be more comfortable, don't you think?" says Noemí.

"Yes, but I'm not sure I can move."

"We'll help. You just hold your daughter, and Miguel and I will help you get up."

Once the placenta is out, Julia and Abel walk away from the delivery room, deeply moved after congratulating Dori and Miguel.

Maternity Hospital.
Doctor's office. 16:30h.

Julia and Abel come into the Doctor's office thrilled about Dori's birth and talking about it. Laura, who is there, asks them:

"Did she already give birth?"

"Yes."

"And, how was it?"

"I found it beautiful. The baby came out on her own."

"Yes, there are babies who get out in one single contraction."

"No, this girl got her head out first, then rotated on her own and was born in the following contraction with the push. Nobody touched her."

"Fine, but don't learn to do it that way because that's how women get torn and that's hard to suture, you will soon find out…"

"This one didn't tear," Abel replies.

"Well, that's not common so don't take it for granted; that's how you get shoulder dystocia[12] and such. When the head is delivered, you should rotate the baby yourselves and help deliver the shoulders. You must get the anterior shoulder first, downwards, and then the posterior, upwards. This midwife is one of the "natural" ones and then, well, things happen."

"What happens?"

"I know what I say, I'm just telling you to watch out for her."

Maternity Hospital.

---

[12] Shoulder dystocia occurs when, after delivery of the fetal head, the baby's anterior shoulder gets stuck behind the mother's pubic bone.

Corridor. 16:40.

Laura meets Celia in the corridor and goes towards her. "The new docs are stunned by your birth."

"It was Dori and Noemí's, the merit is all theirs."

"Don't ever tell me again in front of a woman not to examine her."

"Well, give us a little credit then, if we are telling you how she is and that we've just examined her, trust us a bit. Have you ever thought how vaginal examinations must feel, if they did them to you?"

"But they are necessary."

"Some of them aren't. Some are one too many, as that one you wanted to do. If the birth is not advancing, if you need to make a decision, to diagnose something... but if everything's all right, second stage is coming, she's starting to push... then it will only mean disturbing her, because you won't be getting any information to help you reach a decision."

"Well, I didn't examine her in the end, did I?"

"And I'm really grateful to you for it," replies Celia with a smile.

Week 8

On October 30th, Elena and Javi wake up early. They have spent the night together at Javi's place. Elena's parents think she left the day before for her friend's village. In a couple of hours, Javi and Elena will pick Paula up and the three of them will go to the clinic.

Paula is already waiting for them on the street. She gets her suitcase into the car boot and gets in the back seat.

"Hello," she greets them, "how are you?" she asks her friend. "Nervous?"

"A bit, yes." Elena replies frightened. "I try not to think of it, but I'm rather scared to say the truth."

"Everything's going to be all right," Javi says caressing her leg.

"Quite, but what if it isn't?"

"But how could it not work? These people know what they're doing, Ele. They've done it plenty of times; it's been legal for ages; it's not as it was in our parents' times, when you got it done by a butcher in a hovel: these people are doctors, nurses and such. Hey, look at me!" he says, taking her face in his hands, "everything's going to be alright, do you hear me?

"Yes."

"Repeat after me: everything's going to be all right," Javi says. They always say that in films; he doesn't know why he feels she must repeat it, but if they do it in so many films it must be good.

"Everything's going to be all right," obeys Elena.

Lorena is packing to spend the weekend with Manuel. It's been almost four years since they first met, and he's always behaved splendidly towards her. *He's the perfect customer: rich, cultivated, clean, and with a family he won't be giving up for her. Don't even think about it, for heaven's sake*, she smiles at the thought. *Correct and perfect as a customer he might be, but he's not anyone I could love, not by a long shot. With such extreme ideas and so intolerant at everything. How many times I've had to hold my tongue, and pretend to be on his side despite the atrocities he says? He who pays the piper calls the tune. And now, what? He'll be the father of my child. Tell him or not, he'll still be the father. Luckily, ideas get into your head through time and education; ideas are not genetic,* she thinks with relief.

I don't know what to do. If I don't tell him, I'll have to figure out a way to make a living when the baby is born. I have some savings. Maybe I could start a small business from home so that I can be with the baby. Everything would be much easier if he didn't know, that way it would be just the two of us. But can I do that? I guess he has a right to know he's going to have a child. But if he does know, won't he have some rights over the baby? Obviously, he could help me financially, which would be a huge relief and a guarantee for the future, but… if he dies, what then? Will he legally recognise this baby? Could he do that without his wife's knowledge? I'm determined to have this baby with or without his help, so the best thing is… I have no idea what the best thing is. Why is everything so difficult?

Lorena gets off the train and finds a car with tinted windows waiting for her. The car approaches and stops by her side. Lorena puts her suitcase in the boot and sits on the passenger seat.

"You look beautiful, as always," Manuel says caressing her face. "Did you have a nice trip?"

"Yes," she says, taking his hand between hers and kissing it. "And you?"

"Yes, yes. I haven't been here long. There was a lot of traffic, I was afraid you'd be arriving first."

"Well, I'd have waited for you, no problem."

"You shouldn't keep a lady waiting. Not one as beautiful as you are," Manuel smiles.

"So, we're going to Gredos, aren't we?"

"Yes, to a beautiful country hotel you're going to love," Manuel says as he starts driving.

When Elena, Javi and Paula arrive in the clinic, they are received by a girl who leads them to a waiting room. Soon after, they're taken to a doctor's office. There is a rather aged man there, with a white coat and glasses. *He seems nice*, Elena thinks.

"Come in, come in, sit down. Take that other chair, young man," the doctor tells Javi, pointing at a third chair leaning on the wall, "tell me."

"Well, I'm... I'm pregnant," mumbles Elena, "and I don't want to have it."

"Right. Have you done a pregnancy test?"

"Yes, two: the first result was negative, but the second was positive."

"Do you know the date of your last menstruation?"

"On September 7."

"Very well, lie on the bed which is behind that screen and uncover your belly."

"What for?" she worriedly asks.

"I have to do an ultrasound to see the inside of the womb. You don't have to look."

Once Elena is lying on the bed, the doctor spreads some gel over her lower abdomen and puts the device on top of it. He starts moving it around without speaking. When he finishes, he gives her some paper towels to wipe the gel off and says with a smile, "come with us when you finish dressing. You are about eight weeks pregnant. Pills are the best option when you are at this stage."

Elena sits down again and the doctor tells her, "you're going to have a chat with the psychologist now, and then you'll sign a paper consenting to have the termination done, all right?"

Elena nods without speaking. Shortly, a young woman in a white coat comes in with a paper in her hands. She introduces herself and asks some questions, to make sure that Elena is there on her own free will and hasn't been coerced or forced by anyone. She hands her a paper which Elena signs after quickly reading it. The psychologist leaves, and the doctor gets a small box from a drawer and gives Elena a bottle of water.

"Take this pill with a bit of water. How is the morning sickness?"

"I'm quite alright."

"Will you be able to not vomit for a couple of hours?"

"Yes," Elena replies with security.

"Great," smiles the doctor. "It's an added difficulty for many women, those first weeks' sickness. You can take that pill now. The sooner, the better."

"But I'd rather have the other method, the vacuum one where they put you to sleep."

"Let's see, Elena: this technique is much safer, and having the possibility of doing it like this, what you're proposing is almost madness. What's frightening you? Why would you rather have the vacuum procedure than swallowing some pills?"

"I'm frightened to have the abortion on my own. I'm frightened of going back home, well, to the hotel, and something bad happening to me."

"Nothing will happen to you, Elena. You're only a few weeks pregnant. What's inside your uterus, in quantity, is just a little more than a menstruation. Here is what's going to happen: you'll be taking that pill now and going home, or to the hotel, with your friends. You will do whatever you want, going for a walk, to a restaurant, dancing, jumping… whatever you want, normal life.

"Tonight, around seven or eight, you'll be putting those other pills inside your vagina, as deep as you can, and after a while you'll start feeling unwell. You will start having back pain as if your menstruation was coming, and you'll start getting little contractions, which you will feel as cramps. All this is normal. It's the normal effect these pills have.

"This pill," he says taking the small box from the table, "is going to stop the pregnancy. It's the one telling your body to stop what it's doing. These others," he says as he takes another box, "are the ones you'll be taking home and putting inside your vagina later this afternoon. They will provoke your menstruation. These ones tell your womb: open up, you have to empty. What will happen to your body is the same that happens to it every month, only this time in an artificial way, provoked by these pills I'm giving you. Getting you vacuumed implies anesthetizing you and scraping your uterus, which we should avoid. Its consequences and possible complications are far more serious, do you understand?"

"Yes. Then, I'll take the pills."

"Great. Have you brought some sanitary towels?"

"No," she replies, ashamed.

"It's all right, no big deal, you can buy a couple packs because you are going to need them. Afterwards, tonight, you will bleed a lot, like a very strong menstruation, and in the morning, I want you to come back to see me, to make sure everything has been done correctly and you can go back home."

"Fine; thank you very much, Doctor."

"You're welcome, Elena. Take it now," he says pointing at the pill, "take these ones with you. These are the ones you have to get inside your vagina tonight, and if it hurts a lot, you can have two of these, together, every six hours," he explains as he writes "vagina" and "pain" on each box with a felt tip.

Health Centre.

GP's room.

"So, tell me, Carmen."

"Well, Don Arturo, I've been feeling lousy for the last few weeks. I am tired all the time, I feel sick and listless. I don't know what it can be, I'm normally very active and I've never felt like this," Carmen tells her family doctor.

"Could you be pregnant?"

"No. Well, I don't think so. I've been on the pill since Lara was born."

"Well, it can fail sometimes. We have to consider that possibility. We have to rule that option out first before we start looking for other causes." As he hands her a small container he continues, "we need a urine sample, when you come out of the toilet you can give it to Juani," he says, pointing to his assistant.

Carmen gets into the toilet and as she does what the doctor asks for, she thinks that it cannot be possible. *How could I be pregnant again? Fine, I'll give the bottle to that Juani for him to relax and look for what I really have, which I'm sure is anemia or something of the kind.* After giving the assistant the bottle, Carmen goes back to the doctor.

"How are your eating habits, Carmen?" he asks.

"Fine, more or less, I think. I cook daily."

"Do you eat fruit and vegs?"

"Yes, maybe not as much as I should. Do pulses count? We like spoon dishes a lot at home. But I've been eating less and worse of late. I guess it's a vicious circle: with the anemia I eat little, and as I eat little, I don't get well."

"What anemia? Do you have anemia?" asks the doctor.

"No, I'm not sure; I mean, I guess I must have anemia, which is what people have when they feel like this, don't they?"

The doctor guffaws.

Is he laughing at me? Carmen thinks as she looks at him somewhat puzzled.

Just then, Juani comes in and gives the doctor a paper.

"Well, I don't know if you are anemic on top of it, but you're pregnant, Carmen."

"But, but, but…" Carmen is paralyzed. She listens to that word coming out of her mouth repeatedly, but it feels as if it was another person speaking.

"Look, Carmen, contraceptive methods sometimes fail; even if they have a high reliability they aren't 100% safe. The pill works with 99.9%, which means that out of 1000 women taking it, one of them will get pregnant in a year."

"Yikes, and did it have to be me? I haven't missed any of my periods!"

"Well, you're probably not many weeks pregnant. Ask for an appointment with the obstetrician, for him to tell you exactly, and from there on you can consider things and decide."

"But what's there to decide? I'm pregnant, so I'm pregnant. There's nothing to decide."

"Very well. Now you'll have to feed yourself a bit better, will you? And if you feel sick, take this," he says writing on a paper he gives her. Two at night, and if you still feel nauseous, another one in the morning when you wake up."

Maternity Hospital.
Staff Room. 11:00am.

"Ana, there's a stillbirth[13] coming down for you," says the admissions nurse.

"It's not for me, it's for Marta," Ana replies.

Leyre, the nurse, goes to the board and then she goes to Delivery Room 3. When she comes back she tells Ana, "I'm passing her to you, Marta's still with her patient."

"But hers gave birth before mine!" says Ana irritated as she goes towards the delivery rooms.

"Will you be long?" she blurts out to Marta after coming into the delivery room.

"Well, yes; I'm stitching her, so it will take a bit."

Ana looks at Marta's suture. "Nice mess you've got here," she tells her.

Marta looks at her reproachfully, indicating her to shut up with a gesture towards the woman. On getting out, Ana says, "nothing like a good 'epis'[14] on time to spare this kind of thing," and disappears behind the door.

Maternity Hospital.
Staff Room. 11:20am.

Once Marta has finished, she goes to the staff room and there she meets Noemí and Celia who are talking about Noemí's work options after she finishes her training.

"If I were you, I'd start studying English full blast and would go out in the world, to see how things are done in other countries," she hears Celia telling the student midwife.

---

[13] Stillbirth: Name given to the baby who dies in the womb in the last trimester of pregnancy.

[14] Episiotomy: A surgical cut made at the opening of the vagina during childbirth.

"England's swell, isn't it?" Noemí asks.

"Well, I did my training there, but the way things are going in Europe now, I'd go somewhere else. As a midwife you can afford the cost of living in any country, as you would be working and earning money there; if I were you, there are many places I'd be going before the U.K."

"For instance?"

"For instance, I have a mate who studied with me and is now in Canada; there, midwives work in a completely independent way, they form small teams and women contact them directly and choose where they will give birth with that team: at the hospital, at home or at a birth centre.[15] Midwives care for them throughout the whole pregnancy, and when women start labour midwives go wherever the women are giving birth. Afterwards, the mothers have their postnatal visits at the hospital, and after the hospital they go home. And if they have given birth at home, then obviously all the visits are done there. And the state pays the midwives' team for every woman they have attended, no matter where they've given birth."

"Even if they do it at home?" Marta asks.

"Of course. What they pay for is the work each midwife team has done with every woman, independently of where they decide to give birth. What's more, low risk women don't get to see a doctor during the whole pregnancy, nor at birth or during the postpartum."

"Come on! Way to go before we have that here in Spain," complains Noemí.

"We will never get that far here," Marta says.

"Well, I imagine, with time..." Noemí says.

---

[15] Birth centre: Name given to the baby who dies in the womb in the last trimester of pregnancy.

"I'm with Marta on this," says Celia, "because there's a huge basic difference, which is that our profession, in this country, has always been subordinated to doctors. And even if we have a certain degree of autonomy to assist normal births, reality, in hospitals, is very different. Here in Spain, if you are assisting a normal birth and an obstetrician comes in and they get pig-headed about using forceps just because they want to, you step aside and they get their way. You might fight all you want, but in the end, they are the bosses."

That other way of working can be done in countries where midwives have known how to find their place and separate themselves from the medical profession, countries where they have learnt the difference between sick and healthy pregnant women and doctors have nothing to say in normal births and pregnancies. When those work areas are not separated, as is the case here, doctors supervise every birth, and as in their profession they are not taught to take care of healthy people, but to look for the illness, treat it and cure it, that's exactly what they do. A woman in labour doesn't need a doctor specialized in the pathology of pregnancy, she needs someone specialized in normal births and that's us, midwives.

"If you look closely, many obstetricians, at least in this hospital, are afraid of births. They see it as a process that must be watched attentively, monitored, controlled, with its guidelines and timetables, and if women don't stick to that, they operate.

"How many instrumental births do they perform because the woman has been over an hour in second stage -with a perfect trace and a baby in perfect conditions- just because the clock says so? There aren't many 'midwives' as such in Spain. Most of them work as obstetric nurses, and that way we'll never change. Until we separate our field from the obstetricians, until we don't get a unit managed by midwives where doctors don't come in, forget about getting where Canada or the U.K or the Scandinavian countries stand."

"And where else is our work top notch?" Noemí carries on.

"In some rural areas of South America: many people go there to train with the Mexican midwives. In Africa too, they work well although resources and transfers are limited; and I've heard wonders about New Zealand."

"And in Australia?"

"They are a bit more in-between, let's say they're halfway between what we do here and what it's being done in England. Does Australia attract you?"

"It's a country I've always liked a lot, yes."

"I met several Australians when I was in the U.K., and they were great people."

"Yeah, but it's so far away…" says Marta.

"Yes, but for someone who has no commitments, nor children… if you want to travel a bit, as a midwife you can afford it: you spend a couple of years there, you gain experience, you learn and then you come back or go elsewhere."

"You make it sound so easy…" says Marta.

"Because life's much easier than we think. Besides, the demand for midwives there is high, so they take care of your visa, help you to find a home, open a bank account… in short, they pamper you so that you don't lack anything and adapt easily. But, for that, you really must work on your English now. If later you decide not to go, don't go, but you'll have mastered English language, which will always come in handy for the future, for travelling, for life in general…"

Maternity Hospital.

Delivery Room 1. 11:20am.

Ana goes inside her delivery room; she has to care for the couple whose baby has died and she's rather upset.

"Hello, I'm Ana, your midwife."

Soraya and Vicente look at her. Their eyes are red and swollen, they are holding hands, sitting on the delivery room bed.

"Hello," they both reply.

"I'm going to read your records because this is too painful for you to tell me. I'm very sorry for your loss."

Both nod and Ana starts to read. Once she's over, she explains, "we're going to induce your labour and try for you to give birth to your baby."

"Can't she have a Cesarean?" Vicente asks. "Please, I don't think my wife can take labour, I really mean it."

"Even if making Soraya give birth to your baby looks barbaric now, it's much better for her, especially in the long term. If we perform a C-section, her recovery would be much longer; every movement would remind her of the baby for weeks, and every time she'd see her scar she would remember this for the rest of her life. I know you want this to be over as soon as possible, but giving birth is really a much better option, even if it takes a few hours. Besides, in this case she won't have to go through any contraction, because before starting we'll give her an epidural so that she doesn't feel anything."

Vicente looks at his wife and says, "you'd better have the epidural first, will you?"

Soraya nods, bursting into tears again, and Vicente hugs her, as they both sob. Ana stays there by their side in silence, looks at her watch and thinks, *half past twelve, even if everything goes slowly I'll be the one delivering, it's a second baby… I won't get rid of this.*

As she goes to the door, she tells them, "I'll be right back."

Maternity Hospital.

Staff Room. 2:30pm.

Ana enters the room seething and gets herself a coffee.

"Hey, Ana, you really went too far before," Marta reproaches her.

"Don't talk to me, I'm not in the mood; I have a stillbirth."

"And is that why you came into my delivery room? To see if you could pass it to me, didn't you?"

"Yes, I did. You had delivered half an hour before me and it was yours. And besides you were stitching a tear; well, it pisses me off, yes, because I loathe stillborn labours and it should have been yours."

"No, it shouldn't because I wasn't over. You are over when women get out of the delivery room door, not when they have given birth. Besides, you have no right to make a remark like the one you did when I was suturing her."

"What remark?"

"Damn it, that I should have done an 'epis'. You have no idea. You weren't there, you don't know what that labour was like, so you have no right to say anything. And even if you did, that was hardly the place to do it. The woman was there, although I'm not sure if you realised that because you didn't even say hello or looked at her; and you allow yourself to make remarks about my work, as if what happened was a consequence of something I could have prevented. That's no good even if it was true, which it wasn't."

"But you could have prevented that tear with an 'epis'."

"Look, Ana, no; you have no idea. You who cut all of them, don't know how much a perineum stretches or not. Anyway, that's not why I'm angry with you, it's the fact that you said it there, in front of the woman.

"And for your information, let me add that she gave birth in one push; I didn't even have my gloves on when the baby popped out. But an episiotomy is not something you do perfunctorily: there must be hundreds of women remembering you every time they fuck!"

"Well, sorry. I was cross because I didn't want to get the stillbirth."

"So, tough shit and you take it in your stride. Nobody likes a stillbirth and when you get one, you get one."

Just then a bell rings. It's from Ana's delivery room and she leaves, running and saying, "that's mine."

"I can't stand her," Marta tells Celia and Noemí. "She gets on my nerves."

"C'mon, sit down and have a rest. Shall I make coffee?" says Celia hugging her.

"Hello, my girlie, how did school go?" Carmen asks her daughter, hugging her in the schoolyard.

"Well. I'm going to play with Alma a bit, right?"

"No, dear, not today."

Lara grabs her sandwich, drops her backpack at her mother's feet and runs out to the swings without taking any notice.

"Lara!"

"Just a bit, Mom!" cries her daughter from a distance.

"Let her play a little while, I'll take her home if you want," her friend Marina tells her, approaching.

"Hey, Marina, babe! I didn't see you. No, thanks a lot, I want to take her home and put her to bed early. Get her into her routine. Even if she's been here for one month already, with this good weather, her cousins' birthdays, (all of them this time of the year), one thing and the other, she goes to bed at a different time each day, it's crazy. It's impossible to get her up in the morning. And me neither, with the nights she gives me… Besides, I only have a few months to get her used to falling asleep on her own."

"Are you pregnant?"

"Ssssht, I've just been told and nobody knows; I haven't even told Luis yet."

"It's great, my congratulations, girl! I imagine you must want a boy, after the girl…"

"That's the thing, we weren't after another one, but… these things happen."

"Oh, Carmen, don't you worry, I'm sure everything will be alright in the end. Look at me, I was all stressed with Alma, and since I had Yolanda, as I cannot be keeping an eye on Alma all the time she's much better, more responsible, more obedient. You see, I'm convinced if we only have one, we spoil them. And I don't mean just whims and suchlike, well, also: I mean we don't let them live. If we only have one, we are breathing down their necks all the time: we don't go down the slide because our ass is too large, but if we could there we'd go, to sit them on our laps so they don't get hurt.

"When you have another one, the eldests then get their own time for exploring without having our eyes on their backs all day. And yes, they'll come every now and then with bumps on their head, but they will have to get up and go. Next time you go to the park, just watch and you'll see in a minute which ones have no siblings: they are much more fainthearted, let me tell you."

"Hey, you, I remind you Alma was an only child just a year ago!"

"And that's why I know what I'm talking about. She's much more determined now, like, more mature. And it's not a coincidence, it's because now she doesn't have her tiresome mom over her all the time, because she profits from all the time I spend with her sister to do her own thing. Cheer up, Carmen, this is great news. You'll see. Lara! Alma! We're going home! Did you come by car?"

"I didn't, let's walk and I'll stop by the shop to get some dinner, there's nothing at home. Please don't say anything yet, until I tell Luis."

"Say what, Mom?" asks Lara.

"Aha, look how quickly you appear now, don't you?" her mother tells her, "I always have to call you three times, but Marina calls you once and here you are."

"I was left on my own, as Alma came…"

Marina winks at Carmen and smiles at her.

"You'll prove right in the end!" Carmen replies smiling back.

Maternity Hospital.
Delivery Room 1.

Ana enters the delivery room and smiles.

"We're ready. Could we start as soon as possible?" Vicente says.

"Of course. I'll run your drip quickly," and looking at Soraya she adds, "while I call the anaesthetist to give you the epidural; and, once you're anesthetized, we'll start with the induction."

Ana is performing a vaginal examination on Soraya, "you have dilated seven centimeters. Not long to go. Can you notice anything?"

"A kind of pressure on my back passage."

"That's the baby's head, pressing with the contractions. When you notice that, you may push if it relieves you. Your baby will be born soon. Will you be wanting to see him?"

"No." Vicente says swiftly.

Soraya looks at her husband surprised, but says nothing.

"It's obviously your decision, but if you let me advise you, it's usually the people who chose not to see their babies that have regrets."

"Do you know why?" asks Vicente.

"Because they weren't able to start their mourning properly, they couldn't say goodbye. Not knowing what their baby was like, the face they had, proved a heavy load later on. It might have such an impact that some people might even distort reality and think their babies didn't die and were stolen at the hospital."

"I'm not sure," Vicente says insecure, looking at his wife. "What do you want to do?"

"I want to see him, but if you don't…"

"We'll be seeing him," Vicente says, "but will he be very damaged?"

"No, I don't think so," the midwife replies. "If you want, I'll tell you when I get to see him and you can decide then, ok?"

"I think he's getting out," Soraya says.

Ana spreads sheets over Soraya's body so that they cannot see the birth. She tries to hurry, for she can already see the baby's head showing with the contraction. She has no time to call for the assistant for help, but it's too late: she will have to do without her.

"Try not to push now, blow, blow," she says as she opens the delivery pack containing everything for the birth. "Don't push," she tells Soraya.

"I'm not pushing," she replies.

The head has already been born, and the body is starting to do so. *I haven't done an episiotomy*, Ana thinks. *If she gets a tear, she'll be remembering me for the rest of her life.*

The baby has been born and is lying at the bottom of the bed between Soraya's legs. Ana looks at him and thinks that he's a really beautiful baby.

"Is he born?" Soraya asks.

"Yes," Ana replies.

"What does he look like?" his father asks.

"Beautiful. What's his name?"

"Sancho," says his mother.

"Won't we be calling the next one Sancho?" an upset Vicente asks, lovingly looking at his wife.

"No, Vicente. This is Sancho. We've been calling him Sancho throughout the whole pregnancy and this is Sancho. His future brother will have his own name."

Ana wraps the baby among towels and cleans his head and face with some pads.

"Are you ready?" she says looking at Soraya and Vicente.

They both say yes. Ana puts Sancho in Soraya's arms, and she starts crying the minute she takes her baby. Vicente presses her shoulder, mumbling: "how beautiful he is" and bursting into tears.

"My love, my beautiful Sancho, why? We wanted to meet you so much. We had everything ready for your arrival: your cradle, your clothes, your toys… Even your brother Hugo had chosen a soft toy for you: what are we telling Hugo now? He was so thrilled to know you, he was so happy when he knew you were a boy! Why us, why did you die, my beautiful son, why?" Soraya cries inconsolably and her husband hugs her. They both sob, with their baby in their arms. Ana waits patiently. She wants to go out and leave them alone, but she doesn't want to do it just like that. She wants to tell them something before she goes and she can't find the moment.

Once their crying has subdued, Ana tells them, "I don't know if you have thought about Hugo and if you think he might like to meet his brother. How old is he?"

"Seven. But," stammers Vicente, "are you proposing that Hugo meets Sancho?"

"Yes, that's what I'm saying. You can ask him if he wants to see him, give him a kiss, give him the soft toy he chose for him…"

"We're baffled," says Vicente after a swift look at his wife. "We left Hugo with his grandparents and we haven't even told him Sancho is dead. We still have no idea what to tell him or how, but I find seeing him is a bit too much, isn't it?" he asks Soraya.

"I don't know. We weren't sure about seeing Sancho ourselves and now I feel glad and content to have him in my arms, to see how cute he is, that he has Hugo's little nose…" she says caressing his face.

"It's simpler than you think," Ana continues. "Tell him and see what he says. In the old times people tried to hide death from children to try to protect them, but now we know that hurts them more, as they notice something terrible has happened from which they are excluded. Children should do their mourning too, understand what's happened, express themselves freely and receive sincere answers. Parents may not know things, not have all the answers. No one knows what happens after death, but you can tell him his brother went to heaven, or that he's a star, a drop of water, a tree... For a child it's easier if he has a place to look at, talk to, remember him by. You don't have to do anything now. Sancho is staying here with us until tomorrow, and you'll be going home and seeing what Hugo wants to do. If he wants to see his brother, that's not such a bad idea: children's imagination knows no bounds, and especially in something as delicate as his brother's death we must explain everything that needs to be explained to him. I'm leaving you three alone for a while. I'll be back in about twenty minutes: if you need something before I'm back, just ring the bell for me."

Maternity Hospital.
Staff Room.
Ana enters the staff room and Montse, the maternity assistant, asks her: "how dilated is the stillbirth woman?"
"She's already given birth," replies Ana.
"Why didn't you call me?"
"Because the baby was born practically on its own, I had no time to call you. She noticed something and the baby was already coming out. I had no time to put her on lithotomy, to do an episiotomy, anything. I could barely put the gloves on and open the pack."
Montse gets up and Ana asks her, "where are you going?"
"To get her ready to go up."
"No, they will call. They are with their baby, and they'll be telling us when they're over."
"I can't understand it."
"What is it you can't understand?"
"That business of hugging and seeing off a dead fetus. Some people even kiss them."

"Sure, they do! It's their baby. Wouldn't you kiss your son if he died?" intervenes Marta, who's in the room reading a book.

"Of course, I would, but it's not the same," replies Montse.

"How can you say it's not the same? It's exactly the same. It's your son, and unfortunately he died before you could see him, but it's totally normal and understandable for his parents to hug him, rock him, kiss him and say goodbye to him, as any parent whose child died would do," Marta adds.

"They have another son, seven years old," Ana says, "and he might be coming to meet his brother."

"What? A seven-year-old? But, are we crazy or are we crazy? That boy's going to develop a lifelong trauma if he sees his dead brother. That's sheer madness!" Montse exclaims.

"No, Montse, it isn't. Children must be included in anything that happens in the family and asked what they want to do; and if they want to see their dead brother and give him a kiss, their decision must be respected."

"When I was four or five, the neighbour's baby died and they took me to see him, and it was horrible: that poor baby, lily white, with those purple lips… I still get the willies when I remember it."

"You're acknowledging I'm right, then: you were taken willy nilly to see the neighbour's baby, you were completely out of place there. Nobody asked you, and I think it shouldn't be done that way, because that baby was nothing of yours, he didn't mean anything to you."

"I don't know, I think it's terrible for a child to see his dead brother."

"Only if he wants to, you're not keeping that in mind. He most probably won't want to see him, all he'll want will be to have his parents back home and little more; and if he sees him, his reaction is most likely to be surprisingly normal."

"And where did you learn that?" a sceptical Montse inquires.

"In a fabulous seminar on perinatal death we went to last year, didn't we, Marta?" Ana replies while Marta nods. "You should come to the next one. It'd be good for you."

"Us, Maternity assistants aren't allowed to apply for anything."

"And why not? Have you tried it?"

"We have, yes. Mary tried to go to that foot massage course last year and she couldn't."

"Here we go again. As Mary didn't get to go to the reflexology course, the conclusion is that assistants are not allowed to take courses. Us midwives also get negative answers, you know. Look at the pelvic floor one, many of us couldn't go because, simply, all of us cannot go: some will have to stay behind working, don't you think? If you're interested in a course, talk to the supervisor and I'm sure she'll do all she possibly can for you to go. But do talk to her first, and once she's got you to go, then tell your workmates, because if all of you request it at the same time she won't allow you," Ana tells her.

"I can't do that to my mates."

"Do them what, exactly?"

"Requesting a course without telling them anything and then telling them later when I've got it: you must be really twisted to do something like that!"

"Suit yourself, sweetie. But I'd say you must be real dumb not to do it."

"Are you calling me dumb?"

"Are you calling me twisted?"

"I'm just saying I don't find it fair not to tell my mates."

"Look here, Montse, there's a course you're interested in and you sign up for it. You get it, and afterwards you tell your workmates 'I just got granted for this course, in case there's somebody else interested'. It sounds much more logical than 'there's a course I'm interested in, but I'm telling all my mates, of whose interest or knowledge I have no clue, so that I reduce my possibilities of getting it'. It's not being twisted, Montse. That's how most people think and it's the most normal and logical way of doing things. You do things without telling your competitors to do them too. What you're proposing is utopian, it's for an unreal, ideal world."

"Yeah, well, here goes *Miss Know-it-all*."

"No, baby, no. I'm just telling you what's normal. If you want to tell everyone to have your possibilities reduced, go ahead, darling, suit yourself."

Just then, Ana's delivery room bell rings, and she goes out of the staff room to see what Soraya and Vicente want.

Maternity Unit.

Delivery Room 1.

"Here I am," says Ana coming in.

The eyes of Sancho's parents are red from crying, and when Ana comes closer they tell her,

"thank you very much, Ana, you have helped us a lot."

"I'm happy to hear that," she replies smiling.

"We think we'd like to go home as soon as possible: could we leave already? Really, I don't want to go to the ward if I can help it; I don't want to meet other mothers or pregnant women.

"I'm not sure. Let me ask if you can. Mothers in your situation spend less time here than the rest, but I've never heard of anyone going home straight from the delivery room. I'll ask. Anyway, you wouldn't be on the Maternity floor, don't worry about that."

"Really, all I want is to go back home, see Hugo, and go back to normality as soon as we can."

Doctor's Office.

Ana goes into the doctor's office and finds Dr. Casona there in front of the computer; she looks up and greets:

"Hello Ana, what can I do for you?"

"Hello Nuria. I'm with the stillbirth girl. She says she wants to go home straight from here. She doesn't want to be warded."

"Not surprising," says Nuria getting up from the chair. "What's their name?"

"Soraya and Vicente. And the fetus is Sancho."

"Ouch! Don't call him fetus, it's an awful word. Especially for a baby who's already been born.

"You're right, it sounds terrible. Why do we call them cross fetuses?"[16] Ana asks.

"Not a clue about who thought of that, but it's horrible. Besides, it's used everywhere, at least it was in every hospital I've worked in. I guess it's a way of saying he died inside the womb, but I don't know, it's just a guess," Nuria replies. "It's ok. What else? Do they have more children?"

"Yes, Hugo, seven years old. I've already told them to ask him if he wants to say goodbye."

[16] Stillborn babies are called "cross fetuses" in some Spanish hospitals.

Nuria stares at Ana, who asks: "what?"

"I'm surprised that you say that. Not many midwives nor obstetricians know about the importance of including children in death processes. I'm gratefully surprised, that's all."

"We were talking about that a moment ago in the staff room. We had a seminar last year about perinatal death and we learnt a lot. I think they're doing it again this year."

"It should be compulsory for the whole hospital staff. Well, I'll go meet them; Soraya, Vicente, Sancho and… Hugo, the brother?"

Ana nods and follows Nuria to the delivery room.

"Good morning, I'm Nuria Casona, the obstetrician on call. I'm very sorry about your

loss," she says approaching the family and adds, "Sancho is beautiful." After a short while looking at Sancho, Dr. Casona goes on, "Ana tells me you'd like to leave as soon as possible."

"Yes, please."

"I have to examine you before that, and, if everything's all right, we'll do all the paperwork for you to go straight away. I suppose you must be anxious to go back to Hugo."

"Quite."

"Well, everything's all right," Nuria Casona says after examining Soraya. "You can put your clothes on while I discharge you, and then you may leave."

Soraya kisses her baby and gives him to Ana, who puts him into the cradle.

"What do we do now?"

"The hospital will take care of everything," answers the midwife.

"Thank you very much, Ana: you've been a great help in a very difficult time," says Soraya, hugging her.

"I am ever so sorry," replies Ana holding her in her arms. "There's a Spanish book called '*The empty cradle*' which can help you very much in these moments. I think it would be a good idea if you read it. It won't relieve your pain, but it will help you to take it better, to be aware and accept what you're feeling."

"Thank you; we'll read it," answers Vicente.

"How's the best nurse and husband in the world?" Carmen asks her husband as he arrives home from the health centre.

"We've had one of those fine, wondrous afternoons when everyone's at their best behaviour and we get practically nothing: a couple of feverish children and little else. In short, I've been in the staff room the whole afternoon. Which was peculiar, because Aurora has split with her boyfriend and Nieves, the new assistant, is starting a relationship: they haven't stopped chatting the whole afternoon, my head's ringing. It's so funny how we all take a book for our free time but the girls just take their book for a walk, and besides they won't let us guys read in peace either. They were asking for my opinion all the time. What do they care about it, I wonder! That capacity women have to speak and connect everything creeps me out: one gets a boyfriend, the other leaves hers, and nevertheless they find it a common subject to be chatting about for hours on end. And you, how are you?"

"Fine. I went to see Don Arturo."

"Anemia, was it?"

"No. I'm pregnant."

"But darling, that's great news! Difficult to believe, but great news."

"Are you happy?"

"Sure, I am, how could I not? And, how could it happen?"

"Well, Don Arturo says it can sometimes happen with the pill, even if you make sure you take every single one and all."

"Well, I've never seen it at the clinic, but, look, here's that famous 1% they always mention in contraception."

"One in a thousand, Don Arturo said; it works in 99.9 % of the cases."

"Wow, what precision! If it wasn't because we've been the lucky ones, I would never have believed that. Every time a pregnant woman who was on the pill comes to the doctor we discover in the end she didn't take all of them, she forgot some... Seeing is believing. Are you happy?" Luis asks, taking her by the waist.

"Yes, I'm happier now. I guess the first fright has passed."

"Sorry, darling. Had I suspected anything I'd have come with you."

"Don't worry, I'm all right."

"And Lara? Have you told her?"

"No, I was waiting for you to be there. I'm sure you'll want to be there when we tell her."

"Thank you, my love. I love you to bits, you know," says Luis kissing her.

"I love you too."

Elena, Javier and Paula register at the hotel. Once in the room, Paula asks Elena,

"what do you want to do?"

"I'm not sure," she replies.

"Shall we go for a walk? Explore a bit?" Paula suggests.

"I don't know. What if we find someone we know?"

"In this godforsaken village?" Javier says. "No one we know can be here. And even if there was, which there won't: we are three friends spending the weekend together, that's all."

"Well, all right. Let's go see what's like over here. Maybe it's a beautiful village and all," Elena says.

Around seven o'clock in the afternoon they decide to come back. They've bought some cold cuts and beers to have supper in their room.

Once they're there, Elena gets the pills from the box and puts them on the table. "They don't have any directions," she says.

"Normal, Ele; if they did, people would know what they are for, and would start having abortions at home at the drop of a hat," her friend tells her.

"Do you think that's the reason? Or is it for people not to get terrified by the side effects?"

"C'mon, c'mon, don't get paranoid. I'm sure the reason's what Pau says," Javier chips in. "If it wasn't, we could start an online abortion business tomorrow, knowing the name of the pills: we'd buy them in the black market, and sure people would pay to get them just like that, without clinics or anything!"

"Fuck, the sanitary towels!" Elena yells. "One thing, just one thing we had to buy, and we forget."

"Hey, take it easy, I'll go," Javier says putting his jacket on. "Which ones should I get?"

"Whatever they have. It's the same. With wings, better, if they have them. But get two packs. Three, get three just in case."

The minute they stop at the hotel parking, Lorena knows she's going to like the place: it has a rustic feeling that reminds her of her childhood, when she spent her summers at her grandparents' home.

As they register at the hotel, Lorena notices that the girl at the reception desk is uncomfortable, as if she knew or felt something. *Are we so obvious? It's a considerable age gap, but there are more and more couples with a twenty-year difference or more between them. Maybe he comes here with more women? No. She would know. He's not that kind of man. She's certain she's the only 'other woman' in his life."*

They go up to their suite, which occupies the whole top floor of the hotel. Looking around, a stitch reminds her that this life will very soon come to an end. She can't go on like this, for her child. She must leave it as soon as she can. *This will very probably be my last encounter with Manuel, so I'll try to make it unforgettable for him*, Lorena thinks.

Manuel phones asking for champagne, giving instructions not to be disturbed.

"Just leave it outside, knock at the door and go away."

He is extremely cautious, and the fewer people see them together, the better for both, but especially for him.

"Undress and get this ready," he tells her as he throws a silver little box at her.

Shit! thinks Lorena, *and now what? I can drink a little champagne, but this? I should have known, I know he loves to fuck like this. Think, think, think,* Lorena's mind is bubbling as she starts getting the lines ready on the bedside table.

There's a knock at the door. The champagne's already there. Manuel takes it and opens the bottle as Lorena gets the tube inside her nose and noisily snorts some air. Manuel comes closer, smiles at her and gives her a champagne glass.

"Here's to you, princess," he kisses her and takes her trousers off.

Manuel looks at Lorena, fascinated "I want to take you far away for a few days. I want to take you somewhere where we don't have to hide or stay in a hotel room all the time." Lorena gulps and replies, "It'd be wonderful. Any place in particular?"

"I don't know, I really haven't thought about it. It just came into my mind. Where would you like to go?"

"No, Manuel, this is for you and about you. I don't get to choose. It's you who decides where you want to go with me. Not the other way around."

"Well, I'd like to know your opinion."

"To the Maldives," Lorena tells him.

"Excellent option. See how I was right to ask you? An exclusive paradise, far from the people, where Spanish bumpkins don't go…"

"Don't they? It's where my cousin went for her honeymoon. That's why I said it. I've been in love with the place ever since I saw her photos."

"Well, she can't be a bumpkin if she's a relative of yours. I meant the Caribbean: crowded with Spaniards, wherever you go. Ask any redneck what's the place in the world he likes better and he'll tell you the Mayan Riviera, Punta Cana or Cancún."

"That's probably the farthest they've been, that's why."

"Well, that's what I mean, Lorena; I wasn't expecting less from you, on your choice. Have you ever been to the Caribbean?"

"Yes," she replies with uncertainty.

"Where?" smiles Manuel.

"The Dominican Republic, Puerto Rico, Margarita Island, Florida… I think that's all."

"Well, I'm sure you noticed a great difference in the number of Spaniards in some places and others, didn't you?"

"Not really," says Lorena recalling those places.

"Lorena, are you telling me the hotel in the Dominican Republic wasn't crammed with Spaniards compared to the ones in Venezuela or Puerto Rico?"

"Let's say in the hotels where I was I couldn't notice that difference. Although not everyone can afford them."

"That's exactly what I mean: all Spaniards go to those hives like hotels where they're all crammed together, and given an all-inclusive with cheap rum, a piece of pineapple and a paper umbrella in their glass to make them think they're in a film and that's paradise. And, you know what? They'd better stay there, all together, and leave the rest of the world to us. These are the new ghettos of the XXIth century. Ghettos for rednecks. And besides they're so stupid as to pay for staying there."

"I see: so, a person who goes on a trip once or twice in his life is a bumpkin because he's choosing a popular holiday destination; one where they speak his language on top, so that he'll be feeling more at ease and will be able to enjoy his stay much more. Is that why he's a bumpkin?"

"Exactly."

"Have you been to those places?"

"Yes."

"And you are not a bumpkin because…" Lorena knows very well that she's reaching the limit. That Manuel always wants to be right, and she shouldn't argue with him. Just enough for him to enjoy the conversation, for him to think it's a real conversation and, as usual, after a bit of push and pull, let him be right.

"Lorena, please. You forget that I have a wife I take on holidays every year, and what places do you think she chooses? Those places to show off in front of strangers, to wear the most expensive bracelet there is and show all those strangers that she's not like them, that her room is much more expensive and that the rum she's getting in her glass is twenty years old, even if she couldn't tell the difference from the cheapest one. I've spent many holidays in places like that, I sure know what I'm talking about."

"Nobody could ever take you for a redneck. Not even in your swimsuit and in the middle of a crowd," Lorena smiles approaching him.

Manuel smiles, his ego boosted: he loves being adulated that way, the way Lorena does.

"Speaking of bracelets," he says haughtily, "Clarisa once got angry in a hotel because us VIPs didn't have one, that's how they differentiated. So, she told them she wasn't taking it, and they had to find a bracelet in a different colour just for her. She was the only one in the whole hotel with a different bracelet and she was showing it off to everyone all the time, happy as a child with a new watch: pathetic!" he says, throwing her on the bed with a shove.

"Well, just a cigarette won't harm much; besides, with all I've smoked so far, one more won't make a difference. And I do need it, with all the fright," Carmen tells herself as she wraps a towel around her head. "That's it, like this it won't smell, Luis is like a hound, he can notice any smell from miles, and surely for the baby this anxiety I have has to be worse than any cigarette I smoke".

Carmen climbs atop the toilet bowl, opens the window and lights her cigarette.

Hmm, and why does it have to be so bad? she thinks breathing out her first puff. She looks at her cigarette packet, counting them. *Four. Gee, only four good ones and then I'll have to get the pregnancy ones, there's no way to smoke that, they're totally flavourless. How do people stop smoking? Because I can't, I simply can't. I've tried everything, but every time I try I get sick and I can't; and that can't be good for the baby either...If I had known, I could have started to quit before getting pregnant, but I can't make the poor baby go through this: neither him nor me. Mind you, I'm going to smoke the minimum: three a day maximum, one after each meal and that's that. Not even one more. Well, maybe four, I cannot go to bed at night without the last one, but that will be all.*

She finishes her cigarette and starts getting down the toilet bowl, but she climbs back up and lights another one. "Well, I can do this because it's early pregnancy. And two fags together are better than two of them apart, they say it's more harmful…"

Javier goes back to the hotel and he sees Elena's father with a woman in the lobby. He looks at him and he turns his back as if he had never seen Javier at all.

He hasn't recognized me, Javier thinks, and he hurries to the stairs. *Fuck it, holy shit! Well, we've just barely caught a glimpse of each other a couple of times, he probably hasn't even realised. But what's he doing here? And with that woman? Wasn't he at some convention or something? No way, he's cheating on Clarisa, the bastard. And with that hot chick, too! Fuck, fuck, fuck… and what do I do now? What if he's recognized me? I don't think he has*, Javier thinks in front of their room's door. He tries to calm down before coming into the room. He hears someone coming down the corridor and gets in, swiftly closing the door behind him.

"What's wrong?" Paula asks. "You look as if you've seen a ghost."

Javier looks around for Elena.

"She's having a bath," says Paula nodding towards the bathroom door.

Javier approaches her and hurriedly whispers, "Elena's father is at the hotel."

"What?" Paula says, terrified.

"Shh, be quiet," admonishes Javier. "He's here, with a woman. He's cheating on his wife with her."

"But, are you sure?"

"Sure, I'm sure. It was him, I swear to God."

"And did he see you?"

"I'm not sure. I mean, yes, he has, but I don't think he recognized me, I bumped into him at the reception, but I don't think the bloke's sussed out anything."

"But hadn't you two met before?"

"Hardly. As they won't see me in that family, we have seen each other like, twice, and from a distance. I don't think he recognized me."

"Fucking hell, man, what do we do?"

"We don't tell Ele anything, that's what we do."

"But she'll get wind of it, fuck it! We can't get out of the room, if he sees us we're in for it!"

"Well, we'll think about it. So far, we'll tell her nothing and when we need to we can tell her there's someone who knows her, I don't know, a teacher or something. I know, the bald one who's a friend of her parents."

"Damián?"

"That one, we'll tell her that he's at the hotel and that we cannot get out of the room if we don't want to be caught."

"But we tell her nothing for now, not until everything is over."

Javier goes to the fridge and opens a beer bottle. His hands are shaking so much he can't put the beer into a glass, so he gives up and drinks straight from the bottle. He knocks on the bathroom door.

"Are you all right?" he says, poking his head round it.

"Yes, yes, I'm coming out."

"Want a drink?" he asks, showing her his beer.

"No, I don't feel like it, thanks. I'm coming. Wait for me outside, please, I'm coming."

Well, here we go. Let's put an end to this asap, Elena thinks. She gets out of the bathtub, takes a towel, dries herself and puts her pyjamas on. Once out of the bathroom, she looks around for the pills' box.

She spots it on the table and takes it back into the bathroom.

"Don't you want to eat something first?" Javier asks.

"No, no, I don't," she says disappearing behind the bathroom door.

Lorena and Manuel are going out for dinner. There's a small restaurant some three miles away where he loves to go whenever he has a chance: game, wild mushrooms and a good Ribera wine are, for him, the perfect combination for a discerning palate. When they are about to get out, Manuel sees him. He ignores him, as if he didn't know who he is. Even so, his heart is racing so it feels like it's coming out of his mouth, which has gone completely dry. Manuel goes straight to the car and gets inside hastily. Lorena, surprised, follows him.

"Anything wrong?" she asks.

"That chap is my daughter's boyfriend."

"What chap?"

"That nobody we just bumped into, just now, inside."

"Are you sure?"

"Of course, I'm sure, for Chrissakes!" he bellows, hitting the wheel. "Of course! They are here together. He's here with her. The girl lied to us, she told us she was going to some pig slaughter thing festival, we believed her, we let her go, and look what a pair of scoundrels they turned out to be. They're here for the weekend as if they were two adults, those shameless children. She'll find out what's coming when she gets home, let me tell you. She'll never see that bastard again in her miserable life," he says repeatedly banging the wheel.

"Manuel, take it easy," Lorena tries to calm him. "You have to think about this carefully. I think you're the one who'd be the biggest loser in this business. Keep in mind you have only seen him, but he has seen you with me."

Manuel's expression shows he's panicking. He begins to inhale deeply, repeating once and again, "this can't be happening, it just can't, it just can't…"

"Chances are he won't be telling her: you men are much more discreet and reserved than we are. Being her boyfriend, he surely doesn't want to hurt her. He won't be telling her; not for some time, at least."

"I'll kill him if he does, I will."

"What are you saying, Manuel? Don't say nonsense."

"No, it's not nonsense. I'll kill him and that's that. It's the only way out. If he hasn't told anyone, it's my only way out, isn't it? I can't let that imbecile have any control over me. Something easy, a car running over him, an overdose," he says with a nervous chuckle… "and Bob's your uncle."

Lorena has never seen Manuel like this. She guesses it's the reaction of someone used to always have everything under control. It's the first time she sees him in a situation where he cannot. She's starting to get frightened. She doesn't think Manuel can be talking seriously, or is he?

"Look, let's do something: I'll go up and collect our things. You stay in the car, so as not to be seen by him. We check out, and we leave."

"How was school, princess?" Carmen asks her daughter.

"All right," she replies.

"What have you done this afternoon?"

"Drawing."

"Only drawing?"

"And we've sang a song in English."

"That's great! And what's the song like?"

Lara starts singing and doing the song's routine, and when she's done her parents clap.

"You know, Lara? In a few months we'll be having a baby."

"A baby? For me?"

"Yes, for you and for dad and for me, for all of us."

"And why can't we have it now?"

"Because we must wait for him to grow up, he's tiny now and is here inside me and we have to wait for him to get out."

"And what will his name be?"

"We still don't know because it's very early, but in some time, when we know what it is, then we'll think of a name for the baby."

"But I want a baby!"

"Yes, darling, and a baby it will be, but we don't know if it will be a boy or a girl."

"I want a girl."

"You do?"

"Yes, to comb her hair."

"Right, we'll see what it is, okay? And you can also comb his hair if it's a boy."

"But boys have short hair!"

"Yes, but they also comb their hair, don't they?"

"Yes, but I want a girl."

"All right, sweetie, says Luis, taking her in his arms. "You know Mom and Dad love you lots, don't you?"

"Yes."

"And we'll love you lots when the baby comes," her father says as Lara tries to get rid of his arms. "Will you give me a kiss?"

"No."

"What do you mean no? Give me a kiss and I'll let you go to play."

"No."

"So, you don't want to play?"

Lara kisses her father and runs to her bedroom. Luis kisses his wife, who shuts her eyes. Now she knows the reason for her exhaustion, she's starting to feel much better. As tired as she was, but better.

As Carmen is sleeping on the sofa, Luis goes out to smoke on the balcony. It was very hard for her to reduce tobacco when she was pregnant with Lara, so he guesses it will be as hard now, or even worse. She should try to stop smoking, as it's so bad for the baby, but the sheer mention of it makes her wild. Luis doesn't know what to do or how to face the situation. Maybe it would be easier if they both tried to do it at the same time. *Perhaps, as I don't want to stop smoking, I can do it when I'm not home, she's the one who's pregnant, at the end of the day; and if she doesn't notice she won't miss it that much.*

He finishes off his cigarette and goes back into the house. Just then, Carmen sleepily asks him, "What are you doing?"

"Nothing; go on sleeping, I know you're tired. Rest all you can now that you're sleepy."

"You were smoking," she says.

"Yes, but I went outside not to bother you. C'mon, forget about it: sleep for a while so that you don't think about it."

"Of course, I think about it," she states as she sits up and wakes up completely. "I think of it all the time because I can't help thinking about it. I think I want a cigarette all the time, and then I realize I can't and within minutes, I feel like it again, and it's horrible. I won't be able to quit, darling, I won't be able to because I simply can't."

"But you're doing very well!"

"What? What am I doing well? Being horrid day in, day out? Only thinking about not smoking, when it's the only thing I want? No, Luis, that's not doing well."

"Just try not to smoke till you can't hold it anymore. And then, if you really must, smoke just a couple of puffs to kill the craving and then put out the cigarette."

"But that's not the answer. Gimme a cigarette," she says, putting her coat on.

"But Carmen…"

"No 'buts', you just smoked one and feel so comfy because you're not feeling the pressure of not having to smoke, and it's damn easy to speak on someone's behalf. Just give me a cigarette."

"But I just want you to try…"

"To try bullshit. Tell me something I don't know. Gimme a cigarette, Luis," she says impatiently, her hand open in front of her husband.

"I'm sure we can try to find an easier solution," Luis insists.

"Luis, either you give me a cigarette or I'll go to the shop and won't be back till I've smoked the whole pack."

"But, what nonsense! Carmen, please breathe deeply and relax for a second."

Carmen is still with her hand stretched and Luis knows there's no way to change her mind now.

"We'll share it," he resigns.

"But I'll light it," Carmen insists, already halfway to the balcony.

Luis goes out to the balcony and gives his wife the cigarette pack and the lighter.

Carmen lights a cigarette and takes a huge puff.

"Mmmm," she says exhaling the smoke… "I was dying for it!" She takes another long puff and Luis stretches his fingers to get the cigarette.

Carmen pushes his hand away. "Wait," she says taking the fag to her mouth again and taking two deep puffs.

"Well, 'Miss Anxious', don't you smoke it all in four puffs. We were supposed to be sharing."

Carmen gives Luis the cigarette, while reproaching him that he just smoked one five minutes ago.

"Right, but we have to try for you to smoke as little as possible."

"And why don't you try to smoke as little as possible yourself?" she replies, trying to snatch the butt from between his fingers.

"But Carmen, darling, there's something you don't want to see: you are pregnant and you have to smoke as little as you can. Stop comparing yourself to me and reproaching me that I smoke too. We are both hooked, and to stop smoking is very hard for both of us. But we obviously must do something for the baby, and 'as you smoke then I smoke too' is a useless excuse."

Carmen puts the cigarette out and goes back inside.

"Well, we'll talk about it, don't crush my pleasure. I've just smoked one cigarette, please don't ruin it."

Luis stays on the balcony, considering what he could do for Carmen to smoke less. While he's pondering, he opens the pack and lights another one.

Lorena is packing in a hurry. *He's even crazier than he seems,* she thinks while she closes her suitcase. *There's no way I'm telling him I'm expecting his baby. I wouldn't put it past him to make me have an abortion. He got so wild! It must be a hard blow for him all right, his daughter is precious to him and the boy who's fucking her has him by the balls. It must be difficult to take… but he's talking about killing him because he saw him with me! I mean, he could always deny it and that's that.*

When she arrives at the front desk, she sees Manuel there. He puts his wallet into his pocket and they go out to the car together while the bellboy puts their luggage in the car boot.

"He's here with two girls," Manuel tells Lorena, once inside the car.

"What?" she replies, surprised.

"The son of a bitch, he's come with two girls. He's cheating on my girl with two women. I'll kill him. I don't know how, but I'll kill him. Just watch out, boy, because I'm coming for you and I won't rest until you're dead," he says starting the car.

Lorena says nothing. She just wants this nightmare to be over. To get home and be as far as she can from this monster. She can't believe what's happening: the degree of selfishness Manuel is showing goes far beyond any expectations. He's never wrong, he never makes any mistakes, and when something like what's just happened happens, he only thinks of himself, of being able to carry on living his lie. To the point of speaking of killing someone so that nothing around him changes. She hopes he's not talking seriously and it's just the aftermath of the bewilderment he's just experienced, but she's not so sure, and the doubt is terrifying.

"Are we going back to Madrid?" she asks.

"Yes. I need to think about what I'm going to do."

"We can think about it together if you want."

"Don't worry about things that are not your concern, Lorena. This is my business."

"And mine, too. I'm also involved and I want to help you."

"'*Oh, I'm also involved*', says the fucking saviour," exclaims Manuel in a falsetto voice. "HOW? HOW DOES THIS INVOLVE YOU?" he hollers.

After a short silence, Manuel takes Lorena's hand. She'd like to take it away, but holds on nevertheless.

"I'm sorry. Excuse me, Lorena. I'm very nervous. I don't know what I'm saying."

"It's all right," she replies, terrified. "I'm just saying you are very upset, which I understand, but you have to keep a cool head. That boy's probably much more frightened than you are right now. You might never see him in your life, even. You are his girlfriend's father, and he's cheating on her: do you think he feels like ever seeing you again? In a few days, Elena will be telling you her boyfriend has left her, you'll see."

"You're right. Sure, she will. You know what? We're going to spend what's left of our weekend at the Villa Magna.[17] I bet you've never been there!"

"No," lies Lorena, feigning excitement.

Elena takes her trousers and panties off.

---

[17] Villa Magna: One of the most exclusive hotels in Madrid.

"And now... how do I go about this?" she wonders, looking around for an unexisting bidet. She takes the towel she has used to dry herself, spreads it on the floor and sits on it. *The last thing I need now is to drop them in the toilet...* she thinks as she opens her hand and sees the four pills there. "As deep as I can... I don't know if I'll be able to stick all four of them together, much less pushing them too".

Elena puts a finger inside her vagina and starts introducing the pills with the other hand. "Bloody hell, this would be much easier with an applicator, like tampons."

Someone knocks on the bathroom door.

"Fuck off!" she yells, "I'm not fucking stupid, I'll call you if I need anything," she mumbles.

Once everything's ready, she puts her clothes back on and curls up on the bathroom floor. She doesn't want to get out to the room. She doesn't want to be with them.

She realises she's left the sanitary pads outside and doesn't know if she's going to need them already or if it will take some time.

"Pau," she calls out loud, "the pads."

The bathroom door opens instantly and her friend appears with a pad pack. Paula smiles shyly and asks her, "are you going to stay here?"

"Yes, at least for now."

"Shall I bring you some pillows?" she suggests, looking at the bathroom floor.

"Right. Thanks."

As Paula comes back into the room, Javier stands up from his chair and looks at her questioningly.

"She's going to stay in the bathroom. I'm bringing her some pillows to make her comfortable."

"I'll take them," Javier says, going towards the beds.

"Javi," Paula says holding his arm, "I know you want to help her. It's the only reason for us to be here. She has called for me. Let me be the one to bring them. She knows you're here and have no doubt that if she needs us she will tell us. Don't pester her. This is crappy. Just trust her to ask for your help. It seems that she wants to be alone for now. She's got enough in her hands to have to take care of us, on top of it."

"Yes," Javier says sitting down again, "I'm so nervous…"

"Quite. So am I; but much less than Ele is, I'm sure."

Paula returns to the bathroom. Elena is sitting on the floor, her arms around her knees. Paula puts a couple of pillows behind her friend's back, while she opens the pack.

"Wow, they're thick! I've never used one of these in my life, mate."

"Well, they'll sure be more absorbent," her friend smiles.

As Elena gets up, Paula leaves the third pillow on the floor for her to sit on.

"Shall I ask the reception for more?" she asks.

"No, don't go. Stay here with me, right?"

"Of course."

Both friends are sitting on the bathroom floor in silence.

"Javi's scared shitless, isn't he?" Elena asks.

"I wouldn't say that. I think he's worried about you. He wants to help you and he doesn't know how."

"Leaving me alone. I bet it was him who knocked on the door, wasn't it?"

Paula smiles condescendingly.

"Why can't blokes be of any help in some matters? Javi's great. He's wonderful to me; as you have seen, since I told him he's done nothing but worrying about me, looking for a solution, being attentive… nevertheless, I don't want to be with him right now: I feel as if I had to explain to him what's going on, what I'm doing, how I'm feeling… and I just don't feel like it, you know?"

"Yes, I know."

"However, you do know what to do. Even if you've never been in such a rotten situation."

"I guess this is, simply, a women's thing."

"I'm so glad you're here, Pau. Sorry about your pig slaughter fest thing."

"Well, there are many of those; friends like you, not that many."

"It's starting," Elena says, taking her hands to her belly. "Bloody hell, it hurts, lots. Bring me the pills, the painkillers. No, don't leave me; Javi!" she yells, "bring me the painkillers!"

Javier comes in straight away with the pills.

"Give me two," says Elena, surrounding her belly with her arms again. "Owww!"

She takes the pills hurriedly, then she looks at her boyfriend and smiles.

"I'm fine," she says caressing him. "Again," she bends over herself. "I'm going to be sick," she adds getting close to the toilet bowl. As she sits with her head over it, she feels a strong cramp. "Fuck off, get the hell out you two!" she yells getting up to sit on the toilet. Elena feels she's asphyxiating, she's pooing and she's retching non-stop. She vomits onto the bathroom floor: there are the two pills she has just taken. *Great, no painkillers*, she thinks as another cramp comes.

"No, no, help!" she screams.

The bathroom door opens.

"Close that bloody door, damn it! Leave me alone, will you?" Elena says, flushing the toilet without getting up from the bowl. After a wave of cramps, everything seems to calm down. Elena stretches, takes a towel and dries her face.

"Shit. This is really tough. If I have much longer to go like this, I don't think I'll cope."

She takes some toilet paper and cleans herself.

Will it be out already? she wonders as she gets up and looks into the toilet bowl. Blood, just blood. *Please, God, let it be over already.*

She remains standing up leaning on the basin for a while.

"I'm fine!" she cries out to the others. She spots the painkillers box and reads: "Paracetamol". "What! I've been given just fucking paracetamol for this agonizing pain! It's outrageous! It's clear as day as a man, that doctor has no fucking idea just how painful this is".

Elena gets out of the bathroom. Her friends are sitting at the table. They both look at her.

"Are you feeling alright?" a worried Javier asks.

"I think so," Elena says sitting on his lap. "Hold me tight," she asks him nestling in his arms. Paula gets up, takes the dinner bags and starts preparing the food, as far from them as she can.

Villa Magna Hotel.

"Did you take the coke?" Manuel asks in anguish.

"Where was it?"

"No idea. Somewhere. Where did we leave it?" Manuel inquires as he starts to messily unpack his suitcase. "Here it is!" he says relieved, opening the small box. Lorena approaches him and takes it.

"I'll get it ready." She sniffs some air once more and passes Manuel the tray, who gives it back to her after snorting two lines.

"C'mon, have another one. The more you have, the dirtier you get."

"You want me dirty? You'll get to know what dirty is," she says tying him up to the bed and blowing the lines on his face.

"Well, Elena, we are done. There are no remains in your womb," says the obstetrician after the ultrasound. "Now you'll be bleeding for a few days, like a menstruation. How was it? Did it hurt much?"

"Yes, it was short but it was hell. I thought I would die. I'm happy it's all over now."

"And how are you feeling?"

"Fine. Glad it's over. I can finally relax."

"But? I find you a bit sad."

"No, I'm fine, I really am. I feel much more relieved, but I still have to get used to the idea of what's happened. I still have to get rid of all the tension I've accumulated these last weeks. It's as if I've had a nightmare and have just woken up."

"I understand. It's very common, and logical, to feel that way: you'd be the first woman leaving this place cheerful and merry. This is a difficult decision nobody likes to take. That's why you should be more careful from now on. You see how, even if the fact *per se* was not complicated, being in this situation shakes you up and changes you."

"Yes. Undoubtedly, there's a before and an after in my life now. Thank you very much, doctor. You've been very kind and a great help."

"Take care, Elena. I expect never to see you here again; but if you need us, you know where we are."

"Thank you very much. Bye."

The weekend is over and Manuel is taking Lorena where he thinks she lives.

"I meant it about taking you to the Maldives. I really like to be with you, Lorena. I want to take you and spend some days there together, forgetting about everything else."

"Of course. Whatever you want. Although I don't know what you can elaborate on to tell your wife. So soon…"

"No it wouldn't be now, it's impossible. In some months. May, June… That would give me time to get her ready. Do you have any plans for those months?"

Having your child, Lorena thinks as she replies, "No, not so far, I haven't planned anything yet."

"Well, now you do. We're going to the Maldives, you and I. Thank you for a fantastic weekend. You always succeed in making it wonderful, and this was a tough one. If it wasn't for you, I don't know what would have happened to that kid." Manuel gets an envelope from the inside pocket of his jacket and gives it to her. "I'll call you as soon as I can," and he kisses her.

Lorena gets out of the car and takes her suitcase. She blows him a kiss and waves to him as his car disappears into the traffic. She goes to the main street, where she gets a taxi home. In the taxi, she opens the envelope she has put into her handbag. *How can such a mean chap be so generous at the same time?* she wonders distressed. *What am I going to do? Tic tac, tic tac…*

"I'm totally bewildered. What is it that they say about reality surpassing fiction? Is that it?" Luci says after hearing the story of Lorena's weekend. "I mean, what are the possibilities of that happening? You didn't tell him, did you?"

"No way! That's not going to happen. You should have seen him, the state he was in, how he talked about killing that boy. I swear he was serious about it. Imagine I told him I'm expecting his child! It's obvious I can't tell him. I don't know what I'll invent not to see him again, but I'm not telling him."

Week 9

Carmen gets up from the bed full of energy. *I'm pregnant and with this baby it's going to be different. I must quit smoking, no matter how, for this baby deserves it.* She goes down to the kitchen and brews some coffee. She touches her belly as she smiles and thinks, *my pretty baby, it's incredible that you're here and I can't notice you growing inside me. You'll see, I'm taking care of you the way you deserve.*
Carmen gets herself a coffee and an olive oil toast.
"I love this time of the day, when I have a few minutes on my own. Luis and Lara are still sleeping, and these moments are just for me alone, -and now, for you-," she adds stroking her belly, "although in a few months I shan't be having them anymore, shall I? And the chaos of having a new-born will return, with no schedules and no free time… Phew, and besides the first time was much easier, even if we had a bad night we could sleep in the morning. But now I'll have to get up to get Lara ready for school, get her breakfast, take her to the bus stop and so on, even if I haven't slept a wink all night with you, baby. Well, it doesn't matter, we'll sleep when we come back, we have until one o'clock to doze a bit. Don't think I don't love you, baby, but it's been a shock you appearing like this, without a warning, but we are very happy about you being here…"

The oven clock marks 7:14. *I've got 16 minutes until Luis gets up.* Carmen goes to the living room, puts her dressing gown on, wraps a bath towel around her head, takes a cigarette and a lighter from the table and goes out to the balcony. She lights her cigarette as she inhales her first puff deeply. "Mmm…" she says exhaling the smoke, "how can something that sits so well with me be bad?" she wonders. "Besides, as the baby's so tiny it can't affect him that much…" she finishes the cigarette and goes back inside. She gets herself another coffee, and as she takes the mug to her mouth she feels the smell of tobacco in her hands. 7:26. She drinks her coffee, washes her hands thoroughly and brushes her teeth. *Done, just as if I hadn't smoked anything*, she tells herself as she exits the toilet.

Maternity Hospital.
Outpatient Service. 9:30.
Estela is sitting in the waiting room. She's on her own because Pablo couldn't ask for a free morning to come with her, and Tina, the friend who was to come with her, couldn't make it because her son had a fever last night. *I'm so nervous*, she thinks, *I'm going to see my baby, or whatever it is, I'm not sure what you can see this early. I hope I can see something.*
"Estela Gutiérrez Cao," says the nurse out loud.
"That's me," she says standing up.
"Come in," the nurse says pointing at the room.
Once into the room, Estela sees a man sitting at his table reading some papers. *He must be the doctor,* she guesses.
"Good morning," she says.
The doctor keeps on reading. The nurse tells Estela to sit down.
"Herminia, put her down for next month upstairs in High Risk, and she must bring first morning urine," says the doctor as he scribbles something on the papers and gives them to Herminia. "Good morning," he says, looking at Estela from over his tiny glasses, which barely sit on the tip of his nose.
"Good morning," she repeats.
"Is this your first pregnancy?"
"Yes."
"Date of last period."

"Well, you see, I'm not sure, because my periods are very irregular and…"

"You don't know when your last period was?" the doctor cuts in.

"Yes, but I've been having them every two or three months."

"And when was the last one? It's a very simple question."

"The sixth of October," she says doubtfully after thinking a bit. "Yes, that was the last day."

"The last day of what?" the doctor asks arrogantly.

"Of my menstruation," Estela mumbles.

"The important day of menstruation is the first, not the last. It's hard to believe, how little these young people know of the only thing they should know about," says the doctor, addressing himself to the nurse as if Estela wasn't there.

"You said "last period day", Estela defends herself in a tiny voice.

"No, I didn't, I said "date of last period", and that date is always the first day; the day you got your period, which was…?"

"October 2nd, then," replies Estela, while she thinks, *but what's wrong with this man? Why does he get like that for a small misunderstanding?* She's nervous, she doesn't like one bit the way the doctor's treating her and she doesn't understand why he does. There's no need to get huffy about it.

"Herminia, get her on the bed," he tells the nurse without even looking at Estela.

"Come this way," the nurse tells her, "take your trousers and panties off and get up here, my lovely."

Herminia helps her to get her feet on the footrests and puts a small sheet over her. The doctor comes. He takes a device that looks like a bristleless toothbrush, spreads a transparent gel over it and covers it with something that looks like a condom. Then, Estela feels him introducing it in her vagina. The doctor looks at the screen in silence and she feels the device moving inside her.

"Ouch!" says Estela, very uncomfortable with the procedure she's being subjected to. "You're hurting me," she adds.

"Stay put, please," replies the doctor without looking at her and carrying on with what he's doing.

Estela feels a lump in her throat and her eyes start swelling with tears. *Shit, I'm going to cry, on top,* she thinks. *I was so thrilled with this visit to the doctor and now I feel horrible, as if I had done something wrong. What an asshole, he's a mean jerk. And besides he tells me nothing, he doesn't speak to me, doesn't look at me… how can he do this job being like that? Maybe his wife left him or something and he's bitter or something…*

"There's no heartbeat," she hears the doctor say.

That moment, Estela feels as if time had stopped. She waits for the doctor to say something more else, maybe he's talking about something else. She doesn't ask. She doesn't dare, or maybe she just can't. The doctor extracts the probe from her vagina and as he takes the condom off it, he looks at Estela and says, "There's no heartbeat. No fetus."

"What do you mean?" Estela babbles.

"There's no heartbeat, there's no fetus inside the bag. You have to get hospitalized for a procedure to clean the uterus."

"But… right now? It can't be."

"No, madam, it hasn't got to be now. Herminia will explain what you have to do. Don't worry."

The doctor disappears behind the curtain and Estela stays with the nurse who, kindly, helps her get down from the bed; while she gets dressed, the nurse looks at her and says:

"I'm very sorry. There's a book called 'The forgotten voices'.[18] It's about women who lose their babies in the first weeks of their pregnancy. It might do you good.

And here they come, tears now start running down Estela's face. She looks for a tissue inside her pockets and, swiftly, Herminia passes her a box. Estela looks at her through her tears and thanks her, although she can hardly see her. She goes to the other side of the curtain, where the doctor is sitting at the table, writing what she guesses must be her records.

---

[18] "Las voces olvidadas" is available only in Spanish.

The doctor raises his head and, seeing her crying, tells her, "come on, come on, it's hardly the end of the world, lady. These things happen quite often. What happens is that people don't talk about it, but many women have several failed pregnancies before they have a baby. You're young, you have no difficulties conceiving; don't cry, lady, you'll be able to get pregnant again in a few months."

He gives her the papers and directions, and Herminia walks her to the door. When it closes, Estela bursts into tears. *The worst thing is that I'm feeling worse for the way that moron's treated me than for my baby… he wouldn't even let me cry about my baby*, she thinks as she sobs unrestrainedly. Then, she turns around and yells towards the closed door: "Asshole!" and runs away.

06:50.

Carmen wakes up. *Ouuuch, I feel terrible; I already feel sick, and I'm not even up yet… I don't want anything, to eat, to drink, I want nothing when I feel like this; I don't even feel like getting up. Why does being pregnant have to be so disgusting? And why are there women who don't feel anything wrong and don't have the least bit of trouble? Well, there are also those who say they didn't feel any pain and those who want their labour without the epidural because they want a natural birth… Oh, well, it takes all sorts, and my fate is feeling sick the whole of my pregnancy and the long labour with a ventouse and an XXL stitch. Hopefully this one will be better, because if it's like Lara's I'll have a heart attack. And to tell the truth, the start is being quite as bad.*

Carmen gets up, goes to the bathroom and washes her teeth. Brushing them makes her gag and she vomits in the sink. "Shit!" *There's nothing worse than having nothing to vomit. I'll make myself a … I don't know, I don't feel like eating or drinking anything. Not even a juice, a biscuit. Some herbal tea, let's see if that will settle my stomach.*

Still gagging, she tries to make the tea. *Where's that one without any theine?* she asks herself, as she messes around the tea shelf.

"Here, here it is," she says taking the box and getting a bag out, which she puts into a mug with boiling water. She sits at the kitchen table and takes the tea sip by sip. *It's awful, all this vomiting and sickness. Some women even get hospitalized, no wonder, it's such a wretched feeling... I should go see Don Arturo, to see what to take for the nausea I can't remember...* Carmen jumps feeling her husband's arms on her shoulders.

"Sorry, I didn't mean to startle you."

"I didn't hear you coming. I was minding my business and you scared me."

"How are you?"

"Lousy. I know I have to go through it, and once you have the baby it's wonderful and you forget, but these first months, if we could, we would all go back. It's really awful."

"Why don't you take some Cariban?"[19]

"Yes, I will; don't I need a prescription? I was going to see Don Arturo straight away."

"No, you don't. You buy it over the counter at the chemist's, without a prescription or anything. I can get it for you when I finish, if you want."

"Can't you go before that? Now? I feel terrible, really Luis, I wouldn't ask you if I weren't."

"Relax, babe, I'll look for the one on-call and go."

Luis takes his jacket, his keys and his cigarettes. Luckily, the chemist is not far away and he can walk there. When he gets outside, he opens the cigarette pack and realizes there are several missing. *The pack was fuller yesterday*, he thinks as he lights the first one of the day.

I'll have to start leaving my cigarettes at the mailbox, as I did before. It must be very hard for her, and I'm hardly helping if I leave them around within her reach. In a short while, he goes back home.

Carmen has gone back to bed. Luis goes to her and gives her a kiss.

"You smell of tobacco," Carmen tells him.

So, do you! Luis thinks, but he says nothing. "Shall I call your office?"

---

[19] Cariban: Drug used for pregnancy nausea.

"Yes, please. And ask Don Arturo for a sick note. Take my card, it's in my wallet."
"Ok. I'll take care of Lara. Try to rest."

Maternity Hospital.
Obstetric Triage. 11.40am.
"Marta, there's a woman here who says she wants to go home," says the nurse sticking her head out of the staff room's door.
"And what's the problem?" replies the midwife.
"Her waters have gone; can you talk to her?"
"Yes, I'll talk to her; but if she wants to go home, I don't know what the problem is."
"Can they go home with a broken bag?" the nurse asks doubtfully.
"They can go home in the middle of labour, if they want. This is a hospital: a place where people choose to come and can leave whenever they want. We explain, we give information, and 'patients' -who are not patients at all, for they are healthy- decide what they want to do."
Marta smiles at the nurse's expression and tells her, "All right, don't worry, I'll go talk to her now."
"Hello, I'm Marta, the midwife. I've been told your waters have broken and you want to go home."
"Yes. I want to avoid another induction at any cost."
"Very well, I completely understand."
Cristina looks at Marta, astonished and tells her, "But...?"
"No buts," Marta replies. "I'll just give you some advice as to what to do and not to do and when to come back here."
"You are not going to tell me that it's extremely dangerous, that my baby will die if I leave, that I'm crazy and completely irresponsible?"
Marta smiles. "Wow, you've really done your homework! What a pleasure! The same thing happened to my sister, and she stayed home for two days before coming here when she was already in labour," she tells her with a wink.
"And didn't they give her a hard time at birth?" Cristina asks incredulously.

"I was with her, and as she came with me and she was in labour, they didn't have a clue. Anyway, we didn't tell anyone either. We spared that information."

"May I hire you to be with me?"

"No, but I'll be here today, tomorrow and the day after. So, we'll probably coincide. There's a small problem, however: an obstetrician must see you before you leave."

"Again? And will I be getting the 'dead baby' sermon?"

"What?"

"That my baby will die if I go home."

"Possibly, but you are at an advantage here: you are ready for it," Marta smiles, as she goes to look for the doctor.

"Hello," Marta greets coming into the Emergency Room where Ángela, a doctor, is.

"Hello. Tell me." Ángela replies.

"The girl you just admitted with SROM[20] wants to go home."

"She wants to go home? Well, she can't."

"Come on, Ángela, of course she can. She can do whatever she wants."

"But she has been admitted. If she wants to go, it will be at her own responsibility."

"Well, everything people do is at their own responsibility. Or are you going to take the responsibility if anything happens?"

"No. Well, I'm not going to discharge her. If she wants to go, she'll have to sign a self-discharge form, I'm not discharging her."

"She can go home with the recommendations for SROM but I suppose you have examined her."

"Of course, I have: since when don't we examine admissions?"

"Since their waters have gone and there isn't any uterine activity."

"Aren't you making that up?"

---

[20] SROM: Spontaneous Rupture of Membranes.

"Let's see, Ángela: a woman who SROMs may wait twenty-four to forty-eight hours before her labour starts as long as nothing gets inside her vagina. There are studies corroborating this and you know it. What information do you get from examining a woman with SROM and no contractions?"

"It gives me a Bishop score,[21] knowledge of how the cervix is…"

"It gives you no information. It's a non-labouring multip's[22] cervix. Nothing else. Nevertheless, in pushing towards the interior of the vagina all the germs that might be around, you are exponentially increasing the risk of infection."

"But to justify an admission, or to send someone home, I have to examine and know how that cervix is…"

"Do you? Why is that? You can use a speculum,[23] see if there's any liquor, and there's no problem if you don't see the cervix. Have you ever examined a woman with no contractions and found a dilated, fully effaced cervix… or a labouring cervix, in short?"

"It could happen…"

"Oh, yes?" Marta looks at her, ironical.

"A grand multip, for instance."

"But the cervix would not be effaced. I think you are defending the indefensible just to be right. Let's leave it at that. Take the self-discharge papers and don't be hard on her, she's very well informed and has made up her mind."

"Let's see, the midwife tells me you want to go home," Ángela says to Cristina.

"Yes."

"Do you understand that you could get an infection now that your waters have gone?"

"Yes. And so, could I before," Cristina replies.

"Yes, but your baby was protected before. Now he's not, and neonatal sepsis is very serious. Your baby could die."

[21] Bishop Score: Scoring system for the cervix conditions (effacement, consistency, position…)

[22] Woman who has previously birthed.

[23] Speculum: Device used to see the inside of a body cavity.

"And if I stay, can you guarantee a hundred percent that my baby won't die?"

"Well, not me nor anybody can guarantee that. Everything has risks."

"Absolutely. And the risk of anything happening to my baby if I go home won't be much higher than if I stay and let you induce me," Cristina replies.

"Right, then you have to sign your self-discharge papers, as you have already been admitted."

"What alternatives to induction do I have?""

"You can wait in the antenatal ward."

"Are you trying to tell me that if I go home my daughter is at risk of having neonatal sepsis and the alternative to that is to stay in the building with more bacteria in the whole town?"

"In the ward we monitor both you and your baby and we can detect in no time if you're starting any infectious process…"

"Oh, do you? And how do you do that exactly?"

"By watching your vital signs and monitoring the baby's heart rate regularly."

"And exactly how often is it regularly?"

"I'm not sure, I'd say twice a day," replies a visibly uncomfortable Ángela.

"Well, I don't believe it," Cristina retorts. "In my previous pregnancy I spent two days at the ward, also with a broken bag, and you monitored me twice in the whole two days. You were supposed to give me an induction in twelve hours, but as you were very busy you didn't take me to the labour ward until two days after my waters broke. If nothing happened to me then, much less will happen at my home. So, tell me where I have to sign; I'm leaving, because I have another daughter to care for."

"Very well, as long as you sign you are responsible for this decision, it's fine as far as I'm concerned," a hurt Ángela replies; she doesn't like her ideas refuted, and much less by a patient. "I have to check it with one of the consultants."

"And why is that? I really want to go now," Cristina asks annoyed.

"I'm not allowed to process a self-discharge."

"But I'm the one signing it, not you!"

"Well, things must be done properly. I'll be right back."

"Wait!" Cristina says. "Please, tell the doctor you're checking it with that you have already discussed with me all there is to discuss and, even so, I want to leave. I don't want another sermon."

Ángela speeds off to look for the consultant. She goes to the doctor's office, where she meets Carlos, the consultant, and Mercedes, the registrar, talking. Ángela explains the situation and Carlos stands up and goes to triage to see Cristina, followed by Ángela.

"Hello, I'm Dr. Ramos. My colleague here has told me what's going on. Do you fully understand that you're leaving at your own responsibility?"

"I do, yes."

"And that, if in these hours while you're home, something happens to you or your baby we will not be held responsible?"

"Yes." Cristina replies, making a clicking sound. She's starting to get truly annoyed.

"You can't have sex nor take a bath. You must take your temperature every three hours, even through the night: if it goes up, you must come here immediately. If you don't start labour, you have to be admitted tomorrow morning to be induced."

"All right, where do I sign?"

"Here," answers Dr. Ramos, and he goes, leaving Cristina with Ángela and Marta. Once Cristina has signed the papers, Ángela disappears behind the screen, while Marta stays with her.

"You were great!" she says admiringly. "You've been very brave."

"They're dreadful, really. But just as well I know how things are, because if I didn't, I'd have fallen into the trap again. I hated so much what happened with Laura two years ago… they admitted me to the antenatal ward, then completely forgot about me. They didn't pay any attention to me for two days, and now they are raising hell because I want to go home."

"Well, just take it easy. Go home to your little girl now, and tomorrow morning, if you are not in labour before, we'll meet again."

"Between you and me, I'm not coming till I'm in labour, even if it's not in five days."

"Fine, no hurry. Just take things as they come. Take your temperature twice a day, and if you see you're starting to feel unwell, as if you were about to catch a cold, you come over here."

Before leaving, Cristina urges Marta once more, "please, I'd love you to be with me at my birth, even if you're not working: I'm willing to pay what you make for an extra shift, or whatever you ask me for; please, I want you to be my midwife, please, please, please…"

"But I can't do that, we are not allowed to bring our private customers to the hospital."

"But no one needs to know! From now on, I am your friend and you're doing me a favour, as you did with your sister, for which I'll be awfully grateful afterwards. This is my phone number," she says, giving her a card, "please call me when you end your shift and we'll talk more calmly. "You'd be doing me an immense favour and lifting a huge weight off my shoulders. Just to arrive here knowing you'll be my midwife makes everything much easier."

"Fine, I'll be calling you tonight," Marta smiles as she keeps the card in her scrubs' pocket.

Luis comes inside the Health Centre where he works, walks into the changing room and changes into his uniform. He goes to the staff room where he meets Arturo, his lifelong doctor. *What a stroke of luck!* he thinks. Arturo works at a different Health Centre, and he comes over to this one from time to time to cover for another doctor, but that happens once in a blue moon.

"How are you?" Luis asks him.

"Fine, and you?"

"Carmen's not doing well, she's just started with the Cariban and you should get her a sick note, she's feeling very poorly."

"Oh, I had no idea she was pregnant, congratulations!" says Aurora, one of the GPs[24] working with Luis.

---

[24] GP: General Practitioner.

"Yes, thank you. It's been a bit of an unexpected thing. Well, more like totally unexpected. That's one of the reasons for her to be in a state, she's smoking like a chimney and I don't know how to help her."

"Well, she has to stop, that's awfully bad for the fetus, Luis, for heaven's sake!" she scolds him.

"Sure, I know, Aurora, but she's in total denial: you tell her not to smoke, and she will smoke two one after another."

"So, get her to a shrink or to some kind of therapy," Arturo comments, "I always tell those patients who say they can't stop to smoke as little as they can, and most of them succeed in bringing it down to two or three a day, but smoking two cigarettes one after another… at that rate she'll end up smoking more than before she was pregnant! That's crazy."

"Something has to be done," says Luis.

"And you stop smoking too," Aurora tells Luis, "it's difficult enough to stop it, but when your partner smokes too it's practically impossible."

"I know, I know… I have no clue what to do, really. Each time I've tried, I've failed miserably."

"You can quit smoking," Aurora says. "It's hard, it's difficult, but you can. I've done it three times, the last one six years ago already. You just have to make a firm decision and stick to it and not smoke another cigarette ever again, whatever it takes. You try to overcome withdrawal as best you can and that's it. The first weeks are hard and then it gets better. But to stop smoking is something that must be done sooner or later, because it's awful and it kills you. You as much as Carmen, both of you. Smoking is for idiots, get that into your head, Luis. And every time you feel like smoking one, just think: "I'm not an idiot, this is killing me, these cravings will soon pass", and take several deep breaths until it goes away. It will eventually become less and less difficult, until you learn to take it more or less well."

"Yes, yes you're right. Smoking is for idiots."

"I'm telling it to you like this because it worked for me. Neither the patches or chewing gum or anything else. Straight to the ego. I don't remember where I heard it, but it did it. Even now, whenever I go out for a drink, or after having dinner with friends I still feel like smoking a cigarette sometimes, but it quickly comes to my head: "I'm not stupid" and the craving goes away."

"Could you stop by our place and tell Carmen? I'm sure she'll pay more attention to you. Me, she just doesn't believe it. She thinks I won't stop smoking even if she does, and she just won't listen to me."

"Sure, I'll drop by, I haven't seen her for a while."

Maternity Hospital.

Staff Room.

"Celia, can you come over for a minute?" Marta asks Celia, who's consulting her off duty and taking note of her shifts in a small notebook.

Celia gets up and comes to Marta.

"Yes?"

"No, not here," she takes her to one of the empty rooms, to tell her what Cristina -the woman who went home with SROM- proposed to her some hours ago, and to ask for her advice.

"But do you want to do it?" Celia asks her.

"Yes, I think I do; she seemed very nice, but I've never done anything like this. And if I do, I won't be charging her anything."

"That's where I think you're mistaken. If you don't charge for your work, you are detracting from it yourself."

"But how am I going to charge her for doing my work in the hospital if I'm already getting paid for it?"

"But you will be doing more than that. You'll be on call for one person, and that's worth a lot. You have to be at her disposal and be with her whenever she calls you: what if she calls you at 3am and you start work at 8? You'll have to stay your whole shift, plus the five extra hours, having slept for just a few hours. And if you're just out of a night shift, completely knackered, and just when you get into bed she calls you telling you she's in labour?"

"Yeah, well, considering it that way… but what if she calls me while I'm here and everything happens when I'm working?"

"Well, good luck for you, then! But that shouldn't stop you from getting paid. Don't you get paid for the days when nothing's going on here and you go home having done practically nothing? You get paid for being on call. That woman is paying you for your availability, so you should charge her."

"Fine, but how much do I charge her? I haven't got a clue…"

"One shift every 48 hours?"

"Or just one and that's all…"

"Marta, if she is full term with SROM, she will most likely start labour within the next forty-eight hours; but what if it takes six days? It would be maddening, you'd be sleeping worse every day, you wouldn't be able to go anywhere on your free days, or doing any shopping, because you might have to run to the hospital any minute… and if she ends up with an induction you might spend fifteen hours with her. Follow my advice and put a price to a period of time: it's not the same being on call one day, or five."

"All right, all right, thanks a lot."

"And don't tell anyone: she's your friend and that's that."

"Ok, thank you Celia."

Luis and Aurora arrive at Luis' home. Carmen gets up to greet them from the living room, in her dressing gown.

"How are you? Are you feeling fine?" Luis asks her while kissing her.

"Yes," she says kissing him back. "Aurora, darling, what joy!" she exclaims, hugging her.

"I've come to see you, as Luis tells me you have been feeling poorly."

"Indeed, I have! I'm better now, but this morning I thought I'd die. I even considered having a termination, I felt so awful."

"C'mon, you exaggerate," her husband tells her.

"It's true, just imagine how I was feeling, I actually did consider it! But you know I would never think of having an abortion in my life. Even if I was told the baby had a problem, I could not. Poor creature."

"And how are you doing with your smoking?"

"Terribly. Very very badly. Sure, I do know it's bad for the baby, but I just can't stop it. I tell myself I will, I must stop it, and within hours I'm smoking again. I'm a bad mother..." Carmen weeps.

"Don't torture yourself," Aurora says fondly. "It's possible to stop smoking. I did it six or seven years ago and I haven't smoked since."

"Is it really that long since you left it? And how did you do it?"

Aurora tells Carmen her strategy, and Carmen nods, her hopes high. "But you're absolutely right! We can't let this shit that's killing us have so much control over our lives, Luis."

"Yes, I'll be quitting it with you too. The two of us will do it together, won't we, sweetie?"

"And it's going to be tough. And some of the craving moments make you very cranky. But each one of them you pass will bring you closer to victory. And when you are about to give in, remember the long journey you have already done, and that if you smoke that single cigarette all the bad moments you've been through will have been fruitless, and you'll have to start all over again. Because one thing is clear: you must stop smoking sooner or later, and the sooner the better. If you don't, instead of having bad weeks you'll be having those weeks multiplied by the number of cigarettes you have smoked, talking about real torture," Aurora warns them.

"I have stopped smoking already," a thrilled Carmen says. "Sure, I have. Damm! Are cigarettes going to win over my love for this baby? Never, not at all!"

"Well, it seems we've stopped smoking," Luis says grabbing his wife by her waist and kissing her.

"That's great, guys! That's fantastic. Now give me all the cigarettes, I'll take care of them: even if you are so determined it's never a good idea to have any lying around the house."

Luis opens a drawer and gives Aurora the three packets he keeps inside: then, he looks into his jacket pocket and gives her the one he had already started.

"Done! We don't have any more tobacco, do we, Carmen?"

"I have two packets in the kitchen drawer. Wait, I'll give them to you too," she says as she goes to get them.

"Well, I'm awfully proud of you two," Aurora says, "you will go through very bad moments, but you have to face them, whatever it costs, and not smoke anymore: think of the baby, of Lara, of not being idiots… whichever works for you, or everything at once. Also, look for a substitute, like chewing gum or mints; I was a great fan of liquorice sticks, I loved them. And don't hesitate to call me for whatever you may need. Just ring me and I'll give you a hand, right?"

"Thank you very much, Aurora," they both say, feeling really grateful.

Marta takes the phone and calls Cristina.

"Hello Cristina, I'm Marta, the midwife, how are you?"

"Marta, how great! I wasn't sure you'd be calling me."

"Well, I've been thinking about it and if I can, I'll be your midwife if you still want me to."

"Sure, of course, I do!"

"How are you doing? Any contractions?"

"None. With Laura, I went two days after my waters had broken and I was induced in the end."

"Well, let's hope history doesn't repeat itself."

"It won't, because I'm not letting them give me an induction again. I'm not going to the hospital until I'm in labour."

"You're feeling well?"

"Perfect."

"And the baby? Is she moving a lot?"

"Yes, she doesn't stop for a moment."

"And is the water still clear?"

"Yes."

"And the B strep?"

"Negative."

"Everything's perfect then, isn't it?"

"How do we do it, then?" Cristina asks.

"I'm working an early shift tomorrow. I'll be out at three. If you haven't called me before, shall I drop by your place to meet you around half-past four?"

"Perfect. And what if I start labour tonight?"

"You call me; I'll leave my mobile on the bedside table."

"And at work, will you have it with you?"

"Yes, of course: much more so knowing you might call. Now you go to bed and rest all you can, it will do you good. And call me whenever you want."

"Perfect, thank you very much, Marta. You really have taken a huge load off my shoulders."

"I'm happy to hear that; goodnight, I'll be seeing you soon."

Marta goes to the kitchen to get some dinner ready. She's not very hungry, so she makes a cucumber and tomato salad and turns on the TV. Today is the start of the new American series she so much wants to watch. She's happy. She's going to have her first private customer, and that fills her with satisfaction, although she is a bit nervous too. *I hope everything goes fine and nobody realises anything. And I hope she starts labour spontaneously, because I don't dare to think of her getting an induction. And what if it ends up in a C-section? I could die, poor woman, I won't charge her anything in that case.*

Sara arrives home. She hangs her coat on the wardrobe and goes up to her bedroom to lie down a bit. She's been feeling queasy all day, with that damned nausea she's been suffering for over a month. Besides, today she's been feeling particularly uncomfortable. Her lower back was aching, as when her period is due but less acutely. "It doesn't matter, I'm so happy, I'm finally pregnant, I don't care if I keep vomiting until the baby's born, I will take any pains and troubles this pregnancy brings. I don't mind. I'm finally going to have a baby!"

After the molar pregnancy[25] and all the waiting, and the two failed IVFs[26]… she's finally pregnant with a baby. They had seen it a few days ago. Ten weeks gone, and there he was, her baby, jumping inside her womb. How much did he move! And Juan asking, "but don't you notice him?"

"No, I don't, I don't notice anything."

---

[25] **Molar pregnancy:** Abnormal cell mass made from placental tissue.

[26] In vitro fertilisation: Technique by which an egg is fertilised outside the mother's body.

"Blimey, with all that jumping I thought you should."

"It's too early yet," the obstetrician said.

"How happy you were at the scan! We are finally going to have a baby!"

Juan walks towards his car as he gets his mobile from his pocket, dials and puts it to his ear. He's just closed the sale of the golf course for the damned hotel. It had taken months, but they had finally decided to go ahead. He's anxious to tell Sara. "C'mon, pick the phone up," he says impatiently. It's been a long time since he was so happy. Finally, everything is starting to go well. He takes the car keys and as he gets close to it he thinks it's about time to get a new car.

One of those spacious ones, much bigger, with a huge boot to keep everything, we'll be needing lots of space when the baby comes. Besides, now I can afford any car I want. We must go to the car dealer, to see which one Sara wants.

Where are you? After so much time trying, we are finally going to be parents. I want so much to make you happy… After everything you've been through, my sweetie… I'm going to pamper you as you deserve. You're not answering? Well, we'll be meeting in a minute. This time it's real, this time we're going to have a baby. Nothing can stop us now. It's our turn now. So many people have children they do not want… Seven years! It's easy to say, already seven years since we decided we wanted to have a child. The journey has been difficult, but here we are. Finally, you are pregnant and this time it's for real, this time you have a baby inside, tiny, about two centimetres, the doctor said, but you could see him perfectly, hopping and jumping in there, and with a strong and fast heartbeat. This time I saw him with my own eyes, he was there, my child. Not like the last time you were pregnant, when it wasn't a baby but a mole.

That was horrible. We were so thrilled, especially you, my darling girl. I still remember your face and how you grabbed my hand when you were lying on the bed for the first scan and the doctor told us. And how your face started to change as you realised the way things were. Dr. García told us, it was as if instead of creating a baby your womb was creating some kind of grapes, some bags full of liquid reproducing themselves non-stop, as if the action of making a baby had somehow got stuck in the process and the body kept repeating the same function once and again.

I didn't understand it very well at the beginning; I even asked the doctor if we couldn't give you something to reverse the process, to carry on with the pregnancy. But that would have been pointless, because there was no baby there, and besides it was dangerous. Everything inside the womb had to be removed, and the worst was that we had to wait for a year before trying for another pregnancy. Your face was ashen, your expression was frozen and the only thing you did was squeeze my hand. So much so you were digging your nails, but I said nothing because it was the only thing to remind me I still had blood running down my veins. That pain kept me standing up, made me pretend to be strong and avoided my collapse. After that, when we finally could try anew, you never got pregnant again.

Then came the fertility tests, and we found out that I had almost no sperm cells. But how could that be, if you had gotten pregnant before, if my ex Maribel had a termination because we had a slip many years ago? Raquel, your homeopath friend, explained that very likely my body was reacting to the impact of seeing you suffer so much, refusing to make you go through it all again. I always thought that theory was bullshit, because it's the opposite to what we want: how am I going to stop producing sperm because I don't want to get you pregnant when what we've been wanting for years was precisely that? I never gave Raquel much credibility anyway, with her hippie theories and her house full of dropper bottles for everything.

Well, in the end we had to turn to IVF, and besides with a donor's sperm, but that doesn't matter because a child is from whoever nurtures and cares for him; and I'm going to love him as if he were mine, because he is. All I want is your happiness and I'll be there, always, to try and make it possible.
I'm so anxious to be home! To tell you about the hotel! To hug you, kiss you and take you out to dinner. To celebrate I've sold another course, thank God, for with this fucking crisis… I was starting to get really worried.

18:40.
Wow, if that wasn't a long nap! Sara thinks upon waking up. *I really needed that!* She turns the light on and as she stands up she feels her panties getting wet. *I have a lot of discharge. I'm going to the doctor tomorrow to see what I can do.* She goes to the toilet to pee. She feels some cramps. *If I'm practically eating nothing, how come I have diarrhoea.* Another cramp, a strong one. And another. While she's sitting on the toilet, she feels like vomiting. *I can't control it. Shit, I have nothing here to vomit.* She stands up quickly, leans over the toilet bowl and vomits. With the first retching, she feels something coming out of her vagina and slipping down her leg. She can't take her face out of the toilet bowl, and when finally, the nausea recedes she can see what's happened. As she looks at her legs, she knows. "No, it can't be. Not this time". Then she sees it on the floor, she takes it and she presses it between her hands. "No, it can't be. Some days ago, you were jumping inside me, full of life. What? What's happened? Why didn't you wait, baby? Mommy loved you with all her heart… No, no, my baby, no, no."

Juan gets into his home. *Sara is already here*, he thinks; her keys and her handbag are on the hall table. Her coat hanged; however, there's no sound. No TV, no radio… *She must be in the bathroom.*
"Sara?" he calls her. No answer. He goes up the stairs and sees that the room's light is on. "Hello, darling," he says entering the empty room, "Sara?" There's no reply and he starts to get worried. "Why don't you answer?"

The bathroom door is ajar, but the light is off: as little as Sara likes dark places, Juan doesn't think she will be there. He sticks his head in and finally he finds her, sitting on the floor.

"What are you doing? Why are you here? Why don't you answer? Sara, are you all right?" he says crouching down beside her and taking her hands.

They're wet. As his eyes get used to the little light coming from the bedroom, Juan starts seeing his wife clearly.

Sara lifts her head and looks at him. She's been crying and her face is dirty.

"What's happening? Please tell me something," Juan begs in anguish.

"We've lost him. It's over, again."

"But, are you sure? I'm sure the baby's all right. Come on, get up, I'm taking you to the hospital. Come on, baby, lean on me," he says, trying to pull her up.

"No, he's not, he's here," and as she says this she opens her hands very slowly and Juan sees it: a little bag, like a small egg with a red yolk, and a tiny baby, about two centimetres, as the doctor had said. Their baby is there, in the bloody hands of his wife, and he can't do anything else than hug her and cry.

Week 11

Marta wakes up at 7:20. She has slept rather badly waiting for Cristina's call. She quickly jumps over her mobile. *No, she hasn't called, nor texted or anything. Thank God, I wouldn't have noticed if she had ...* She gets up and goes to the shower.

When she arrives in the ward, the board has good news for her. It's half empty, and besides there's Celia, Eirini, Cande, Nico and Ashley. *Super! All of them are great people. What a good day I'll be having!*

Her working day starts, and she gets Delivery Room 3. Araceli is there: a girl with an induction because of suspected macrosomia. Marta enters the delivery room and greets her, has a look at her records and just then, there's a deceleration of the baby's heart. Marta explains to Araceli what's happening, manipulates the oxytocin pump, and immediately the medical team on call comes in.

Araceli's baby soon recovers and the team leaves the delivery room, after giving Marta some instructions.

A few hours later, Nico comes into the room:

"Hello Marta, hello Madam," he says, first addressing Marta and then Araceli. "Look, I have to go see the supervisor: would you mind taking care of my room while I fix my holidays?"

"Yes, sure, no problem. What do you have?"

"No, I haven't got anyone, but as the next admission is for me, it's just in case; I don't want to go downstairs without telling you first, and this way I'll make the most of not having anyone now."

"Ok, go, no problem."

"Nico? Nico? Has anybody seen Nico?" Marta hears Eirini, the midwife at the door with the new admissions, asking. Marta goes to her encounter to explain to her that Nico isn't there and she's in charge of his delivery room until he comes back.

"We're passing him an induction, twins."

"Right, get her in and I'll take a look at her until he comes back and gets her ready."

"She can't wait. The CGT is suspicious. You'd better monitor her, they're rushing her because the first twin is not very happy. They want you to break her waters, to see the liquor and to monitor her."

"Gosh, what a mess-up."

"I know, girl, I'm sorry."

Marta returns to her delivery room with Araceli and looks at the corridor clock. *Twenty past one. I'm almost finished*, she thinks. Just then, she remembers Cristina and thinks it's strange that she hasn't rung her yet, but she guesses that means she is all right. She'll drop by this afternoon. Just then, she puts her hands in her pockets and she freezes. She starts running towards the staff room, where she has her handbag. She can't believe she has forgotten her phone and she hasn't realised all morning. She takes her handbag and starts looking inside, frantically.

"Where are you?" she repeats nonstop, rummaging through the bag, taking everything out and putting it on the table. "I can't have left it behind; no, no. I'm sure I took it. Here!" she yells at finding it.

She looks at the screen, and there they are: four missed calls.

"Shit, shit, shit, shit," she grunts. The calls are from Cristina. She's been calling the whole morning. "Well done, Martita, well done. Your first private customer and you totally mess it up. That's being on call, my lovely, well done," she tells herself as she calls her back.

"The number you have dialled is not available, please try again later," says Cristina's phone.

Just then, Eirini comes into the staff room and tells her: "there's a woman in Triage asking for you."

Carmen wakes up feeling queasy. She takes a biscuit from her bedside table and sits up. She's still feeling unwell. This trick Luis told her of eating a bit before getting up is not working too well. But she doesn't dare not to eat the biscuit, in case this unpleasant daily feeling gets worse. But she hasn't felt any better since she's been doing it. She starts rummaging in the table drawer, because she can't find her pills. As she does, she finds a cigarette. Instantly, her pulse speeds up and she starts salivating.

"Shit!" she exclaims. "What is this doing here? As well as I was doing, I've already been five days without smoking… and all the craving has come back just like that, all of a sudden. I am not an idiot, I am not an idiot," she repeats, closing the drawer firmly.

While she's having a shower, Carmen can't stop thinking of the cigarette she's found. She wants to smoke it, she so much wants to smoke, it and she knows she very probably will. She thinks of throwing it away, and she gets the idea out of her mind at once. *If it's the only one I've got, I can't throw it away. And if I just smoke this one and start all over again?*

Aurora's words come back to her head. She remembers her saying that the important thing was not to smoke that cigarette, because everything starts all over again and those five days of torture would have been pointless.

"But they haven't been pointless, it's five days when my baby hasn't smoked. My baby, MY BABY," she repeats as she dries her belly with a towel. Then, she starts running naked to her room, opens the drawer, takes the cigarette and, returning quickly to the bathroom, she throws the cigarette into the toilet bowl and flushes it.

"Yes, yeees, I did it!" she says, thrilled. "Sure, I did, my baby, look what your mom just did! I've been about to throw everything down the drain, but I've behaved. Whoopee!" she cries out. "How right Aurora was in taking all the cigarettes out of the house. Look how silly I got just because I've seen a cigarette in the drawer. Now I can really say I've stopped smoking. I am not an idiot!" she yells, laughing.

Maternity Hospital.
Outpatient Service.

"Soledad Prieto Monzón," the nurse calls.

"Yes, that's us," Sol says as both get up from the waiting room chairs.

Both get into the room where Dr. López is writing something.

"Sit down, please," the nurse tells them pointing at the two empty chairs.

"Very well," says Don Jesús, the doctor; he finishes writing and gives the papers to Herminia, the nurse. "Who's the patient?"

"I am," says Sol.

"Tell me."

"I'm pregnant, and I'm here for the first time."

"Very well. Date of last menstruation?"

"September 5."

"Are your cycles regular?"

"Yes, 28 days."

"How long are they usually?"

"Six days, more or less."

"Are you healthy? Any illness or condition in yourself or your family?"

"No."

"Diabetes, hypertension, heart problems…"

"No, nothing."

"And your partner? Also, healthy?"

"Yes," Sol hesitates looking at Sonia.

"Yes, the father is also healthy," Sonia replies.

Dr. López looks at Sol from over his tiny glasses and asks her, "Do you have to ask her whether there are illnesses in the family or not? Who is she? Your sister in law?"

"No," she replies uncomfortably with a hint of a smile.

Dr. López lets some seconds pass, waiting for an answer that doesn't arrive.

"So?"

"No, the father is also healthy," Sol repeats.

"And his family?"

"Also; extremely healthy, all of them."

"How lucky this baby will be!" says the doctor ironically. "Not a single diabetes, nor a heart problem, or depression… in none of his two families. Every single parent and grandparent alive and kicking, and the rest died of old age…"

"Well, my grandma died of cancer," Sol replies.

"Of course, and cancer as we all know is indicative of health and not of illness."

"Then what do you need to know?" an obviously annoyed Sonia asks.

"This kind of thing. I mean, I'm asking about the family illnesses, you tell me nothing, and when I delve a bit I find there's cancer in the family. I need to know what your direct relatives have died from."

"But that has nothing to do with the pregnancy, as far as I know," Sonia replies again.

"So, listen to me, miss, that's called taking the medical history and I need to collect all this data."

"Whatever for?" Sonia asks irritated. "What difference will it make in the pregnancy monitoring that my mother in law's mother died of cancer or is still alive?"

"We're talking about your friend here," says Dr. López pointing at Sol. "Not about you."

"She's not my friend. She is my wife. And you are treating her as if she were a child who doesn't know the answers to the exam, so please go on with the checking up and try to treat us as equals and not as inferior beings, which we aren't."

"Then, who is the father of this child?"

"This child has no father. He has two mothers. Four breasts. Lucky for him."

"But he must have a father, because you can't have produced the sperm, if I am not mistaken."

"Of course not. But let's call things by their name and talk about the 'donor'; or are sperm donors called fathers too?"

"Well, we have to talk about the donor's health, then," says the doctor, uncomfortable.

"And we are talking about him."

"Sure, that's why you have doubts about the father's health," he says looking at Sol, "because you don't know him."

"Precisely." Sonia replies again.

Sol looks at Sonia, annoyed.

"Is everything all right?"

"Yes, yes; everything's fine."

"Ok, come to the bed, then, and we'll do the scan."

After following the nurse's directions, Sol is lying on the obstetric bed and Sonia is holding her hand.

The doctor introduces the probe into her vagina and looks at the screen in silence for a couple of minutes. Then, he turns it towards the couple and says, "This is the baby and… this, too."

"What?" says Sol, "They are two?"

"Yes. You are going to have two babies."

"Oh my God!" says Sonia kissing Sol.

"They will suit you well, those four breasts you mentioned before," Herminia butts in with a knowing smile.

"What do you mean?" Sonia asks, astonished. "But I'll have no milk."

"It's more difficult, but you can also produce milk and breastfeed them…"

"What a thing to say, Herminia!" Dr. López cuts her. "With all the splendid milk varieties there are nowadays on the market, there's no need to complicate their lives with hormone treatments for breastfeeding."

"But she wouldn't have to take hormones…"

"That's enough," the doctor cuts off. "That's your opinion. I find it logical for a mother to want to breastfeed her baby; but to want to breastfeed without having any milk is crazy. Well, let's get to the point. You are eleven weeks and two days pregnant," he says putting the probe back in its stand; "get dressed," and he disappears behind the screen that divides the room.

Sol and Sonia, happy, hug each other and Sonia asks Herminia, "that thing you said about me breastfeeding them…"

"Induced lactation. Relactation. Look for it on the net," and she takes a finger to her lips for her to keep silent as she points with her head to the screen, meaning the doctor is behind it.

"Thank you," Sonia whispers to her.

"Well, you have to have these blood tests done, ask for two appointments downstairs. One for the tests and another one to come back here, once you get the results."

"Thank you," Sol says, taking the papers the doctor is handing her.

Once the door is closed, Dr. López says to Herminia, "Sluts."

"What?" she asks, astounded.

"Lesbians are sluts, all of them. And you, besides, telling the one with the father role to breastfeed them, how gross, the mere thought of it is repugnant…"

"But what are you saying? If a mother adopted a baby, would you find it repulsive too?"

"Yes. No. I don't know, it's not the same."

"It is the same. A mother who hasn't gestated her child and who wants to breastfeed him."

"No way, Herminia! An adoptive mother is a normal woman, but this is a lesbian, who wants both to be a man and breastfeed. Call the next one," he says pointing with a gesture of his head to the door. "Frankly, I don't get it."

Yes, that's quite true. There are a good many things you don't get, Herminia thinks getting out of the room.

Maternity Hospital.
Obstetric Triage.

Marta is frightened. She's convinced the woman outside is Cristina and she's pretty anxious. *I hope there's nothing wrong with her*, she thinks. She's angry with herself for making a mistake as silly as leaving her mobile behind in her handbag. She walks to her and asks her how she's feeling.

"I've been calling you. The waters are yellow and as I couldn't find you I got frightened and came here."

"I'm sorry. I left my mobile in my handbag and I couldn't check it until now. Are you sure they are yellow?"

"Yes, my waters look yellow-greenish now."

"Any contractions?"

"Nothing much: my belly is getting hard, but not much."

"Have you been examined?"

"No; I've come to look for you, to see what you told me, because I really want no induction, unless it's unavoidable."

"Let's see, Cristina; if your waters have changed colour and it's over twenty-four hours since they broke, getting rid of the induction won't be easy. You know you're the boss over your body, but in these circumstances thinking about an induction is far more sensible."

"I don't want anything to happen to the baby," she sobs covering her face with her hands.

"I know," says Marta kneeling before Cristina. "Let's do this: I'll put you on the CTG, without admitting you or anything, and we see how your baby is doing. Wait a minute here. I'll be right back."

Marta goes in to look for Eirini and she explains to her what's happening to Cristina. She's frightened because she wants to do it well, but she doesn't know how to advise her correctly. She doesn't want to let herself be carried away by Cristina's wishes to end up with something happening to the baby.

"Fine," says Eirini. "I will put her on the monitor and if someone comes, I'll tell them whatever. You go monitor the woman with the twins, she's already in and Nico is not back yet."

"Thank you," Marta says, kissing her, and she goes to Delivery Room 1. "She's the one with the red glasses," she shouts from the end of the corridor, to which Eirini replies with a gesture.

Marta comes into the monitoring room and sees Cristina amicably chatting with Eirini. "Phew!" she inhales deeply, "that means the baby's all right, for sure". She approaches them and looks at the CTG from the last thirty minutes.

"This baby is as happy as can be," she tells Cristina.

"Then we're going home."

"Are you sure, Cristina?"

"Yes, I want to avoid an induction at all costs. Don't tell me I can't, because I can't let them induce me again," she replies with total certainty.

"I'm on your side a hundred percent. Yours and your baby's, but I just want you to take a bit of perspective and analyse the situation in a rational way."

"No, Marta, please; don't you give me the dead child sermon also."

Marta takes Cristina off the monitor, looks up and sees it's 14:50.

"Look, Cristina, I'm out in ten minutes, why don't we go over to your place and talk about this calmly?"

"That's my midwife. The one who tells me what I want to hear. I'll wait for you outside." Cristina replies proudly.

When Cristina goes out, Eirini comes to Marta and asks her, "what are you going to do?

"No idea. Explain everything very clearly to her.""
"Be careful, lovely, will you?
"Yes," she replies.

"Listen, the woman who SROM'd yesterday is here, the one who went home. Why isn't she in a delivery room? Isn't there one available?" Ángela, the registrar, asks approaching Marta.
"I don't know," Marta lies.
"Well, I'll find out, I'm on call today. This one will end with a C-section, mark my words," she says, disappearing through the double doors.
Fuck! Marta thinks.

Sol and Son are at home.
"Are you all right?" Sonia asks her wife.
"Yes. No. Worried."
"Why? Aren't you happy?"
"Yes. Yes, I am, but after the initial joy of having two babies I'm growing pretty worried."
"But why? We'll be doing splendidly. There are many parents of twins out there, girl. It's not the end of the world."
"Right, but I've started to think of the birth, and I guess now it will be impossible to give birth: it will have to be a cesarean and, well, I'm a bit terrified of surgery."
"Why, Sol, don't you worry. If it has to be a cesarean, so be it. Anything for our babies' good."
"Right, yes, anything for their good, of course, but: wouldn't you be afraid if you knew you'd have to go through surgery to get your babies out?"
"But does it have to be a cesarean for sure? How do you know? If you're pregnant with twins, is that the only option? I think some celebrity gave birth to twins…"
"Did she? Then it must be for being famous; they will have a heap of doctors and paediatricians in case anything goes awry. The National Health Service here doesn't deploy such resources."

"Fine, let's check it," says Sonia as she gets up to get her laptop. "Look, Sol. In this forum they say it doesn't necessarily have to be a cesarean: great! It says here that most doctors recommend trying for a vaginal birth, even with twins. It seems it depends on the babies' position too, at the end of pregnancy."

"Yeah, but look," Sol remarks, "here they say that there's a possibility that one twin is born vaginally and the other needs a cesarean. What a mess!"

"Take it easy, don't fret. It says that's just in a small percentage of the cases."

"Can you imagine? Having given birth and undergone surgery at the same time? Horrors!"

"You're right, that must be awful. But that's just talking: it doesn't have to happen to us. We must trust that everything will be alright, and think positive. Just as you don't think the babies are going to have an illness or that something horrible is going to happen to them, we shouldn't be thinking labour is going to be a butchery. We are going to look for a good doctor, who knows about these things, who makes us feel safe and explains things to us clearly."

"If I get a cesarean, what are we going to do with two babies and me unable to move?"

"Sol… you are worrying before time. I think that, even if it's a natural birth, I'd like to try to breastfeed them myself too, as the nurse at the doctor's told us."

"That would be wonderful, Son, really. For everyone, really: for you, for me, and for the babies."

"Yes? Do you really find it a good idea?" Sonia smiles.

"But, how could it not, darling? I had no clue that was possible. If the nurse had not mentioned it, it would never have crossed my mind. The fact that it's possible that your breasts work like mine to feed our children? I don't know the exact advantages of a baby having two mothers, but this is undoubtedly one of the best. Especially when we are expecting two babies. One more baby? Here come two more breasts! Any mother would do anything for her partner to be able to breastfeed too. Besides, I think that as the non-gestant mother it will bond you much more to your babies, there's no possible comparison between breastfeeding them and giving them a bottle."

"Sara, please let me take you to the hospital."

"Juan, forget it. I don't want to discuss it, I don't want to talk, and I don't want to go to the hospital."

"I know, dear, but what if anything happens to you?"

"Please, Juan, that's enough. I can't. I'm not going to the hospital. I can't go, I just want to lie down and that's all. I'm exhausted. I'll die if I have to go. How many times have we been there? How many? And what for? For nothing, for having hopes in vain. And if we go, what are they going to do? The usual, an ultrasound, a sad face -more because their failure than for us and our baby- and then I'll be admitted there, to spend the night in that hell of happy women, with their huge bellies. I can't, my love, I simply can't go there. Don't worry, I'll tell you if I bleed, but not today, stay with me today, lie down, hug me and don't say anything else."

Juan hugs her, worried and impotent. *And what if anything happens to her?* he thinks. *With you I can do anything, I can face anything by your side, but if you leave me, I'll die. I understand it's hard, it's hard for me too, my dear, but if anything happens to you I'd never forgive myself.*

The telephone rings and Juan gets it as he breathes deeply and sighs.

"Hello," he says.

"Hello, son, I'm your mother, how are you?"

"Fine, Mom, and you?" Juan replies looking at Sara.

Sara throws him a brief glance which he interprets perfectly.

"Are you all right?"

"Yes, Mom, we're fine."

"I've been calling all day and you didn't answer the phone."

"Because we weren't here, Mom."

"But you're always home, where were you?"

"Just out and about, Mom."

"That's right, making Sara tired, you must be proud! with all the trouble you're taking to give me a grandchild, I don't want us to have a disappointment for your nonsense."

"Mom, please, not now. "

"Not now, what? All I'm saying is you should be careful, because we cannot afford any nonsense."

"Right, Mom, what do you want?" says Juan, feeling tempted to hang up on her, because he's starting to feel dizzy. Sara is sitting on the sofa looking nowhere and he doesn't feel up to his mother. Not today.

"Nothing, son, just to tell you I'm making paella tomorrow, for you to come for lunch."

"No, Mom, thank you very much, but not tomorrow."

"Why not?"

"Because we can't go tomorrow, we're going somewhere else."

"And where, if I may know? Because if you're going somewhere you could come here instead, your father and I are feeling rather neglected of late."

"Look, Mom, I can't tell you now, because you'd be spoiling my surprise and that's as much as I'm saying," lies Juan, now quite impatient and feeling like hanging up.

"A surprise, for whom? Are you coming? Oh, darling, what a joy!"

"Mom, can't you think of anyone but you? No, it's not for you, and don't wait for us tomorrow, because we cannot go."

"Then you can come today for supper."

"Mom, no we can't, we are rather busy these days; today doesn't suit us. You have to learn that 'no' means 'no' and stop insisting."

"Come on, son, how can you say that to your own mother… your father will be utterly disappointed when I tell him."

"So, don't tell him, you are the one who's going to upset him."

"Me? I'm dying to see you, you're the one who doesn't want to come."

"Mom, really, I can't go on with this conversation now," says Juan, really angry now.

"But you never come and now we can't even talk on the phone, I'm going to start writing you letters so you can read them when it doesn't bother you, when you have time for your mother, who has given you everything and look at the way you…"

"Goodbye, Mom!" says Juan and he hangs up the phone, seething with rage. He inhales deeply and lets the air go slowly to calm himself. He usually knows how to cope with his mother's reproaches with humour, but not today, today he's upset with her.

"What did she want?" Sara asks.

"The usual, to keep on ordering about and controlling my life, as she has always tried to do. She's simply exhausting, and she will never learn. Everything has to revolve around her, and if you say something she doesn't like she keeps harping on and on with her 'you don't love me' emotional blackmail. She wears me out."

"I know, look at your sister, you don't find many families where a daughter doesn't care a fig about her mother."

"She had to… if she does this to me, imagine her, being the youngest it was much worse…"

"No, no. I find it totally normal, knowing your mother and how she has smothered you… I think Silvia has been very brave and has done what she had to do."

Juan doesn't want to go on; he's really hurt about the situation and it's very rare for him to hang up on his mother, but Sara is talking and that's the important thing, for her to talk, even if it's not about what's going on.

"There's no way to understand your mother. She's had everything in life, she married a great guy, all she does is twiddling her thumbs, she's had two kids she doesn't deserve and, even so, she insists on being unhappy, in smothering everyone around her. I don't know how your father bears with her. Why, he's earned a place in Heaven just by putting up with her…"

Juan doesn't very well know what to say or do, he wants Sara to talk, but not about this. But as she's so distressed he can't say no to her, even if her favourite sport is tearing her mother in law to shreds. It hurts him when someone picks on his mother, even if she's terrible and even if he's the first to do so. But, at the end of the day, she is his mother…

"And she's forever tormenting your poor father," Sara goes on, "she doesn't let him live, criticizing him all the time, always picking on him, making his life impossible, even when she owes everything she is to him; because your father is a self-made man, he worked his way up from the bottom up to where he is now…"

"You sound like you are in love with my father," says Juan sitting by her side and putting his arm over her shoulders.

"Don't say nonsense. But I'm very happy that you take after him. Only you are a better version, more handsome and cleverer and much more independent; you don't depend on me as he depends on your mother."

"Yes, I do," Juan says, leaning his head on Sara's shoulder and bursting into tears.

"But darling, what's wrong?"

"Nothing, baby, nothing, it's only that," he says among sobs, "these last days have been horrible, and everything has been adding up, and I'm sorry but I can't take anymore. Last night when we were holding each other I thought you could die and it'd be my fault, for not taking you to the hospital…, and yes I depend on you, my love, if you left me I couldn't go on on my own, because I live for you and I don't know what to do to make you happy, because you deserve everything, you deserve to be happy, and I don't know what to do to achieve it."

"Don't worry, my love, cry all you want," Sara says caressing his head. "There's nothing wrong with me. I'm sorry you are suffering, but I can't… I can't take care of you these days. I feel dead inside," Sara says while she also starts to cry. "I can't explain it, but I have this feeling my body's rotten. The image of a burnt, dry, deserted field where nothing grows keeps coming to my mind all the time. And I don't understand, I don't get why us, why can't I become a mother, not even with another man's sperm. Why can't we be parents, Juan? So many undesired children in the world, and we seem to get everything, but to the rim. Getting pregnant twice, we were thrilled both times and every time has been worse, because if at least I wouldn't have succeeded in getting pregnant… but no, we did get pregnant, and twice, and twice we lost the baby…"

Both of them cry inconsolably. Juan gets up; they kiss, they hug, and they spend a while embraced between cries and sobs.

Cristina's home.

"Do you want anything? Coffee, juice? Have you eaten?" Cristina asks Marta.

"No, I haven't. I've had a very busy morning and I didn't have time to eat."

"What do I fix you then? What would you like? There is…"

"Nothing," Marta says, taking a plastic container from her handbag, "but if you tell me where to heat this I'd be grateful."

Cristina brings Marta her warm food and sits in front of her. "It looks scrumptious. Did you make it yourself?"

"Yes. I prefer it, because food at the hospital is not very varied and you get bored quickly. Want some? There's plenty."

"No, thank you. We ate two hours ago, before going to the hospital. But please eat up. It's almost four pm, you must be starving, woman!"

Marta starts to eat and Cristina asks her, "what are we going to do?"

"I think induction would be the most sensible thing, Cristina."

"But can't we wait? As you have seen, Raquel is perfectly all right."

"So, her name's Raquel? I didn't know. Raquel… I like it," she says with a smile. "Well, I'll give you all the information and you decide, but I have to tell you. The first thing is there's been a significant change between yesterday and today, which is that Raquel has pooed. Babies poo inside their mothers for two reasons: one is because they are already mature and they play and investigate and they push, and meconium[27] gets out; this happens often, especially if the pregnancy is over forty or forty-one weeks."

"I'll be forty-one tomorrow."

---

[27] Meconium -colloquially called "mec"- is a dark green substance composed by dead cells and secretions from the liver and the stomach inside the new-born intestine. They are the earliest stools and their formation starts at the fetal stage.

"True. The other reason babies poo is because they suffer. When there's fetal distress, one of the things babies do is poo."

"But her heartbeat was fine."

"As you say: it was. What the baby's CTG tells us is how your baby is at that moment. The minute we stop the monitor we cease having information on her condition."

"But the CTG was done after she pooed, so that means the first option is the right one, doesn't it?"

"I don't know. Nobody does. It's not that easy. Meconium is a sign that makes us suspicious: it might not mean anything, it might do. Raquel may be suffering and we are not listening to her."

"Don't tell me that, Marta."

"Cristina, I have to. It's important that you know, and to decide you need to have all the information, because you can't make the right decision if you don't."

"What do you think I should do? The truth, right? Keeping in mind how much I want a natural birth and that I want to avoid induction at any cost."

Just then they hear the door and Santi, Cristina's husband, comes in.

"Hello," says Santi, approaching to kiss Cristina.

"Hello Santi, this is Marta, the midwife. She's here to help us decide what to do with this little poopy babe," she says caressing her belly.

"Hello," greets Marta.

"Hello," replies Santi sitting beside her. "And what have you decided?"

"Nothing yet," Cristina says; "Marta was going to give us her opinion right now."

"Yes," Marta smiles nervously. "You must know I cannot and should not give an opinion, because I'm not you, Cristina. You are the one in this situation and only you, the two of you, can decide what to do."

"But you can tell us what you think, at least, can't you?"

"I'll try not to, Cristina. Really, I can't say what I would do in your place, because I've never been pregnant. I don't have your previous experience with Laura's birth and my opinion would be based on my experience and my knowledge as a midwife, not as Cristina, so it wouldn't be reliable."

"Fine; then, as a midwife: do you think it's a good idea for us to stay at home and wait until the birth starts?" asks Santiago.

"I think, as I told Cristina before, that we don't know why Raquel has pooed. It might have been just because or because she had had a little oxygen deprivation incident resulting in the expulsion of meconium. As we can't know the cause for this mec, it looks as if the most sensible thing would be an induction."

"Even if the heartbeat is alright and I'm feeling fine too?" asks Cristina.

"Yes. Your waters have gone over twenty-four hours ago and there's no sign that labour is coming. You don't have a single contraction... I'd love to tell you the opposite. I'd love to tell you that we can wait relaxedly, but I don't think so. It's possible, if we wait for you to start labour on your own, that you will, and everything will be alright and you will have no problem. But what if you don't? What if Raquel is suffering? What if there's something we don't see and the only sign is Raquel's meconium? You are the only ones who should decide. The decision has to be a hundred percent yours, and I will stand by you, whichever you take."

"You will?" Cristina asks, surprised.

"Yes, of course. My job is to be with you and to stand by your decisions, whatever they are."

"Do you have anything to listen to the heartbeat here?"

"Yes. I put my doppler[28] in my handbag yesterday in case I had to come to see you."

Marta looks inside her handbag and she takes a small bag.

"Please lie down," she tells Cristina pointing at the sofa.

---

[28] Doppler: A hand-held ultrasound transducer used to detect the fetal heartbeat for prenatal care.

After feeling her abdomen, she puts a bit of gel on the doppler's probe and, warning Cristina that it will be a bit cold, puts it on her lower belly: Raquel's heartbeat is quick and strong, and they all smile.

"She sounds like a galloping horse," says Santi.

"Yes. It often reminds me of that too," replies the midwife.

"Is she all right?" asks Cristina.

"She sounds well and happy."

"When do you have to go back to work?"

"Tomorrow morning."

"See what you think of my idea," says Cristina. "You stay here with us," she says looking at Marta, "we get the guest room ready for you, you go home to get what you need and we wait and see. We listen to Raquel's heartbeat every now and then and if I'm not in labour in the morning then we all go to the hospital."

"If that's what you want, it's all right by me," Marta answers.

Santiago nods and Marta goes home to get her things ready.

Iberian tavern, 20:40.

Manuel rushes into the tavern. Marcos makes a hand gesture from the end of the bar. Everyone else is there, he's the last one to arrive.

"You're awfully late, mate!" Ramón tells him. "What are you having? Come on, we're several drinks ahead of you."

"I'll have what you're having. Yes, I'm late, I was with the deputy."

"These politicians!" says Marcos, "What were you thinking to change medicine for politics?"

"Don't listen to him," says Tomás, putting his arm on his shoulders. "He's just plain jealous, as are all of us, seeing the good life you lead."

"You are the one who's jealous!" Marcos jokes.

"Me? Let me remind you that I'm the only one who studied Obs and Gynae…" rebukes Tomás as they all burst into laughter. "Thus, I'm the one who's the least jealous of Manuel. You are the ones who chose Derma, GP and Haematology…"

"Serve another round, please," Ramón tells the waiter.

"But I've just started this one," Manuel replies.

"That means you're drinking very slowly," he retaliates. "Come on, drink up."

After a while at the bar, the four friends get into the dining room. They have been friends since university and, if not very often, they try to meet when they can.

After dinner, Marcos tries to egg Tomás on:

"Let's see, you are the obstetrician to be jealous of. Tell us something to make us drool with envy."

"Go on, go on," he replies shyly. "What do you think? That I only get bimbos? I remind you obstetricians get all kinds of women, the old ones, the ones who don't wash, the ugly ones…"

"And the bimbos!" says Ramón hitting his hand with his fist, "so just tell us about them, we all get the old ones."

"Well, there's this girl I have known since she was fifteen or sixteen, who is by far the utter sexpot I've ever met in my life, mates. She's Brazilian, although she's lived here most of her life. She's a Spaniard with a Brazilian body. Best of the best. Tall, blonde, golden skin… and with such boobs, I've examined them so many times… Every time she goes for a check-up, it's been hell for me not to eat her pussy on the spot…"

"Ha, ha, ha," they all laugh.

"Haven't you tested the water? Maybe she's dying for it," Marcos urges him.

"What do you mean, chap? My relationship with her is strictly professional. I love it. At the minimal insinuation and if she wasn't interested, she'd leave me. And, believe me, I haven't the slightest intention to let the chance to see her naked and get my hands all over her pass, even if it's just once a year. Well, it will be much more now because she's pregnant. I don't know who's banging her, but he's a lucky devil, the bastard! Besides, it looks as if they don't have a very romantic relationship. She looked rather annoyed when I asked her about the baby's father. Never mind. Eat your hearts out, on the 20th of January these little hands will be on her glorious body," he says showing his hands and smiling proudly.

"Fuck it, mate, do you know your appointments by heart?"

"Of course not, but I know when she's coming. As if I wouldn't," he smiles.

"And what's the name of that stunner?" Manuel asks.

"Who cares?" Marcos laughs.

"Do you know her?" Ramón asks astonished.

"No. Just curiosity. I'm sure she'll have a beautiful, exotic name. I can't imagine that bombshell being called Facunda, isn't it?" he says, nudging Tomás.

"You're absolutely right. Her name's Lorena."

"Lorena…" mumbles Manuel leaning back on his chair.

"And what time do you say she's going to your clinic?" asks Ramón.

"Don't even think of it, I can picture the three of you there to see her."

"What the hell, to see her! I'll take my coat and examine her with you" Ramón laughs.

"No way. I'm not sharing my time with her for all the gold in the world."

Week 12

Cristina and Santiago's home.

06:00 am.

"Marta," says Cristina coming into the room. "The waters are greener. May you listen to Raquel?"

Marta gets up and sees Cristina with the doppler bag in her hand. She applies the sensor to Cristina's belly and again they can hear the gallop of Raquel's heart.

"She sounds all right," says Marta. Then, Cristina starts having a contraction and Raquel's heartbeat goes down. Automatically, Marta turns the doppler off. She doesn't want to alarm Cristina and she knows that, during contractions, little Raquel goes through a heartbeat deceleration. That information is enough.

When the contraction is over, Marta puts it on again: 95, 103, 111, 129, 146, 152, 138, 126, 132…

"When did the contractions begin?" she asks.

"Around three o'clock, more or less. Is she all right?"

"She's starting to get tired. I think we should go to the hospital."

"Right. I've got everything ready. I'll wake Santi up."

The three of them get into the car. Santiago is driving, and Marta and Cristina are sitting behind. Just then, Cristina has another contraction. When it's over, Marta listens to Raquel's heartbeat: 87, 85, 92, 97, 106, 126, 138, 142, 134, 138…

"Is she all right?" Cristina asks, worried.

"Yes. Tired. She doesn't like contractions much; but she gets over them quickly when they're over."

Arriving at the hospital, Marta leaves them at the Triage waiting room and goes in, looking for anyone on call. She knocks at the doctor's room and there's Ángela, the registrar.

"Hello Ángela, how's the night going?"

"Fine, without trouble. Rather calm, really. What are you doing here? Is there anything wrong?"

"I've come with Cristina, the girl who 'SROMed' and didn't want an induction. She's here. I think we should take her in now. Green meconium."

"But where is she coming from? I had a look yesterday and she wasn't admitted."

"From her home."

"But it's been two days since her waters went! She should have been induced yesterday!"

"Well, she went home and she's back now, her waters are green. She has the right to. She would also have that right if she had stayed home now. Please, she's an acquaintance of mine. Treat her well."

"I'll treat her as I have to treat her. She disobeyed us."

"Hey, you are not her owner! She doesn't have to obey you or anyone. She can go home in the middle of second stage if she wants to. You should get it into your head that a doctor is not an authority, nor is a hospital prison: people can come in and out as they please; we are the ones providing a service, not the other way around. People don't have to comply with anything we tell them here," she says, furious. "Look, Ángela: this woman is frightened. She has opposed a medical indication and her baby might now be suffering from fetal distress. You can opt for being a great pro and treat her as she deserves, without bad feelings or anything of the kind; or you may opt for being an authentic tyrant bitch and show her what bad girls get when they don't follow like sheep the specific protocols of the hospitals they have been appointed to."

Ángela sighs, "Come on, tell her to come in…"

Cristina comes into the room with Santi and Marta. Ángela offers her a chair and in that moment, Cristina has another contraction and presses Marta's hand as she lets out a long, uninterrupted blow from her mouth.

"How long have you been having contractions?" Ángela asks.

Cristina closes her eyes and gestures with her hand for her to wait.

"For the last two or three hours," he replies, smiling.

"The midwife tells me your waters are green now: when did you realise that?"

"I'm not sure," Cristina says and she looks at Marta for help. She doesn't know whether to tell the truth or not. She'd rather Marta did the answering.

"I'm not sure. What time did you call me? About two hours ago, was it?" Marta chips in.

"Yes, when I got up to pee: yes, two hours, more or less."

"Fever?"

"No."

"Take your clothes off from the waist down and lie on the bed," Ángela tells her, putting sterile gloves on.

Ángela examines Cristina in silence; as she does, Cristina has another contraction and tries to get up.

"Please stop," she asks Ángela.

"Wait a minute, I'm not finished yet."

"Not like this, I have to stand up. Stop it, please!" Cristina begs trying to get up.

"Take a deep breath," says Ángela without taking her fingers out of her vagina.

"Ángela, stop, you'll go on later; let her stand up, it hurts more like that," Marta intervenes, helping Cristina get up.

"Done. This is significant mec, see?" she says showing Marta the stained glove. "To the delivery room," and she goes out to do the admission.

"But, how is she?" Marta asks following her into the corridor. Ángela disappears behind the Triage door.

Marta enters the staff room and looks at the board. Cristina has got delivery room 2 and her midwife is Cande. *Thank God*, she thinks as she greets the people in the room.

"Marta, how come you're here?" asks Celia.

"I've come with a friend, she 'SROMed' and now she's got meconium…"

"It's Cande's turn," Celia says, "shall I call her?"

"Where is she?"

"I think she's sleeping. It's being a very quiet night…"

"No, don't disturb her then; I've come to stay with her anyway, so it's all right. I'm going to get changed quickly and I'll be right back, ok?"

"Of course. Is there anything I can do?" asks Celia.

"Yes, please monitor her, this looks a bit awry."

Juan wakes up and sees his wife lying by his side, her eyes open wide.

"How are you?" he asks her.

"What do you mean how are you?" Sara replies.

"Physically, how are you?"

"Not fine, still knackered, nauseous and upset, I guess it must be the hormones still running around."

"Are you bleeding?"

"No, I haven't bled at all."

"Won't that be dangerous?"

"What? Not bleeding?"

"Yes, I'm not sure…"

"Well, it must be the first time ever not bleeding is a sign of alarm," she replies ironically.

"Right, of course, but don't you think we should go to the hospital to get you checked?"

"Juan, don't start, I'm not going anywhere."

"But what if you still have some remains inside and you get an infection or something that can be helped now but not later?"

"Well, I'd feel unwell or have a temperature if I had an infection, wouldn't I?"

"I don't know; please, darling. I'm worried, do it for me, let's go see a doctor. I just want to make sure everything's right and you haven't…"

"Nothing is right, Juan, nothing is right; we have lost our baby and I can't take it, I can't do anything that reminds me of it, I'm not ready to go to the hospital, or to Dr. García's or anywhere else that reminds me of any of this."

"Then let's go to a different doctor's, one we don't know at all, to ask him. Please, Sara, I know you don't want to and it's very hard, but it's also hard for me and I'm very frightened that anything could happen to you. I'm afraid of losing you, and if anything happened to you… I don't want to think about it, but please, consider it just for a moment. Try to understand me."

"There's nothing wrong with me, darling, I just can't do it. And if we go to the doctor's and in the waiting room we meet a pregnant woman, proud of her belly, and she asks us if we are going to have a baby too? I don't know, there's a real possibility of that happening and I swear I couldn't take it, I really couldn't, my love, I couldn't."

"Look, let me take care of it, tell the doctor what's happening, get the first appointment without even passing through the waiting room."

Juan remains waiting, and on seeing Sara is considering it he doesn't dare to let her say anything, for fear she refuses again.

"Really, darling, let me be in charge; I'll talk to the secretary and she will organise everything. We'll go as private patients and you'll see how as we'll be paying there will be no problem and they'll treat us wonderfully, please," he begs her kneeling by her side and taking her hands.

"All right," Sara says, "but I'm doing it just for you, for you to relax, because I love you and I don't want you to suffer; but you must know that for me this is a huge effort and a great pain."

"I know and I love you, I love you, I love you... thank you, darling," says Juan stretching to kiss her as tears start running down his face.

Maternity Hospital.
Delivery Room 2.
Marta comes into the delivery room and there she sees Cristina and Santiago. Celia is with them.

"She has done a couple of typicals,"[29] Celia says, showing her the five-minute CGT.

"What's wrong with her?" asks an anguished Cristina. "Is Raquel all right?"

"She's tired; she doesn't like contractions much, but she does recuperate all right after them. It looks like you're in labour," Marta smiles.

"I am? How do you know? Did that doctor tell you?"

---

[29] Typical deceleration: A kind of deceleration of the baby's heartbeat.

"No, but your contractions are very close together. Now, the minute we get your papers, we'll see how many centimetres you have dilated. You did it! You started labour on your own," Marta smiles again.

"Yes? Yes, I did it! These contractions are nothing compared to Laura's. Are you sure they mean labour?" she asks as another contraction comes and she starts to blow.

"Well, if they aren't labour pains they are very close to it," Marta jokes. She looks at the monitor attentively and Celia puts the volume down, as the baby's heartbeat decelerates. Just then, Ángela comes in followed by Laura, the consultant on call.

"But, what are you doing? Make her lie down, come on, on the left side. Oxygen. Come on, madam, lie down," Laura says nervously.

"Relax, Laura," Marta replies. "It doesn't get much better in left lateral."

"Shh," whispers Laura, annoyed. "Madam, lie on your left side right now. Your baby needs to be born on the spot. You're going to have a C-section."

"What?" says Cristina.

"Why? 48 hours since your waters went, significant mec, variables on the CGT... What else do you need?" replies Laura angrily as she dons the sterile gloves and prepares to examine her.

"Her consent, basically," Marta replies.

"Whatever, whatever, but please let nothing happen to my baby, please," says Cristina, frightened.

"You should have thought of that before, when we told you that we had to induce your labour and you refused and went home. Or do you think we say things and operate just because?"

"Hey, Laura, watch it," Marta cuts her. "She decided to go home and when things went wrong she decided to come back. We have to respect her decision."

"Well, if anything happens to this fetus I'm reporting you two, mark my words. Open your legs," says Laura, introducing her fingers violently in Cristina's vagina.

"Ouch!" she exclaims.

"Get her ready for theatre. Emergency C-section," Laura says as she goes out of the delivery room followed by Ángela.

Cristina starts crying inconsolably. Santiago, Marta and Celia move closer to comfort her.

"My little girl, oh my God! What have I done? My little girl… It's all my fault. Why didn't you convince me, Marta? Why didn't you drag me here yesterday when I went home? My girl, my pretty thing, I didn't want this…"

"Relax, Cristina," says Marta, holding her hand, "Raquel is exactly the way she was before these two came to see you. If they had not come in, we'd be here just as we were. You'd be standing up and happy; we'd be keeping an eye on Raquel's state. Yes, contractions are affecting her and the CTG is suspicious, but that's all. You won't be getting a C-section, or at least not right now. Breathe deeply, take it easy and let me examine you, because I still don't know how far dilated you are. None of these two doctors have told us anything after examining you."

"But that doctor said I'm having an emergency C-section," says Cristina in tears. "I don't want anything bad happening to my child, for God's sake, Marta. Take me to the theatre now, I'd never forgive myself if anything happened to Raquel. Really, what was I thinking? My poor girl was trying to tell me she was feeling bad and me all pig-headed, stubborn as a mule, 'I want to stay home, I want to stay home, I'm not going to the hospital…' Santi, please, I want her to be taken out right now," she begs, distressed, pressing her husband's hand.

"Cristina. Hey, Cristina. Listen to me," Marta chips in, "Raquel is all right. Don't be afraid. It's true she's not liking contractions, but there's a long way from that to saying she needs to be born straight away."

"But the doctor…"

"That doctor," Marta cuts her, "is one of the worst we have here. She just wants to make you feel bad for not having obeyed a medical order yesterday. You've given her a very good chance to show her power and show off, and she's profiting from it to the maximum. In her mind it's something like: You have defied us? You get a C-section. So that you don't dare to do it again. If you have a normal delivery after discharging yourself, going home, not coming back the next day for the induction and coming forty-eight hours later with your waters green, you are destroying the foundation she has been standing on for all these years. For her ego and for her pride you can't win. If she coerces you into getting a cesarean, not only she will have won, but she will also be hurting you and many women coming after you.

"Imagine the next woman who comes here leaking water and wants to go home as you did two days ago. The doctor will be telling her something like 'yes, like the last one who said that, and we had to do an emergency C-section with an almost dead baby'. You will see how she will want to take Raquel to the Neonatal Unit, but not because there's anything wrong with her; just to give you a lesson, to make you feel guilty, for you to learn that you can't play with her."

"Another one," says Cristina trying to get up as she gets a contraction. Marta helps her stand up, and then, Cristina utters a guttural sound very familiar for the two midwives, who look at each other astonished.

"Son of a …!" Marta exclaims.

"What's up?" Cristina hollers, "What's that?"

"That's you pushing, Raquel is being born now. You'll have her in your arms in no time, Cristina," Marta smiles, crouching before Cristina and putting several Inco pads on the floor.

"Another one," Cristina says as she pushes. Raquel is born in just one push. Marta takes the baby and gives her to her mother, as she checks the girl's heartbeat by touching the umbilical cord.

"Is she all right?" Cristina, uneasy, asks Marta.

"Yes, she is; a bit soiled form all that mec, but fine."

Cristina bursts into tears, hugging Raquel, who opens her eyes and looks at her mother placidly. Santiago is staying by her side, visibly moved. After a few minutes, Cristina asks, "they won't take her away from me, will they?"
"They might try, but if that's the case, you just stand firm, right?" says Marta with tears in her eyes.
"Thank you very much, Marta. I couldn't have done it without you. Thank you very much, truly," says Cristina, crying.
"You're welcome. Thank you for your trust," she hugs her.
The theatre porter comes into the delivery room, pushing a theatre trolley.
"You may leave. We are not going to need it," Celia tells him.
"Who was that?" asks Cristina, who could not see him because her bed is not facing the door.
"The theatre porter. He was coming to take you for that C-section."
A few minutes later, Ángela comes in through the door.
"I'm bringing the consent for you to sign it," she says approaching Cristina. "But, what's that?" she asks, astonished on seeing the girl in her mother's arms.
"This is Raquel."
"But, but… and 'Paeds'?[30] We must take her to the neonatal unit. Take her up straight away."
"Apgar's score[31] 9, 10… and I'll give you the ten minutes one in five, but something tells me it will also be 10. This girl is perfect." Marta replies.
"Right, but she has been over 48 hours with prolonged rupture of membranes with no antibiotics, significant mec and so on. This girl has to be admitted for an infection screening and observation."
"My girl is not going anywhere without me," Cristina states defiantly.
"I'll get Dr. Gómez," says Ángela walking out the door.

_____

Doctor's office. 7.30am.
[30] Paediatricians.

[31] Apgar's score: First examination of new-born babies performed in the first, fifth and tenth minutes of their life to assess the idoneity of their adaptation to extrauterine life. Maximum punctuation is 10.

Ángela enters the doctor's office where she finds Laura with Nuria Casona, who's just arrived.

"She's given birth," Ángela announces.

"Who?" asks Laura.

"The woman in number two, the one with the prolonged SROM, the mec and the variables. The one for the C-section."

"What?" exclaims Laura with a start.

"I'm telling you, she just gave birth. I went in for her to sign the consent and there she was, the picture of happiness with her baby in her arms!"

"Shit!" says Laura. "Right, that baby goes to NNU."

"That's what I told her, but she told me she is not going to be separated from her baby."

"But we must put that baby on the risk of infection protocol."

"Sure, I told her that myself and that's when she told me the baby is not leaving her side."

"I'm calling the judge, if need be," says Laura vexed.

"But, what's up?" asks Nuria.

"This woman came two days ago with SROM and she got cocky with Carlos and Ángela, saying she was going home. One of those who think we do things just to pester people here. Those who have read everything, and say 'this study recommends to wait'. The same thing happened to her in a previous pregnancy, and it looks like it was heaving then and no one took care of her here... in short, she went home with the instructions of coming back the following day for an induction. But she didn't show up. And now she's come, two hours ago, with a very significant mec and tremendous variables. When I examined her and I saw she's not in second stage yet, I told her she's getting a C-section, and that stupid midwife, that Marta, started questioning me, saying the woman will have to consent and so on. There, right in front of her! And now she has given birth."

"So, what's the problem?" Nuria asks, "if she has given birth, all the better, isn't it?"

"No, it isn't, Nuria, not at all. What this woman has done might be very dangerous and besides she's getting off scot free."

"Dangerous for whom? Because I still can't see what the problem is."

"That she has done exactly the opposite to what we do here! She's throwing every protocol out of the window!"

"And we're risking… everything being alright for her?" Nuria asks ironically.

"Right!" Laura replies annoyed, "I'm getting that baby to NNU even if I have to call the judge."

"And what are you telling the judge? 'I have a disobedient mother here who won't allow me to take her perfectly healthy baby from her by force to take him to NNU'?"

"Perfectly healthy? With atrocious variables and horrible mec!"

"Laura, we have been discussing this for ten minutes, and I guess Ángela would have told us by now if that baby needs a paediatrician urgently," says Nuria looking at Ángela, who says nothing. "If you are going to admit the baby to NNU just to apply a protocol to her, her parents have every right to refuse and I even think the judge would not be amused, and rightly so, if you call him because of this."

"Then what? Shall we let her go home with her baby to tell everyone that she opposed one medical order after another and they are both as fresh as cucumbers?"

"'Fraid so, babe. Either that and you try to forget it, or you get as frustrated as you want on the subject, because you are not right. C'mon, go home. That way at least you won't be seeing her again. Or Marta."

"That's another matter too. How to put up with her and the 'flower-power' on top."

"Come on, Laura, go home. If you could realise what you're just saying...! It looks as if you'd rather something bad had happened to them. People make their own decisions, like it or not. This woman did, and she has given birth to a healthy baby. Good for her. Stop going on about it."

"I don't understand how everything seems so easy to you," she says picking her handbag up.

"Because it's easy. They are not our enemies, they are not opposing us. They are simply people making their own decisions over their bodies and their babies. The rest does not matter."

Maternity Hospital.
Outpatients department.

María Elena is waiting alone in the obstetrics clinic. José Luis can't come with her, they haven't even dared to tell Mr. Vidal anything, the way things stand here… José Luis has had his job at the cafeteria since they arrived from Lima and they have to do all they can to keep it. If they don't, what would they do with a baby and no work? It doesn't pay much, but it's better than nothing. They both have university degrees, but her husband has spent the last seven years with him at the cafeteria and her as a cleaning lady and looking after elderly people, because her nursing degree is not recognised here in Spain.

Once at the doctor's office and after her ultrasound, Dr. López addresses her, "María Elena Pérez. You are nine weeks pregnant," he says without looking at her.

"Yes, sir."

"Are you just passing through?"

"No, I've been living here for seven years."

"Are you working?"

"No, not at present."

"Is this your first pregnancy?"

"Yes, sir."

"Will your baby be born in Spain?"

"God willing, he will, yes."

"God has nothing to do here, it will be if you and your husband want the baby to be born in Spain."

"Yes, sir, yes."

"Are you married?"

"Yes, sir."

"And why is your husband not here with you?"

"He is working."

"Of course, and he couldn't come with you, could he?"

"He had an important meeting today," replies María Elena, uncomfortable, feeling harassed by the obstetrician's questions, "is it necessary for him to be here?"

"No, no, it's just always the same story. You come here to take our jobs from us and you can't even ask for a free morning for the really important things."

"Dr. López, calm yourself; she's not the first woman to come alone," intervenes Herminia, the nurse.

"Right, but what annoys me is that we have so much unemployment in this country but the one who's sweeping the streets is black; the coffee barista is Moroccan; the one who phones to sell you I-don't-know-what, Indian. Isn't it, María Elena? You won't happen to be unemployed?"

"Yes, sir."

"And getting paid from the money that comes from my taxes, aren't you?"

"No, sir, I don't get paid."

"How surprising, or are your benefits payments already expired? And your husband, where does he work?"

"At the Embassy," says María Elena knowing there's no way back now. But she won't tolerate being treated like this by a guy who's had everything easy in life, who has no idea what it's like to spend your life suffering and begging because you come from another country. Despite having university degrees, both she and her husband are doing the jobs nobody wants. Yet they are treated as if they were taking something from someone. This happens every day here, and she's fed up with people abusing her in this way just because she's not living in the country where she was born.

"Oh, yes?" says the doctor sarcastically, "and what is the position your husband has at the Embassy?"

"He's the Peru ambassador to Spain."

Time seems to stop just then. Dr. López stands paralysed for a second, as well as the nurse and María Elena, who looks down as she's feeling humiliated. She has been forced to lie, she doesn't know how or why she's done it, but she has felt completely cornered, and right now she's into this mess with no clue about how everything will end up.

"Your husband is the Peruvian ambassador?" says the doctor, astonished, "why didn't you tell me before? Here I am, treating you as scum, understand what I mean by scum, with all due respect, when you are a lady. I'm sorry, I'm not used to attending to personalities like you here in the hospital. You should come to my private practice, where I'll take much better care of you: you can come in the afternoon, if you prefer, or whenever it's more convenient for your husband, and that way I'll be able to give you a much more personalised treatment."

"Don't worry, sir, I prefer to come here; it's more convenient for me and I don't want to abuse my husband's position."

"Come on, come on, don't say nonsense, that's hardly abusing, I'm giving you my card and you just call me whenever you want."

"No, really, doctor, excuse my insistence but we really need to do it this way. Due to the relationships between our countries, we must have total confidence -which of course we have- in the Spanish public health service. Our duty is to be attended to by the state health system to show our fellow countrymen that we have faith and trust in this system that embraces us."

"Come on, but the public health service is crap, excuse my language, but private service is much better, and besides…"

"I don't doubt it, doctor," María Elena cuts him, "but we have to comply with the pacts between both states, and that's the way it is."

"Well, Madam, María Elena, I feel very honoured to have you in my practice, and you'll see how your pregnancy will be taken care of by one of the best professionals in this country. I'm giving you my private phone number, and any doubt you might have, anything you might need, just call me without any hesitation. We don't want people thinking they're not welcome in this country. Those who come here to work will always find us with open arms; but those who are criminals should better stay in their countries, don't you think? I'm sorry I've been a bit harsh with you; I had no idea you were someone of importance. Come back in two weeks for your first scan and blood tests. Herminia here will give you an appointment," he gestures towards the nurse, who takes María Elena's records and proposes,

"At 11 on the 17th of this month?"

"No, no, Herminia, at the time that's convenient for her. For her and for her husband. What time do you want to come? Or maybe another day, would you rather come another day? As you want, madam. Maybe whenever it's convenient for your husband," he repeats.

"No, no. On the 17th at 11 will do."

"Really? You can change it, whenever it's good for you."

"No, that day is fine. We cannot count on my husband until the last minute, because as you know he may have meetings all of a sudden which he cannot cancel."

"Yes, yes, of course, I can imagine. We'll be meeting in two weeks, then we'll see this little Spaniard you're carrying inside."

"Well, little Peruvian," María Elena smiles.

"No, no, children are from wherever they're born; so, a full-blooded Spaniard through and through."

"Very well, I'll be seeing you then," says María Elena as Dr. López sees her off from this office door. As she's walking down the stairs, she can't help but smile. She doesn't usually lie, but for the first time in her life she's glad she's done it.

"Fuck, what a cock-up, Herminia!" says Dr. López after shutting the door. "How could I know she was the ambassador's wife? They all have the same poncho and flute face to me. She was content when she left, wasn't she?"

"Well, I think she was astonished," Herminia smiles.

"Yes? Why? Did I go too far? Not that much, did I?"

"Well, boss, you were rather rude."

"No, but I mended it afterwards, and I gave her my mobile number and all. Go get me a coffee, come on, and with cold milk, not piping hot as you always do. And tell the next one to come in when you go out, let's see if we finish once and for all."

Dr. Casona's private practice.

"Hello, good afternoon, please come in. Dr. Casona is waiting for you," says the assistant on opening the door.

The doctor walks towards them and shakes Sara's and Juan's hands as she introduces herself and shows them into her office.

"How are you feeling, Sara?"

"Awful; I'm dead inside, I want to die and I have no idea how I'll get out of this."

"Even if I can't be in your shoes, I share your pain and I can imagine what you must be going through. I'm very sorry; I mean it. Losing a baby is always painful; I had a miscarriage myself a few years ago so I can relate. But the path you are going through is very hard, and it's only yours. I am really sorry."

"Thank you," replies Sara.

"Well, I'll be as brief as I can: Juan tells me you didn't want to come at all, so I'll try to make everything as swift and comfortable as I can. Come with me and I'll give you a quick scan to make sure there's no risk of infection."

Sara enters the room and she feels very distressed when she sees the scanner there. The last time she saw it, it was the bearer of such good news… The same machine that now is going to search her empty womb to confirm that her baby has completely disappeared. Through her eyes, glassy with tears, she observes the screen has been positioned so that she can't see it from the bed. "Thank you, doctor, thank you."

"You're welcome. My name is Nuria," she says with a smile.

Sara cries out of gratefulness as she lies down on the bed. She likes this woman; she looks at her husband, who is also moved. He is proud to have hit the mark with the doctor.

"Right. Are you comfortable?"

"Yes."

"Let's go, then. If you notice or want to tell me anything, do so in all freedom, right?"

"Right."

Dr. Casona starts moving the probe around Sara's abdomen. Juan holds his wife's hand as she looks to the wall. Juan looks at the doctor and frightens: she looks worried, although he has no clue why. He doesn't dare to ask so as not to frighten Sara, but something's clearly going on.

"Sara, I don't know how to tell you, but I think this is something that speaks for itself and you should see it yourselves."

Sara turns her head; the doctor turns the screen and… there it is. A baby. A baby moving and kicking. The doctor puts the volume on and they all can hear the heartbeat, clear and strong. The three of them remain silent, surprised, stunned. Juan and Sara press their hands, their eyes glued to the screen. None of them is able to utter a sound.

Juan starts sobbing and jumps on his wife, who starts sobbing too. Both melt into an embrace. The doctor turns away from the scan to leave them alone. As she raises her eyes she sees her assistant Nati's face, astonished to see what's happening.

Nuria leaves Sara and Juan for a minute as they embrace and kiss and cry with happiness. Their baby is there, their baby is still alive, they are going to be parents. Everything has turned upside-down in the most incredible way, but never mind that. They are seeing him, they can hear him: their baby is healthy and strong, growing inside his mother's belly.

Nuria comes back into the room where she left Sara and Juan. "Well, let's see how this baby is, all right?"

"Yes, yes, sure, of course," says Sara among sobs. "But how can this be? I lost my baby, I saw him, I had it in my hands, a tiny baby, as if inside a small egg. I know what I saw and I know it was a baby. That's why I didn't want to go anywhere: because I knew what I had lost. If I had had any doubt, if I had not seen it, I'd have run to the hospital to see if he was still there, if he was fine... what's happened, doctor?"

"Well, the only explanation I can find is that you were pregnant with two babies, you lost one of them and the other is still growing inside you."

"But when they scanned me for the first time they didn't tell us there were two babies, there was only one. Is it possible not to see two babies?"

"I don't know, it's pretty difficult to miss, but apparently something of the kind has happened. Who did that first scan?" asks Nuria.

"Doctor García," they both reply.

"If you had said any other... but he is one of the best obstetricians I know. It's rather strange. You should go visit him and talk with him, to see if he has any explanation for what's happened."

"But I want you to take care of my pregnancy from now on; after the way you have treated us, I don't want to see anybody else."

"I'll be delighted to be your obstetrician from now on. Although I think you should go and see Fermín, so that he knows what's happened, and that you have decided to come with me. If I am not mistaken, you really have nothing against him or the way he has treated you, do you?"

"Of course not, he has always been very nice and has treated us wonderfully. All right, we'll go to see him. The problem is that his office is in the fertility clinic, and like it or not, it's a rather cold place that constantly reminds you where you are," reflects Sara.

"Well, it does remind you that you are in the place where you got your IVF, where you got pregnant, my love," says Juan. "Remember that you're still pregnant, dear. That everything you didn't want to know, see nor remember is welcome again in our lives."

"It's true, Juan, I just can't believe it. It's a real miracle."

"And how many weeks pregnant am I, the same I was before?" asks Sara.

"Well, you are twelve weeks pregnant, does it fit?" Dr. Casona asks.

"I'm not sure, I guess so," answers Sara. "I've completely lost track of time these last weeks."

"Yes," says Juan. "It took me two weeks to convince you to come here and you lost the baby when you had just passed week 10. So, yes: today is Tuesday, you're due on Saturdays, you are 12 weeks + 3 days pregnant."

"Impressive!" Nuria exclaims. "That's splendid, what a fantastic husband, Sara, he knows everything! That's not very common, you know?"

"Aha, Juan is my steering wheel. I don't know what I'd do without him. He's forever reminding me when I've got appointments, asking me if I've taken my pills…"

"So, we know who's going to go to school meetings, to remember every word teachers say about your son," jokes Dr. Casona.

"Or daughter," Juan smiles proudly.

"Well, take a last look at your baby, so far, and you can go celebrate. Will you be wanting to take the triple screening tests?[32]

"Which ones are those?" Sara asks.

"The Down syndrome ones," Juan replies.

"Indeed, they're done to see if the baby has any kind of anomaly, such as Down syndrome, spina bifida…"

They both look at each other and Sara replies, "I guess we will, we'll be taking every test we should take, won't we?"

"Sure," her husband nods.

"The option's there," Nuria clarifies, "even if this is not a diagnostic test as such. It doesn't tell you yes or no for sure, but it puts you within a risk group. We will know if you have a high or low risk of having a baby with these conditions we're talking about. If the risk is high, and at your age it will probably be, then you can have an amniocentesis, which is a diagnostic test that tells us exactly what your baby has, in case they have something."

"We will, won't we?" says Sara looking at her husband for approval.

"Let's see, the reason I'm telling you all this is because everything has its risks. Amniocentesis has a miscarriage risk of one percent, which can be considered as a rather high risk. The screening, by putting you within a risk group, may worry you without reason, because it would tell you something like you have a possibility of one in 40, 70, 180… of having a baby with problems. So, if you decided not to do the amniocentesis[33], you'd go through the whole pregnancy with the anxiety of not knowing exactly whether your baby has that problem or not."

They look at each other confused, without pretty much knowing what to say.

"In short, I have made it very complicated. You must consider if you would terminate this pregnancy if your baby had a problem. If you'd go ahead with the pregnancy at all risks, then there's no point in taking any of these tests."

---

[32] Screening tests: Tests that tell the pregnant woman a statistical value of the risk of having a baby with a given pathology, anomaly or syndrome.

[33] Amniocentesis: Test in which a small sample of the amniotic fluid surrounding the baby is taken to be analysed.

"I think I'm speaking on behalf of both of us if I say that, with all the pains we've taken to get to this point, we'd be having this baby even if it was made out of cardboard; and that I won't be having a termination for anything in this world."

Juan kisses her forehead.

"It's decided, then," says Nuria; "now, you go and enjoy yourselves. Tell Nati to give you an appointment in a month as you go out, and we'll be meeting then. If you need anything in the meantime, you know where I am."

"Thank you very much, Nuria, we are so grateful!"

"Nothing to thank me for, I've just been the bearer of good news."

"You know it's more than that," says Sara kissing her.

The moment they are out of Dr. Casona's practice, Juan and Sara look at each other and hug again.

"We're back to having a baby," says Sara. "That's totally incredible, my love. You are the best husband anyone could have. Thank God you insisted on coming. If I hadn't accepted, if you hadn't insisted so much... now we still wouldn't know I was pregnant and our baby is healthy and strong, growing inside me. Darling, I have never been happier, and I owe everything to you."

"I'm so happy, Sara. I'm ecstatic. I just wanted you to see someone to make sure you were all right, and look at the news we've received! What do we do? What would you like to do to celebrate? Shall we go to Mario's for dinner? Shall we go to your sister's? Do you want a seafood dinner? What would you like to do?"

"And what if we pack and spend a few nights at our hotel?"

"Yes, of course, let's go home, take a couple of things and go away. I'll call Sebas, tell him I'm disappearing for a couple of nights and it's done."

Maternity Hospital.
Staff room.

Marta, Cande and Celia are in the staff room. Cande is brewing coffee. Ana comes in and turns the TV on. On screen, there's a famous Spanish singer with her baby in her arms, typically posing at the door of a private clinic after having her baby.

"She has already given birth?" asks Cande.

"Looks like it," replies Marta.

"Give birth, my ass," replies Ana, "C-section, I bet my life. They all do, these celebrities. Just look at her, she can't even move!"

There's a silence as all of them look at the screen and listen:

"The baby is a boy and he weighed three kilos. He was born by C-section last Monday morning. Both mother and son are in perfect state".

"You have to be daft to let them do that to you," Cande says. "Do they really think it's the best for their babies? Does anyone in their right mind really believe that a C-section is better than a vaginal birth?"

"It depends on who for," Marta replies, "I know some who, at the first chance, do a C-section because it's the best for them."

"Yeah, well, you're right. But that's the lazy, unscrupulous doctor (I won't deny they exist) who gets rid of a woman by sectioning her the minute he has the chance to, just to have a quiet night. But that's not the case here. The obstetricians of the celebrities don't do it in order not to be woken up at three am. They do it for other reasons, which are also very clear to me. What I don't get is what makes a woman believe that a C-section is better than a vaginal birth. To her, who's suffering it on her own flesh: how do they sell it to her that a cut in her belly is better than what nature intended? Are they all stupid?"

"I don't think they're stupid," replies Marta, "I think they're victims. As are all the women who, for some reason or another, have an *'unne-cesarean'*."

"These ones are more the victims yet," adds Celia, pointing with her chin towards the TV, "because they are completely used by the private hospitals. As they're famous, the reputation of whoever does the C-section will soar like a rocket. Can you imagine one of these doctors saying at a press conference: "There's nothing to tell, we just let nature follow its course and this is the result. Oh, and as us doctors only act when things deviate from normality, here's the real expert in normal births, the midwife who was with them…?" she says, taking Marta by the arm to stage the hypothetical situation.

"No, no, please, don't take photos of me, all the merit's on the mother and the baby, I just did my job giving them what they needed…"

"Girl, for the one time in your lifetime that you are at the birth of a celebrity, promote yourself! Direct her pushes, do an 'epis' to her or say you gave the baby a bottle because the mother was too tired to breastfeed…" says Cande, and they all burst into laughter.

"Well, there's the crux of the matter. In what you just said," says Celia pointing towards Cande. "What professional, presented with such a chance to get recognised, would say the merit is not theirs, that they were just there? Or, in the case of a doctor, that he didn't even enter the room because it was not necessary? Believe it or not, the least important in this case are that woman and that baby."

"That's why I'm asking you again, because I don't get it. If the fact that a C-section is harmful for both mother and baby is a proven thing and if it's also proven that the baby needs," says Cande stressing the word, "… their mother's birth hormones for their correct emotional development; if there is no real benefit for birthing and being born by C-section, but all the opposite, how do you convince a woman that she must go through an operation, when there's a much better alternative?"

"By turning things over," Ana butts in. "By lying to her. You sell her birth as something bad, full of possible things that can go wrong, dirty, for poor people: 'Your baby coming out of your vagina is for riffraff'. You tell her that a C-section is much better, that she can choose the date, that she won't have to wait until the fortieth week, that this way her skin won't stretch anymore in the last weeks…"
"What nonsense," Marta mocks.
"That you won't go through labour pains…" Ana goes on enumerating reasons.
"No; you just go through a much more painful recovery period for weeks, when you won't be able to hold your baby or laugh…" adds Cande.
"Hey, I'm only recounting the things they say to convince them, I don't agree with them," Ana complains and she goes on with her sequence, "…that you recuperate much better, your body gets less spoiled, your pussy won't lose firmness, whereas after a natural birth you piss yourself all the time…"
"Seeing it that way… And they believe all that?" Cande inquires, saddened.
"See, there's your answer. They all end up with a C-section. The princess, the singer, the model, the football player's wife…"
"Not all of them," Celia intervenes, "the singer from 'El sueño de Morfeo' has birthed at her home; one of the Bosé sisters did too; Melanie Olivares tried to; Eva Hache[34] birthed without drugs and you should listen to her speaking about birth, oxytocin, breastfeeding… she's awfully well informed, that woman. And Cindy Crawford, Demi Moore, Meryl Streep, Pamela Anderson, Gisele Bundchen…"
"Who's that?" asks Marta.
"The best paid model in the world. She birthed at home, I think twice, and you can see her on social media with her baby hanging from her tit as they make her up and, besides, she remarks she's being made up and nothing else. Completely normalising breastfeeding a child while she works."
"Damn it, those are the models society needs. Women who live off her bodies, who

---

[34] Different Spanish celebrities.

give birth and are proud of it," says Cande. "I knew nothing about these celebrities. How do you know these things?"

"Through Facebook," Celia replies. "But you see, that's exactly what happens with birthing women, these things are not told, they aren't voiced because private hospitals could lose their business if women birth naturally, speak about it and some of them even enjoy it. What a pity these experiences are stolen from women, just for the money…"

"I'm not on Facebook," Cande says.

"There are also forums for professionals, midwives or women looking for truthful information when they get pregnant," Celia replies.

"Yeah, well, those from 'El parto es nuestro'[35] who call us "midwifesaurus" and who think they know something because they have read a book by Michel Odent," Ana replies.

"Well, that's our fault, Ana," Marta tells her, "If we have gotten to this point where a woman has to inform herself by reading lots of books and fight half the hospital to have a normal birth, it's because people on this side are not doing it well."

"Are you defending them?" Ana replies, incredulous, "I wasn't expecting this from you."

"Me and practically every midwife I know. And the ones who don't, it's because they fail to understand that what these mothers ask is absolutely legitimate and is their right, as users of the public health system."

"What? A woman telling me not to get an IV access on her, not to monitor her or not to do an episiotomy has a right to it?" asks Ana, stunned.

"Absolutely," say Marta and Celia almost at the same time.

"It's her body," Celia adds. "And over your body, you decide."

"Well, but there's also a baby in the equation," Ana protests.

"Over whom the mother has legal authority and power of decision, in anything concerning them. And that's when it has been born; babies have no rights before."

"Well, if I get one of those telling me not to do an episiotomy to her and then her baby dies, I'll denounce, mark my words," Ana replies.

---

[35] "El parto es nuestro" means "Birth is ours". It is a Spanish association that fights for mothers' and babies' rights during childbirth.

"That's what you don't get, Ana," Celia tells her. "What these women ask for is for you not to do anything to them that's not strictly necessary; no routine episiotomy, no IV just because. But they do ask you to give them their baby straight away when it's born, to delay cord clamping…"

"But then, if anything happens, I'm not taking responsibility for it."

"But she is the one who's responsible for it, always, whatever happens. The one who will have her body cut open, or will take a baby with a problem home will always be her. The things they stand for and they ask us not to do to them are the ones that are avoidable. What mother doesn't want the best for her baby? What mother would say "No, I want a natural birth" when you tell her she needs an emergency C-section because her baby is in danger?" Celia goes on.

"Those pains in the neck? All of them!"

"What nonsense you say, Ana, for heaven's sake!" exclaims Cande, "every mother wants what's best for her child, and those women do too. And that's why they fight the system, because they always want the best for their babies. You have given birth yourself. What would you think if you go back home minus a leg because the person taking care of you considered that was the best for you and for your future births?"

"Come on, that is really nonsense," Ana replies.

"That, exaggerating, is the same as doing a routine episiotomy, the kind you like so much."

"No way. It's been proven that a clean cut is more…"

"A clean cut is more what?! More of a hell for the future sex life of that woman?" interrupts an indignant Marta, "do dare: put yourself to shame saying the words that follow. Think about it before you do. Tell your workmates you haven't read a single book or an article since you finished your studies. It's been more than twenty years that all the scientific evidence has been adamant about the routine use of episiotomy: that it shouldn't be done except for very isolated cases. Look for a study from this century in favour of routine episiotomies."

Ana stands up, ashamed, and leaves in a hurry.

"And don't you do another one ever again before you find it!" Marta yells furiously.

After a long silence, Marta says, "I overdid it, didn't I?"

Nobody replies for a few seconds.

"I don't think you have," says Cande finally, "she's a show-off, we all know how she works: 'Same ole, same ole'. If a woman asks her for anything, she tries not to give it to her with any excuse, and if in the end she does, it's reluctantly, as if she were doing her a favour. If she can, she'll take it away from her in the next moment with any excuse. Whatever it is: the ball, walking, standing up, a different position from lithotomy[36]... and on top of all that, she is proud of being more behind the times than black and white TV. Good for you. She needs someone telling her things as they are. So, my answer is: no, you haven't gone too far. She deserves it and the women in her care deserve a brave woman like you telling her what you just did."

Celia nods in agreement, "and as you can see, nobody went running after her. We all stayed here."

"It's clear whose side we're on," Cande goes on, hugging Marta. "We need brave
people like you standing up against people like Ana."

"Thank you," says Marta, hugging her back.

Nuria Casona comes into the room and pours herself some coffee.

"Gee, that woman's birthed already?" she says pointing at the TV.

"C-section, Nuria, C-section," Candela corrects.

"Sure, *natürlich,*" Nuria replies.

"I'd love to know your opinion on all those celebrities' C-sections," asks Celia.

"There's nothing to have an opinion on, Celia."

"But you obstetricians must also be taught in university that vaginal birth is better than having a C-section, that you must only operate if the birth goes really wrong. That C-sections are there as the last resource, not as something to be offered to women as an option... *Primum non nocere,*[37] Nuria," Celia complains

---

[36] Lithotomy: A position of the body with the legs separated, flexed, and supported in raised stirrups.

[37] Primum non nocere: Hippocratic oath doctors sign: "First, do no harm".

"Money talks," Nuria replies.

"They do it just for the money?"

"Money, prestige, avoiding legal complaints… if anything goes wrong after a birth, you are in deep trouble. If anything goes wrong after a C-section…"

"Which is much more likely to happen," Cande cuts in. "The rates of infant and maternal morbidity and mortality are much higher for C- sections than normal births."

"But if anything goes wrong after a C-section," Nuria continues, "they can always say: 'We did all we could'."

"Even if it's a lie?" protests Celia, "even if the C-section is what killed that mother, or the main cause for that baby to be admitted to NNU and get a chest drain?"

"Yes, but how do you prove that?" Nuria asks her.

"But there are more mothers and babies in hospital due to C-sections, so these surgeries must have an influence on those results."

"Of course, Celia, we all know that C-sections can cause iatrogenia[38] and that there's lots of people out there damaged by a C-section that shouldn't have been done. But if as a doctor you do one, there are upsides. First, it's more difficult for you to get a complaint because it's being perceived that you have done everything you could. Second, in case you get a complaint, how can anyone prove that the C-section shouldn't have been done? It's practically impossible: you could always have an excuse: fetal distress, cephalopelvic disproportion… Third, can't you see that for us a bad result is practically synonymous with disqualification and maybe jail?"

"What a pity we have got to that stage!" Celia says.

"It happens in many professions, but it's true that now -more than ever- we practise defensive medicine. And the whole society suffers the consequences."

"But if you got one of these in your private practice telling you she wants a normal

birth, what would you tell her?" Marta asks her.

"I'd tell her to go on, of course, that we'd make everything possible for her to have it."

---

[38] Iatrogenia: Damage caused by a drug, medical or surgical procedure done by the doctor within a correct indication.

"So, why don't they get more information? Many of them have studied! They are cultured people!"

"Right, but I can't think of anyone more vulnerable than they are. If they 'sell' you the best professionals in the country, it's normal you have blind confidence in them. If they tell you the best for you is a C-section, because you can fit it in your husband's agenda to your convenience, because your pregnancy will be weeks shorter, because… it's the same, you know as well as I do how many things you can tell them to convince them a C-section is the best of the best, make them believe you and stay convinced they have been better treated for being who they are."

"The worst thing is that that's just the tip of the iceberg," Celia laments.

"What do you mean?" asks Cande.

"I mean if they do elective C-sections to celebrities, the rich will also come asking for them, and then the rest of society will demand C-sections too and will claim them as an option, not just an emergency solution. And this lousy patriarchal society we have, instead of advancing towards equality will go farther and farther away from it, and women will get C-sections they think they have freely chosen… But the thing is, if you don't know your options you don't have any. I read a quote from Gloria Lemay, a Canadian midwife, not long ago, which said that roses open each one at its own time and nobody would think of forcing a bud open, because we all know we'd destroy it. However, that's what we're doing to babies. Because we think we're gods, because we don't know that birthing that way, forcing births that way, will have dire consequences in their future life. And when we all know about those consequences, there will have passed decades in which babies will have been extracted from their mothers, who will have been deprived of one of the most joyful moments in their lives. And this is such an aberration, and will have such an impact in the future, that we will come to be remembered in posterity as the society that emptied wombs, the society that forced their most precious buds open."

Week 20

Lorena and Luci go together to the clinic where Lorena's pregnancy is being followed up. She's so thrilled… She loves having ultrasounds and being able to see her baby.

"Good morning, Lorena", greets Tomás, her obstetrician, as she walks into his office. "How are you doing?"

"Very well. Happy."

"Any distress, nausea, vomiting?"

"No, the truth is I feel wonderful. No problem at all."

"And she eats everything. Tell her something," her friend Luci intervenes.

Lorena looks at her friend, annoyed, as Luci goes on, "there are many things pregnant women can't eat, aren't there?"

"Not so many, really. Be a bit more careful with raw things, wash any fruits and veg you'll be eating raw, have sushi -if you eat it- with a lot of wasabi… even if it's now compulsory to freeze fish beforehand in restaurants if they're serving it raw."

"And cured ham?" Lorena asks.

"You can eat ham and cold cuts during pregnancy without any problem," the obstetrician replies.

"Are you sure?" Luci asks, "they always say pregnant women can't eat ham, don't they?"

"That was before, when we knew less. There was less hygiene in general and people killed their pigs with little or no sanitary control. Nowadays, all pigs undergo many controls before they get to the shops. The possibilities of getting toxoplasmosis, which is the illness infected meat would cause, are very, very low. Besides, extreme temperatures would kill the eggs, so, if it makes you feel more at ease, you can freeze cold cuts for a couple of days. One thing you should be careful with though is cat excrement."

"I don't have a cat."

"Right, but you don't know where your neighbour's cat might have passed through, or any street cat. So, if you have any plants outside or a vegetable patch, you'd better wear gloves if you touch the soil, and wash your hands thoroughly afterwards. Soak lettuce and tomatoes and add a drop of bleach to the water, but with a dropper, right? Better dilute a bit of bleach in a dropper and every time you clean veggies you add a couple of drops of that dilution to the water. Aside from this, eat whatever you want, without any excess, whatever you feel like."

"Even a hamburger?" Lorena asks him.

"Sure, girl, why shouldn't you eat a hamburger?"

Lorena sticks out her tongue to Luci and mocks her.

"Go to the other room, Lorena, and take your clothes off from the waist down," the obstetrician tells her. "We're going to do a scan, I guess you'll want to see your baby."

When they get out of the doctor's office, Lorena and Luci walk towards the bus stop.

Manuel has parked his car practically in front of his friend Tomás' clinic and he sees Lorena going out with her friend. He has no doubt it was her Tomás was talking about. Nevertheless, he had to see it for himself. Lorena is pregnant. From him. He is going to have a baby with her, the woman of his life. They could be happy together, for sure she'd be delighted to have him by her side, to be a family the three of them. Send Clarisa to hell, now that Elena and David were grownups and practically raised... He imagines a scene from his possible new life with Lorena by his side, the baby sleeping peacefully in its cradle, by the fireplace.

Yes, he'd do that for her. He'd leave Clarisa and her ridiculous views on life: she was nobody, and look what he had turned her into…! And he would live happily with this wonderful woman he loves being with, and would walk her arm in arm and people would look at them and envy him and think: *this is the bloke who's fucking her.* Besides, with a baby; so, nobody could think she was a whore. Because she wouldn't be one anymore, of course, they'd be a family and live together and… Fuck it, the vaccinations, the paediatrician, the nights of endless crying without any apparent reason, the sagging breasts, the hairy legs and dirty hair… No, no, no. Not Lorena. He'd get her a nanny from the day the baby was born; so that she didn't ruin her looks, so that she'd go on being who she was, always, magnificent for him, every day. That's what happened to Clarisa, and to Carlos' wife, and to his sister and every woman he knows; but only because they haven't had the right man by their side. If he gets her a girl to take care of the baby from day one, she'd go on being the bombshell she is and he'd have her home every day and she'd be his wife. Yes, he could ask her to marry him, if she likes the idea… but how could she not like him, if that's every woman's dream? Getting married to a rich guy if possible… *Yes! I'm going to have a date with her and I'll propose it to her. It's impossible that she says no*, he thinks as he gets lost into the traffic.

Maternity Hospital.
Outpatients department.
Dr. López has just finished Sol's ultrasound, and Sonia and Herminia are helping her up from the bed.
"We've been having a look at the induced lactation," Sonia whispers to the nurse, "we are going to do it."
"Great! I'm glad, for you and for your babies. They are very lucky. Breast milk is the best thing you can give them," says Herminia with a huge smile.
"Well, everything's going splendidly," says the doctor as they approach his desk, "I'll be seeing you in a month."
"Yes, quite. What about the antenatal classes?" asks Soledad.

"Oh, they won't be necessary. As we're checking you in the hospital, you don't need them. That's for learning how to breathe and suchlike, but as we take care of you and you'll be getting the epidural straight away, it's not necessary that you waste your time with those matters."

"Ahh!" says Sol, annoyed.

"Right, but they teach you many more things," Sonia butts in, "from what I hear, they give you quite a lot of information about the babies' first days, how to bathe them, how to make them burp, how to breastfeed... we are first time mothers and we'd like to go."

"I don't know about that, because as we look after high-risk pregnancies nobody has ever asked to go to classes. As the low-risk ones don't see their doctor half as much, classes are a follow-up more than anything; but as you're high-risk, your follow-up is much more continuous. What I mean is, you don't need any classes."

"Ask in the GP practice that's closest to your home," intervenes Herminia, "I'm sure the midwife there will have a gap for you. These classes are very good for first time mothers, and if they want to go, let them go."

"So, you just heard: your Health Centre will inform you," says the doctor, leaning back in his chair.

Sol and Son get out of the doctor's.

"It's amazing how difficult it is for this doctor to give some information, depending on what it is," Sonia tells her wife, "as if he should care that we go or don't go to antenatal classes."

"Yes. It's true that he doesn't appreciate things not being done his way," says Sol, "I'm going to call María, that way instead of going to class anywhere, we can go together and have fun, the four of us."

"Good idea. As we'll be the only couple of mothers, at least we'll go with someone we know."

Luci is looking for her mobile inside her handbag as the bus approaches. She can't find it. She has no clue what she's done with it, but it's not in her handbag.

"But when was the last time you saw it?" asks Lorena.

"I don't know," her friend replies, "I had it, that's for sure. I had it in the waiting room, because I was checking my Facebook… Sorry, Lore: I think I left it in the waiting room."

"It's all right. We'll go back and get it. It's a doctor's practice, not a bar: I'm sure it will be there.

When they turn the corner, Lorena sees him and stops dead. Luci looks at her and asks, what's up? You look as if you've seen a ghost."

"That's him," Lorena says grabbing her arm.

"Who's him?" Luci asks, confused.

"He knows, Luci, he knows."

"What are you talking about? What do you mean? Who?"

"That's his car. That sports car over there. He's just left from there, right in front of the clinic; he knows, Luci, he knows."

"But what makes you say that? It has to be a coincidence, come on…"

"No, Luci. He's just gone away from the clinic's doorstep, I've seen him with my very own eyes, it can't possibly be a coincidence. I don't know how he did it, but it's obvious that he knows."

"But maybe it's simply…" Luci goes on.

"Luci. We are in Madrid. The father of my child leaves in his car from the doorstep of the clinic where I just had my pregnancy check-up, and you think it might be a coincidence? It's impossible. I must disappear, I have to get out of here. I have no clue how he got wind of it, but he knows and I don't trust him an inch. I must disappear. Shit! I have to vanish off the face of the earth."

"Well, I don't know, maybe… what a fuckup! And what are you going to do? It's been so sudden, just like that…"

"I don't know, I don't know, but I have to disappear. Remember what I told you? When he saw his daughter's boyfriend in the hotel and he said he was going to kill him? I don't want to have anything to do with him. He meant it, Luci, he wanted to kill him because he had seen him with me… If he knows I'm pregnant with his child, which he does for some reason, he does know, he'd kill me, I'm telling you. I mean it, he knows and he's after me."

"Right. Let's go get my mobile and go home. There we'll think of what to do."

Manuel has been thinking about how to tell Lorena for several days. The more he thinks about it, the more he likes the idea: starting a family with Lorena. He wants to do it right, but he doesn't know how. He could buy her a ring and invite her somewhere for the weekend. She'll like the idea for sure. *And besides, the poor thing, she still hasn't dared tell me anything because she must think I'd hate the idea. She's going to be stunned when I tell her I'll leave Clarisa for her.*

Week 23

"How are you?"

"Frantic. I haven't slept a wink all night. But she's almost here, my girl is coming. I'm dying to see her! One year; one whole year travelling around the world and me, on tenterhooks every day because, even if she knows what she's doing, well, she's so far away and if anything happens to her…"

"Well, Alicia, she's back safe and sound."

"How I asked her and begged her not to go, or at least not for so long! I told her a year was far too much, but she kept going on and on: that time overwhelmed her, that freedom this and that… and when Ingrid starts talking about freedom, there's no stopping her. In short, I'm dying to see her. She's here and I'm going to smother her with kisses, and I'm not letting her go anywhere for a long time; I have to make up for this lost year of hugs I've missed."

"Well, let's see how long she lasts, your daughter is not one to stand still for long…"

"I understand everyone wanting to live their life, but why can't her life be more or less normal, as everybody else's? She could look for a job in the city, fall in love, live happily and come home for lunch on Sundays. Like yours; well, like everyone else's, is that asking too much? But this child of mine: a trip around South America, aimlessly, she gets a ticket to Bogotá and from there she will see… To Bogotá! With the quantity of people they kidnap down there, especially foreigners! You have to be crazy. Remember the other one they kidnapped, she had the same name and all. Who knows, they could mistake my Ingrid for her or something…"

"Alicia, that's enough: Ingrid is 32, she knows what she does and danger is everywhere, Colombia is no more dangerous if you're called Ingrid; it's just a coincidence."

"Ouch, yes! Mili, you're right, but as I've had such a hard time... Well, you know it better than anybody, you've been my shoulder to cry on. I guess as I won't be able to complain anymore I'm profiting from these last moments."
"C'mon, Ali, you're a piece of work... what time is she arriving?"
"In a few hours, although I'm already taking a shower and leaving to wait for her there."
"Don't go too early, airports are very tiresome."
"Don't worry, I'll have breakfast relaxedly, get ready and leave. Big kiss and I'll be calling you. Maybe not today, but soon."
"Ok. Kiss, and another one for Ingrid."
"I will. Ta-ra."

Manuel has been thinking of Lorena for some time. He takes his phone and rings her. He feels like hearing her voice, talking to her. See her reaction on hearing him. Then, he hangs up quickly: he'd better call her from his office. The poor girl must be so frightened that she might not answer her phone because she doesn't know what to say. He's always been very careful with his calls, so this would be the first time he'd be calling her on her mobile from his office.
"Hello?" Lorena answers the phone.
"Hello princess, how are you?" Manuel replies, "I am delighted to hear your voice, as usual. I want to see you. I've missed you so much. I haven't seen you for so long..."
"Fine, yes. We'll meet whenever you want. Me too, I'm dying to be with you," Lorena lies.
"We'll meet this Friday then. In the hotel, at six o'clock."
"See you then, Doctor," says Lorena before hanging up.

Madrid-Barajas Airport.
"Moooom!"
"My beautiful baby! What a joy!" Alicia exclaims running to her daughter and hugging her between her arms.
"How beautiful you look, Mom!"

"You're the one who looks beautiful! Let me see you. But you're even a bit more plump and all! That's great! And me thinking that you'd be skinny, you must have been eating so badly…"

"Mom, you always manage to remind me how thin I am, even when you're telling me I'm plumper," her daughter tells her with a smile.

"No, dear, I'm telling you as a good thing; you look beautiful, I love you a lot and I'm very happy that you're here. God, how I've missed you," she says hugging her again, "how was the journey? Are you tired?"

"Yes, Mom, I'm knackered. I didn't sleep at all on the plane and, besides, there was this man by my side taking all the space he could and I could hardly stretch my legs. So, I've spent half the flight walking up and down the aisle."

"Don't worry, we'll take a taxi, go home, eat something and you go to bed."

"Well, and you? What do you tell me? Have you gotten any boyfriend while I was away?" Ingrid asks her mom.

"Not really, dear, some flings, that's all, but nothing serious."

"Well, if you've had some joys from time to time, that's very good. We'll find you a fantastic guy one day."

"And you?" her mom asks.

"Like you, nothing serious. But lots of wonderful experiences, I'll be telling you."

"Good, I feel more at ease now, dear. I was afraid you'd have done one of yours, like going back there to live in the jungle half naked because you were in love with a huge black bloke or something."

"But Mom, where do you think I've been?" Ingrid smiles, "I'm not surprised you had such a hard time. C'mon, you silly-billy, don't worry. My plans right now are staying around here and not straying too far."

"Welcome home, dear," says Alicia opening the door.

"Home! How good this house always smells. You don't know how much I've missed this smell. The smell of my home. I wanted so much to be back here!"

"Dear, you sound as if you missed your home more than your mother."

"Don't be daft, Mom! Remember that I've been homeless for a year, and that's been the hardest. You, I had when I wanted to, even if it was by phone. But this feeling of rest you have when you have a home, that I haven't experienced for a year, and it's a wonderful feeling being in your own four walls."
"You see? You shouldn't have gone."
"Mom, please don't start. I'm glad I went away, it's been wonderful. Taking this year for me has been the best thing I've done in my life, but it's normal to miss some things, to have bad moments sometimes… but the scale tilts in favour of the trip, so don't pretend to be its victim. I'm back, and I don't want to start having arguments this early. Let's enjoy each other a bit, before falling back to our fighting routine."
"Of course, dear, I don't want to fight with you. I've made 'cocido',[39] shall I heat some up for you?"
"Of course! Mom's 'cocido', how wonderful! I'll have a shower as you get it ready, okay?"
While Alicia is preparing the meal, Ingrid is humming in the shower. She feels happy and she's delighted to be back. She just has to tell her mother, and she's been putting together how to tell her for some time, so everything will be fine. She won't be happy to start with, but she will come to understand. She's a fighter, her mother, who raised her on her own, and with her head held high!
Ingrid closes the tap and wipes the water off her face with her hands. She opens her eyes, and there's her mother, petrified, her mouth agape.
"But, my dear…!"
"Sorry, Mom, I didn't want you to know this way."
"But, weren't you going to tell me?"
"Sure, I was, Mom, I was going to tell you now at lunch. Telling you in the middle of the airport or in the taxi wasn't right. It's something big and wonderful and I wanted to tell you here at home. I'm going to have a baby, Mom."
"But, whose baby?"

---

[39] Cocido -literally "boiled"- is a traditional Spanish winter dish, consisting of different vegetables and meats boiled together -hence the name- with chickpeas.

"Mine, Mom; mine and yours. There's no huge black bloke waiting for me anywhere in the jungle. Don't worry about that. This child has no father. That's how I wanted it and that's how it will be."

"But does he know?"

"No, Mom; not even I know who he is. Stop worrying. My story won't be like yours. This baby will have a wonderful mother and grandmother and nobody giving us headaches. This is what I wanted, it hasn't been an accident and I want you to be happy for me, because I am. I love you, Mom," says Ingrid hugging her astonished mother.

"Me too, dear, me too."

Manuel goes into the lobby of the hotel where he usually meets Lorena when he can't spend the night with her. He invents a long meeting or a dinner with his mates, and this way he can meet her without Clarisa suspecting anything. Although he doesn't care anymore. She may suspect all she wants, because everything's going to change when he talks to her. This very night, he'll be telling Clarisa to leave home. Or maybe he'll be the one to do it. He won't mind if his wife wants to keep the house anyway when he's finally with Lorena. If he's going to start a new life, better not to do it in that house. They should start in another one, both of them together. From zero.

While he's in the lift, he notices he's getting nervous. When was the last time he was? He can't even remember. "Frightened she might reject you?" he smiles and replies, "that's impossible. She's just a whore and: weren't all women so crazy some years ago with "Pretty Woman" they even found being one was glamorous, in case they found their Richard Gere? So, there's no better Richard Gere than me, who can afford to give her anything she wants."

Manuel enters the hotel room. He's surprised to find it empty: Lorena has always been on time. *How strange!*

He looks at his watch: five past six. Well, five minutes are forgivable…

18:15. Manuel looks at the time, impatient. "What's up with her, why is she this late?" he wonders, considerably annoyed. He takes the phone and dials Lorena's number: '*The number you have dialled is not available, please try again later*' he hears.
"But, where the hell are you? Just you wait till you arrive! All the money I pay you and you're making ME wait!"

18:40. Manuel presses the redial key for the umpteenth time. Lorena's mobile is still off.
"Is she all right?" he wonders. "Maybe something's happened to her and she's gone to see Tomás."
He takes the phone again and calls his friend.
"What's up, Manu?" Tomás answers instantly.
"Hello, Tomás," he replies, suddenly shy. He has not realised he hadn't thought about what to tell Tomás, but it's too late now and he's there, on the other end of the line.
"Look, I'm calling you because I'm looking for that girl, the one you mentioned the other day. The Brazilian with the perfect tits…"
"Lorena?"
"Yes, Lorena. You won't happen to have any news from her?"
"Err, no. But, do you know her?"
"No; well, yes. It doesn't matter, I just don't know how to find her and I thought maybe you did. Never mind, forget it."
"Well, I do have her data, but…"
"No, no, it's okay. It was nonsense. We'll be meeting soon, right?"
"Yes, sure. Call me whenever you want and we'll have another dinner."
"Yes. Goodbye."
Manuel hangs up and looks at his watch: 18:50. Maybe she didn't get it right and she thinks we meet at seven.
"C'mon, Lorena, why are you so late? Do come, I'm going to make you the happiest woman on earth."

19:15. Manuel pays for the room and leaves the hotel. He gets into his car and goes to Lorena's house: she'll have to see him, if she wants to or not. He deserves an explanation, and this won't be the end of the matter.

22:00. Clarisa calls him for the third time and Manuel rejects her call once again. *Shit, Clarisa, always calling at the worst moments; you only think of yourself.* He sends her a WhatsApp message explaining he's in a meeting and he'll come home as soon as he can, but it will be long.

He tries Lorena's number again: it's still off. *But, where are you?* he wonders. *You're clearly not at home, if you were your phone would be on… Are you with another man? No. It can't be. We agreed that you'd be just for me, that I'd always come first; that's why I pay you what I pay you, so that's not possible. But if it's not that, I can't understand it. It's true that your phone has never rang when we were together. Have you found anyone better? No. Never. It can't be. You'll see next time we meet, you're in big trouble, you fucking bitch. I was about to offer you the garden of Eden and you're fucking around, playing to make me jealous. No, Lorena, baby, no, you don't do this to the father of your child. This is not a good way to start our life together. There are many things I will have to make very clear to you when we talk, like I'm the boss here and you're the one who obeys. Period.*

At twenty past eleven, Manuel leaves what he thinks is Lorena's home after calling her one last time. *You'll see what's coming to you next time we meet*, he thinks as he disappears into the traffic.

Lorena and Luci are together at Lorena's home.

"You know what you're going to do?" Luci asks her friend.

"No, I don't know yet. The only thing I know is that I'm not going to see him ever again. It's obvious that he knows. The other day he called me from a landline, which is something he has never done, ever. As he got me by surprise, I agreed to meet him, not wanting to go through a bad moment over the phone, or that he could notice I sounded weird. So, I said yes, of course, as usual."

"When did you agree to meet him?"

"Today. At six. Same place."

Luci has a look at the clock on her friend's wall.

"It's ten past ten," she says.

"Yes. He must be climbing up the walls by now," Lorena smiles.

"He might think there's something wrong with you…"

"Him? Possibly. He could never imagine anyone taking a decision not good for him. I bet he still hasn't realised he'll never see me again."

"And do you think it's safe for you to stay here in Madrid?"

"So far, yes. Carefully, until I decide what to do next. I think I'm staying here for a few more months and then, maybe, I'll go back to Brazil. To Rio, maybe, as I have many relatives down there and it's a good place to start from zero."

"But isn't it taking too much of a risk? I'm not sure; and if he's waiting for you where he thinks you live one night and you arrive with another customer?"

"Well, Luci, we've been in more difficult situations. There's nothing easier than moving from a false address… from now on, I'll tell everyone to drop me off at a different place, that I've moved, and that's it." After a short silence, she tells Lucía, "I'm going to have a shower and go to bed. Are you staying?"

"No, I'm going home; I'm going to the hairdresser's tomorrow and I prefer leaving now than having to hurry tomorrow morning."

"So, do me a favour, go around my "non-home" and tell me if he's there."

"Right. Do you think he will be?"

"He might. He's capable of that and much more. Look, I'm even frightened to turn my mobile on, I must have over twenty missed calls. I won't do it until tomorrow; that way, I'll get some sleep. By the way, call me from a number I know, because I won't be answering any calls from unknown numbers anymore."

"Whatever you say, babe."

Maternity Hospital.
Staff Room. 8.10 am.

"Celia, can you help me, please?" says Begoña, the nurse working in the Postnatal Ward as she comes into the staff room.

"Sure, tell me."

"See, I have the English girl with the adoption and the cocaine in my bay, and as I speak no English…"

"And I don't understand your Spanish. Slow down, what? I don't know what you are talking about," Celia cuts her with a smile. "An English girl with an adoption and cocaine? What's that?"

"Oops, sorry, I thought they had told you on the shift handover."

"Just about Labour ward, they don't tell us anything about Postnatal."

"Ok. So, I have this English girl who just gave birth and is giving her baby up for adoption. And her records say she's been drinking and taking cocaine during pregnancy. And the people in NNU asked me to find out how much she's been taking, to evaluate what they should give the baby for her abstinence syndrome. Could you please ask her?"

"What's her name?"

"Kaa tee eh," reads Begoña showing Celia her records.

"Keh ee tee, it's pronounced Keh ee tee."

They both walk together to the postnatal ward and Begoña says as they come in, "she's the one in bed four."

"Hello Katie. My name is Celia; I'm one of the midwives on duty today. How are you?"

"Ok," Katie replies shyly.

She must be just past twenty and with her there are a boy and a girl about her age.

"I need to talk to you about a few things regarding the baby. Are you happy for your friends to be here while I do?"

"Yes, they're ok."

"Ok. So, you're giving the baby up for adoption, right?"

Katie nods.

"I don't know if you know this, but the baby might develop withdrawal syndrome. So, it is very important for us to know how much coke and booze you have taken during this pregnancy."

Katie nods shyly again.

"Have you taken coke every day?" continues Celia.

"Almost every day," nods Katie again.

"During the whole pregnancy?"

"No, only the last four, five months, since I arrived in Spain."

"And before that, how much did you take?"
"Just the weekends."
"You have been drinking, as well?"
"Yes."
"What?"
"Vodka."
"And how much would you say?"
"A bottle."
"A bottle a day?"
Katie nods again, ashamed."
"Anything else? Any other drugs?"
Katie shakes her head in denial.
"I guess this must be very difficult for you. You have helped your baby a lot by being so honest. Thank you, "Celia tells her.

"Your baby's blood results are positive in cocaine," a loud voice can be heard saying in the ward. Celia turns her head and sees a guy about thirty years old in a white coat waving some analysis in his hand and walking towards them, "we have to take your baby for some tests…"
"Stop it, stop it," Celia tells him getting up from the bed where she was sitting. "Wait a minute, come here," and she takes him to the corridor, which is empty.
"Man, you can't just come in yelling like that about such a delicate matter, even if it's in English."
"Yes, yes, excuse me, you're right. I didn't realise."
"Who are you?"
"I'm Miguel, registrar, Paediatrics."
"Fine. You can never say anything about a patient without their consent about who may listen to it."
"Sure, sure, you're absolutely right. I'll never do it again. I've learnt the lesson."
"Well, I've been talking to her and she's been drinking a bottle of vodka and taking cocaine practically every day since her second trimester. How's the baby? Have you seen it?"
"Yes. She's all right. She won't get the syndrome for a couple of days yet, and so far, she's happy and content."
"Where is she?"
"In 6 of NNU 2."
"And are you there?"

"Yes."

"Can you do her a favour?"

"Whom?"

"The baby."

"Yes, of course," he replies, surprised.

"Make sure she's held in arms, hold her yourself when you have some free time. She's just been born, lost her mother and she will start with the syndrome in two days. What a start. At least, let's try for her physical contact to be a bit more than nappy changing and bottles…"

"What's your name?"

"Celia."

"You know what, Celia? You've taught me two things today, and this one I find mighty important. I would have never considered it. We always see babies as patients and nothing else, and I would have never thought of holding and hugging that baby. And I think you just did her a huge favour by telling me this; do you have a boyfriend?" he jokes. "No, I mean it. Thank you very much."

"When my shift ends I'll go up and cuddle her a bit, if you're not there doing it yourself," Celia smiles.

"What time do you finish?"

"Ah, no! I'm not going to be that easy. You stay holding the baby in your arms as much as you can. And just you wait if she's in the cot when I go up!" threatens Celia as she goes walking backwards smiling at Miguel.

"Hello.

"Hello, Ali. What's up? How's Ingrid? Everything's all right, isn't it?"

"Yes, everything's fine."

"How come you're calling me so soon? I thought you wouldn't call me for a few days, but just a few hours after your daughter has arrived… are you sure that…?"

"I'm going to be a grandma."

"What? That's great! Congratulations! You're happy, aren't you?"

"Yes, I guess, I'm not sure yet. It hasn't sunk in enough, you know?"

"And the father?"

"Well, it seems this baby has no father: she's going to raise him on her own. Although considering the help I got from her father, it'd have been better if he had never known I was pregnant. Bless my soul, as much as I've suffered to raise her on my own and now she goes and does the same!"

"No, Alicia, it's not the same. You can't compare this to what Julián did to you; you just said it yourself, the situation is very different. What your daughter has done is much better than having a husband who gives you headaches and frightens you for years; your daughter will never have to face such a situation."

"Yes, that's true; and I'm going to help her as much as I can; this baby won't be lacking anything, let me tell you, I'll treat him with kid gloves, and my daughter too; I'll care for them all I wasn't cared for."

"Sure, you will, Alicia, I have no doubt you'll be a great grandmother. You are happy, I can tell."

"Yes, I am, ain't I? I think I needed to call you to realise I was. Thank you, Mili, a big hug."

"Another one for you, and for Ingrid and the baby... ha, ha, I've come from sending you one hug to sending you three in one go! How swell! I'm very happy for you two."

"And when is the baby due?" Alicia asks her daughter.

"In four months."

"I'm calling the doctor, he'll have to see you, I imagine, won't he?"

"Yes, Mom, but give me a few days to get over the jet-lag at least."

"If you're five months gone, you have to do a lot of tests and things and you have to start taking vitamins too..."

"Everything's all right, Mom, it's ok. This is a sought pregnancy, prepared and very desired. I've been taking what I have to take since before I started my trip, I've been careful with my food, the places I went to, what I've drunk... and I even had an ultrasound in Buenos Aires one month ago. Everything's fine, it's a beautiful baby with everything in its place."

"Do you know if it's a boy or a girl?"

"Who cares?"

"Well, of course it's the same and I'll love it whatever it is. I really love it already. It's just for the sake of knowing."

"It's a boy, Mom."

"A boy, that's great! That's beautiful, I'm going to have a grandson! I'm calling the doctor for an appointment and to get those tests done and such."

"Fine, but ask for a day next week or the one after; not before, right?"

"Have you thought of a name already?"

"No, Mom, we can do that together."

"What do you think of Miguel? And Juan? Mario? I like Mario a lot."

"Mom…"

"Right, dear, right; but at least you'll give him a normal name, won't you? There are such weird names nowadays…"

"Well, we'll see, it has to be a name with some meaning; besides, what's a normal name? Because if it's a common or frequent one, I pass. I want a special name."

"Fine, but don't choose a foreign name you can't even write afterwards."

"As if mine was very normal!"

"Right, dear, a name like yours: normal and beautiful, not very common but known, not like those names of today they have to tell you several times until you get them and when you have to say it again you've already forgotten."

"Well, we'll see, Mom, we have plenty of time for that."

10.10am.

The phone rings. Lorena sighs and she looks at the screen: it's Luci.

"Hi darling," she says, "how are things?"

"Fine. I'm calling to tell you that you were right, and he was there, the rascal, when I went by in the taxi. I don't know how much longer he stayed, but it's clear you have to take a lot of care. He's looking for you, Lorena. This guy is obsessed with you."

"Yes. I know. He's tried to contact me twenty-three times and he's sent me thousands of WhatsApp. I've blocked his number and all. He's furious."

"You can't go anywhere he knows you used to go. You'll have to look for a new doctor, as he knows the one you go to, he was waiting for you at his clinic the other day."

"Yes, I'm coming over to the Health Centre to see what they tell me and to have the rest of my pregnancy follow-up done there, until I decide what to do."

Week 25

"Hello, good morning, how can I help you?" Dr. López asks Ingrid.

"Well, I'm twenty-five weeks pregnant."

"But, why didn't you come before? Or were you living somewhere else? Do you have your medical records?"

"No, but I have an ultrasound I got in week nineteen, in Buenos Aires."

"And the tests' results? The screening?"

"I only have the nineteen weeks scan."

"But then, has your follow-up not been done down there, in Buenos Aires?"

"No, I've been travelling around South America and when I arrived in Buenos Aires I had a scan with a private obstetrician."

"I'm astonished… you've been pregnant for five months and you haven't worried at all about your health or your baby's…"

"Not quite; I've been taking folic acid for several months before getting pregnant and I've taken a lot of care of myself during these last few months."

"But if you haven't done any blood tests or tests of any kind, your son could have problems or malformations…"

"Something that none of those tests you mention would have avoided."

"No, but you could have decided if you wanted the baby or not. Now it's too late."

"Late for what? Well, you'd better not tell me; I don't want to hear it. I don't even know why we are discussing this at all. I'm a pregnant woman coming to your practice for the first time. Just do my papers for whatever tests I have to do at this stage of my pregnancy: analysis, scans, etc."

"But the date for your screening is past, we won't be able to do it."

"Well, if it can't be done there's no point in worrying about it then. Just do the routine tests for a five-month pregnant woman who comes to the doctor for the first time."

"Are you going to tell me how to do my job now?"

"No, doctor, it's just the opposite. I'm telling you not to give me hell for things that cannot be changed. Nothing you tell me will change the fact that I'm twenty-five weeks pregnant and I've just arrived in Madrid. So, please do your job and don't give me your opinion, as I didn't ask for it."

"Ingrid, please," says her mother.

Ingrid raises her hand slightly, indicating to her mom not to get involved.

"Go over there, we'll do your ultrasound."

"Come," says the nurse, showing her where to go.

The doctor starts doing the ultrasound and after being silent for a while, he turns the screen towards Ingrid to show her her baby.

"Mom, come," says Ingrid.

Alicia shows her face from behind the screen and Herminia invites her to stand by her daughter.

"Everything's fine, here's the head, the spine, the ribs, and this is the heart, see how it beats?" says the obstetrician turning the scanner sound on for them to hear the heartbeat.

Alicia takes her daughter's hand, moved. "It's a boy, isn't it, doctor?"

"Yes, it is; everything's all right."

Dr. López goes back to his desk as Alicia and Herminia help Ingrid getting up.

After sitting at his desk again, the doctor starts asking questions about the family records.

"Any important illness in the family?"

"No, not as far as I know."

"In the father's family?"

"Neither," she hesitates.

"Anything wrong?" asks the doctor, intrigued.

"No, I just had to think about it. You always know better about your own family; you tell them just like that, without thinking."

"Well, you have to ask for an appointment downstairs, at the entrance, to get these tests done, and another one for the next follow up, two weeks after your blood tests."

"And when do I have to go to the midwife?"
"We don't have midwives here at the hospital. That's just for the big Health Centers."
"But I'd like to be followed up by a midwife."
"I think it would be better to have you followed up here, because you're about to enter your third trimester and you haven't had any previous control, so your pregnancy will be classified as high-risk."
"High-risk? Why?"
"Because you didn't get any tests done on the dates they should have been. There are many things we don't know yet. It can be a fetus with malformations, you may have an illness during pregnancy, rubella, toxoplasmosis, pregnancy diabetes…"
"But supposing everything's fine; if I want to be looked after by a midwife, what should I do?"
"You go to a Health Centre where they have them and you register there," answers the nurse.
"But don't go until we get the results of all these tests; you don't want to go to a different place for nothing."
"Thank you very much," says Ingrid, taking the papers the nurse is giving her, and she says goodbye.
"These "Miss-know-it-all" are the worst," the doctor tells Herminia when Ingrid and her mother have left the office.
"Yes," replies Herminia smiling. She likes this girl. Not many people have the guts to stand up to Don Jesús.

Maternity Hospital.
Staff Room.
Celia, Marta and Nico are in the staff room. There's just one woman on the labour ward, so most of the midwives have nothing to do.
"I'm going upstairs to see how the English girl's baby is doing, ok?" asks Celia.
"Yes, go wherever you want, this is as calm as glass today…" replies Marta.

Celia enters the NNU and goes towards cot number 6. There's a beautiful baby girl there, awake, who looks at her with huge eyes.

"Hello beautiful, hello baby," she says, getting her out of the cot. "I am Celia, my pretty one."

Just then an assistant worker comes in with a bottle, which she offers to Celia, "do you want to give it to her, or shall I do it?"

"I will, I will!" she replies, thrilled. "But give me a hand, I haven't given a baby a bottle in my life."

"What are you, a student?"

"No, I'm a midwife."

"And you've never given a bottle to a baby? Not even as a student? Didn't you rotate here?"

"No, I studied in another country, and there it's the mothers who feed their babies, or the fathers, but not us."

"For the normal babies I understand that, but is it like that too for the babies who are admitted to the unit?"

"Yes, it's also parents who do."

"But every three hours?"

"Yes, in the hospital where I studied parents could be twenty-four hours by the incubator if they wanted. And many of them did, or they took turns with the grandparents. But most babies are always with a relative by their side. Same as any grown-up."

"Well, it must have been larger than this, because we couldn't possibly fit that many parents here."

Celia doesn't want to start a discussion with this woman about the quantity of babies who are admitted to NNUs in Spain when they should be with their mothers instead. Babies who are under observation and whom nobody observes, who just get their obs done every six hours, or babies who are there because they need IV medication twice a day and stay here all day instead of being with their moms and getting that done in the maternity ward. *That way, there would be room for the parents of the ones who really need to be here*, Celia thinks.

"It's easy, you just get the teat into their mouth, making sure it's full of milk so that they don't get any air. If they are swallowing, you'll see tiny bubbles. If you don't, turn it around a bit and that'll do the trick."

Celia sits down and takes the bottle. When the baby opens her mouth, she puts the teat inside it. The baby starts sucking mightily. "How hungry you were! Drink, drink your milk, even if it's this powder one, eat up, eat up my darling." *If we don't even have open doors for the parents here, we really have a long way to go before we have a milk bank. As good as that would be for you and for other babies like you...* Celia thinks.

"How shall I call you?" she asks her. "Claire?" she suggests after thinking about it for a few seconds, "do you like Claire? I like it too. I think it agrees with you a lot. So far, until your parents decide what to call you, you're Claire to me."

Claire goes on sucking her bottle and Celia talks to her, "you know, Claire? Right now, your parents want to meet you very much; although you'll be spending some time here before going home to them. But they've been waiting for a long time and when they know you're here they'll be thrilled. They are going to love you and care for you a lot. I'm sure they'll be fantastic parents. And your other mom, Katie, also loves you lots; but she can't take care of you. She needs to take care of herself. But you haven't done anything wrong. You're priceless, you're precious, and you're going to have a life full of love and warmth. Even if the start is going to be a bit shitty and you're going to be a bit lonely, but everything will get better soon."

Celia looks up and sees Miguel leaning on the door frame smiling in tenderness.

"Were you spying on us?" Celia tells him.

"Sorry. I didn't want to interrupt, so I stayed here. Do you think she understands you?"

"Sure, I do. Well, not literally, I don't think so. But she can do with some sweet and kind words. We all need to have what's happening around us explained, and much more a baby like Claire."

"Claire?"

"Yes. I like it, and so does she."

"But her parents will give her a name, won't they?"

"Of course, but I find it cruel that she stays without one for a whole month, so she's Claire for me."

"One month?"

"Yes. They stay one month in custody before they are given up for adoption; in case the mother changes her mind and wants to come back for her."

"Well, this one clearly isn't. Even if it's for the shame of it. How can you get that high practically every day? And being pregnant, besides?"

"I guess it must be to escape reality, to forget, to avoid facing what she's going through. Each person solves their problems as they can, and who knows what she's going through!"

"In that case, she'd better…"

"Shh!" Celia cuts him, "Claire is here. She's beautiful. She's going to have parents who'll give her the best, and she'll be most grateful to Katie for having given her life."

"That's the only thing."

"It's a lot."

Celia looks at Claire, who's fallen asleep. She leaves the bottle on the table and keeps her in her arms.

"I'm going down for lunch, are you coming?" says Miguel.

"I'm staying here with her a bit longer, I've already had lunch," she smiles at him.

"I'm not coming back here, ever," Ingrid tells her mother as they come out of the doctor's.

"But why?"

"Because I don't get why this man has to mind things that are not his business and tell me such things."

"Well, it's his job."

"No, Mom, it's not. His job is to perform tests to confirm my pregnancy is going well, not to frighten me by telling me about hypothetical illnesses or mortal risks for not having come running to the doctor's the very moment I knew I was pregnant."

"Well, my dear, but doctors are the ones who know things about pregnancy, what's good for you and your baby…"

"No, Mom, the ones who know all that are midwives. Doctors should be there only when there is a real illness. You don't go to the doctor when you're fine; and I'm fine, I'm not ill."

"It's the first time in my life I hear something like that, love; when I had you, it was the doctor who followed your pregnancy, and you just obeyed and kept quiet. And I thought it was still like that."

"Unfortunately, yes, it's still like that; in this country. But no, in many others it isn't. In England, for instance, a pregnant woman doesn't go to the doctor unless something's wrong."

"And who does the pregnancy follow-up and the tests and scans?"

"The midwives, Mom, as they are specialized in normal pregnancies without problems."

"Well dear, that must be in other countries; here it's the doctor who takes care of everything. And to tell you the truth, I think that's the best, because you'll be much better taken care of by a doctor, because they are the ones really specialized in pregnancy; midwives are their nurses, aren't they?"

"No, Mom, it's not like that. Each part of the body has its specialized doctor, and when you get sick, depending on what's the affected part of the body, that's the specialist who cures you: the ear specialist for the ear, the ophthalmologist for the eye, the oncologist for cancer..."

"And the obstetrician for pregnancy," adds her mother.

"That's where you are mistaken. Pregnancy would be a doctor's matter if you had, let's say, a sick pregnancy. But most women have healthy pregnancies, as most people are healthy and not ill. But as pregnancy and birth are special situations, they need a specialist. Those are midwives, Mom."

"The things you've got to know these months with your pregnancy, dear! Where have you learnt all that?"

"Before I left I got into a forum, an internet group of pregnant women who fight for respect in births, for the birth of their children to be theirs and not of those who look after it. They aim to take decisions over their own body without anyone deciding for them. What they're claiming is being the owners of their births and deciding what they want for themselves and their babies."

"Oh dear, and how do you find something like that?"

"Just like everything, Mom, searching."

"You have to show me, because Mili tells me amazing things from the internet. I want to know about it too."

"Right; let's go to a Health Centre to get me a midwife first and then we'll see if we can find how to get internet at home, and I'll show you how it goes."

Week 28

Health Centre.

Midwife's clinic.

"Let's see, get on the scales, María, you're getting far too fat and that's no good," the midwife tells her.

María takes her shoes off, ashamed, and gets on the scale. Rosa, the midwife, approaches and looks at the screen.

"75 kilos!" she exclaims, "but, what are you doing, woman?"

"Nothing. I'm eating rather well. Quite a lot, but no sweets. Lots of nuts, I feel like them all the time lately."

"So, you'll have to eat less. Nuts have many calories and that's not good for the baby at all. Besides, the fatter women are, the worse their births are. What do you drink? Coke and soda?"

"No."

"Cream?" she asks sarcastically.

"Some juice from time to time, but that's good, isn't it?"

"Natural ones, and just from time to time. The bottled ones are just sugar. Well, you'll have to watch your weight because getting this fat is not convenient for you at all. From now on, you'll walk one hour every day. Drink only water and have just one serving when you eat. If you're hungry, eat fruit or veg sticks: carrot, cucumber, celery… any veg you like, raw. You are taking the iron tablets[40], aren't you?"

"Yes, but I'm awfully constipated."

"Yes, it's one of its side effects, but you have to go on taking it; all pregnant women have an iron deficiency and then if there's a haemorrhage it's better to have reinforced it during pregnancy."

After measuring her blood pressure and writing it down in her notebook, María asks the midwife,

"when do the antenatal classes start?"

"In two weeks, every Thursday at six, for two months."

---

[40] Some professionals put all pregnant women on iron tablets.

"Could my sister-in-law and her partner come, too?"

"Who are they?"

"You don't know them. They don't have a midwife because they are going to have twins and in the hospital where they go they've been told to ask for antenatal classes in a Health Centre. As we are in the same weeks of pregnancy we'd love to go to classes together."

"Well. I don't know if there are any vacancies," the midwife says, dragging her feet, "what can't happen is one of my couples not being able to go because some outsiders want to."

"No, no, I was just asking in case they could. If they can't, all right. They'd love to come with us, because it's easier that way, all together."

"All right, they can come. But don't make a fuss, right? Couples who know each other often do."

"No, no. Of course not," says María, "thank you very much."

"I'm having a homebirth, Mom," says Ingrid.

"What are you telling me! Here?"

"Yes. Here."

"No, dear, no. Anything but that. What if anything goes wrong?"

"I'm having the baby at home with a midwife who'll make sure everything's all right."

"But my dear, this is not a hospital. What if anything happens? If anything happens to the baby?"

"That's what the midwife is there for. To make sure and keep us assured that everything will be fine. If it's not, then we'd go to the hospital, but that's her work. She's the one who knows about this, and if she suspects that anything's going wrong, then we'll go to the hospital."

"Darling, please. Don't do this to me. If anything happens to you I will never forgive myself for not having stopped you. In the hospital they have devices, doctors, theatres and many things within reach."

"Yes, Mom. And they also have this indiscriminate use of technology, and many women end up with a Cesarean or a cut in their vaginas they don't need."

"What utter nonsense! Why would they do a Cesarean to a woman who doesn't need it? They do it because it's necessary. I don't believe doctors go around operating people all over the place with no need."

"Look, Mom. I've been preparing for this pregnancy and this birth for a long time. I've contacted a midwife who takes care of women in their homes and I like her lots. Her name is Esther and she's wonderful. I'm meeting her tomorrow and she'll be coming here to see me."

"She's coming here, home?"

"Yes. That way, you'll be able to ask her all your questions directly to rule out any doubts. She'll know how to explain things to you much better than me."

"Oh dear. But what have I done for you to do this to me? Why do I have to be the one with the weird daughter?"

"Mom, please. Don't start."

"I start, of course I start, yes," her mother replies, angry. "You leave on a one-year trip, on your own, you come back pregnant you don't know by whom," she says, enumerating with her fingers, "and now you say you want to give birth at home. What do you want, to make my life a misery? How can you be that selfish? You only think of yourself, or what?"

"Well, yes, Mom. I'm mainly thinking of me and my baby. You're the one who's selfish when you think I must live my life according to what you think is right. You did and do with yours what you find more appropriate. Why shouldn't I do the same?"

"Because you can die, dear, that's why."

"But do you really think I'd take such an important decision as where to give birth lightly? What do you think? That I just woke up this morning thinking I'd give birth at home? Please, Mom, have a bit of respect. Listen, try to understand before hurting me. I've been reading for months, looking for information, surfing the net in forums and suchlike, and after having considered everything for many months, I've come to the conclusion that I want to give birth at home, that it's the best option for me and my baby."

"But I'm just telling you to think about it well, dear, that if anything happened to you…"

"That's what makes me angry. That you don't seem to understand. That you're telling me to think about it when I've given it a lot of thought already. You may think that I just thought about it, that it's not a well-considered decision, and that's what makes me angry. Mom, you have no idea about giving birth at home, apart from gossip and things you might have seen on TV, which mostly aren't true. You have to try to listen before rushing into judgement."

"It's not that, love. It's that I worry about you and the baby."

"And do you think I don't? Do you think I could make a decision like that if the probabilities of anything happening to any of us were higher at home than in a hospital?"

"And aren't they?"

"No, Mom, they're not."

"Well, I had heard that with all the progress we have nowadays, giving birth at home was backwards and dangerous."

"And who did you hear it from? From someone who hasn't a clue. The hairdresser? In that TV program you like so much?"

"Everybody says so, dear…"

"No, not everybody, Mom. There are many people giving birth at home, and they are, normally, the ones who consider things carefully, who look for information, who see beyond, investigate… Trust me, Mom. Please. I need you by my side. I need your support and I don't want to fight you over this."

"Of course, I want to support you and help you, dear. But you must understand my worry, and that what you're asking of me is not very normal."

"I understand, Mom. It's normal in some places. I know here it isn't, not much. But that's because they've frightened us so much with birthing that it seems as if our bodies were all defective and we needed a doctor to save us no matter how."

"You hear so many things…"

"Like what?"

"Well, people's births, what you can hear around… Most of them are horror stories."

"That's precisely what I want to avoid. I want this birth to be wonderful, not a horror story. Believe it or not, the start of this horror story is written with uninformed women who arrive at their labour trusting the people in the hospitals will make every effort for their and their baby's wellbeing."

"And that's not true?"

"No, Mom, it isn't. They'll do what they think is best… for everyone. Whatever simplifies things, the easiest way."

"I don't understand it, love. Where did you get such loathing for doctors and hospitals?"

"Well, from reading, from getting information, from seeing things are not as they should be. They've been telling us that a thousand calamities could happen in birth for so long that we believe it blindly. So much so that we have lost all confidence in our bodies and we need a man in a white coat who sees us for five minutes to tell us we're fine to feel safe. Fear is a very powerful weapon. They frighten us, they make us doubt our own capacities, they make us believe we need them because something terrible could happen without them. Thus, we all end up following that path they impose, because they've made us believe it's the only one that's safe."

"I really don't get what you're telling me. Why should doctors want us to be afraid?"

"It's not anything conscious, Mom. They don't do it on purpose. They've been like that for a long time. But what is clear is that, this way, they earn more in every sense."

"Do they earn more for a Cesarean than for a natural birth?"

"In private clinics, they do. In many of them, the Cesarean rate is incredibly high. If a pregnant woman goes to a private clinic, the probability of her ending up with a Cesarean is almost twice as high than in a public hospital."

"But that's terrible! But they do need a reason to do a Cesarean, don't they? And don't you have to sign a paper giving them your permission?"

"Yes Mom, of course you have to sign a paper, but that's not a problem. They don't come and tell you: 'Look here, madam, as a Cesarean is better for us than a natural birth, you're getting one. Besides, we finish sooner and can go home earlier. Only us, of course, because you will have to stay here for five days instead of two and afterwards you'll be suffering the consequences of a post operatory just when your baby needs you most… Also, you won't be able to breastfeed him because of the pain and the discomfort of the stitches. But we'll give him a bottle and that way the rest of us will take care of him, as you'll be busy enough with the consequences of the Cesarean we did to you'. This would be the most honest, but no one would be giving their consent, would they? So, they come and tell you something like: 'It seems you can't dilate well and your baby's starting to get tired, it seems your pelvis is narrow… but don't you worry, because we can end your suffering as well as your baby's in a second with a Cesarean. You'll be awake and will be able to see your baby when he's born'."

"I'm beginning to understand many things now. Damned money. How can they do something like this just for the money?"

"It's not just the money, Mom. It's convenience, misinformation, fear of a legal complaint… Doctors are experts in pathology. Generally speaking, they know how to do their job wonderfully, so they are much better at performing a Cesarean than patiently waiting for a birth to happen spontaneously.

"We've had this notion that we'll be much safer giving birth with an obstetrician for so long that it sank very deep in people's minds. So deep, that it seems impossible that a birth can go well if there's not a doctor there."

"That's true, dear: even I was of that opinion until five minutes ago when you explained all this," says Alicia with a certain degree of sadness.

"Don't be sad, Mom. Look at what I've just told you and how your opinion changed in a few minutes. I've been compiling data on birth at home and in hospitals for almost a year: hospital statistics, information from other countries… I have decided to give birth at home because it's the best for me and my baby. Don't worry, everything will be alright. Esther, the midwife, is coming to meet us tomorrow at eleven, and you'll see how she will shed light on many more things. Think about all this a bit and write down the questions you may have, so that you can ask her tomorrow."

"I love you lots, dear," Alicia says, taking Ingrid's hand, "I'm sorry I was so pig-headed. I was very frightened."

"It's all right, Mom. I understand. A couple of years ago, my opinion would have been the same. When they make you believe something, you do, and until you start scratching the surface you can't see what lies beneath."

"You're a good one to scratch every surface," she says, embracing her.

"Just as it should be, Mom. Just as it should."

11:00am.

Ingrid opens the door of her house and smiles at the girl in front of her.

"Esther!" she says as they greet each other with two kisses.

"Hello Ingrid, pleased to meet you."

"Look Esther, this is my mother, Alicia."

"Pleased to meet you, I'm Esther," she kisses her on both cheeks too.

"Would you like anything to drink?" Alicia offers.

"Yes, please. Do you have any coffee made? If you don't, I'll have some tea."

"I'll do it in a second, I have one of these capsule coffee makers. But I never know which capsule I should use."

"I don't mind. Just get the first one you find, with a bit of milk. Thank you, Alicia."

Ingrid and Esther sit in the sitting room.

"How great that you're here! I was longing to meet you."

"So, here I am. I'm all yours," Esther smiles, "how's your mother? Did you tell her?"

"Yes. Fine. Just as I told you: at first, she was very worried, and when I started shedding some light on her doubts, she began to understand. I've got a splendid mother, I really do."

"That's great! You are very lucky. Not everyone has the same support. Many women don't even tell them until after the birth, because they don't want any mother-daughter fight during pregnancy."

"Yes, but surely they have a partner and can afford to do that. My only support is my mother, so I have to be able to count on her for this."

"Of course. I'm very happy for you."

Alicia arrives with the coffee tray and puts it on the table.

"Esther, I'm leaving everything here, you just serve yourself to your liking," says Alicia as she takes a coffee cup and sits next to her daughter.

"Thank you very much, Alicia," says Esther, taking the other cup.

"How do you find her, Doctor?" Alicia asks Esther.

"Midwife, Mom," Ingrid corrects her.

"Ouch, yes, force of habit! Midwife."

"Esther is all right."

"All right," Alicia smiles. "So, how do you see her?

"Well, I haven't seen her much, but she looks all right; and you, how do you see her?"

"Fine, too, but you're the one who knows about this."

"Well, Alicia, I think in this case Ingrid knows more than you and I. Ingrid, how are you?" Esther asks her.

"Fantastic. I'd love to have a coffee instead of a pineapple juice, but aside from that, fine."

"Yes, dear, I have to get some decaf for you. As nobody has ever had it in this house... I had everything ready for your arrival, but of course wasn't counting on this."

"It's all right, Mom, don't worry, we'll get it."

"Have you got any papers? Scan? Analysis?"

"Yes, everything's here," she says, opening a small green folder and giving her its contents.

"Ahh, but you've got everything!"

"Yes, the doctor asked me for every possible test when he knew I was twenty-five weeks gone and didn't have any previous papers."

"Horrors! A pregnant woman with no papers!" Esther jokes putting her hands on her head, "he must have had a heart attack."

"Quite, yes. He even put me down as high risk."

"Why?"

"For being naughty," she says with a huge grin.

"You're joking!" Esther looks at both of them.

"Yes. She was very cheeky with the doctor. Told him to just do his work, not to give his opinion as he had not been asked…" Alicia shows her daughter off.

"You've just become my heroine," says the midwife, astonished. "Most of us just become tiiiny when a doctor scolds us, and you faced him. Who was he? López? Nooo! You confronted Dr. López? I'll do this for free," smiles Esther. "It's a great honour being the midwife of the woman who actually gave Dr. López a bit of his own medicine."

A proud smile comes to Ingrid's face and also to her mother's who, until now, wasn't too sure about her daughter's behaviour at the doctor's. Now, recalling it and seeing the midwife's reaction, she realises it was her daughter who was right, and the doctor was very rude.

"You have to tell me exactly what happened later; I want to know every juicy detail of that conversation. Then, he put you as high risk, why?"

"Just because. For arriving twenty-five weeks pregnant with just a scan under my arm."

Esther has a look at her papers and says, "but everything's all right, you are as healthy as a horse! All that's lacking is the glucose tolerance test."

"Which I'm not going to have done. Do I need it to give birth at home?" asks Ingrid, worried.

"No, no, you don't. Well, I won't demand it from you. You can do whatever you want. If you don't want to do it, I'll respect that."

"What else do you need? What's essential to give birth at home?"

"Well, apart from what you have here," Esther raises the papers in her hand, "knowing that the baby is head down, that he's growing well, that he's fine and… little else."

"And for that, do I have to go back to the hospital?"

"No, I'm the one who'll check that. If you decide you want to give birth at home with me as a midwife, I'll be taking care of you from the moment you make the decision till one month after the baby's born, or for as long as you need."

"Really?" says Ingrid with a huge grin, "I don't need the glucose tolerance test,[41] I don't have to go to regular CTGs[42] nor controls, or fight with anyone else or such like?"

"No. That's the point of having a private midwife: you don't have to go to the hospital."

"But won't she be needing more tests?" says her mother. "She's only six and a half months pregnant. The sugar test?"

"The tests she has are enough for me. The sugar test is not necessary. I can see she's taking care of herself, the test has a lot of false positives and if she doesn't want to have it done, it's all right by me. From now on, I'll do everything that's necessary, and you might have to go to the hospital to be checked, but only if I detect something strange. If I don't, you won't have to."

"Hired!" says Ingrid pointing at her with her finger.

"But, do you have the necessary devices to do all that?" Alicia asks.

"Yes, Alicia. I have some of them here, in that bag. To take her blood pressure and to listen to the baby's heartbeat, which is the way we midwives have to know how the baby is," she says as she opens her bag and takes a smaller one from within. She opens it and shows them what looks like a small box with a screen and a microphone.

"And you can know that the baby's all right all the time with that?"

"All the time it's on, yes."

"And you use it during birth?"

"Of course, from while to while I listen to the baby to make sure he's fine."

"You won't be listening all the time?"

---

[41] Glucose tolerance test: A medical test in which glucose is given and blood samples taken afterward to determine how quickly it is cleared from the blood.

[42] In Spain, pregnant women have routine CTGs every few days from 37 weeks onwards.

"No, that's not necessary, Alicia. During birth, I'll be using it every twenty minutes or so."

"And what if something happens to him during those twenty minutes when you're not listening?

"If the baby is fine when we listen to him and nothing different happens -for instance, that Ingrid's waters break or she notices something strange or a different kind of pain-, there's no reason why he won't be well twenty minutes after."

"Then, if you listen with that device and two minutes after that, her waters break, do you listen again immediately, or do you wait another eighteen minutes?"

"I'd listen after the waters broke and every time it was necessary. The twenty minutes are orientative. I won't be having a stopwatch at hand, either. We listen to the baby every now and then to make sure he's all right, but if the birth is going normally, the baby will be fine."

"And what if suddenly, just imagine, you're listening to the heartbeat and it tells you that the baby is not well, what happens then? Shall we run to the hospital?"

"That depends on many factors," replies Esther, "first we'd listen to see if he recuperates. That's the first. Often, babies in there fool around a bit, you must know. For instance: you know if you put something into a baby's hand, they close it, right? Sometimes, what they get in their hand is the umbilical cord, and that squeezing of the cord will make his heartbeat slow down; but the minute the baby starts to feel unwell, his muscles get less oxygen and relax, the hand opens and he lets go of the cord. That happens quite a lot. There's not that much space in there as to prevent that from happening from time to time.

"But imagine it's not that, imagine the baby has the cord around his neck and it's very short and when the baby starts his way down to the vulva the cord compresses too much and slows his heartbeat. Then we'd have to see how's dilation, how long we have before the baby's born, how he is recovering after every contraction... There are many factors to observe before deciding.

Alicia, it's very difficult for a baby who's fine to be poorly five minutes after without any extra signs, poorly enough to make us take the decision of transferring. Think of any effort, any sport… nobody starts running and suddenly collapses. They start getting tired, they measure their energy, their body goes telling them it won't hold for much longer. Exactly the same as a baby during birth."

"But what if anything happens all of a sudden? The placenta comes loose, the baby or the mother have a heart attack…"

"A placental abruption is hard to happen. The baby, and also the womb and the placenta, are usually very ready for this moment, and they don't fail under normal conditions."

"What are normal conditions?" inquires Ingrid.

"A physiological birth. Without synthetic IV oxytocin, with freedom of movements, without an epidural… well, normal conditions are the conditions you have in a birth without external factors or drugs. It's very difficult to have a placental abruption in such conditions. If, in spite of everything, it happened, you'd notice an intense pain and it wouldn't become detached in one go. But naturally, if that was the case you'd be immediately evacuated to the hospital.

About the heart attack, that's very rare, and of course if it happened it would be better to be at the hospital. But keep in mind that zero risk does not exist. Everything in this life implies a risk: going out to the street, riding in a car, eating an olive, giving birth… It's very difficult for something to go wrong in a physiological, normal, low-risk birth… but if anything does, it's better to be in a hospital. Undoubtedly. That's where you have to contrast the pros and cons and see what's the best option for you."

"But studies say the results of mother and child deaths are very similar in home-births and low-risk hospital ones, and that the degree of interventions is lower at home, and that's what I'm looking for," Ingrid adds.

"And that's splendid, Ingrid. But that's something I have to explain to you. I need you to be sure, to understand and assume your responsibility in this process. I need you to understand that I can't assure you -no one can- that everything will be alright, wherever you choose to give birth. And that if you choose to give birth at home, you're the one who's taking that decision freely and who assumes all responsibility for that decision and its consequences."

"And if I go to a hospital, who's responsible for my birth?"

"You are. You are responsible for anything happening in your body, for anything that is done to it. If you go to a hospital and something goes wrong nobody will be declared responsible, because you're the one who is."

"But how is she going to be responsible if in the hospital they take her baby out with forceps and break his head, for instance?" Alicia asks.

"That's different, Alicia. Here we'd be talking of malpractice. Of course, in that case, someone must take responsibility for their mistake. What I mean is when something goes wrong without malpractice: with everyone doing their work well but nevertheless getting an undesired result. The responsibility, when there's no malpractice, falls upon the person assuming the consequences, and when it comes to birth this person is always the birthing mother. Whatever happens, it happens either to her or her baby, for whom she has parental authority."

"Well, but that's living. Taking decisions, assuming risks, consequences, responsibilities…"

"Indeed. You assume responsibility for your life, your body, your birth and you decide what you consider to be the best for you and for your baby."

"And what happens if we have to go to the hospital halfway through labour? How does that work? Do we have to call an ambulance?"

"Normally, we don't. We get there by our own means: in your car, or mine, or by taxi... All the transfers I've had so far have been for failure to progress. The woman stopped dilating at some point and labour didn't progress for hours. Every time, we went to the hospital by car. If we had an emergency, we'd call an ambulance, which would always be better than driving ourselves."

"But by the time the ambulance arrived, they'd both be dead!" Alicia exclaims alarmed.

"Alicia, don't be afraid. As I told you, labour is not more dangerous than any other physiological process, as eating, for instance. You eat without fear, and when you choke, your body reacts quickly for everything to go back to normal. How many people do you know who have choked?"

"We all have, haven't we?"

"Yes. Everybody, and more than once. And how many deaths by choking you know of?"

"I don't know. Sometimes you hear that someone has choked with a chicken bone and died."

"Exactly, and we go on eating without fear; at the most, maybe after reading the news we'll be more careful the next couple of times we eat chicken, and that's all. Now, imagine someone who has choked with a chicken bone starts a campaign and spreads the word that we should go eat at hospitals because there's people there who know about this, who can even avoid it by putting a tube in your stomach and giving you purees three times a day; and, besides, if anyone insists on eating normal food, there are doctors there who will perform every possible manoeuvre to get the bone out, including surgery if necessary. This may sound like a joke, told like this, because we see the act of eating as a normal part of life. But labour is just as normal and physiological an act; only we've been convinced for several decades now that a hospital is the most appropriate place for births, and thus, we don't find this circus around it that crazy.

When I come to your home when you start labour, I'll be coming with lots of things just in case. I'll be bringing fluid bags and everything I need for an IV, to stop a haemorrhage, for stitching, resuscitating, and so on. Every homebirth midwife carries this, and, really, I have never used it. Most of the drugs I carry I change because they pass their expiration date. It's very rare for us to need anything, but nevertheless we are always ready for anything. Our main job at a homebirth is to make sure everything's going fine, and to act promptly if there's any emergency, as we have the knowledge. In most home births, anyone could do the visible work of a midwife, because we basically support, cheer, facilitate, relax, help, eliminate barriers, calm and let things happen as the woman wants. In many births I haven't even put my gloves on because I haven't touched anything, the one to receive the baby wasn't me. But should anything go wrong, a midwife will be able to identify it.

"And if there's an emergency, which is very rare, you'll be happy to have a midwife there with you."

"And do you think I'll be needing a doula?" Ingrid asks Esther.

"A what?" asks Alicia.

"A doula, Mom. It's a woman who's with you during labour, looks for what you need, gives you water, dries your sweat, helps you doing whatever's necessary for me and Esther not to lack anything during labour, and later helps you once you've had the baby too…"

"But that's what I'm here for, dear! I know nothing about births apart from having had you, but all those things I can do…"

"I know, Mom. It's in case I need you, to hug me for instance, and besides we have to prepare the bathtub, or get water, or prepare some towels and I don't want you to let go of me…"

"They don't know what to invent… I would have never thought there were people doing that as a job."

"As you want, Ingrid," Esther intervenes, "I don't need one, but if you think she'll come in handy for you…"

"I don't know. As I've never given birth, I have no idea if I'll be needing her. I'm afraid of needing my mother by my side all the time and what if we need anything, then?"

"If it's anything like you mentioned before, like filling the tub or getting you a glass of water or something to eat, I can do that, as long as it's inside the house, of course."

"And if you want, I can always call Mili for her to come and give us a hand..." Alicia suggests.

"No, Mom. I don't know if I'll be wanting Mili to be at my birth. For a doula, that's her job, so I know she'll just be with me, she won't judge me, she will know how to be at a birth, in silence... To Mili, I'd have to explain I'm having a home birth, which will probably frighten her, so I don't want to be taking care of her in my labour. Besides, if she's anxious or afraid she'll pass it on to me."

"I know several doulas, if you want I can give you their contact details and then you decide."

"You're not anti-doula?"

"No. I think they do wonderful work. Decades ago, when a woman was in labour there was a whole tribe of sisters, cousins, aunts and so on around her. But these days many of us are away from our families, and we don't have those women to hug them and to be held by them during labour. I mean, I'm obviously not going to be sitting on a chair looking at you. And if you need hugs, contact and tribe, I'll be giving that to you, of course. But I will also have to be paying attention to the more technical side, making sure that you and your baby are fine at every moment. A doula is a 100 percent tribe, because she's there just to be with you."

"I had heard midwives didn't like them..."

"Let's see: there are opportunist people and intruders in any trade. Most midwives like doulas who act like doulas, because we understand their realm. However, when there are women who usurp our competencies... we don't like that as much. A doula cannot give antenatal classes, or do a pregnancy follow-up or assist a birth. She's there just to be with the mother, to listen, to support her... I know there are doulas out there who attend births without a midwife, and even if I disagree, if the women they're with have chosen that freely and well informed...I cannot interfere. Every woman is grown up enough to decide what and who she wants at her delivery."

"The problem is that most people don't understand this, and the day something goes wrong, and it will… then home births will be in the thick of things and might even be forbidden," Ingrid observes.

"Well, I'm not sure. Things would really have to change a lot to make women birth in a determinate place," says Esther.

"Look at Brazil," Ingrid responds.

"Is it compulsory to give birth in the hospital in Brazil?" says Alicia surprised.

"A few months ago, Mom, the police went to get a woman from her home to take her to hospital, where she got a Cesarean."[43]

"But the baby must have had a problem, didn't he?"

"Mom, do you think there's a mother in this world who, knowing the life of her child is at risk, rejects a cesarean and stays comfortably at home?"

"No, dear, I don't think so. But why did they take her, then?"

"Because it was a breech birth and they had scheduled a Cesarean for her. She didn't refuse it, but she wanted to wait to be in labour to have it done, which is totally understandable."

"But if she was going to have a Cesarean anyway, why didn't she go?" asks Alicia, confused.

"For a good many reasons, Alicia," Esther intervenes, "to give the baby a chance to turn around, for him to be born when he's fully ready, for him to get the birth hormones, which are wonderful for both baby and mother in their relationship…"

"And are you trying to tell me the police went to this woman's home to take her to hospital to have a Cesarean the day the doctors had decided she should be having it?"

They both nod.

"That's terrible! What's the world coming to?"

---

[43] Since this book was written, several cases have happened in Spain where women who wanted to have a homebirth have been unlawfully taken to the hospital by force.

"Do you understand now, Mom, why I don't want to have my baby at a hospital? Why I don't want some people who have nothing to do with such a huge moment in my life, who don't know me or give a damn about me, decide what's supposedly the best for me and my son? Because once you enter a hospital they apply a protocol to you as if you were on the conveyor belt of the assembly line of births."

"Yes, love, sure I understand it. What I don't understand is how it is possible that nothing gets done about it. Can't this be stopped? How can we tell everyone about that?"

"The same way you tell them about any other thing: little by little and with patience, because it's been many decades that this way of doing things has been ingrained in people. So many decades in fact, that we see it as something good. But the most important issue is information. If people are informed, then they'll choose other options. They will demand a change in society. There are many people nowadays who, like Ingrid, are getting informed and looking for alternatives. If we continue along this path, if there's more and more information available, if more and more women know these things… that's how we'll get to change it."

"But I want to think that there are many good professionals and people in Spanish hospitals…"

"Of course, Alicia," Esther adds, "I don't think any of the professionals working in hospitals and labour wards act in bad faith. I'm convinced that all of them do their job thinking that's the best way to do it. I myself, for many years, worked like that. When I studied, and during my first years as a midwife, I broke my neck every day doing things as I had learnt them. Utterly convinced it was the right way and that doing what I did was the best for both mother and child. It's very difficult to take the blinkers off, to see that there are other ways to do things and, above all, to go upstream. Because even if you realise it, changing the system is a loadful and it's very difficult. And the usual run of things is that all the midwives and obstetricians who have taken their blinkers off, after a few years of disappointing work, end up leaving that unit and looking for jobs in places more akin to them, or working only privately."

"Like you," says Ingrid.

"Like me. Look, one of the last days I worked in the hospital, I was taking care of a woman in labour and eight doctors came into the delivery room, like that, all together following each other."

"Good heavens! What was wrong?" Alicia asks, alarmed.

"Absolutely nothing. But I had had too many conflicts with everyone of them, each time with a different one… They came in and took decisions that weren't for them to take, when everything was going normally. They told me to do this or that… I sometimes ignored them, other times I told them no, they had nothing to do there, they weren't needed… Just imagine the expression of that poor woman when she saw such a white coat battalion coming in: 'What's wrong?', she asked, terrified. With you and your baby, nothing, I replied."

"But what did they come in for?" asks Ingrid, annoyed and not understanding.

"To shut me up. I had clashed with them too many times separately, so they all came together to join forces and be eight against one."

"What a bunch of brutes!" Ingrid says.

"Indeed. But that way of acting is what they've absorbed along their whole training. Each time they say this or that, they are really convinced it's for the best. In that hospital, for instance, the obstetrics director was a great guy: progressive, driven… and they had to give him explanations the following day for every single C-section done. He worked Monday to Friday, so the rest of the doctors, all of them an inferior rank, took their friends and sisters to have their births over the weekend so as to get their C-sections done just for the sake of it, without having to give the boss any explanations, because they knew he wouldn't be there on Sundays."

"But why did they do C-sections if they knew that wasn't right?"

"Because they didn't know that, Alicia. Because they really believed that practising medicine and performing surgery on someone, even if they didn't need it, was the best they can offer."

"Good Heavens!" says Alicia, taking her hands to her mouth.

"Well, men are blind in their own case; so, what happens is that many of the seers end up having to leave, because they suffer too much working in such a hostile environment."

"I'm never going to a hospital again, mark my words," says Alicia.

"C'mon, Mom, don't you turn more catholic than the Pope, now!" laughs her daughter, "you'll have to go if you need to."

"Then I'll be calling you, Esther, and asking you what I should do. Or are you only for births?"

"Of course not, Alicia, I'm specialised in women's health."

"Then, what's the difference between a midwife and an obstetrician? That's what I don't fully understand."

"Well, the main difference is that one is a professional of physiology, that is, the 'normal' state of things, whereas the other is specialised in pathology, the illness. All normal things related to women, as pregnancy, contraception, menstruation, menopause… are within a midwife's competence, as they are physiological processes. As women, we go through them as a natural thing. But whenever any of them shows a complication, an Obs & Gynae doctor should intervene."

"But then, we shouldn't be going to our yearly gynae check-up? What I wouldn't give to get rid of it!"

"Of course not; in this country, what gynaecologists do is not well understood, not to mention what midwives do, of course."

"And could you do my yearly revision?"

"Sure, I can, but as I'm telling you a yearly revision is not necessary."

"Well, but the mammograms and all that jazz…" Alicia adds.

"Alicia, it's more than proven mammograms are useless. They're an unnecessary expense which, in all these years when they've been implemented as a routine, haven't been of any use to save any lives, but only to upset many people and amputate many breasts."

"Really? Oh my God!" exclaims Alicia turning towards her daughter, "where have you found this gem? But, is that true?" she says incredulously.

"I had no idea either, Mom, but if she says so, I believe it. I think she knows a lot."

"I believe it, too," Alicia says, "please understand me, Esther, darling, I absolutely believe what you say, but what you are telling me is so... While we've been here, you have dismantled health's structure, telling me about the doctors, midwives, mammograms... I still can't believe what I'm hearing! Not because I don't believe you, but because I'm astounded, and even if I feel liberated by the information you're giving us and for having you in our lives, I'm also rather annoyed to see how we are constantly fooled. One thinks it's just politicians, and then finds out it's everywhere!"

"Alicia, you don't have to apologise. It's perfectly normal for you to feel that way."

"But then, how come people don't know about that? How come nobody tells women to go to the midwives and not to the doctors when they're feeling alright? Because I don't know a single woman who likes going to the gynaecologist, much less getting your breasts squeezed with that bloody device..."

"Look, Alicia, midwifery schools were closed for about ten years in Spain."

"But why?"

"Because they thought they weren't important, that what midwives did could be done by obstetricians or nurses and they weren't necessary. This led to a huge lack of midwives, which is still present nowadays, where there is always a large need of them throughout Spain. And in the whole world, if you ask me. And what happened then? That, as we were not enough, every midwife who qualified went to work in the labour ward, because that's where we were considered most necessary. Then we were getting jobs in GP surgeries and after that, the crisis came. Then, midwives stopped being hired and their work is being done by other people, while there are more and more jobless midwives."

"And who are the people doing those jobs?"

"Doctors and nurses, mainly."

"They should do their own job."

"Yes, sure. But it isn't that easy. You can't change a society from one day to another. Most people believe everything will be much better, and the risk of anything going wrong much lower, with a doctor at the birth, when, as we discussed before, we know that's not true. Women get their mammograms done because they blindly believe that's what they should do. They go to the obstetrician once a year because they wrongly believe they'll be healthier that way, or anything they might have will be detected earlier. Look, I had a boyfriend who was an obstetrician, and a couple of years ago he told me they had been told in a symposium that what increases the risk of a normal labour becoming a pathological one is the presence of a doctor."

"So, they know it themselves," Ingrid remarks.

"What does pathological mean?" Alicia asks.

"To go awry, to become more difficult," clarifies Esther.

"So, they do know and they go on doing it?"

"Yes. It's convenient for them. If obstetricians got forced to operate only when they were necessary, they would be far too many, and who wants to bite the hand that feeds you, as you will understand..."

"Do you mean they operate that much in order to prove they are necessary, then?"

"Not exactly. As I'm trying to tell you, everything they do, they are convinced they have to. I don't know any obstetrician who openly says: 'I'm going to do a C-section to this woman so that I can go to bed early and have a relaxed call'. Maybe some of them think like that, but they don't say it out loud. But there's more than one who are too lenient and do a C-section whenever they have a chance, yes."

"But why?" says Alicia.

"Because that's exactly what their work is meant to be. They are there to perform surgery, to do something. An obstetrician hasn't been trained to hold on patiently, to wait, to care, to be with the mother and wait for things to develop at their own rhythm: he has been trained to correct, to repair, to sort things out, to solve.

"That's why they shouldn't join in the follow up of healthy women, pregnant or not, at any stage of their lives: because that's not their job and they simply don't know how to do it. And it's not just me saying so, it's the president of the WHO and lots of world famous obstetricians: healthy woman, midwife; ill woman, gynaecologist. If you're healthy and go to a doctor, the possibilities for you to end up with a C-section are pretty high."

"See what misinformation can do!" says Alicia, "from now on, I'll be calling you for everything. And you'll help me see what I can do."

"Fine. Now, let's get back to business," Ingrid smiles, "I'm convinced Esther has many things to do and has no time for that much conversation."

"Yes, you're right," she replies, "however, I can always find some time to criticise the system, can't I?" she smiles, "please, lie down, then" she tells Ingrid as she takes a measuring tape from her bag.

After having checked they both are perfectly healthy, she asks her, "what are you doing about the antenatal classes?"

"I'm not sure; I'd like to go, but Dr. López said it wasn't easy. I'd like to go to the Health Centre ones. Any recommendations?"

"Which is your GP surgery?"

"The one on Market Square."

"Why don't you go there and ask the midwife to let you come to the next group? You tell her you've been considered high-risk and that you'd like to go to her antenatal classes. I don't think there'll be any problem."

"But do you do antenatal classes?"

"Yes, of course I do. I do it at home. I'll do it for you when I come to see you. When I have several couples with similar dates I do them for all of you together, but I don't have anyone with similar dates to yours, so you'll be on your own."

"Well, I'm going to see the midwife if you don't mind, because I'd like to be with more pregnant women, I don't know, belonging to a group… You don't mind, do you?"

"Of course not! Why should I? I'm sorry I don't have anyone else to do it with you, because those groups work really well. Besides, as you want a home birth, it's always better to get together with people more akin to you, because the Health Centre group may deceive you a bit."

"How come?" asks Ingrid.

"Well, because they'll probably be women who haven't contemplated most of the things you have, they don't consider it or they don't know it could be necessary; in these months, they'll most probably have been gathering more information about clothes, prams, high chairs and bottles than about the hospital where they'll be giving birth or their alternatives. But please do go. It will be good for you and for the others, for what little you say might be a great help to someone."

"Right; and you and I, when are we meeting again?"

"When do you have your next hospital appointment?"

"In three weeks."

"So, call me a couple of days before and we'll meet just after," Esther hugs Ingrid and Alicia to say goodbye to them.

"See you soon, and call me if you need anything."

"I sure will," Ingrid says with a smile and she closes the door as Esther starts to go down the stairs.

Week 30

Dr. Casona's practice.
"Well, Sara, Juan. This baby is doing splendidly. Happily growing in her mother's tummy."
"That's great! We are very happy too."
"I think we should start talking about your birth options. What will you be wanting?"
"A baby!" says Juan with a grin.
"Yes. That wish is already granted," smiles Nuria, "I mean if you want everything to develop the normal way, waiting for things to happen, or you prefer to program a C-section as soon as possible."
They both look at each other without knowing what to do or say.
"We don't know," Sara replies.
"In normal situations, the most rational thing is to wait until you go into labour and try to have a vaginal birth. It's the best for both you and the baby. But in cases where conceiving has been very difficult or there have been previous losses, when the baby is as desired as yours is, we offer you the possibility of a C-section in week 38 or 39."
"Ahh," replies Sara, "I had no idea. I don't know what to say. I had never thought about it."
"But, isn't a C-section worse?" Juan butts in, "for Sara, I mean."
"That's irrelevant," Sara cuts him, "whatever's best for the baby, without a doubt. If it has to be a C-section, let them do it. No problem."

"Let's see," Nuria Casona starts explaining, "that's the complicated part. It's an option that's given to you and you should consider it. One more option is simply that: one more to choose from. If a vaginal birth is possible, you should always give it a try. The only reason a C-section is offered in your case is for you to rest assured that your baby will be born when he is fully mature and ready to get out. There are babies who, after having been conceived without a problem, aren't born alive and we don't know why. This happens in a tiny percentage and this is what we want to avoid. We don't know either if this is really a good idea, but it's done as something exceptional. The moment the baby is ready to live outside, we get him out, just in case, for everyone to relax."

"It sounds a bit like using a sledgehammer to crack a nut," says Juan.

"Maybe it is, yes," Nuria says.

"I don't think it's such a bad idea. And if anything happens to him if we wait? And if he dies during birth or as Nuria says, in the last weeks of pregnancy? We'd never forgive ourselves, Juan."

"That's why we give you this option and that's why not even professionals agree about this, because surgery also implies a risk for both."

"Well, but if we'd make sure the baby would be fine with a C-section…" adds Sara.

"Here's the dilemma, Sara, that a C-section is not risk-free either. Babies born by C-section have more respiratory problems, for instance. And mothers are the most affected, of course. But that's not something you have to decide right now. You have a lot of time. I've told you early for you to consider it, to talk about it and decide what's best for you. Go home and you can tell me at our next appointment, all right?"

"Of course," says Juan, as Sara nods.

"I wanted to ask you something," says Sara, "the antenatal classes, where should we do that? Do you do them?"

"No, no, it's midwives who do that, they are the ones who know, I wouldn't know how to begin! Go to your GP Centre and the midwife there will inform you; but go right now, because that's usually done in the last two months of pregnancy and you're on your last stretch!"

"Rosa asks me if you'll be going to the antenatal classes," Luis tells his wife.

"Sure, I will, I don't remember anything," Carmen replies.

"All right. I'll tell her you're going, then."

"We" are going," she corrects him, "I already went to most of Lara's on my own and I don't want to be the only one on my own, you never know what people will think."

"I can go with you, but what do we do with our daughter?"

"When are they?"

"On Thursdays, I've been told."

"She has English on Thursdays. Your mother can pick her up and we'll go get her when we get out."

"Right, as you want. I thought maybe with the second child you wouldn't be going, because these classes are more for first time mothers…"

"Luis. I don't remember how to breathe, what the epidural was about and all those things they tell you. I know how to raise a child, but I don't remember anything about the birth anymore."

"Sure, darling, I'll tell them we'll be there, we'll be starting next Thursday already."

Health Centre. 17:55.

Rosa comes into the Health Centre. Today's the first day of the antenatal classes. She turns the room lights on and tells the couples they may come in.

María, Guille, Sonia and Soledad enter together.

"Take a mat and two pillows per couple," Rosa tells them.

Ingrid comes in with Alicia and approaches Rosa to ask her where to sit, when Rosa smiles at someone who's behind her.

"Carmen, darling, you look great!" Rosa says as she goes to her.

Ingrid looks around, takes a couple of mats and puts them next to María and Guille. "Take some cushions, Mom," she tells Alicia, who's standing by the cushion box.

Juan and Sara enter the room. They stop by the door, not knowing what to do. Sara takes a look and sees everyone has taken their shoes off.

"Shoes off, Juan," she says, pointing at her feet. Juan takes his shoes off and helps Sara do the same.

"Come on. Just one mat and two cushions per couple or we won't have enough for everyone," Rosa tells the room.

"Luis, Carmen. Sit somewhere and we'll talk later. I think almost everybody is here now."

Lorena comes in with Luci. They smile shyly and sit next to Carmen.

"Well. Let's start, I think we're all here already. If anyone isn't, they'll soon be here," says Rosa looking around the room. "Gee, six big tummies and only three men!" she exclaims. "It will finally be true that just one man would be enough to save humanity," she jokes, "I'm Rosa, I'm the midwife who'll teach your antenatal classes. I'd like you to introduce yourselves so that we all know a bit more about who we are. We're going to be together for quite some time in the following weeks, so, if you don't mind, tell us your name and if it's your first baby and such..." says Rosa pointing at Sara.

"Hello, I'm Sara. This will be my first baby, even if I've had several pregnancies, so this baby is very special. This is the first time we've got this far, and we're thrilled. This is Pedro," she says touching her belly, "and this is Juan, my husband," she points with her head to Juan, who smiles at her.

"Well, that's it. I'm Juan —he says shyly—. And Sara already told you everything.

"Hello. I'm Ingrid. This is my first baby too. It's a boy, although I haven't thought of the name yet, and this is my mother, Alicia."

"Hi, I'm Alicia. This will be my first grandson. And I like Mario a lot for a name."

"Ha, ha, ha." they all laugh.

"Hi, I'm María. This will be my first baby too. It's a girl, although we still haven't decided on a name yet, and I'm thirty weeks pregnant."

"Cheers, I'm Guille. I'm Maria's partner, and the father of this baby girl. And I've come to see what we can learn here about birth and being parents and suchlike..."

"Hello, I'm Sol. I'm also thirty weeks pregnant, but I have this huge tummy because I'm going to be the mother of two. They're twins. Two girls: Sofía and Diana."

"I am Sonia, and I am Sofía and Diana's 'other mum', and I'm also the aunt of this other baby girl," she says pointing at María, "so, we're all very happy!"

"Wow, those grandparents must be thrilled!" says Rosa, "are they the first granddaughters?"

"Yes," say the four of them.

"The house will be all joy! No babies, and now three of them all of a sudden!"

"Yes, three girls," says Sonia.

"Gosh, that house is going to be so pink... just like Barbie's house!" says the midwife, and they laugh.

"I'm Carmen. I'm also thirty weeks pregnant. This one will be a boy, and we already have a girl at home."

"I'm Luis, I've been a nurse at this health centre and a workmate of Rosa's for ages and I'm Carmen's husband."

"Hello, I'm Lorena. I'm thirty weeks pregnant. Well, most of us are, aren't we?" she says looking at the rest, who nod in agreement.

"Yes. You're more or less all at the same stage," Rosa confirms.

"Hello, I'm Luci. I'm not her partner nor her mother," she says gesturing towards Sonia and Alicia, "I'm just Lorena's friend."

"Well, so here we are, all of us. I'm going to tell you a little bit, and then you can ask me all you want at the end. Anyway, we'll be starting with what everyone finds the most interesting. Before, when I gave these classes I used to talk about the exercises, the breathing… but we spent the whole afternoon talking about the epidural. So, I've decided to start from there, and thus you'll be paying more attention to the next classes.

"Epidural is an analgesic that's injected here," Rosa says, taking her hand to her back, "in your lower back, in the epidural space, hence its name. The sooner you ask for it, the better. I'm telling you this because many women say things like: 'oh, I only want it if it's necessary' or 'I want to give natural birth a try, I can always get the epidural later'... and that depends on so many factors that, sometimes, when you ask for it the anaesthetist is busy, or it's too late because the baby is about to be born, or whatever. The best thing is to sign the consent, which depends on every hospital, but they're all rather similar, so that it's already in your records when you arrive in the hospital," she looks inside a folder and gives every couple a sheet, "this is the Maternity Hospital's consent, but as I told you they're all pretty similar. In a few weeks, you'll have to go to get your anaesthesia tests done, and when you're there and talk to the anaesthetist you sign the consent, because many times they won't give it to you later if you haven't signed."

"How come?" asks Ingrid.

"For many reasons: Sometimes the anaesthetist is busy somewhere else with a woman who has signed it and, of course, has priority. Other times, because you have to pass some blood tests that are required before an anaesthetist can do anything. Last, some anaesthetists say a woman in labour is not able to make such an important decision, so many refuse to give it to you in case something happens and you give them hell later."

"And why would we give them hell?" asks Sara.

"Well, for anything... because things don't work out as you expected, because there is some side effect... and you decide to sue him; one must be very careful with these matters nowadays."

"Naturally: if I got some side effects from an epidural I'd be denouncing it too," says Sol.

"That's my point," continues Rosa, "people didn't denounce before, but now you get a complaint for anything."

They all look at each other, puzzled. On seeing their faces, Luis intervenes, "what Rosa's trying to say is that the way things stand now with complaints, it's better to do things well from the start, for if you don't, anaesthetists might be afraid to give you the epidural and refuse to do it. It's called defensive medicine, and it's the way medicine is implemented now in this country, well, and in most others too. Due to the increasing number of complaints, what's done now is not the best for the patient, but the best to avoid legal complaints."

"But that's terrible!" says Sonia.

"Yes. It is," replies Luis, "but it's the only way."

"How is it going to be the only way?" Sol adds, "doing their job well done is the way, and is what they should do."

"It's not that easy. You see it that way because you regard it just as patients. But if you could put yourselves in their shoes, you'd view it differently," Luis goes on, "if you were to see your workmates having problems all day, reading stories about doctors and nurses who've been sentenced and so on, you'd do whatever it takes to prevent that."

"Even if it's the rest of us who pay for it," adds María.

"Yes," Luis explains, "that's the way some professionals do their job, and if anything happens, they try to wriggle out of it. People now will complain at the slightest chance, even if it's nobody's fault. When a baby's born with a problem and dies after a few days, parents will very likely look for the culprits, even if there aren't any. And the first people to go after are those who took care of the woman at birth and, if they find no irregularity there, because there simply wasn't any -imagine, for instance, a new-born with a metabolic problem he already had in the womb-, then they'll go after the obstetrician who took care of the pregnancy for not having detected it."

"It's just as Luis tells you," Rosa intervenes, "but let's go on, because if we carry on discussing that, we'll get nowhere: we don't have that many classes and there's a lot to be told. As I said, ask for an appointment with the anaesthetist and sign the consent form, so that you don't come across any surprises later and have to do without the epidural just for not knowing this."

"What are the cons of having it?" asks Ingrid.

"Well, your legs might go numb, or you can't pee, or you can't push well, but that has a solution because if you are in bed you don't need to feel your legs, you're not going anywhere anyway, being monitored. The midwives in the labour ward will catheterise you every few hours to empty your bladder. When your birth time comes nearer you'll be learning how to push here. As you can see, they're just minor inconveniences.

"And for the baby? It doesn't have any drawbacks?" Ingrid insists.

"But what drawbacks could it have for the baby? It's you who is having the labour pains, not him," says Rosa.

"Right, well, but they say the number of C-sections and forceps increases after having the epidural," adds Ingrid.

"Fine, but you cannot have everything. If you want a painless birth, you'll have to assume what an epidural entails; besides, how can you know what would have happened in those cases without one? Maybe they would have ended the same way."

"Well, I imagine people doing those studies know how to do them," Ingrid points out, "if you compare the number of women with and without an epidural and you find a significant difference, it's clear that it must have some influence."

"Well, be it as it may, the baby is hardly affected by the mother having an epidural during the birth, because as I told you, birth doesn't hurt the baby. You should get the epidural," Rosa continues, "once you're in labour and more than 4 cm dilated."

"What happens if you get it before?" asks Sara.

"Then you'd have to get the oxytocin drip too. Oxytocin is the hormone that makes you have contractions. If you get an epidural before you're in established labour we'd have to accelerate your contractions. We can't keep you in labour for three days. Anyway, don't worry, because midwives and doctors take care of everything and check your dilation before they give you an epidural. No one would give it to you without checking beforehand."

"But if they have to induce you, do you also have to wait?" asks Sol.

"It would be the best, but it's different in your case, because they'll give you the oxytocin from the start, so your circumstances would have to be considered. In some cases, it's possible to give it without any dilation."

"In my case? Am I being induced? I was asking in general!" Sol says.

"Well, with twins the likelihood of being induced is much higher than in other cases, yes."

"I didn't know that," she says with obvious distress.

The midwife, realising it, tells her, "don't worry, whoever takes care of you will do the best for you and your babies, that's for sure."

"But you just said a moment ago that each one will help himself more than helping us," Sol replies.

"Well, it was just a manner of speaking, luv. There are wonderful teams with very good people in our hospitals who'll be doing the best for you and your babies. Don't worry about anything, because you are in good hands. You as much as the rest of you, right?" she says looking around at them.

Maternity Hospital.

"Nico, you are taking an induction for postdates," says the Triage nurse.

Nico takes her records and walks towards the delivery room. He starts leafing through them and he sees the woman is 41 weeks pregnant. He goes to the doctor's office. There are several registrars there and he goes towards Laura, the only consultant he can see in the room.

"Hello Laura; look, they're passing me an induction for postdates and the woman is 41 weeks pregnant."

"So?"

"So, she still has one whole week to start labour by her own means."

"I guess she must have had a scan and they've seen it's the right moment, then," she says as she leafs through the records, "here's the scan and the Triage report, Jesús saw her yesterday… I don't know, they must have had their reasons. Maybe she doesn't have much liquor. I don't know, what's the difference between 41 and 42?"

Nico looks at her incredulously. "I can see there's no difference for you. But for that mother and baby it might make a big difference. As if there wasn't any difference between a normal birth and an induced one!"

"And who told you she'll be having a normal birth if we let her wait till 42?" she says arrogantly.

"No one, but at least we're not prematurely taking away the possibility that she might. That's the reason why we don't induce all of them at 37 weeks, because letting the birth develop by itself is infinitely better for everyone, especially for babies and their mothers. Do you really need someone to explain this to you?" says Nico with snide.

"Look, Nicolás. This woman was admitted yesterday. She has already been administered 'Propess'[44], and now, we're going to carry on with the induction. Are you going to defy the colleague who has taken this decision and knows more than you do about this?"

"...And who knows more than I do? What about? My area or his? Because it's clear that inducing a woman who is 41 weeks pregnant just because is not knowing more. It's believing you to be more, believing you can decide at your whim to ruin a birth for two people because you simply don't care. It's not having informed that woman about her options, it's deciding on her behalf because you feel like it for something as transcendental and important as is the birth of her child, which will have repercussions for the rest of their lives. And this proves that you know very little."

"So, if you are not inducing her we'll pass her to another midwife."

"I'm not the one inducing her, that's not my job I'll be taking care of her. And go on: don't listen, don't reflect. If I face you with something you don't like, just in order not to challenge another colleague's authority, and not because of any sound reason, you just pass the hot potato to another one. Well, no, Laura. This woman has been assigned to me and I'll be the one taking care of her. And within that care comes defending her from any abuse, which is what I've just tried to do. You are the Labour Ward consultant and you say to go on with this induction, well, so be it. I have to try to do my job well. And I think so do you. Do we go on with the induction?"

"Naturally," replies Laura defiantly.

---

[44] Propess: Medication given in the vagina to soften the cervix.

"So, write it down on the records," Nico says, giving her the folder.

After scribbling something on the record, Laura gives it back to him and Nico reads what she has written out loud, "'Induction at 41/40 for postdates pregnancy and scan-verified placental ageing.' Sure, like all 41-week placentas. You're very brave, Laura," Nico tells her, and he leaves.

"These are the worst ones," says Laura to her junior colleagues, "these little midwives who think they know more than we do and dare to defy doctor's orders. You have to put them in their place, or they will go all cheeky on you."

"But why are we inducing her on 41 if here we do it at 42? Any clue?" asks Mercedes, a registrar.

"I have no idea," Laura laughs, "my guess is Jesús was on call and you know he doesn't like evolution that much."

"What?" asks Abel, the junior doctor, puzzled.

"Jesús is about to retire," says Laura lowering her voice, "he's been inducing at 41 all his life, and even if the last protocol says we have to do it at 42, he carries on doing his will, and I'm not going to oppose him. Besides, how do we go about telling that woman to go home? That could mean trouble for us... there are enough complaints already; we should help each other when we can."

Nico enters the delivery room and there's Susana, sitting on the bed.

"Hello, I'm Nico, your midwife. How are you?"

"Very well. You're the midwife?"

"Yes. Do you mind?"

"Sure, sure. It's just I had no idea there were men who were midwives. I mean, look at the word 'midwife'..."

"Yes. I am a midwife, or that's what it says on my diploma. You don't say "firewoman" or "carpentress" either, it's just a matter of habit. Do you know why you're here?"

"Because this one won't get out —she says touching her belly.

"Well, maybe his moment hasn't come yet," Nico tries to sound her out.

"He should have been out a week ago, I can't take it anymore."

"That was your estimated due date; that means he'll be born around that date, fifteen days up or down, but it's not exact. Few babies are born exactly on the day their mothers are forty weeks pregnant."

"He's just like his father and he hasn't even been born yet! He always keeps everyone waiting," Susana laughs.

"You know what's going to happen next?"

"You're putting me on a drip to provoke contractions."

"You had the prostaglandins yesterday, didn't you?"

"Yes, they gave me something, yes."

"And have you noticed anything?"

"Yes, some aches like strong menstruation pains, back here in the kidneys."

"Well, I'm going to monitor you now to see how your baby is doing and in a while we'll start the induction with oxytocin. What will the baby's name be?"

"Brian."

"Is there anyone out there waiting?"

"My husband and my sister."

"We'll ask them to come in if you don't mind."

"Both of them?" the maternity assistant asks.

"Yes, both of them. Susana, you're going to be here for quite a long time. Starting birth is not easy. We're talking about a few hours here, alright?"

"Ahh, I don't know if I'll hold on, I didn't want to have the epidural, you hear so many things about it… I want a natural birth."

"Well, if we induce you it's not going to be very natural to start with…"

"Right, but only if it's necessary, because I don't want an epidural."

Nico feels terrible. Poor Susana doesn't want an epidural. There are few women who don't come through the door already asking for it. The contractions provoked by synthetic oxytocin are much more painful than the ones produced by the body if it starts labour on its own. She'll be having the complete pack of interventionism just because; because she had the misfortune of getting "Mad knife" in a check-up and he decided, with no medical indication whatsoever, that this baby would be forced out today.

"Then we'll do all we can so that you don't need it," Nico smiles.

Susana has had contractions for several hours. It will soon be twelve hours since she has started with the oxytocin. Ana, the midwife who came in last night taking over from Nico, is about to examine her.
"She's the same," Ana tells the assistant, "tell them to come see her."
"What?" Susana asks, "am I not dilating?"
"No, love, you're not. It is the same as before."
"I can't take it anymore, I want the epidural, I can't take it. I've done all I could," she says, starting to cry.
"Come on, come on, darling. Don't worry, the anaesthetist will be here in a sec and will take that pain away."
Laura, the consultant on call, puts the gloves on and examines her.
"We're going to deliver the baby by C-section, Madam."
"What?" Susana asks, frightened, "the baby, is the baby all right?"
"Calm yourself, he is. But you're not dilating, we've given you everything but you won't, you don't want to dilate. So, don't worry, we'll do a C-section."

Maternity Hospital.
Labour Ward Staff Room.
"Where are the docs? There's no one at the office," says Marta coming into the room.
"In theatre," answers Cande. "She's bleeding. They have already asked for blood."
"Have they?" Ana asks, alarmed. "My lady?"
"A failed induction who's been here all day."
"Why was she induced?"
"Postdates at 41."
"And something else," says Marta. "We have not been inducing until 42 weeks since the new boss arrived."
"I don't know, I haven't seen anything else on her records…"
Nico arrives in the morning and leaves his bag in the room. Ana comes in and he asks her, "how is she? How did it end?"

"C-section for failed induction and hysterectomy[45]. She's being transfused in Recovery."

"What?" he bellows furious and frightened, "what?"

"Yes, babe, yes; she nearly dies over there."

Nico runs to Recovery. He meets Laura in the corridor and addresses her, livid with anger,

"you are responsible for her nearly dying, you are responsible for her not being able to have more children. Do you still think you were right? Do you still think she had to be induced just for the sake of it? Do you still think week 41 and week 42 are the same? If you had waited for a few more days maybe she wouldn't have been induced, or the conditions would have been more favourable and the induction would not have failed."

"You don't know that," Laura stammers.

"Oh, so you carry on? You dare to carry on? The only thing I know and you know it too is that this woman should not have been induced yesterday, and here you have the result of your pride. '*How am I going to listen to a midwife and change a doctor's order*'," he imitates her in a falsetto voice. "This woman almost dies and we both know why. So, I hope you put this to good use and whenever you take such a futile decision in the future you remember that your arrogance almost killed Susana."

Nico goes to Recovery to see Susana, and Laura runs to the changing room, where she bursts into tears.

"Hello Susana," says Nico, taking her hand. "How are you?"

"Water, please," says Susana, looking with her tongue for some moisture inside her mouth.

Nico soaks a gauze in water and puts it in her mouth.

"You can't drink anything right now, but you are having blood and fluids through the drip and your thirst will soon go away."

"How's Brian?"

"I don't know, I haven't seen him yet. Where is he?"

Nico looks at the Recovery nurse.

"At NNU."

"But is he all right?" Nico asks.

---

[45] Hysterectomy: Surgical removal of the uterus.

"Yes. He's there because we don't take responsibility for babies here in Recovery. When you go up to the ward, they take him to you," says the nurse looking at Susana.

"What? How do you mean you don't take responsibility for babies in Recovery? But there's absolutely nothing to do to them, they just need to be with their mother. I'll go get him," Nico tells Susana.

"Well, I'm not taking any responsibility for that baby!" he hears the nurse yelling as he's going towards the lifts.

Maternity Hospital.
Intensive Neonatal Care Unit.

"Hello. The baby from tonight's C-section, where is he?" Nico asks the first person he meets at NNU.

"That's him," says the nurse, "shall we take him up already?"

"No, I'm taking him down to Recovery, his mother hasn't even seen him yet."

"But is he coming back here or not?"

"Is there any reason for him to be here?"

"No. They always bring C-section babies here because they can't stay in Recovery."

"And why can't they?"

"Not a clue, for their mothers to rest? So that they don't disturb?"

"More like the second option, methinks," says Nico pushing the baby's cot, "where can a new-born baby be better than with his mother?"

"You can say that again," agrees the nurse, "besides, we don't do anything to them here. They're simply there, waiting."

Maternity Hospital.
Recovery Unit.

"Look who's here," says Nico as he approaches Susana's bed pushing Brian's cot.

"Oh!" exclaims a thrilled Susana, trying to sit up.

"Wait, wait, don't move, I'll give him to you," says Nico, taking Brian's blanket away and positioning him near his mother's face. Susana smothers him with kisses and starts to cry.

"Hello sweetie, hello my love, my sunshine, how beautiful you are. Please put him a bit farther, I can't see him well so close to me… But you're beautiful! Brian, baby, I'm your mom. Has his father seen him yet?"

"I don't know," says Nico, "I'm not sure."

"How can I breastfeed him? I cannot even move," says Susana, slightly raising her arms, which are one of the few parts of her body still responding to her orders.

"Susana, you've lost a lot of blood. You're very weak. Wait until you get a couple of blood bags inside you, rest a bit and then you'll feel much better and you'll be able to start breastfeeding him."

"Then someone give him a bottle, please, the poor thing must be starving!"

"Well, let's go step by step," Nico says, "Brian has been fed right until the moment he was taken out of you. If you want to breastfeed him, you'll have to insist. Most babies don't even eat in these first hours; they just play around with the nipple a bit and that's it. I'm leaving him here on the bed by your side, and you just rest peacefully. When you have rested for a few hours, ask for someone to help you breastfeed him, but don't ask for a bottle yet. You have lost a lot of blood and we must watch your breastfeeding very closely, and how Brian is sucking. If you want to breastfeed him, the important thing is for him not to have a bottle. Brian needs a bit more of breastfeeding control, as your body is very weak to produce milk. If he needs some kind of milk reinforcement, it's better if he takes it from a cup or with a spoon or a syringe. If he doesn't, it'll be very difficult for him to breastfeed later. Besides, if he takes some artificial milk, it has to be under control and for a few days, to avoid that he develops any allergy or intolerance. If you have any doubts, ask for them to call me to the Labour Ward and I'll come here to see you, all right?"

"All right. You're the best midwife I could have," says Susana with glassy eyes.

No, I'm not the best. The best wouldn't have let this happen, he thinks distraught, kissing her on the forehead.

"I'm not taking any responsibility for that baby," the Recovery nurse tells Nico when she sees him leaving.

"What do you mean?" asks Nico, turning to her.

"Just that, that I'm not taking any responsibility. If anything happens to him…"

"Like what? Is he going to explode? He's a human being, on his first day of life, who's perfectly healthy and whose only need is being with his mother. Of course, you're not responsible for him. Nor are you for me, whom you've never even met. Where did you get that nonsense here in Recovery? It's the parents who are responsible for a baby, not a nurse or a midwife or a priest. The only thing that could happen to this baby is falling from the bed, and I already have put the cot as a stopper. Nevertheless, and even if you're not responsible for him, I guess you'll try to stop it if you see he's about to fall down, merely as a human being if not as someone responsible for him."

The nurse bends down her head and says nothing. Deep down, she knows Nicolás is right and that that's just something constantly repeated among her workmates, but she has just realised she doesn't even know what it means.

Nico goes to the labour ward. He looks at the clock. Twenty-five past eight, and he has already had two fights today.

"What a crap day," he mutters, "and it's only just started!"

Week 38

Health Centre 17:50.

Sara, Ingrid, Sonia and Lorena are talking.
"What's your hospital?" Lorena asks Ingrid.
"The Maternity Hospital, and yours?"
"The same, but I'm considering going to a private clinic," says Lorena, "I haven't decided yet."
"How come?"
"Because I have insurance and private clinics are much better, aren't they?"
"Well, that depends on what you consider to be better," Ingrid points out.
"In those clinics you have your own doctor, you don't need to share a room, you can have a friend with you, they have more means if anything happens…" Lorena enumerates.
"The last one isn't true. They have less means. What's more, if something goes wrong, they put you in an ambulance and they take you to the Maternity Hospital at full speed."
"Really?" Sara butts in.
"Oh yeah," Carmen says, "private clinics don't have the really expensive devices. It's not very relevant for a birth, but if the baby needs an incubator, Public Health is much better."
"I always thought private meant better too," says Sara, "I mean, I'm going to the MH myself, but I always believed private clinics were the best."
"But if it isn't a premature birth and you don't need an incubator, private's better," Lorena insists.
"Don't be too sure, Lorena," Ingrid replies, "you have a higher chance of ending up with a Cesarean section in a private clinic than in a public hospital."
"Well, but that's probably because in a private one you can choose to have a Cesarean and in public ones you only get it if you need it, isn't it?"

"It's not only that. There aren't that many women choosing to have a Cesarean as for that modifying statistics. Most don't want to go through surgery if they can give birth."

"Come on, you see celebrities having them all the time," says Sara.

"Yes, but not all of them had it planned. What I mean is that if the C-sections percentage is some ten points more in private clinics, the number of women choosing a planned C-section doesn't impact that percentage much. The main reason for that difference is, like it or not, money. The clinic earns more with a C-section than with a vaginal birth."

"I have to decide whether I want an elective Cesarean or not," Sara says.

"How come?" asks Sonia.

"Because as I've lost many babies and I've never gotten this far, they give me the option of choosing if I want the baby to be born when he's ready, instead of waiting for labour to start."

"And what are you doing?" Ingrid asks.

"I'm not sure yet. I'm still thinking. I prefer a vaginal birth, but I couldn't live with it if something happened to my baby because I waited."

"And if something happened to him because you didn't?" Ingrid points out.

"What do you mean?" asks Sara with curiosity.

"What if anything goes wrong with the Cesarean?"

Sara remains deep in thought for a while and whispers, "I had never thought of that."

"I don't mean to frighten you, Sara, but you should consider that too. C-sections are not a hundred percent safe answer. What you say about something going wrong with the baby because you took the wrong option is there whichever option you choose."

"Sol is terrified with the twins," says Sonia.

"Where is she giving birth?" Ingrid asks.

"In the Maternity also."

"And what did they tell you?" asks Sara.

"That they'll induce her in week 40 if she gets there and she'll be getting an epidural, and that she'll possibly end up with a C-section because of it being twins, you know…"

"And why don't you look for more options?" Ingrid says.

"Like what? Another hospital? You said private ones are even worse, didn't you?"

"And a private midwife?" asks Ingrid.

"But a midwife can't take twins, can they?" says Sonia.

"A private midwife can help you get whatever you want, she'll give you the relevant information for you to decide what's the most convenient to you. If you just go to one place and don't look for alternatives, the one on the other side tries to sell you the typical 'That's the way things are done here', not 'Here's all the info with every possible option you have and I'll be with you along the whole process whatever you decide'. It's like a lawyer. If you have a legal problem, you put a lawyer in charge of the matter, because you know nothing about law and that's what they are there for. It's the same with a private midwife."

"Gee, I had no idea about all that," Carmen butts in. "As Luis is in the trade, I've never worried about anything. I didn't even know there were private midwives. I had heard there were some who did home births, but I didn't know you could hire one for a birth in a hospital."

"Hello everybody," says Rosa the midwife, "sorry, I'm a bit late today. Let's start."

"Do you know any private midwife?" Sonia asks Ingrid as they sit down.

"Let's talk later," she nods.

"We'll be talking about the birth today. About what you have to do when the moment comes," Rosa starts, "you're all first-time mothers, aren't you?"

Carmen raises her hand.

"Naturally, Carmen. Well, except for Carmen you all are, right?"

They all nod.

"Well, I'll be talking, in general, about first-time mothers; you're the majority and you Carmen also have Luis. But whenever there's any difference I'll be telling you, Carmen. When your contractions start, don't go running to the hospital because you'd stay there for a long time. Wait until they're regular and they've been so for a long time. Not all births start the same way: some start little by little, you feel a bit upset, then they stop, then they start again, then they stop again... And others start without any notice, just like that, one contraction after the other nonstop until the baby comes. That's why it's very important that you know the difference between the latent phase of labour and established labour, as we said last week. The moment you should go to the hospital is when you have re-gu-lar contractions," she says stressing each syllable, "and you've been having them for at least one hour. I'll explain: if you start with a contraction, then another one twenty minutes later, then after ten minutes, then two almost together, there's no regularity there, there's no rhythm. You'll know you're in labour when you have strong contractions every five minutes, strong enough to make you stop what you're doing. When you've been like that for one hour, and they're becoming stronger each time, more intense, then it's time to go.

"Once you're there, come to Triage, go to the counter and tell them you're in labour. They'll take care of everything.

"Your partner can take this chance to go park the car then, as cars can't stay at the entrance.

When you come in you'll be received by the on-call obstetrician, who'll start your record: you know, how long have you been having contractions, if your waters have broken... afterwards, on the bed, she'll examine you to see whether you're in labour or not, and depending on the result of that examination you'll come in, you'll be taken to the ward or you'll be sent back home if you're not in labour yet.

"Once admitted to the labour ward they'll give you a hospital gown and if you want an enema, they'll give you one too."

"If you want?" asks Ingrid.

"Yes, if you want. It's not compulsory. But let me tell you, everything you have inside is bound to come out. So, you decide if you prefer doing it in the bathroom or in front of the people in charge of your birth."

"But I thought during the last days of pregnancy or the first hours of labour your tummy gets quite loose and the intestines empty themselves?" adds Ingrid.

"Yes, that's why I'm telling you it's your decision and nobody will make you do you anything. If you don't mind pooping in public, don't get one."

After a few seconds of silence, María asks, "and what about pubic hair, do we have to get waxed?"

"That's also your decision, you don't have to if you don't want to."

"But they'll shave it at the hospital," adds Carmen.

"No, not anymore," says the midwife, "unless they have to do something to you. If you end up with a C-section, they will, of course. Or if you have hair in the episiotomy area also; but if you are not shaved, they won't do it, not anymore."

"Well, I do recommend waxing," says Carmen looking at everyone in the room, "because you know the difference in the way your hair grows after waxing it and after shaving it. That area will be very painful with the episiotomy stitches, and it's what I remember most about the first days after Lara was born, it truly is. And it's very sad that when you remember your first days as a mother the first thing to come to your mind is how you suffered when your hair started growing. So, this time I'll get a Brazilian waxing."

"Me, I'm convinced pubic hair is there for a reason, that it has its function," says Ingrid, "and I'm sure it will have its relevance in the birth too."

"But what function could it possibly have?" asks Carmen.

"I don't know, I don't have a clue. All I can say is that the only time I shaved it all out of curiosity, for a change…, whatever, every time I peed the wee went down my leg, so, I don't know, maybe to channel the amniotic fluid, to catch it, to avoid infections… I have no idea what it might be for, I just wonder: Won't it have some use?" Ingrid carries on.

"Well, I don't think it does," says Rosa, "I'm of Carmen's opinion, it's better if you wax it beforehand. As you'll be showing quite a lot of people your private parts, it's better to have them nice and neat, don't you think?" she asks the others, "well, let's go on. So, once you've had the enema, you go to the toilet to do your business, and when you come out they monitor you to see how the baby's doing, they put an IV line and start you on a drip."

"Just like that, right from the start?" Ingrid intervenes again.

"Of course, when are they going to do it? Once you start haemorrhaging?"

"But if you drink water you don't need a drip, or an IV, unless it's strictly necessary, isn't it?"

"No way, absolutely not!" says Rosa raising her voice, "that's something no obstetric service in this country will take. They're letting you get away with a good many things already: walking, the ball, having music, having a companion, cutting the cord, skin to skin… Not having an IV is a terrible imprudence nobody will accept, all right?"

"But you will be able to say if you want it or not, won't you?" says Sonia, "It's your body!"

"But if you go to a hospital, you'll have to accept its rules, won't you? It's as if you come to my home and start destroying everything."

"No, it isn't. It's as if I go to your home and you open a wine bottle and just because I'm there I have to drink it even if I don't want to," says Sonia.

"Well, but you cannot expect going to a hospital and being allowed not to have an IV line. Some things are acceptable, but others are not," Rosa adds.

"And what are the alternatives?" Sonia asks.

"Well, staying at your home. Although I don't recommend it, home births are totally backwards well into the 21st century," says the midwife.

"But Rosa, then you're saying that either we go to the hospital and obey or we'd better not go," Sol intervenes.

"I am. That's the way things are and it's better if you go there prepared, because hospitals have their norms and their protocols. And they are updating themselves lots, and giving you more things that were unimaginable before."

"Like what?" Ingrid asks.

"Like the ones I mentioned before: the ball, walking, playing your own music… in many of them, you can even drink water! In the maternity ward the baby is with you in your room… However, those are things that have been considered reasonable with time. Not having an IV is just crazy, as are those birth plans which are the latest fashion, with so many women saying, 'I don't want a C-section' or 'I don't want an induction'. So, what do you think, that they do it for pleasure?"

"What's that birth plan thing?" asks Lorena.

"It's a paper which is the latest craze now, where women say what they want in their birth and they put it in writing, so that they don't have to be saying 'I want this or that' during the birth,"

says Rosa. "But it's absolutely useless. Well, to be held in contempt, that's what it's useful for, and many hospital people say: "here we have another one of those weirdos who thinks we're here just to annoy her".

"But it's a completely legal document, with full legal capacity or whatever it's called," Ingrid points out, "you express your wishes on it, what you want to be done, or not done, to you and your baby."

"Like what?" asks the midwife.

"Like nobody coming into your room, freedom of movements, being free to go to the toilet…"

"But all that's already happening, do you think you're going to a prison or what? You can move around all you want, nobody comes into your delivery room unless they must. They don't do it just because; they do it for your own good. And as for going to the toilet, before you go in, when you can, of course they let you go. Afterwards, when you have all the wires on you, you can't, but the Maternity Assistant will come with a bedpan; it's her job and she's seen it a thousand times before."

"Yes, but I haven't. I don't pee or poo in public, much less with someone I don't even know," Ingrid complains.

"So, you tell her to go out for a minute. What I mean is all you must do is say it. And it's much easier to tell the Maternity Support Worker to go out for a second than having everything written on a piece of paper. Because what they can give you, they will. And if they can't, there's no point in having it written, even if it was written in gold."

"And what about the Group B strep?" Ingrid asks again.

"What about it? There's no getting away from that: if it's positive you'll be getting the antibiotics. If you passed it to the baby he could die, and I'm not joking here."

"But scientific evidence suggests the opposite and says it has not been proven that antibiotics are efficient in preventing neonatal sepsis. Whereas it's a fact that they have many disadvantages, such as destroying the mother's intestinal flora, and the baby's too, and giving you a mastitis that will probably prevent you from breastfeeding."

"But where have you heard all that?" Rosa snaps.

"Well, I've read it. It's from the Cochrane library, I think."

"Look, don't read so much because in the end it'll do you more harm than good. Because if every single hospital gives antibiotics to women with a positive streptococcus, there must be a reason for it, mustn't it? And if that article was published yesterday, there will be another one tomorrow stating you all should get antibiotics, with or without streptococcus.... Get my drift, girlie, I can see you're very young," Rosa says without hiding her annoyance, "you can read anything on the internet, and if later at the hospital they perform something that even if it's good for you you had read it was bad, you'll be upset for no reason, you see? Where are you giving birth? What's your hospital?"

"The Maternity," answers Ingrid.

"So, listen to me: if you want things to go right, you'd better not take a birth plan. For when we see a woman with one in her hand we know she means trouble, and you'll be kept on a much shorter leash, because we know we have to be extra cautious with birth plan mothers, they're very likely to denounce us for anything."

"I expect I won't have to."

"Of course not, dear! You won't need that, I'm telling you. You have to understand the team at the Maternity is wonderful -as they are at all the other hospitals, of course- and they'll be doing what's best for you. All you have to do is let them lead you and advise you, they are the experts."

"I've hired a private midwife, she'll be taking care of my dilation at home."

"Ah! Who is she?" the midwife asks.

"Esther."

"The one who attends home births?"

"Yes. But she does much more than home births. She follows up on your pregnancy, explains every test, helps you to understand what you've been told at every visit with the doctor, choosing… She also stays with you during labour. And when you're reaching full dilation she takes you to the hospital. After the birth she comes to the hospital and to your home to help you with the baby, breastfeeding, postpartum… I'm delighted."

"So am I," says Alicia, "she knows a lot. And not only about births, she's helping me loads with my old lady matters…"

"Fine, but when you start dilating, go to the Maternity, right? You have no idea about the cases that midwife has brought to hospital. Everything looks hunky-dory at home until it stops being that way and then, yes, then we all want a hospital, don't we? For them to get us out of the mess we've got into for being so irresponsible," says Rosa.

"Well, that's what hospitals are there for, for whenever things go wrong. If you're having a home birth and something goes wrong, of course she should go to the hospital, shouldn't she?"

"There shouldn't be any home births, that's what I mean. I can't understand how in these times there are still people risking their lives for such things. And not just their lives, because if it was only theirs… but when a baby's life is at risk you have to be very selfish to take that decision for your child when you can give birth surrounded by all the necessary technology to help him being born. And what if anything goes wrong? It may happen. And a baby dying at a home birth nowadays deserves that woman being denounced, and the midwife, and everyone, for complicity," Rosa says angrily.

"I think you're mistaken there, Rosa," Luis butts in, "I think when a woman chooses a home birth she does it thinking of her baby above all. I'm one of those who would never think of doing it, and if Carmen wanted a home birth I'd do all I could to change her mind. Be it because I am biased due to my work, be it because in my nurse training I worked in the labour ward and saw many things that frightened me. Even though I'm convinced the decision to have a home birth is not one women take heedlessly. And if a woman decides to do it it's because she has pondered over it a lot and she has thoroughly considered both the pros and the cons."

"Maybe, Luis. But that's not the point. The point is that many things requiring immediate attention happen at birth. Exposing yourself to that happening at home, when you can have a theatre, a NNU and an excellent technical and human team if anything goes wrong is an unnecessary risk which should not be taken today. It should be forbidden by law."

"But Rosa…" says Sonia, "I'm not sure whether I'd like to give birth at home or not because, obviously, with the twins, we haven't even considered it. But like abortion, like having cosmetic surgery… that should be a free option for women to take. No outsider should decide over another person's body. If you're not in favour of home birth it's all right. Just don't do it, don't support it. But from there to say it should be forbidden, there's a world of difference."

"All right, all right, I overdid it, but I find it so crazy that with all the resources we have nowadays… people have died from home births! In a hospital that is solved in a second!"

"Or maybe not!" says Ingrid, in a louder voice than she would have liked, "don't mother and babies also die in hospitals? Aren't those teams and those NNUs many times unable to solve the conflict and there are deaths as a result? Aren't there babies who have died as a direct consequence of being born in a hospital?"

"What utter nonsense!" exclaims Rosa visibly annoyed.

"Is it? Every few years we can see in the media babies destroyed by misused forceps. Not so long ago, a baby got an injection that should have been for his mother and it killed him. Then, we have that baby who was in the hospital and died because somebody made a mistake and gave him his milk through the IV drip… and we could go on, Rosa."

"Yeah, but that's taking things to the limit. You're talking about human error here, that's overdoing it. We all understand that if anything goes wrong it's better to be at a hospital, and the cases you're talking about are few and far between."

"Well, but if anything's happening to you it's always better to be at a hospital, always. If you have a heart attack, it's better to have it at a hospital visiting a friend than in your home's sitting room," says Ingrid.

"Yes, of course. It's always better if you get it near a hospital. Now you're saying I'm right. What I mean is, if anything happens, being at a hospital is better no matter how you look at it," says the midwife.

"That I understand, Rosa. But there's a long way from that to restricting a woman's capacity of deciding about what happens to her body. Hospitals use too much technology; and that hyper-technification brings too many undesired consequences."

"And at home, too!"

"No! There's no technification at home. It's much easier for something to go wrong when we try to manipulate it than when we respect everybody's timings. When did we stop respecting ourselves and each body's nature?"

"Nature is not as wise as you think; nature fails."

"Few times. And that's not an excuse to intervene in births as a routine."

"Fine, let's all go and give birth in the jungle with a stick between our teeth," says the midwife, annoyed.

"But why do those who are against home births always have to use that birth-in-the-jungle or in the stable arguments! I don't want to give birth in the jungle: I want to do the necessary tests to know we are both fine to then freely decide what I want. And I decide that, if everything's all right, I want to give birth at my home, with my sofa, my bed, my nightie and my privacy, just the people I want there and my midwife."

"Oh, yes? So, you just want technology for some things and not for others? To have a scan it's quite all right, but not to give birth."

"Of course! Absolutely! It would be very silly not getting its benefits for the things it can help us with! One thing has nothing to do with the other: the fact that I use technology in my favour doesn't mean I have to use all of it. You wear earrings, right? Why don't you wear them in your nose, eyebrows and lips? If you use earrings, either you use them everywhere or not at all. That's more or less what you're saying."

"Well, ladies," Luis cuts in, "it's clear that we're not going to agree here because positions are very different. But we've been discussing something that'll take us nowhere for a long time; this is like making an atheist and a believer discuss, each one has their arguments and neither will be convinced by the other…"

"Yes, you're right, Luis. Let's go on, or there won't be any class today," says Rosa relieved to be taken out of the mess she has gotten into.

Ingrid looks at her mother, who kisses her and presses her hand.

"You're the best mother in the world," she whispers to her daughter.

"No, Mom: that's you," she says with tears in her eyes.

"Well, where were we? Ah, yes! You have already got your enema and your drip. Then you're taken to the delivery room to dilate. There they monitor you to hear the baby's heartbeat and check the intensity of your contractions, and then they let your companion come in."

"And not before?" asks Sara.

"No, it'd be complicated: it's just a small room and there are several women there, so it's not right for everyone's husbands to be there."

Sonia clears her throat noisily.

"Well, or the partners… ranting a lot today, aren't we?" says the midwife, irritated, "and once inside they'll use the internal monitor."

"Just like that?" Ingrid asks.

"It's much more comfortable."

"For whom?" Ingrid comes back, "because I don't think babies appreciate having their heads pierced that much."

"That's hardly a pinch, come on, they just catch their skin a bit, they don't even notice!"

"What?" says Sol, alarmed. Do they pierce the babies' heads to monitor them?"

"It's very superficial, they don't even notice, come on," the midwife tries to calm them.

"Oh, yes? Just google 'baby's head internal monitor' and you'll see. Your hearts will sink."

"Look here, girl… what was your name again?" asks Rosa patronizingly.

"Ingrid," she replies.

"What are you in these classes for, may I ask? Because the only thing you're doing here is frightening these people with things of dubious veracity. So, if you know everything, don't come back anymore, because you're interrupting me all the time. Questioning every single word I say is making my job difficult here. Because this is my job, ok?"

"Rosa," Luis tries to calm her.

"Let me be, Luis!" she says gesturing with her hand towards her workmate, "I just can't understand it. As if I were here just to annoy you and not to inform you! It's the system that works that way, not me. You're making me responsible for all that happens at hospitals, when I don't even work in one of them!"

"You're responsible for what you say, not for what others do. But don't worry, I'm leaving and I'm not coming back. Because, as for teaching us anything, that still remains to be seen," says Ingrid standing up.

"Great, lovely, the argument of the weak: as I'm not right, I discredit you as a person."

"No, Rosa, it's you and you alone who discredits yourself without any help from me. You still haven't taught us anything. In every class, all you've done has been to tell us what others will be doing to us, to be like sheep, not to question or ask anything, to comply with and obey orders. I came here to learn what's happening in my and my baby's bodies, how we work, about hormones and the importance of letting them flow. I wanted to learn how to bathe my baby, to cure his umbilical cord, to breastfeed him…"

"Well, we're talking about the birth now, but you already want to know what will happen when the baby's out," Rosa defends herself, "we still have many classes left, you know?"

"At least I have Esther, who will really inform me. Your classes are not only a waste of time, but counterproductive, too."

"Jeez! Anything else?" she says with an ironic smile.

"Yes, now that you mention it: do you know who Michel Odent, the French obstetric researcher, is? Because maybe you don't have a clue."

"Of course, I know who he is."

"Fine. He says the only thing that should be done for a pregnant woman is to make her happy and not to worry her; and you don't even do that."

Alicia follows her daughter towards the door, and halfway, she turns and says, "this is my daughter. She makes me proud I gave birth to her."

Once outside, Alicia hugs her daughter, who bursts into tears in her arms.

"No, no, my baby. Don't cry. That silly woman doesn't deserve your tears. Shhh. You're the best mother in the world, and this baby is very lucky that you are the way you are. I'm very proud of you."

Both are still hugging until they feel the door open. It's Sonia.

"Excuse me, but I didn't want to let you go, because I admire you a lot and I think you're very brave and a great woman, and awfully well informed. You have been an example to everyone in there. Not only to that old school midwife, but to everybody. For we don't have a clue; we had never heard about the immense majority of the things you were bringing up there. I'm ashamed even of saying it. We are going to have a baby and we have gathered less information than we do when we go on holidays."

Ingrid smiles, flattered.

"Gimme your number, please, I'd like to see you and also to get your midwife's contact," Sonia tells her.

After copying Ingrid's number on her mobile, she hugs her and kisses her and tells her goodbye by saying, "I'll be calling you. Alicia, you must be very proud!" and goes back inside.

Week 35

It's been months since the last time Manuel saw Lorena. She's not taking his phone calls or replying to his messages. He waits for her near her door any time he has a chance, but to no avail. He doesn't understand what's wrong with her. Why doesn't she want to be with him? He has even texted her via WhatsApp about his intentions, but he's got no answer. She has vanished. She's not at her place or she never goes out, for he has waited more than once at different times of the day hoping to see her but without success. It's as if she has disappeared into thin air. *Who could have any news from her? Who, who, who…?* Manuel thinks, *there must be a way to find her… Of course! Tomás! I'll call and ask him. No, I'd better drop by his practice and take a look at her records to see when she has an appointment...* Manuel thinks, thrilled. *Why didn't I think of that before?*

Dr. Salcedo's practice 17:30.
Tomás is doing an ultrasound when the nurse comes in and tells him, "Mr. Manuel Martín is here to see you."
Tomás frowns, surprised. *What's wrong with Manuel?* he thinks. *This is very weird. The other day he calls me out of the blue to ask me about Lorena, and now he comes to my practice just like that, without a warning. Will it be him?* Tomás thinks *Will he be the bastard that's shagging her? No, it can't be. Although, come to think of it, he's loaded and he's not that bad looking...*
"Everything's fine, Madam," he says, putting the scanner probe back in its place to give the nurse some instructions.
Tomás goes out to the waiting room and sees Manuel standing there.
"Hi, Manu, what are you doing around here?"
"Well, I was in the neighbourhood and as I had some time I thought I'd come up to see you. Are you staying much longer? I'll buy you a beer. Take a break and we'll have a chat."

"Sure. I'm with the last one. I'll be done in five minutes. Wait a moment here and…"

"Look, where do you keep your records? I want to check something about Clarisa; she'll be coming for her check-up soon and I'd like to have a look if you don't mind."

Manuel is nervous and Tomás knows he's lying. Clearly, there's some relationship between Lorena's disappearance - she has not asked for an appointment for months- and what Manuel is looking for. He feels uncomfortable. He doesn't know what to do or what to tell him. He shouldn't let him access that information, but what can he do?

"Have a seat and I'll tell Concha to look for it."

"No, it's all right, I can do it myself…"

"Concha," Tomás tells the girl coming up the corridor, "help Manuel here to get his wife's records. Clarisa… well, he'll be telling you her family names. I'm going to say goodbye to my patient and I'll be right back," he says, returning to his office.

"Tell me her full name," says Concha.

"Da Silva Costa," says Manuel in a low voice.

Concha looks inside a drawer and says, "here it is! Oh, no it isn't, this one's called Lorena."

"Yes, yes, it's her," Manuel tells her, "Lorena Clarisa."

Concha goes to the shelf and gives Manuel a folder.

"Thank you," says Manuel. He opens the folder as fast as he can, looks for her data and there it is: Soria Street, 14. 6A.

Bitch, he thinks.

"Yes, it's time for her to come," he says out loud as he gives the folder back to Concha.

"Shall I leave it out here?" she asks.

"No, no, put it back. I don't know when she's coming, I just wanted to check it's time for her to. Keep it, keep it."

Tomas comes into the filing cabinet room where Manuel and Concha are.

"Ready. Concha: give her an appointment for next month. Let's go, Manu," he says, showing his friend the way with a gesture. Once at the door, he says, "wait, I've forgotten something. Go downstairs if you want, I won't be a minute."

Tomás goes back to the filing cabinet room and looks for Lorena's record number in the drawer: 2311. As he goes to the shelf, he sees a folder slightly askew, as the ones that have just been put back there usually are. He takes it and sees, unsurprised, that it's Lorena's.

"What are you up to, Manolito, what are you up to?" he whispers as he puts the folder back.

Alicia opens the door to Esther, who greets her and kisses her on both cheeks.

"Come in, come to the sitting room. Ingrid's coming in a second, she's in the toilet, I think. Do you want a coffee?"

"Just some cold water, please. Thank you."

Esther is checking her phone when Ingrid comes. After greeting each other, they sit down with Alicia.

"How are you? How are you feeling?" Esther asks with a smile.

"Fine. Huge. And pissing all the time…"

"The usual thing, then, isn't it?" smiles Esther.

"Yes. Just a few weeks before I get to know this little one," she says caressing her belly. "Do I have to take any more tests?"

"It depends. Will you be wanting to do the anaesthesia test, the group B strep or going to be monitored?"

"No, not if I can help it. Is that monitor thing important?"

"No. It's absolutely useless. And if your baby happens to do any mischief just then, they will induce your birth willy nilly. I don't recommend them. What's more, I recommend not to waste any time with them."

"Just like Rosa, isn't she, Mom?" Ingrid smiles at her mother.

"Pfff, don't remind me! Don't even mention her, I get sick just at the mention of it. What a rude woman! Treating us like that in front of all those people…"

"What happened?" asks Esther, intrigued.

"The Health Centre midwife kicked me out of the antenatal class a couple of weeks ago."

Esther looks at them, astonished. "But, why?" she asks.

"For knowing more than she did and shaming her, she couldn't be more ignorant, that lady," Alicia butts in.

"You're joking! She threw you out? But why, exactly?"

"I don't know. We had been to four or five classes already where she wasn't teaching us anything. She was just telling us 'they'll be doing this or that to you', 'you just behave well, they are the ones who know', 'you're in good hands', 'trust them'... and whenever I questioned or refuted anything, she always said things like 'if they do it that way there must be a reason', 'professionals know more than we do'... till she got mad and told me not to come back, as I already knew everything."

"I feel so ashamed on her behalf right now, Ingrid, I truly do!"

"Well, Ingrid left her there, petrified on her chair, after calling her ignorant, I felt so proud… And when we got out, one of the girls -one who's got a good head on her shoulders- came after us and told Ingrid it was exemplary for her to be so well prepared and that she felt ashamed of not being as informed as she was," says Alicia proudly.

"Sonia, yes," Ingrid says smiling. "They might call you, because I told them I had a private midwife, and these two girls are rather lost."

"What two girls?" Esther asks, confused.

"Sonia and Sol. They're a couple, and they are expecting twins. Sol is the one who's pregnant, and from what they tell me the hospital staff are frightening her a lot just because it's two babies. Apparently, the pregnancy is going perfectly well. She's got my number, so if she calls me and asks for you, may I give her yours?"

"Naturally, do, by all means. How many weeks pregnant is she?"

"Like me."

"Well, they'd better call me soon, because these babies will start being born in the next few weeks…"

"Yes," says Ingrid enthusiastically. "I can't really believe it. In a few weeks my baby will be here," she continues after a silence. "What are we doing from now on? When do you start to be on call?"

"From week 37; that's in ten days. But I already am. If anything, at any time, just call me."

"Even if it's in the middle of the night?"

"If it's an emergency, or it's worrying you so much you can't wait till the morning, yes, without a doubt. If I'm not on call, the only thing that could happen is not having my mobile with me and not hearing it, but after week 37 I take it even to the shower, and I sleep with it by my side."

"Excuse me a second, I just got this doubt," Alicia cuts in. "Everything related to home birth is crystal clear to me, and as you say these things are not necessary to give birth here, the anaesthetic, the monitors… but, what happens if anything goes wrong?"

"Which it won't," says Ingrid.

"Let me, dear, this is important. And if things go wrong, we have to know this. What happens if, for any reason, we have to go to the hospital and you don't have those tests that they insist are so important? Maybe it will mean trouble for us, or that midwife has written on your records that you're having a home birth… what happens then?"

"That's a very good question," says Esther. "If in the end you go to hospital and you don't have the group B strep and the anaesthetic test they can annoy you quite a lot. The anaesthetic test can be done right there and then, although that depends on how busy they are. About the strep, they'll probably try to give you antibiotics if you haven't had the test done. You can always refuse, but labour is not a moment to get into fights… but here's something you can do… when should you be doing your Group B strep test?"

"The day after tomorrow or one day after that."

"Let's do this: the day before, you peel a garlic clove and you smash it a bit, just enough for it to break, you wrap it in gauze and you put it inside your vagina. You leave it there for twenty-four hours, and before you go to do the test, you take it out."

"Will that take the streptococcus away?" asks Ingrid intrigued. "So, why don't they put a garlic clove inside the vaginas of women with a positive test instead of so many antibiotics?"

"Not exactly: garlic is a natural antiseptic, and it modifies the results. If you use the garlic, the test will be negative even if you have the streptococcus."

"Incredible!" says Alicia. "Well, consider it, dear. At least, if you have to go to hospital they won't be bothering you for not having that test done."

"I think I will, yes; if I can't have a home birth, going to the hospital would be bad enough without having to be fighting everyone there on top."

After a bit more conversation and having checked everything's fine with the baby, Esther agrees with Ingrid that she'll come back to visit her at the onset of week 37, and she leaves after hugging her goodbye.

María, Guille, Son and Sol are having dinner together at the girls' place.

"Hey," Guillermo tells his sister, "the other day, at the antenatal class, what did you tell that hippie when you went out after her?"

"I went out to ask her for her phone number. Before class we had been talking, and she told me her midwife could help us with Sol's birth to avoid a C-section and to get everything to be as natural as possible."

"You didn't mention anything," her wife claims.

"Well, it was just a conversation, nothing much. As she was leaving and it was clear she wasn't coming back, I asked her for her phone number in case we wanted to call her."

"I wouldn't trust her," says María, "go figure how she'll be giving birth. I've always been wary of her at the classes."

"Why?" asks Sonia.

"I don't know, I don't like her. The questions she made, challenging absolutely everything. I don't trust these people who know everything about everything, frankly. That need of knowing absolutely everything can't be good. You end up being more catholic than the Pope."

"Well, I think we have a lot to learn from her," says Sonia, "I felt rather ashamed every time she talked to the midwife and I realised I haven't prepared myself at all for something this important."

"What do you mean we haven't?" her wife snaps, "we're going to the classes, we have that book on pregnancy and the National Geographic video we watched … of course we have prepared ourselves."

"I don't think so, Sol, not at that level. She has evaluated the relevance of every test, if they are really necessary, why should you get this and that one... We are completely blind and subject to the people who are at the hospital the day we go there, and without knowing them."

"So, what? Don't you trust doctors? Because I do. I'm certain they know how to do their job and they'll be doing what's best for us. And if they decide they have to do a C-section, it will be because it's the best, nobody does such things just for the hell of it."

"Well, if you trust the doctors who will take care of you that much, ahead we go. But that doesn't mean that I don't recognise that Ingrid was miles ahead from all of us with all she's done to be prepared to have her baby."

"Just an obsessive personality, that's all," adds María, "If I'm building a house, I trust an architect If I have a legal problem, I trust a lawyer. If I'm pregnant, I trust doctors. Or are we going to get a diploma for everything we have to do in life?"

"I'm not saying that," Sonia insists, "besides, if she can get so analytical about everything, it's because there's more to probe before automatically assuming everything is being done for our own good."

"Look, Son," her brother butts in, "it looks as if you trusted that girl more than you trust people who have studied for ten years. But if anything happened to your baby, you'd rather have a doctor than having that hippy by your side."

"Holy crap, but that's obvious! I'm just saying that I admire her and that seeing how well prepared she is made me feel ashamed. And I believe many of the things she said more than what the midwife said. I've learnt a lot from the conversations they both had; if it wasn't for her I wouldn't have a clue."

"Like what, for instance?"

"Well, about the epidural, for instance. How can it not have side effects? Or what she said about pinching the baby's head. I had no idea about that, and now I know if Sol is going to be monitored I can tell them not to put that in the babies' heads. If it wasn't for Ingrid, we'd be accepting that for sheer ignorance."

"But what I don't get is: why always be contrary to everything they say? Why believe it's wrong? If they put that on the baby's head it must be because it's the best. They wouldn't do it if it wasn't," María intervenes again, "if the midwife says it doesn't hurt them, that it just pinches their skin, it must be true, mustn't it? She's like the devil's advocate: let's carp on everything, because everything they do is wrong. Well, if this device is made that way, it must be because it's the best way."

"But the best way for whom? That's what we should be getting at," says Sonia. "Who are they selling the machine to? The hospital or the mother? Who's buying it? And who wants it to have a high definition, to see the baby's heartbeat perfectly without any interference, to be able to operate even if the woman waggles, because as the sensor is connected to the baby you never lose contact? That's irrelevant for the one who's buying the machine. It's his job that's relevant for him, not any injury in the baby's head. But if you ask a mother which device she prefers, I'm certain she wouldn't be choosing the one that pinches the baby when they can have the other one that is belted to their bellies, even if it's more uncomfortable for her and has to be repositioned from time to time because it loses contact… What's more, I'm going to do what she said about looking for images on Google," she says, rising from the table.

"But Sonia, that's the problem you don't want to see. If you look at those images, and I'm sure there'll be some horrid ones, when you're in the hospital and they tell you they're going to monitor the girls you'll suffer terribly thinking of your twins and those photographs you saw. They're probably extreme cases that got infected or whatever," says María.

"It's you who doesn't want to see. I don't know how you can have that blind confidence in people who don't give a damn about us or our children."

"And who says that? How are they not going to mind us? If they commit malpractice they go to jail, don't they?"

"Sure. And that's exactly why, María. That's why they pinch the baby's head, cut you, give you an epidural even if later they have to use the forceps to take the baby out... because not going to jail is what they care about, not that you get out of the door walking on your own two feet with your baby in your arms and both of you with as few stitches as possible..."

"Right. Maybe it's like that, like you say. But if it was, there'd be thousands of women disappointed with their births... but look, women do it again, so their experience can't have been that bad."

"Well, many will repeat, others won't. It probably is like with domestic violence victims that they learn to live with it and say nothing because they don't find any understanding around them. They bottle it all up inside and live with that. And they probably think that's normal, that's what happens to all of them."

"Fine; in any case, I'd rather you didn't call her," says her wife, jealous, "maybe, if we had thought about it before... but now it's too late to start looking for alternatives. There's just a month to go. We'll do it better with the next birth, right?"

"Ok, I'm not calling her if you don't want me to, but that midwife could help us a lot with my breastfeeding, for instance."

"What?" an astounded María asks, "you? Breastfeed? The twins?"

"Yes."

"That can be done?"

"Yes. I've been doing some research and as we're having two and they have two mothers, we could profit from the advantage, couldn't we?"

"Well up to you, I guess. I think that's far too complicated. You just feed them with bottles, and that's that."

"Yes, but breast milk is better."

"Yes, right, but you don't have to be such a Taliban, do you? As if there weren't thousands of children out there perfectly raised by bottle feeding! Myself, for instance, and look, here I am."

"Aren't you going to try breastfeeding?" Sonia asks María.

"Yes, but without killing myself. I'll give it a try, but if I don't have milk or I can't, it's no big deal. I don't see the point in these mothers who become obsessed and do it with cracked nipples and all... I don't see the need for that, let me tell you."

"Personally, I would like to be able to breastfeed them," says Sonia, "it's important to me. I think it's a chance to give them all the good I can. As I haven't been pregnant with them, I'd love to breastfeed them."

"Yes?" says her brother. "It gives me the creeps a bit, to tell you the truth."

"My breastfeeding the girls?"

"Yes. You're not their mother. I mean, yes you are, but as your breasts won't be producing milk out of the blue, I find forcing it a bit... well, forced. Of course, everyone's free to do as they please, but... I don't know, it gives me the shivers. I can't explain it. Have you seen "The hand that rocks the cradle"?"

"Yes," they reply.

"Well, ever since I saw it that scene is engraved in my mind, when that woman, the "bad guy", breastfeeds the other woman's baby, and I felt such revulsion...Yuck, my hackles rise just thinking about it."

"Yeah, but that was the baddie who wanted to steal her child. I'm going to be their mother. Their other mother."

"Me, I'm delighted that Sonia wants to make the effort of producing milk and breastfeeding the girls. I think breastfeeding is important, and most twins have to do without their mother's milk because it's very tiresome, whereas anyone can give them a bottle. So, having this great chance it's very lucky for the girls: two breasts for each one, as all children do."

"Yes. I understand the theory, but I can't help it giving me the creeps," Guille excuses himself. "It's clearly my problem, not yours. And if you want to do it, bravo and go ahead, gals!"

Week 37

Manuel is waiting in front of Lorena's house in Clarisa's car, as he has done more than once. He's already starting to doubt she's still in Madrid, when he sees her. There she is, walking towards her door, hugely pregnant. He springs to open the car door and instantly stops dead.

"Stand still. You know she lives here, you know she hasn't left, you know she's pregnant. Now you have to think what to do. If you screw things up now, it will be the last time you see her, that's for sure. So, think carefully about what you're going to do, what you'll be telling her, how and when, but not like that, no matter how. Now think, Manuel, think…" he mumbles as he watches Lorena disappear behind the door.

Week 40

María and Sol are together. Sol is being admitted tomorrow for the induction and she's a bit frightened.

"Shit. They've been telling me all the time not to worry, for twins are always early, and look at me, I'll be going tomorrow for an induction."

"So? You're lucky! I can't take it anymore. I wish they were getting mine out tomorrow!"

"Yeah, you say that because you're not in my boots. But I'm not that thrilled at the prospect of being induced to tell you the truth…"

"But what can you possibly complain about? You'll be seeing them in no time, and you'll be getting the epidural from minute one, so you won't be suffering at all, babe. Think of me. If there's a lot of people I might not even get it. I'm not doing what the midwife said at all. The minute I have two contractions, I'm going there: I don't want to not have an epidural because I went there too late."

"Really? You won't try to have a natural birth?"

"Natural, yes, but not without any help. In these times, it's silly to go through labour pains, babe. It's like pulling a tooth out without anaesthetic. You wouldn't do that, would you? Well, it's the same with labour. I can't understand that obsession some people have for experiencing pain for the hell of it now that we have epidurals."

"Huh. Me, if it wasn't for the twins, I'd give it a try, I really would."

"Whatever for? Everybody says it hurts terribly. What for? Seriously, I don't get it."

"Well, to experience it, to go through that process, to see how your daughter being born from your body feels…"

"It feels tremendously painful. I think that way, with that pain, you cannot enjoy birth, really, you're more worried about the pain than about giving birth. However, if they take the pain away, you're much more into the process, you can experience it much more, because it doesn't hurt."

"I'm not sure. I trust nature a lot. And if it wasn't supposed to hurt, it wouldn't hurt. That pain has to be there for something."

"Well, it clearly isn't, because there's no difference between the women who have given birth with the epidural and those who haven't."

"What do you mean?"

"I mean there they are. Happy mothers all of them, ones as much as the others. I mean you're not going to be a better mother for not having it. It's what I'm telling you: profit from all the technology, it's there for us to use it for our benefit. Don't be daft."

"I don't know, it's just that Sonia has started to read and there are things in which she's right, I find."

"Look here, Sol. I think it's perfect that she's getting all that information and such, but at the end of the day you're the one who's going through labour. So, she can say whatever she wants, but the one enduring every contraction and the birth and all will be you. She has to respect your decisions."

"She does respect them a lot. I'm just trying to tell you things are not as simple as you say. I also agree that we are overdoing it with so many machines and devices. And I don't think it's all beneficial and no damage."

"Well, it's the same. What time are you going there tomorrow?"

"In the morning. We were told to get up, have breakfast and go there."

"You'll see how everything goes splendidly. Maybe you'll start labour tonight, you never know," she says getting up. "Ouch!" she exclaims, "what was that?" she says, touching her pubic area. "My waters have gone, Sol! I'm getting soaked! Call Guille, I'm changing my clothes and we're going to the hospital."

"Easy, María, it's all right. How swell! Your girl is going to be born! C'mon, get ready, and I'll phone Guille."

Carmen's contractions have started, and she calls Luis, who's gone for a walk with Lara.

"It's starting," she tells him.

"Right, I'm leaving Lara with your parents and I'm on my way there."

"Hurry up," she tells him as she hangs up breathing deeply as another contraction comes.

"Luci, I'm starting to stain with some blood," Lorena tells her friend, who's sitting on her living room sofa.

"Right; let's go to the hospital then, shall we?"

"No, I think it's too early. The midwife said we shouldn't go before we were having regular contractions, that these first moments we'd be better at home than in the hospital."

"But you're bleeding. Is that normal?"

"Yes, it's the mucus plug, you expel it before labour."

"And you don't have any contractions?"

"I'm not sure. Some discomfort, some stitch, but nothing much. I think we can wait a bit. If I see things become agitated, we'll go, right?"

"Sure, whatever you say. Shall I check the hospital bag?"

"Again?" she says with a grin.

"Yes," smiles Luci, "well, just in case we are forgetting something," she says, opening it.

Sara and Juan are hugging on the sofa.

"Tomorrow is the day. Tomorrow we'll be seeing his face…"

"Yes. How are you?"

"Happy, joyful, thrilled. Longing so much to see him. To have him in my arms. I can't believe it, Juan. We're finally going to be parents. Tomorrow."

"I'm very proud of you," Juan says, kissing her.

"And so am I, love. You're going to be the best father in the world."

"And you the best mother. You already are."

"You're not angry because I didn't have a C-section yesterday as Nuria suggested?"

"How could I be angry? I think you've been very brave for waiting and giving Pedro these extra days inside your belly, which is where he is best. What mother in your situation would have waited?"

"It's because Ingrid, that girl who knew so much at the classes, made me think a lot when I told her, and that's what made me wait. She was absolutely right. If anything goes wrong in any of the two options, we'll blame ourselves just the same for not having chosen the other one, so I'm very happy to have waited until week forty."

"And you don't want to wait a few more days?"

"No. We already took the decision of waiting till week forty, which is today. If he didn't want to come out, I wouldn't be relaxed now. I prefer having a Cesarean tomorrow, I really do."

"You're very brave. Supermom!" he tells her, kissing her on the head.

"Dear, don't you think we should be calling Esther?" says Alicia as her daughter, sitting on the Pilates ball gestures her to wait and breathes deeply with her eyes shut as the contraction fades.

"It's still early, Mom. Don't call her yet. Maybe there's a lot to wait yet."

"Well, maybe not for her to come. But we should tell her that you're having contractions, she'll probably want to know so that she can get ready. I think it's better to tell her now how you are than calling her in a few hours to tell her to come running."

"All right, Mom, call her. Call the midwife."

About the author.

Yes, this is a very long "About the author" section but well, it's my book and I'd love to tell you more about my life than just when and where I was born and what I studied. This is your book also so you decide what to read. I also warn you that I am constantly creating and moving around so the end of this section might not be correct for very long. :)

The first time I saw a baby being born I was 12 years old. The baby was given to the midwife and she took him to another room, weighed and measured him, bathed him, combed his hair and dressed him. I was as fascinated then as I am terrified now recalling the story of the first time midwifery entered my life. I wanted to be that person, I wanted to do that. I studied nursing as this is the only possible access into midwifery in Spain, but once qualified as a nurse I went to work in the UK, and a year later as I was training as a midwife in this country. I was in a city with such a cultural diversity I learnt so much about birth practices around the world, but mainly about respect for others' autonomy over their own body.

When I went back to Spain after 5 years in the UK people asked me, very hopeful, about midwifery in the latter. I thought it was quite system centered instead of women centered therefore I could not understand the fuss about practising in this country. I worked for 3 years in two different hospitals & I realised how shocking the difference was between the care and respect women received in Spain compared to the UK. That's when I started writing this book.

Then I met an amazing man, my partner, and I moved to Galicia, Spain's best kept secret. I worked as an independent midwife for over 5 years and I taught other midwives about homebirth. Professionally, these have been the happiest years of my life. I just said "yes" to everyone who asked for my services at home: several women who went over 42 weeks, a woman who declined any antenatal care, a woman who I had accompanied for her first birth and the second was breech and they refused to give her the chance of a vaginal birth... I was over 30 weeks pregnant with my second child then and I remember how calm I was (thanks to the wonderful hormones that flooded my body and didn't allow me to worry about unnecessary matters!) ...

I gave birth to both my daughters at home without any professional help. I trusted my body as I've always done... Giving birth to them freely has been the most amazing experience I've ever had, followed very closely by meeting their father and breastfeeding them for years without covering/hiding wherever I was.

When the youngest was 5 months old we left Spain to write our next chapter in Australia. We travelled around south-east Asia for a few months on our way there and one day, my partner said, "I've sent your CV to a job in Bangladesh". We were living in Bali at that time and we all ended up in Bangladesh a few weeks later to help them with the development of the midwifery career. The political situation was quite difficult when we arrived and we found ourselves spending our first Christmas away from home in Nepal. Two wonderful months in a country where midwifery care was the most challenging I've ever come across. After 1 & ½ years in Bangladesh & never making it to Australia, we slowly came back to Europe but we stopped for a few months in Goa, India. My partner wanted to improve his acupuncture knowledge and I remember this time as the freest I've ever been, even though I had a couple of toddlers to look after, it was just the most amazing, relaxing and joyous time.

It took me a while to find a job in the UK, wherever I interviewed they wanted candidates to learn mechanical algorithms; my experience and knowledge meant nothing.

A Spanish midwife, who has become a good friend, taught me these algorithms and I got the jobs then. I worked in a London hospital for over 2 years, most of them in the birth centre where I enjoyed my time very much. However, and as I had been away from the UK for 11 years I had to start working on the labour ward. Can you imagine a vegan working in a slaughterhouse? That's exactly how that time on the labour ward felt for me. Don't get me wrong, I am not saying the labour ward is a slaughterhouse. I am saying that for a midwife who admires birth, women and their bodies, as I do, this is how I felt working there; completely out of place. Then, as Tim Robbins in the Shawshank redemption, I kept writing to the person in charge of rotating us about being moved to the birth centre until I was moved there.

After 18months there I applied for a job at a University. I loved teaching, I loved the relationship with the students. Their feedback was so rewarding... but it was back to rehearsed algorithms again and I was reminded the ladder steps are different depending on where you come from. I got a job as a senior lecturer in a different university where I felt appreciated for who I was and what I could offer.

At present I am writing, organising different learning experiences for birth workers unattached to any protocols or algorithms. Trying to help women in a more global approach.

In the 18 years I've been a midwife I only got to take a baby away from her mother and bath her straight after she was born, once. She was stillborn and that's been the most cathartic professional experience of my life. There I was, 10 years after I had discovered I wanted to be a midwife, bathing the most beautiful baby I had seen when I had heard her heart beating strongly just a few hours before. I made sure the water was warm, I cleaned her and bathed her, I talked to her while I sobbed and thought how I wanted to be a midwife because I had seen one bath a baby and... everything made sense in that moment. I was where I was supposed to be and I was bathing the only baby from another woman I was supposed to bath.

Acknowledgments:
This book would have never been possible without my husband's support. In the dedication I thank him for giving me wings and that's the best thing he could ever have done for me. He's giving me guidance in all my purposes and ideas, he has given me impulse to believe I can do anything I set my mind on. Jose has shifted my "No, I can't" through, "Of course you can" to "Yes, I can". Our daughters are "my" greatest achievement although they are theirs, not mine but I feel so grateful they chose us and how much they teach me, love me and care for me. Two very young women who have supported me so much, calm me down, bring me drinks, massage me, ask me what I need or offer cuddles and "mimos" when they see me tense, look after me while I write, get interviewed, get blocked, sleep little... I am so fortunate!

Thanks to Isabel Ferrán, a friend, who not only revised the Spanish version several times but did the wonderful translation you've just read.

Augustine Colebrook is an independent midwife who appeared in my life in 2020. She contacted me to take part in her wonderful "Worldwide Midwifery Podcasts" and it's been a beautiful love story since; we admire each other and we've become close friends. She's written the most beautiful foreword ever written in history and she's written it to this book. I cannot wait to embrace her in my arms not through a screen and thousands of km. apart.

Ximena Silva is a doula and graphic designer and she's helped me with both versions of the books just because she loved the story and wanted to help it reach as many people as possible. Whenever I asked her anything she did it stat. I can't thank you enough Ximena.

Begoña Songel took my book over the Atlantic and published it in Perú. She liked it so much, she was living there and she thought it would help Peruvian women. I am so grateful. Muchas gracias, Begoña.

Kristin Beylich became a good friend while she got pregnant with amazing Emilia and we've been close friends since. I was her midwife-friend and she edited and corrected this book while pregnant, supported me through a rough patch and share her oxytocin love with me since Emilia was born. Every so often she sent me videos, photos of her, including me in that period which I consider the most wonderful in a woman's life. I cannot wait to hold them both in my arms soon.

To you who are reading this, for doing so, for purchasing my book. For telling others about it for your support so I can keep writing.

You can contact me on:
https://www.facebook.com/irene.garzon.501
https://www.instagram.com/tucomadreirenegarzon/
https://twitter.com/Tucomadreirene

¡Muchísimas gracias!
Con cariño,
Irene (pronounced E réne).

Printed in Great Britain
by Amazon

10936198R00174